THE SLAB

THE SLAB

First edition, published in the UK April 2025 by The Slab Press
The Slab 003 (softback)
10 9 8 7 6 5 4 3 2 1

ISBN: 978-1-7384268-4-3 (softback)
978-1-7384268-5-0(e-book)

Cover design by Paul Alex Condie
Typesetting by Donna Scott

Contents

Introduction

Donna Scott

Solarpunk sits someway between Cli-Fi (climate-centred science fiction) and Hopepunk (speculative fiction concerning radical community action with kindness at its heart as characters fight for positive change). Hope is the upbeat aim of Solarpunk, but what both Hopepunk and Solarpunk have in common is the notion that there is something inherently negative that needs to be overcome, and therein lies the grit in the pearl...

To embrace the positivity imbued by these literary subgenres is a wonderful thing, but even the most optimistic story is by necessity grounded in a needful realism. Our world is what it is: according to the 2024 IQAir World Air Quality Report, only 17% of global cities meet the WHO air pollution guideline; globally, we are facing unprecedented challenges when it comes to climate action. Human activities have been driving the rise in greenhouse gas emissions. Extreme weather events such as hurricanes, floods, wildfires (including within the Arctic Circle) and droughts are both worsening in severity and becoming more frequent. The window for positive action to stop temperatures rising past the point of no return is narrowing. What's worse, despotic governments who have turned against the Paris accord that their precedents signed up to, or who never signed up to it in the first place, are doing their utmost to counter research, education and positive action against polluting industries and climate science in some kind of childish point scoring against 'wokery'. Whilst technological advancements such as solar power, carbon capture, and improvements within high-polluting industries such as cattle farming are certainly helping on one hand, new tech such as AI is proving to be very thirsty, using up to 12 litres of water for each kWh of energy usage according to OECD.

Whilst first termed in 1938 by Vladimir Vernadsky, the term "Anthropocene" has been growing in use throughout the 20th Century to describe our current geological age as one in which humanity has become a planetary force of change. The usage of this term has increased in the 21st century, seemingly in correlation to the visible effects of climate change, pollution, environmental destruction, and the proliferation of microplastics in our water, soil, food, and even our bodies.

As editor of the Newcon Press anthology series, *Best of British Science Fiction*, I have noticed a strong and consistent trend for climate-based science fiction over the last decade, whereas other themes have flashed through the public consciousness in alignment with whatever topics have been prominent in the news (Brexit, COVID-19, reproductive rights, assisted dying, AI etc.). Some of the stories have been hopeful, others less so. It can be difficult to imagine all of humanity extracting itself from the pickle it finds itself in right now because things are far from OK, so writers will often depict an even worse scenario from which the characters will rescue only themselves, or their small sector of society at most. This is not much of a prospect to hang our hope on, but if we have any hope at all, it is that we are innovative, adaptable and resilient as a species, and most of us accept the science and acknowledge that we need to act, even if action is frustratingly slow.

Solarpunk is definitely much more of a specialist topic than general climate-based science-fiction. Hopeful endings are rare. However, I believe they are very much needed.

When I set out to compile this anthology, I was primarily seeking out excellent science fiction centred on human innovation to solve the climate and environmental challenges we are facing today. I also knew what I didn't want to see: whilst Elon Musk is currently talking up manned missions to Mars, which he thinks might be possible in the next five years (and what a grim notion all of *that* is), I knew I did not want any Planet B stories. I can never understand people who profess to "live in a shithole". Honestly, tidy it up, and plant something if it's that bad, though often people just need to adjust their attitude. I don't think we can make things better by pretending we can just leave the mess behind and move elsewhere. There is no Planet B.

Secondly, I knew I did not want any stories where the solution was essentially magic, and I did receive quite a few that were a little too 'woo-woo' for the brief. I do think we need to adjust our attitude concerning our relation to our environment, but I don't think cosmic ordering is going to extinguish the fires in California or clear all the junk in the sea.

I was thrilled with the quantity and quality of the stories that did fit my strict criteria, but I limited the selection to the twenty best stories. The authors whose stories feature in these pages are from all over the world: global voices for global hope. Many of the authors are seasoned writers with many publication credits under their belts. A couple of the writers are sharing their first or second published stories here. I very much hope you enjoy reading them and are inspired by them to do something positive for the planet in your own way.

Donna Scott

March 2025

References:
2024 IQAir World Air Quality Report | IQAir
OECD.AI
Sustainableish.com

Oil and Water

Holly Schofield

A sour slurry of petrochemicals, a sick sludge of carcinogens and hydrocarbons, the consequence of a thousand unwise decisions done with full knowledge of a poisonous legacy. The childhood memory burned though my brain. Grandpa, eyes blazing, plunging my toddler hands into the bucket of gasoline, again and again, over the shouts of my mother and my gasping sobs.

The council meeting erupted into shouts. My eight coordinators and the dozen or so folks in the audience had forgotten all decorum, forgotten that we should listen closely and take turns speaking, forgotten the calm of our gathering space surrounded by pea vines and edible flowers.

Just talking about Oil Day had set us all off. None of us even turned our heads to look at the actual Folly itself. The huge metal tank of gasoline a few dozen metres away, the size of a garden shed, cast its shadow toward us, a squat cylinder of harsh blue rearing above kale and broccoli, a long-familiar part of our Vancouver Island intentional community's landscape.

And the Folly was the problem.

We'd stopped seeing it.

In six years as head coordinator I'd rarely wished for a gavel but I did now. The downside about our community governance system was none of us were career politicians. We all disliked the job, knowing it led to so many compromises, and so we tended to throw our emotions into each and every issue. That was also the upside about it.

Lissa was on her feet, pointing and yelling at the wallscreen where the word "Folly" glared out amid a block of smaller text. Mateo was signing madly, face scrunched up in anger, so fast I couldn't follow his ASL. I touched the wallscreen so his words would appear in text and be broadcast aloud. The other five coordinators variously bellowed, spoke with intensity, or sat glowering with arms crossed.

"OK, everyone, OK." My words were lost in the din so I banged my fist on the table, so out of character that they all stopped cold and stared at me. I flinched at the sudden shift of attention, as autists do, but managed to splutter out, "Let's get a grip on ourselves. I know it's a contentious topic—"

"Kinsley, keep Rogan's Folly out of Oil Day!" Lissa sat down with a thump. "Speeches and memories and vids are enough."

I felt my stubbornness rise like floodwaters. "We don't dip our hands in gasoline anymore. But passing around a bucketful just to smell it, to *know* it, that makes a point. We still need the Folly, we've proven that over and over."

Mateo's fingers flashed in the sun and his words scrolled, "Proof? None! Take it down! Why is it there?"

I shouted, "Because we don't want to return to Hell!" So much for the classes I'd taken in arbitration and negotiation. My form of autism coupled with social anxiety meant I generally got too direct and abrupt. I knew I needed to draw on those lessons now, coldly and clinically, once I stopped shaking.

Of course, that's when Tanisa, over by the nasturtiums and spinach, waved her hand. Raising a smart neurodivergent 14-year-old daughter when I was neurodivergent myself, as well as running my woodshop and being head coordinator, meant I continually felt like a heap of wet sawdust by evening. I gave her a reluctant nod.

Her voice, inappropriately loud and intense, rang out.

"Mom, we should make a list of pros and cons. A table, a chart, a decisional balance sheet using an implementation intentions technique which could achieve optimal goal attainment—"

"OK, got it. Thanks, Tanisa."

She flushed and sat back down.

My sister Jill, sprawled on the bench beside her, smiled ruefully at me and shook her head in mock sympathy. She never seemed to realize the depth of emotion a person could have when teenage angst got coupled with generational anxiety and climate crisis PTSD. Somehow Jill had skipped over all that and actually enjoyed her teenage years, which made her sympathy levels just now rather low. Tanisa was learning to cope with neurotypical society, and our community was learning to accept diversity in all its forms, but we all still had a long way to go.

Time to get back on track. Our council protocol, based on local Coast Salish governing techniques as well as the better of the old-time generic board rules, required each question to be answered before we moved on. I could replay the recording to see the questions left dangling when things exploded—I thought maybe Mina had been speaking about gasoline's potential for contamination of groundwater —but I made a quick decision and grabbed Mateo's question as if it was the next one.

"Why does Rogan's Folly exist? Good question, Mateo! When Rogan's Garage closed down and we all switched to e-cars and public transit and less travel and…"

"And lots of walking!" someone said and we all laughed, breaking the tension a little.

"…it was felt that a permanent reminder needed to be in its place. So that we wouldn't forget. Same reason we have Oil Day each year." I grabbed the communal stylus. "And, yes, let's do an old-fashioned table with advantages and disadvantages, as long as we realize each point won't have equal weight." I cleared Mateo's words off the wallscreen and drew a long "T" in the middle, labelling the left column "+"

and the right column "-", happy to be using my hands for something useful. "Let's start with disadvantages of keeping it. Lissa?" Asking her first might get her off her stubborn mode. I'd learned the hard way that extroverts liked to repeat themselves and felt it of value, the opposite of most introverts.

Lissa scowled but spoke mildly, hands remaining in her lap. "OK, anyway, we know that the Folly has served as a visual reminder of our past foolhardiness. But, as time goes on, the risk of leakage is simply too high. And it's affecting people subliminally to have that nasty thing right in our faces all the time. A simple plaque describing what's wrong with fossil fuels, or small replica of an oil rig, say, would be enough."

We all kept silent a minute, waiting to see if she had anything to add, another Indigenous protocol we'd co-opted. Often, a person's afterthoughts were more insightful than their original words.

But Lissa seemed finished so I wrote "strong reminder" on the plus side of my chart, then "too risky" on the minus side, saying over my shoulder, "That big ol' Folly over there is a war memorial in a sense, already." Then I nodded at Mateo.

I watched the screen, not his too-fast fingers, as his transcribed words overlaid the chart, fading as the audio read each one aloud. "Yes, a war memorial full of loaded guns. Leakage a real threat. Seventy years risk. No more oil refineries, right?"

I nodded as I added "oil/gas production no longer a consideration" to the minus side. That was all true enough. We were doing OK. Since the big Effondrement when Grandpa had been in his 30s, the west coast of Canada had mostly set a new and better course. Solar panels and well-insulated houses and a mixture of permaculture techniques and computerized irrigation systems and far less travel and, oh, a hundred other things meant we weren't hungry and the megastorms didn't bother us as badly as before. Locally, we hadn't lost a crop in fifteen years or more. And we no longer had to wear thick wool socks nine months of the year, although Grandpa always had until the day he died.

William raised his hand and I braced myself. Of all the coordinators he was my least favourite, showing zero willingness to listen or to change his views on anything. "Well, actually, if we cleaned up all ten thousand litres, maybe it could give us enough fuel to run an old-style truck to bring goods from Victoria for the next year or two." He sat down, sunburnt face proud, as if he'd now get congratulated on his so-very-astute suggestion.

Everyone burst into shouts again. Lissa stomped a foot and swore. Tanisa dug into one of the veggie beds and held up a fist of damp dirt, shaking it furiously.

And me? I froze, selective mutism rearing its head at the shock of his words.

What was *wrong* with William? Sure, there weren't any more combustion engines or useable trucks, but to even *think* of using petrochemicals again was contemptible.

I dug deep and found my voice, then outshouted them all. "Horrible, awful logic like that is the *reason* we still need the cursed thing!"

I threw the stylus in the bushes and turned away, needing a moment.

From the corner of my eye, I saw Tanisa let loose with the soil. Others strode over toward William, gesturing wildly.

Sometimes, I despair of people.

I spooned in black bean soup quickly. All across the communal dining gazebo, people's whispers and glances and outright stares pinged off me. Yesterday's meeting still itched, like a rash on my mood, probably similar to what Grandma had gone through. She'd told me stories about when the food ran low one February and the community's only food was a kind of beige vat-generated pulp—a few sealed bags of dried pulp still lingered in one of the storage lockers—and, as a newly elected coordinator making a hundred decisions, all with only bad or worse options, she'd had to impose rations. Her eyes had moistened as she told me.

I raised my eyes to the Folly, just down the way. Gasoline, the last of the evil last, Grandma's way of not only confining a dangerous substance when we'd dismantled a gas station but making use of it by putting it on permanent public display. The large glass window, four centimetres thick, revealed an innocuous amber fluid—a view into a different world, one we hoped to leave permanently behind.

"That soup's getting cold on your spoon." Jill plopped down without asking if I wanted company, as neurotypical sisters do.

I pushed away the soup and pulled my salad closer. "Got to get back to work. No, I'm not going to discuss Tanisa." I stabbed at miner's lettuce.

"Kinsley, come on. She's not trying to make you look bad. She's disdainful and arrogant because she's insightful into how silly we're all being—she sees things for what they are, not how we couch them to be. And with her chemistry interests, she knows how dangerous a leak from the Folly would be. And she's also just being a teenager. Enjoy these years, they'll go fast!"

I refused to raise my head. I didn't need to see her white teeth gleaming at me. Nothing about this was funny. "Suggesting a pro-and-con chart so snottily, like we're all children trying to learn how to make decisions. She embarrassed me, even if the idea worked out fine. And then throwing that clod of soil at William…"

I stopped and tapped my fork on the salad bowl.

Huh. I'd let my ego blind me, once again.

The chart had been more than just a helpful tool; everyone had calmed down after that and, more importantly, had felt heard. The list of pros and cons now was on the community website and had been scrolled through by dozens of people.

And William certainly deserved to have his shirt spattered with mud.

I settled for saying, "hmph", like I was somebody's stern grandparent.

"There you go." She gripped my hand so I'd stop tapping. "Now, make time to talk to Tanisa, discuss what happened until you're both sick of talking."

"What if William or someone tried resurrecting some of those old-timey motor machines in the museum, though? Scraped the rust off, got just one of them working again? It *might* be possible. It's sent my anxieties soaring."

Tanisa came from nowhere and flopped down beside me. "Hi, Mom," she said around a big mouthful. The remains of a flax roll drooped from her hand. "No, a person couldn't revive any of the vehicles or engines, they're all too old and nasty now, seals all rotted, rats have eaten the brake lines, no parts available, and so on. The Folly *does* have enough fuel to heat our greenhouses for several winters, though, if we made a burner that—"

"Don't tell anyone *that*!"

She rolled her eyes at me. "I won't. Think of the emissions, duh! Did you know gasoline is made up of more than 150 chemicals?" She stared into space, set the flax roll on top of my salad, then drew out her tablet and began tapping away on it.

I glanced over Tanisa's curly head at the Folly. The day was sunny and clear and scented with lilac and lavender. I closed my eyes, ears roaring. *The sour sting of gasoline permeating my nose, the icy chill on my fingers, the dour adult faces.* Behind my eyelids, always and forever. Years ago, the annual Oil Day ceremony mainly consisted of opening the tap on the big tank and sticking a bucket underneath, like it was some kind of deadly maple tree. Grandpa had volunteered year-after-year to be the person who submerged people's hands, while a band played music like a funeral dirge. I'd immediately scrubbed my hands afterwards with nearly a full bar of Grandma's special lemon balm soap, but I'd felt like gasoline lingered for months in the crevices of my cuticles. And in my soul. How had people filled their cars every week with the stuff and not seen it for what it was?

"Oil Day's not so serious anymore, anyway," Jill mused, as if reading my mind. "I heard that Rosemary's going to hand out frozen fruit bars, and Jerome's playing their latest guitar solo. It's become a party, a holiday, a nice change of pace. I thought I'd wear my new cape to celebrate. I finally finished weaving it." She beamed.

"Everything's always so superficial to you, it's exhausting." I twisted toward Tanisa. "And as for you, I don't want to hear any more about the Folly. I'm done talking about it. It's not up for discussion." I pushed up and strode over to the dish bins, thrusting my soup bowl too hastily in the wash water and sending a slash of amber fluid across my hemp shorts.

Puttering in my woodshop the rest of the day, accomplishing nothing, I scrubbed my knuckles over my nose so many times that I got a rash.

With two days to go before the annual ceremony and no decisions, I stared at the message from Tanisa that had suddenly appeared in my phone. It shrieked out at me. *STOP THE CEREMONY. DESTROY THE FOLLY.* And then a long diatribe that didn't make sense, jumbled run-on sentences flopping up against one another.

…don't need more risk and threat, we are healing, albeit slowly, is that

spelled right, did you not even see the petition last month, it's a matter of civic urgency, we need to dismantle, dismember, disassemble the—

I stopped there. What petition? I slogged through my past messages. The group petition was dated three weeks ago, signed by every teenager I knew and a few adults too. The kind of adults who usually didn't involve themselves in government stuff. I'd overlooked it, having more pressing matters like the volunteer roster for the greenhouse reglazing having been mislaid, and the weather forecasting equipment being clogged with pollen, and the four specialized pollen-cleaning brushes we have all up for repair or signed out for other tasks.

I re-read Tanisa's message of a moment ago:

… even see the petition, no, probably not since you'd rather have your head inside a piece of wood, than responsibly govern a community that needs you…

There was more, several hundred words more. I picked up the tiny carving of an owl I'd made a while back and fiddled with it. That part of the message was right; I *would* rather be creating furniture or other useful items in my carpentry shop than dealing with people. The craft of melding nature's designs with my ideas on shaping wood had obsessed me since childhood. But I'd forced myself to help the community, doing my duty, taking my turn as head coordinator. Tanisa was wrong there—I didn't "govern". We all worked together now, different than Grandma's era, deciding minor things and putting major things to a referendum.

Oh. I set the carving down.

A *referendum.*

Of course. We'd all been too incensed to think of it.

Vivid Worlds

It took a long tedious meeting with my team that evening but we got it hastily set up for the next day. We mass-messaged everyone who'd consented to be informed, three-quarters of the community. Signage appeared on the notice boards, flashing at a frequency rate of twice an hour, higher than most referendums. I wasn't expecting much—most referendums dealt with the type of fence the communal farm fields should have, or whether we should plant beets or carrots this year beside the reclaimed shopping mall, so a 20% turnout was typical.

The online advance poll and chat room wavered back and forth, opinions flying. Throughout the evening and into the night it stayed about even—half in favour of keeping the Folly, half against.

With Oil Day looming, I wandered the market stalls at daybreak, listening and watching, the crowds making me uneasy in my skin as usual. People chatted and waved their hands. Some buzz about the sighting of a cougar by the river, and a lot of chat about the literary festival happening later in the summer—it seemed like everyone wanted to do a reading of their works-in-progress, whether it was a novel or poetry or just an anecdote about daily life. But nothing much about the referendum.

Finally I stopped at the tool stall and picked up a handsome old plane, all worn oak and aged metal, fitting nicely in my hand. Remi, the wizened carpenter who'd restored tools since I was a kid, ambled over. "Somebody's ground this too thin," I said, fingering the blade. "The first knot that it hits will wreck the edge."

Remi eyed me, one earring glinting in the sun. "Everything has more life in it than you'd think. Even old tanks of gas." They jerked a thumb in the direction of the Folly, three blocks away. "I hear your daughter's been raising a fuss over it. And some other kids."

"And what do you think, Remi? Is it an idea whose time has passed? Or does it serve a need, still?" The plane suddenly felt heavy and I put it down.

"I remember getting my hands shoved in that bucket. I had nightmares for weeks each and every time. Glad we don't do that anymore." Their callused hand rubbed one shoulder as if reassuring themself.

I nodded. "I used to cut my nails really short afterwards, short enough to bleed, just to be sure that no poison lurked under them."

Tanisa suddenly pushed past my elbow. "Hi, Remi. You have that package for me?" She spoke brightly and clearly, making eye contact—or at least looking at Remi's chin—then smiled up at me. She'd been that way for the past two days. Friendly but distant. Faking it. Masking. Is this what I wanted? A daughter who seemed neurotypical in every way? Or the usual Tanisa: impatient, impetuous, unable and unwilling to understand or follow the less common-sense cultural norms. Someone who was her own person, someone who had obsessions with things like *Brassica* species, the Fibonacci sequence, and 3D printers.

"Tanny, I—"

"Gotta go, Mom. Meeting some folks." She took the burlap-wrapped package from Remi with a well-modulated Thank You, holding it in her arms like a baby. A very heavy baby.

She slid past me, oil on water, and was gone.

Remi winked at me and sauntered off to help someone else.

On Oil Day, the poll was at 55% in favour of keeping the Folly. Voting would start at noon and end at sunset. I'd arranged to trade a refinished pine desk for two hand-woven shirts so I wrapped it in an old quilt and hauled it in my ancient handcart, down the woodshop ramp and past the gathering place, the handcart's reprinted tires nicely gripping the cobblestones.

The Folly glowed in the morning sun, its window like a Cyclops's eye watching to see what we foolish humans would do next. Some short stick-like things shone at its base. I propped up the cart and went nearer for a closer look. A hammer leaned against the tank, right under the amber-hued window. I picked it up, recognizing it from Remi's stash of almost-usable-but-we-still-have-better-ones bin. A metre away was another one, this one ballpeen. And over by the bakery were three more: a claw hammer, a tack hammer, and a framing hammer.

And just beyond sat my best upholstery hammer. And my second best ballpeen.

I steadied my breath. Tanisa must have scooped them from my shop when I wasn't looking. And gotten the rest from Remi.

And she'd mentioned meeting people.

What else had she been doing under my nose?

Tanisa was waiting for me in her usual summertime study seat under the big-leaf maple in the south courtyard. I'd picked up six of my hammers as I walked over, and passed forty-eight others, quite a few painted beige.

Her screen displayed chemical formulas but I could see the Folly poll running in the corner—it had dropped a bit; just 47% now were in favour of keeping it. One of the strange beige hammers sat at her elbow.

I set down my carry bag, hammers clanking.

"Did you think I wouldn't—" I stopped. Clearly, she didn't think. Or, at least, she didn't think *that* way. Time I learned that. "Why wouldn't you just discuss it with me and—" I stopped again. I'd told her not to, and she'd taken me literally the way she had her whole life.

I started again. "What if someone had broken the tank's window with one of these hammers? People would have been hurt; soil would have been contaminated. You know how many tree roots run under the gathering place?" I tried to make my voice radiate only concern but I'm sure anger tainted it.

"It's not likely, Mom, the tank metal is super solid and so's the glass, but people will *think* it's possible, that's the whole point, using their stupidity to get them to vote to take it down. And, since I knew you'd worry anyway, I assigned watchers. See, here's the schedule." She tapped her screen and showed me the careful spreadsheet, filled with times and names of teenagers that lived near us.

"Why would they help *you*?" I blurted it out, then tried to backtrack. "I mean, of course, you have friends—"

"Of course I don't. Get a grip, Mom. You know how I am."

"I do." I resisted hugging her. Physical contact didn't reassure her, never had. It just raised her anxiety levels, since it required a social response and since touch of any kind was overstimulating. Just a couple of the things we had in common.

"The other teens helped because they see problems with it too. Different problems, like how we could use that space for something better, like a snack bar."

I started to cross my arms then deliberately forced myself to relax, words coming slowly and thoughtfully for once. "Dismantling the Folly is that important to you? I'm trying to understand here."

"No, Mom." She spoke patiently, probably resisting rolling her eyes. "It's that important to you. You sniff and rub your nose whenever you walk by the Folly or anyone speaks about gas-powered engines or old-timey cars or lawn threshers."

"Lawnmowers," I corrected absently.

"Aunt Jill said something wise the other day." She hesitated.

"First time ever," I said then regretted it. "Go ahead, tell me."

"She said that you older folks think you deserve this thing glaring at you as you pass by, this annual Oil Day suffering, because you still feel guilty for things you weren't even alive for."

"That's silly. I mean, I know there's generationally-carried trauma and my cortisone levels are affected by what your great-grandpa and grandma went through but I don't feel that—"

"Why are you a coordinator when you really hate that stuff and you'd rather be woodworking? Why are you *head* coordinator? You're *punishing* yourself."

"Is that what Jill said?"

"No, Mom." She took a breath and laid a hand on my arm, a light touch that I knew cost her emotionally. "It's what I said." Her voice grew gentler. "You've atoned enough.'"

I sat for a moment, considering.

I picked up the beige hammer, my fingers needing something to do. It weighed too little and felt wrong, like brittle plastic or something.

"Here," Tanisa said. "Give it here." She grinned the mischievous grin of a typical 14-year-old, then took a big bite of the handle and spoke through a spray of crumbs. "Needed more hammers to make my point visually but couldn't scrounge any more. Couldn't let that disgusting food pulp we have stored go to waste. The 3D printer had an easy template."

I laughed for the first time in days.

She broke the hammer head off with a snap and handed it to me. "Try it. It's terrible. We're going to serve them at the Oil Day picnic this afternoon, as a reminder."

"When did my daughter get so wise?" This time, I did give her a hug, just a short one before we both pulled away at the same time.

The vote went through: 23% in favour of keeping it, 71% against, 6% undecided. The council immediately made plans to dismantle and drain the Folly's tank. I don't know if the presence of all Tanisa's phony hammers turned the tide, and I tended not to ask people how or why they voted. I buried myself in the tedium of the logistics—that's one big danger-ous tank. How were we so *very* foolish all these years?

Sometimes I still have the bucket nightmare, frigid poison pouring over my fists, fumes burning my nose, but not as often. I started seeing the community therapist again, which is helping a lot.

Oh, and after Tanisa apologized to William for the dirt flinging and did some chores for him, I assigned her to be part of the task force to figure out how to properly decommission the gasoline, turn it into useful things. It's a real challenge for everyone; the obvious uses like paint thinner or a tool cleaner are a no-go, of course. And simply disposing of it responsibly is even more challenging. But we aren't the type to shirk responsibilities.

Tanisa gets all her instructions by messaging, sends in reports that way too, and she's turning into a wonderful scientist. I even put her in charge of two younger kids doing simple research on repurposing the glass window and she's giving them clear and patient direction.

Don't ever tell her but she'll make a great coordinator someday.

Tractors in the mist
Cécile Cristofari

Dawn breaking on a long straight road, fog resting over the ground, feather-light yet thick and still as stone. On either side, the ghosts of rusty machinery, tractors like skeletons guarding the road in a twin wall. In the middle, figures gathering, placards raised, though one would need to come very close to read what they say.

I stretch my back, aching from the morning damp, and search for familiar faces. Some of them I've lost track of and only meet at this time of the year, cold, short days just breaking out. It is in winter that we protest, when the fields can rest for a day, when we can dangle the threat of leaving our lands fallow when the spring comes or sell the cattle before the young are born. It has been a long time since we've needed to resort to threats, but still we show up, when we're called.

Here is someone I know—Margiella. I wave across the fog. A kiss on each cheek; we already need to raise our voices to talk. I grin, realising this. I can feel it already, the camaraderie, the energy rising. Margiella chafes her gloved hands.

"So what's this about again, this time?" she says. "I heard milk prices?"

"That, and they're bringing up five-hundred-cow farms again," I say.

"Like that's going to happen!"

"Well, better if they know we know it's a terrible idea, isn't it?"

She smirks.

"I'm here, aren't I?" she says. "Not sure that's doing much good, but I'm here."

We stroll together, past a gigantic piece of machinery,

wheels as tall as we are. Margiella looks up at the rusted cockpit. Says nothing. Enthusiasm aside, it is true that the union's demands are rarely met. We still struggle, year after year. But our heads are above the water at least, and that's something to hold on to.

Drums, trumpets and shouts begin rising, far ahead. Slowly, like wheat erupting from its husk, the crowd begins marching.

Long ago

Breaking dawn, in winter, motors rumbling around us as the tractors assemble along the road, blocking traffic. A couple of unhappy-looking policemen pace about, redirecting even unhappier drivers away from the area. Defiant calls from the cockpits here and there, like owls hooting. From my own vehicle, I scan the crowd, looking for familiar faces. Many *are* familiar; it simply does not make me happier to see them, however. One of them waves with a grin that could be more sarcastic than friendly. Our latest conversation about his chemicals contaminating my fields nearly ended up in fisticuffs.

At last a face I am pleased to see. I stop my tractor by the side of the road and step down, relieved. It feels much too high up in there. The time is gone when modest machinery could get you by on a farm. By the time I have finished paying for the monster I now park in the way of incoming traffic, I will be lucky if I can still move around. I wave across, and my old friend Nayla hops down from her own tractor and joins me on the asphalt.

She has shadows under her eyes and her smile looks strained.

"Short night?" I say.

She shrugs and mutters something about feeding the cattle,

then looks around at the crowd. After a while, she lets out a long sigh.

"I suppose we're all in the same boat," she says.

I nod. We are indeed: working the same land, facing the same scorn, wrestling the same corporations, drowning in the same debts. Working together, protesting together. Not that many of us are happy about it. Today we stand side by side on the road; tomorrow we will be back to fighting each other over who has the greater claim to the land—a battle that the little ones, the organic goat herders, the hedge growers and polyculture farmers, keep losing and losing.

Which is why we are here, really. Though Nayla and I see very little of each other outside of protests, consumed as we are by the demands of farm life, the last few weeks has seen us talk a lot more. Nayla looks around. From the corner of my eye, I see another police car loom behind us.

"Has Justine arrived?" she asks.

"I thought you were meeting her this morning?"

She shakes her head and says nothing. I feel sudden dread.

"She *is* coming, isn't she?"

"She said she would. She's talked to her colleagues. She's got five different newspapers coming. Quite the audience." She laughs. It sounds small and afraid.

I squeeze her arm.

"I hope they'll get past the police," I say, though only to make small talk.

It doesn't matter much if they don't. They will want additional images, for certain; but they need little more than what we have already handed to them. Standing in the middle of the road, I keep surveying the growing crowd like a general watching soldiers, though they're not my soldiers and if this is a war (which it may be), I'm more of a traitor than an officer. The thrill of knowing that we might have been found out worms its way into my mind, but it feels energising, more than sobering. This is quite a story we've delivered. Or rather, it is one more story, yet another human and environmental scandal in a country that has had them by the dozen. It's unlikely to change anything, I know, but I also know that Nayla is right: you cannot tell what the tipping point will be unless you're actually tipping.

"Over there," Nayla says.

At first, I think she's pointing to another group of acquaintances, Julian who fitted solar panels to the roof of my chicken coop last year, Margiella the former jurist who brings her sheep to graze down the lawns of public parks. I start waving. Then I see the dark van Nayla is showing me.

They look like police. Or rather, they don't. Not enough.

"What's that?" I say.

"Private security," she replies.

I'm not certain how she knows. But I believe her.

"Shit."

The energy recedes, and I do begin to feel sobered. The law protects whistleblowers, or so it says. But there are no *whistleblowers* when it comes to farming. Only environmental extremists with warped views of agriculture, or so the state says. The police have a dedicated task force for people like us. If the chemical firms we raised the alarm against—are getting to raise our placards about right now, in fact—have sent mercenaries, I doubt there will be a dedicated police force to deal with *that*.

Just like there is no one, and nothing, guarding our profession against looming abyss of debt, land sinking into barrenness under the chemicals we pour into the earth, day in day out, so we can meet market demands that have long passed the bounds of the reasonable or even the biologically possible, our own bodies filling up with poison, and yet with banks still demanding that we make food grow from the ground after it has turned to ashes. I raise the bag where we've stashed our rolled-up banners.

"If we take fright at the first black van we see…" I mutter.

Nayla nods. She's not taking her eyes from them. She holds out her hand and in it I place the pole that holds the banner up. She reacts with a half-smile.

The crowd shifts about us. Some wave and walk closer. Some faces harden, too, and drift away. Over there, to the side, not quite where the line of policemen is, the van opens.

Nayla places a hand on my arm.

"I need to tell you something," she says. Her voice is very strange. "I'm not—I'm not one of the crazies. I've never been. My children—they don't think they want to work on the farm when I retire. They say I'm mad to keep trying. They think not using pesticides is as bad as not wanting to get vaccinated. They'd just like me to get a larger tractor and rip down the hedges on my land, plant wheat in rows, claim whatever money I can from the state and try to get bigger before I starve. I love them so much, and they think I'm crazy. And I'm not. You know that, don't you?"

I gape at her.

"Nayla, are you all right?"

But now she's pointing at the people getting out of the van, strolling about, peering between the assembled machines. Unassuming, drably dressed, people you wouldn't notice.

"I'm all right," she says. "Maybe I did something a little crazy this morning."

I try to keep my eyes on the newcomers. But the crowd is already moving forward along the empty stretch of road. The flow pushes us on. A megaphone blares ahead; I walk closer to Nayla.

"Are you really sure you're OK?" I say. But she just nods.

"You know what they used to say, back in the day? No, I don't suppose you do. Well. They said… if you went out on your own before dawn, on a solstice day, and you walked really far from houses, didn't talk, didn't sing, didn't eat, didn't hear the cock's crow—then maybe, if you did everything right, as you passed by the church on your way back, you would see people walking into mass. But not this year's mass. Next year's."

Voices rise around us, chanting, marching. *Our end, your hunger.* I almost join in. It would have seemed to push Nayla away, however, so I stay quiet.

"Only nobody goes to mass any longer, do they?" she continues, with a wry sound that's not quite a laugh. "I'm not sure I was hoping for anything. And anyway, it's not like there are churches in industrial zones. I just kept walking before the sun rose, and I ended up here. And… look, you have to listen to the end. I'm not crazy. Right?"

I shake my head because there is no other way to respond. We slowly walk past police cars, as one ponderous beast. They have brough riot shields, batons. I know they mean them for intimidation rather than actual use. I still have to fight an impulse to drift towards the middle of the road; I make myself raise the banner higher instead.

"*Traitors!*" someone shouts behind us.

I turn around. Nayla doesn't. My eyes meet a hostile gaze, an older man in a thick padded jacket. I ignore him after a couple of seconds, though my heart is still racing. We knew this would happen. A lot of people in the crowd had come to demand the means to do business as usual without sinking under further debt, as they have for the past fifty years. As for us, we may be farmers, but we're fighting to smash down business as usual. Common interests may impose a truce, but as soon as the protest ends, we will be back to being the enemy, even more so now that we have raised the alarm about what kind of supposedly 'harmless' chemicals our soils are absorbing. I only hope that it can wait until after the protest.

The more we demonstrate, the more the public shrugs us

off as a temporary inconvenience. I hope our whole fight will not sink into indifference as soon as the road is cleared of machinery. I pick up the chant, and for a while, Nayla and I march on, shouting, until we arrive in view of the growing traffic jam we've created, past the police line. The crowd stops there, gathering energy.

Nayla has fallen silent.

"So, was that the end?" I prompt.

"No." She says nothing for a while. "No. It's not. Look, in the end, I walked right up to here. There was just a bit of light. I arrived here, and I saw…" She gestures around. "This. All of this. At first, I thought people had arrived early. And then I saw people I knew, and I called out, and they never seemed to see me, and… and that's when I understood. This wasn't real. It hadn't come to pass yet. I was walking in front of next year's protest."

There is more shouting behind. My hands tighten around the banner. This isn't chanting, or even random insults of the kind we're used to have thrown at us. The calls are mounting, some aggressive, some fearful, some feral. There's a shift, people turning around. Our acquaintances gather close.

Just then, I glimpse a face I know, one of the journalists we have been in touch with. I don't manage to get her attention, though. The crowd is growing tighter, coming to a halt where people attempt to turn their cars around.

"How do you know it was next year's protest?" I ask Nayla, as neutrally as I can.

But she waves me off.

"I can't explain. Look, what you need to know… it's about to work. The tipping point, remember? This is it. We've done it. But we can't let go now. Next year it's going to be us, and they'll have changed regulations, we'll still be pushing but those industrial farms will be on their way out, only we can't stop, do you understand? It works *only if we keep trying!*"

And the shouts behind us grow louder, and I remember the nondescript, unassuming people coming out of a private security van, ready to blend in and stir up whatever they were ordered to, and the crowd shifts like a wave and there are people pushing through, hurling things, whooping and ripping banners out of hands and throwing them at cars.

Something flies past my head. It was supposed to be another protest, perhaps useless, at best a way of keeping our heads above the water. But now the police in riot gear are coming—towards us. *Us*, of course. The little ones, the organic farmers, the idealists from the hippy communes. The ones who paint anarchist emblems on their banners and whose balaclava helmets look like they're meant to shield us from view, not from the cold.

There are calls to stand down. Reflexively, I take a step backwards. Nayla's hand shoots towards me and grabs my arm. When I look at her, she's shaking her head, her eyes wide open, a look of grief and terror on her face.

"We can't give up now," she says.

"This is getting bad. If we're accused of derailing the protest, this could be worse for our—"

"Please."

It feels like being caught in a strong wind. The police's megaphone blares orders again. The riot shields are raised, and smoke already rises from somewhere down the crowd. My eyes water. Teargas, dispersing in the wind.

But Nayla still grips my arm.

"There's another thing the legend says," she goes on, urgently, above the increasingly disorganised noises. "If you manage to see next year's mass, that means you'll see who's sitting in the pews, and who isn't. And so… you'll know who's died, during the year." A policeman is approaching, face shielded, entirely dark. Nayla's laugh is shaky. "It's not like anyone here ever goes to mass, right? But we come here.

We all know who wouldn't miss a protest unless…"

The policeman raises his arm. I pull Nayla back just as the sting-ball grenade flies towards us. Towards the ground, which would be vacant now, if we had indeed pulled back, as the policeman must have thought we would.

Except that Nayla didn't pull back. Eyes unblinking, despairing, she stands right there and never takes her eyes off the weapon, which should have hit the ground and only hurt us enough to scatter us like a flock of birds—and instead hits her right in the chest.

Long after

Margiella makes a face and squeezes my arm.

"Sorry. I shouldn't have said that."

I realise I haven't responded to her comment about the uselessness of protests, and I shake my head.

"Don't worry. I wasn't thinking about…"

I stop, because I was. Walking by the abandoned tractors, I saw ghosts, for the briefest while. Nayla's ghost, of course; her eyes opening even wider when that grenade struck her, then the noise, the blood, the disbelief. The policeman's ghost, too, though I'd seen very little of him, only a brief, horrified flailing, then a voice in a radio, frantically calling for help. And a horde of other ghosts that were not to come back to that site.

We were right, both Nayla and me. I'd known that yet another whistle blown would change nothing by itself. And as it turned out, very few people talked about our leaked data, in the aftermath. No one cared that the newly touted, seemingly harmless pesticides were destroying the soil at an even faster rate than the one before. But they did care about the riot that followed upon Nayla's death, once they saw the pictures taken by the journalist our revelations had brought to the roadside that morning. The looming election was supposed to be a formality, billionaires and their authoritarian allies taking the vote amid general resignation, while other parties bickered and despaired. No one had counted on the turmoil and grief the death of a fifty-year-old mother, and the dozens of wounded, would stir up through the country. Within days, an unexpected alliance had formed. And risen. And won the government.

And the reassurances to us that had thus far been little more than words began to turn into funds, reforms, the long-needed overhaul beginning at last.

We still came back to protest, around the solstice, every year. We had our dead to remember, and a battle that still needed fighting. But we were no longer drowning. It cost us less now to plant hedges than to tear them down, to let cattle graze about fallow fields than to send beasts to the slaughterhouse and scar the ground with machines. Bees came back as peddlers of chemicals were forced to withdraw; farmers rose their heads where industrialists lost ground. When the city, amazingly, agreed to let those of us who now found their gigantic tractors useless leave them by the side of the road as a memorial to those whose blood had seeded change, I brought mine and left on the back of a donkey Nayla's son had brought, after placing a bunch of wild flowers by the ditch.

Rusted, crumbling cockpits poke through the mist like dinosaur bones. And we're marching, a congregation of hope, because our ground needs to be held, because no battle is ever won for good, because the world did not stop overnight believing that those who work the earth are worth less than the dirt they shovel. Sun rising, fog shimmering, another year sinking into winter. The days will grow longer again, very soon.

And we march on across the mist.

Don't Blame the Tanuki Temple Thief

R.J.K. Lee

A farewell haiku, oh-la, but I tried to make it yummy and positive. Feel it? The working title is a bit on the nose but tanukis sure got cute ones.

"Tanuki Temple"
Belly groans. Bells chime.
Take crickets, rice, coconuts.
Storm refuge feeds friends.

So, Gwen and I have left. We're sorry, Moms, Dads, everyone. No offense to the community. It's just that the scaly lurks, the tanuki chimes, and we follow the tug of their promises. I doubt we can prove what we've seen and heard, unless we strike out and explore more than we're allowed here.

Maybe while we're gone, you'll discover what we did—or antsy Ami and Brickell will show you—and if you do, be sure to feed them more. They give as much as they take.

Not sure many will understand me. Understand us, as Gwen clarifies. She's very *on* me about taking no blame. Another reason we agreed to leave. I'm a blame magnet. Sarine understands, I'm sure.

The community does need to stay safe, needs to avoid making a footprint that might destroy what balance we all worked to rebuild. Traveling the wild, we'll keep such respect in mind. Maybe one day, we'll scamper home carefree and drifting on potential discovered. Just like the lizards lurk under rocks then pop out in a flash of sunny colour. Just like the tanukis pat their bellies in the shade, grinning over sweet rice.

Despite what I did, I agree with the more faithful among us. Keep up those offerings.

Know that we're safe and learning plenty in the next commune over. Main reason we're sending a long message on vine net.

One story to share about how we got to this point. Started with me being naughty again, oh-la, playing lone wolf in my explorations, talking about mythical creatures turned alive and magical, not deadly at all.

I'd gotten caught, remember, carrying that statue of a tanuki from one of the temples. Tucked it in my basket of rice and coconuts. Idiotic, I admit. Should've left the statue in its place. I thought it might catch the tanuki's attention.

Sarine took me aside after the adults had a meeting. "Really, Ninako?" She crossed her arms. "Not only ignoring what we said was off limits, started stealing, too?"

"It didn't belong to any—"

"Belonged to the temple. Plenty people fear yokai will punish us for that."

"C'mon! Tell them they're overreacting."

"They understand you're a foolish child."

"I'm fifteen. Damn! And it was just a statue."

"Language. Act responsibly if you think you're all grown up. Wouldn't have to reprimand you, if you'd listen. We're happy if you work in the rice fields and coconut trees. But don't wander the outskirts alone, no matter what wild creatures you think you see. We closed that area for a reason. Show respect. Don't worry everyone."

"There's nothing to...I haven't..."

"Yes? You say we're overreacting, but dear, there's more to this than angry spirits. Understand what happened before you were born. Millions of species gone in the last century and on through this one. We survived by overreacting. By gathering anybody we could, hunching down in mountain hideouts, making these limited communes and adapting controlled farms. The outside world's still a threat. Rules protect us, help us grow stronger together over the decades. We allow what we can. We encourage love and diversity and play, the basics of humanity, you know that. When it comes to the outside world, you understand, not many species remain, and those that do are pumped full of so much poison and sickness."

"Yah, I get it, I do, but I've been...I swear that...aughhh..." I flailed at the annoyance I wanted to express: *duh, I understand, I heard the same speech from every mom and dad.* But I'd been hiding my whole life and wondered if the world hadn't healed enough already to warrant freedom to explore and enjoy the world around us. What hope and joy lay hidden from us in our fear to bounce back from doom?

I bowed my head. "Gomen nasai." A humble apology in my family's native tongue.

Sarine returned my politeness with a slight bow. "I'll schedule you for farm work next week with Gwen. You two look out for each other. Listen to Gwen. A year your elder, and she's been a leader in youth experiments with new foods."

Everyone trusted and adored Gwen. But she had a crush on me, I knew it, and she wasn't about to stop me from showing off what I'd discovered. She'd beg me to show her, oh-la.

And yep, Gwen told me it's OK to divulge that in writing, so no doubt. I mean, I've turned sixteen since then, so leave us be.

We hiked out. Gwen took my hand at the last ridge, and we gazed over the outlying farms near the beach and the dilapidated temple everyone left alone, claiming it was haunted by yokai.

Her big blue eyes latched onto me. "You really saw it out here?"

"A tanuki waddling in the shadow of the temple. Like it was stealing rice to store in its pot. A bell chiming as it ran."

"What's that moving on the beach then? Is that it?"

I saw it, the flicker of movement in the shadows of beach rocks.

"Might be. Let's get closer."

When we reached the palm trees and looked out toward the waves, we spotted a wriggly, scaly yellow-and-black creature about the size of me. It crawled from the shadows of the rock onto a sun-drenched stone.

Pressed against a tree trunk, we held hands.

"Is that it then?" Gwen asked. "Maybe you mistook it for a tanuki when it crept through the shadows before."

"Much different shape. Look at the size, oh-la. Imagine if there are more."

Gwen tightened her grip. "If there are, we're in serious trouble. Let's back off and finish our quota. Then tell the adults what we found."

"The moms and dads will complain that we'll lose half the crop to the next storm. They'll blame me for corrupting you then apologize for their anger and drag me to demonstrations of mindful breathing and capoeira steps for a better self. As if."

"The capoeira's fun. Don't worry. I'll demand they blame me, too."

"Nah, let's do this. They think I need to be the same careful, sad people they are, but I like my weird self just fine. Wait here."

I crept from the palm trees.

Gwen hurried after. "You idiot. Ninako, put this on." She tied my handkerchief around my head, protection against the shining sun. "They'll really get on your case if you don't wear common sense like this." She checked my air filtration mask. "OK, here we go."

I whispered to her as we crept closer. "Everyone down here has to take special care not to breathe the air, drink the water, eat the wrong fruit, touch the rare animal. Most things fatally poisonous, punishment from the capitalist end times our moms and dads survived as babies. But it's been half a century since they survived. Time for healing. We're teens, grown enough to work, travel communes, fish between gaps in typhoons and tsunamis."

Gwen squeezed my hand. "Look!"

A winged creature danced about the stones. A lone, red-shelled crab scurried in shallow water. More movement than usual.

The massive, yellow-and-black scaly lizard curled around the sunny rocks. I breathed deep through my mask, centred myself, and continued over the sand. "I saw one of these," I whispered. "On the day of respect and mourning. An elder collected thousands of images of things lost. Especially extinct species."

"This is extinct?"

Five more steps and we reached the wide stone the scaly lazed upon. It twitched its head in our direction, a triangular chunk as big as five coconuts. Shifting its body to face me, its tail whipped around to splash the water lapping at the stone's rear. With a flick of a forked pink tongue, it dashed off the rock and into the brush along the coconut trees, leaving a flurry of sand dust in its wake.

On the rock, I found a fragment of yellow-and-black shed skin. I tucked it away then we finished collecting coconuts.

"We got to tell the adults." Gwen placed a coconut in her basket. "We both saw it. They'll believe us."

I gazed at the silhouette of the temple through the trees. "They'll take it the wrong way. Let me take the blame."

As soon as we returned, Gwen said we had to tell the adults, so I told her hush again, let me do the talking, and we went to tell Sarine. At least she wouldn't outright deny me like everyone else.

I planted my fists on my hips, proud to show a brave face against the community's fear. "I saw the big lizard right on the beach near that old, eroded temple by the sea that everyone's scared of."

"Seriously? Went to the outskirts again, did you?" Mom Sarine clasped her hands in front of her healthy bosom. She'd been feeding her baby. Milk stains on her chest. She wasn't holding the baby though, which meant she was napping in her cradle. "Fought too hard to keep our mountain safe for you to go out there. Just had this talk, didn't we? Were you there Gwen?"

Gwen nodded.

I held up a finger, stopping Gwen from saying anything. "We were out collecting food to quota," I said. "Coconuts around that temple, too. See, thirty of them in this basket."

"But I just told you." Sarine heaved a huge, breast-rippling sigh. "Well, did you touch this creature?"

"I—"

The wind howled in the treetops. I looked up as if I'd find an answer there.

"Well, you did, didn't you?" Sarine shook her clasped hands at me. "Admit it, then let's drag you and Gwen to the clinic for quarantine. Now I've got to be quarantined too, just talking to you about this nonsense. Really, Ninako, how come I put up with you?"

"You don't put up with much now do you, Mom." I pulled out the shed lizard skin. "I touched this."

Mom shook a finger at me. "Nuh-uh, you didn't. A definite no-no."

I held the shed lizard skin up higher. "I saw this skin, this lizard, when your father had it on the day of respect and mourning. You always talk about him and his research. Don't tell me you're not into this stuff."

"The colours do look familiar. But he left us after that. I'd rather not think about him."

"Maybe he left for a reason."

"I'll pretend I didn't hear that. Fine, quickly, before the storm, show me."

Sarine didn't waste a moment. We led her to the beach where we'd found the scaly. At the palm trees, I spotted the same stones but out in the water with the waves splashing harder. The tide had shifted closer. The lighting darkened. Not a creature in view. No flyer, no shell, no scaly. "Gone."

Gwen took my hand. "I don't see anything either."

"You're sure you both saw it?"

"I wouldn't bring you here if I wasn't."

Gwen squeezed my hand. "I saw it, too, Sarine."

"Storm's on us." Sarine planted her fists on her hips. "Whatever it is, it probably sensed as much and took shelter. We better do the same. Maybe we spot it next time."

There was no next time. The raging storm destroyed outer farms and homes, and over the next few months, shelters had to be constructed, damage repaired, people assisted.

I was placed in a youth rescue team to assist adults in retrieving lost goods from the disaster and storing them in the mountain shelters. So, I convinced the team to visit outlying farms "to see what we could rescue," though really, I aimed to share both my discoveries, the lizard and the tanuki.

The four of us arrived at the trees to find them mostly intact. Fallen coconuts covered the ground so we split up to effectively gather up the fruit. Investigating the inland side were stout Brickell and lithe Ami. Polar opposites in temperament but ever doting on each other.

Gwen and I wandered the beach side. I plucked our third

coconut from the sand and placed it in the basket. "Keep your eyes open. You know what we saw, but you still haven't seen the tanuki."

Gwen bent down to collect our fourth coconut. "Probably gone after the storm."

"That lizard was big and sturdy. Probably burrowed nearby. The tanuki…I dunno."

"Maybe we should stick together. Brickell's big and sturdy, too. If that lizard turns aggressive…" Gwen pointed into the coconut trees where silhouettes of Brickell and Ami cracked through the underbrush.

I spread my hands wide. "We're not too far. If it's still here, it'll run from us like last time, not attack."

She raised a pointer finger for emphasis. "We better not get sick. We're lucky we didn't get quarantined last time."

"Sarine knows better."

"Or she forgot, in the face of that storm."

I climbed atop the stones where we saw the scaly before, then came a swift shuffling whisper. The lizard bolted from a hidden crevice to the trees. Gwen shouted in alarm. I screamed in delight.

Brickell and Ami hollered a unified, "You OK?!"

I charged after the scaly. Foolish, I know, but the thrill overwhelmed any practical sensibilities I might have had. This was my chance to show off my discovery and stop being laughed off by the adults.

Scaly left plumes of dust in its wake. I squinted as I dashed through puffs of the sand clouds and followed the creature into the trees. It tore loose leaves and branches, tossing them in my face. I raised my arms against the onslaught and pressed on, ignoring the screams of "Wait for us!" and "Come back!"

My right foot slammed into a fat coconut, knocking it thumping into the nearest tree trunk. The rest of my body sped forward, thrusting me off-balance. I sprawled through branches and leaves and into the dirt.

I spit out grit, wiping my slashed arms as I stood. I peered about for the lizard and saw nothing but a trashed coconut farm.

A hand clamped on my shoulder. "Wait," Gwen said. "We'll help."

Brickell, Ami, and Gwen hurried on with me through the trail of shredded underbrush, which led us out of the coconut trees and along the overgrown rice fields to the haunted temple entrance. We walked up the eroded steps and into a flat area. Sliding doors had been crunched through and lay twisted, hanging, a dark mould chewing at the edges.

I went in first, fearless. Gwen followed after, fingers on my back. Then Brickell and Ami.

Bells hung around the room. Clumps of rice and fruit and insects scattered along the floor. The massive lizard shuffled around a wooden platform, a baby chair, probably stolen from our community. Or maybe someone had brought it to the temple along with other offerings.

On the platform of that chair sat a fuzzy, chubby rat-like creature with impressive whiskers and ears, brown and black streaks of fur, and a definite male with large balls hanging down…the tanuki, reaching up a paw and tapping a bell that hung before it. *Chime chime chime.*

"I told you! There he is!"

"There they both are!" Gwen squeezed my shoulder.

"Dad always said they're real," Brickell said.

Ami clucked her tongue, then asked, "Does this mean you really did make him mad?"

"I was trying to get his attention," I said.

The tanuki swatted the bell aside, *chime*, then pounced onto the clump of rice nearest us and bared its teeth.

Scaly swivelled around to face us and hissed.

"Careful, Ninako," Gwen said.

I raised my hands and bowed my head. "We're friends."

The tanuki started chittering and barking at me, snapping its jaws as it rambled nonsensically.

The lizard behind it kept hissing and swiping its tail along the ground.

"Let's get out of here," Brickell said.

"Agreed," Ami said.

I heard them backpedalling for the exit, but Gwen's fingers still clung to my shoulder.

"Just wait a second." I reached into my basket and extracted a coconut, which I held out a few centimetres from the tanuki's cute, wet nose.

The tanuki ceased blabbering and sniffed at the coconut. The lizard stopped hissing and flicked a tongue at the offering, too.

The tanuki patted a paw on the coconut and knocked, grinning at the hollow *thwock thwock thwoc*k. Swaying side-to-side, he did another *thwock thwock thwock* then placed both paws on the sides of the coconut and pulled it from me.

I let go, smiling. "Go on and take it, friend."

He carried the treasure to the old baby chair, then he sat with the coconut resting on his ball sack and reached his paws scrambling around the sides and back of the chair. A sizeable rock in paw, he started hitting the coconut until it cracked. He scooped the white meat out and shoved it into his mouth. Then he offered the next portion to scaly, who sucked it from his paw and munched with satisfaction.

After the pair had devoured their coconut, Brickell and Ami still hadn't returned.

"Should we go look for them?"

"Not yet. Look at the tanuki, Gwen. He wants another one."

The tanuki had both paws swinging in the air in front of the chair, watching us with his beady eyes.

"Clearly," Gwen said.

"I can't remember for sure," I said. "I think Sarine's father said lizards eat all sorts of things. Not so many coconuts. I mostly remember insects. Maybe we should fetch some."

"I'll go," Gwen said. "Scream and run if you need help. I'll be right around the entrance. I saw some flies in a web."

Gwen hunted insects for scaly, while I offered another coconut to the tanuki. He took it, but then he placed it on his chair, pounced onto the floor, and started scratching into the packed dirt and rock with his claws. I stepped back in case this turned into outright aggression. Dust rose from his work and seemed to sparkle and flash with images of rice fields, fruit trees, more animals scurrying about, humans collecting food, leaves blowing in the breeze, ocean waves and statues and temples.

By the time Gwen returned, the tanuki had finished and returned to feasting on the coconut. Scaly turned its head away from any more of the fruit's white meat.

"Flies, and found a few crickets," Gwen said. "What did you do?"

She scanned the floor while holding forth a leaf plate of insects in her hands.

"I swear, it was him." I pointed at the tanuki snacking on the chair.

"Whaaa…?"

"The guy scratched this out while you were gone. After I gave him the second coconut."

"Huh." Gwen met my eyes and shrugged. "So, like a gift in return."

"Maybe?" I swept my head across the floor "Looks like a map to me. Water. Trees. Clumpy people."

Gwen squatted for a closer look. "Those triangles look like other temples, don't they?"

"Maybe. Places for us to reclaim. Probably what the little

guy wants, oh-la."

So, oh-la, believe it or not, a tanuki fed the lizard from his mini throne like he owned the temple. He didn't care that I'd kidnapped the statue, whoever it belonged to. The tanuki patted his belly as we decided he must be showing us other temples, other places he'd been.

We'll be looking for more. We hope you take care of whatever we've left behind in the temple, no matter how hard to believe upon first reading. Easier to blame. Harder to accept.

"We'll be back to check on you all," Gwen tells me to write.

"Will we?" I have to ask.

She says we will, and that you'd better stop being sad and paranoid, Sarine and everyone, because we want a better world to live in. We want a world in which we can embrace everything. A little risk is OK, as long as there's a lot of open love to go with.

Kisses from us both, and maybe she's right, we'll return soon enough. Until then, oh-la, another haiku:

"Coconut Wind Sings"

Joined temples chime hope

when storms wash away what grew,

leaves, breeze sighs field, fruit.

Post-Apocalyptic Survey of the Heart of Hokkaido

Toshiya Kamei

"Look, Namika!" I shout into the moaning wind as she climbs out of the spaceship and gathers her pink coat around her. I point toward the snow-capped mountains—the only parts of Hokkaido still above water. "That's Daisetsuzan."

Ever since my dad discovered Otakemaru in the jagged peaks of Mt. Asahidake, the region's rich repository of fossils has sparked scientific interest beyond Earth. Unbeknownst to Namika, that's why we're here. My dream is to help rebuild the Earth. But this time around, we need a more sustainable society. Maybe, just maybe, I can convince Namika to join me.

"Kami, darling," Namika says as white puffs of air rise from her mouth. "Did you bring me here for our anniversary?" She pulls her hood up and tucks her ponytail away, shivering. I follow suit. My cropped cut fails to keep me warm, and I think I'll let my hair grow if I stay here long.

The wind blows biting snowflakes in our faces. Namika cries out and squeezes me.

Wait. I freeze. *Did she say anniversary?* My brain feels sluggish. Is this what two weeks in cryosleep does to you?

"That's so beautiful," Namika squeals. "Thanks, Kami!" Her eyes shine in the feeble light. I struggle to recall why she's thanking me. The smell of the cryopod comes flooding back. Stinging antiseptic and steel. Pleistocene Park Inc. The company logo of a woolly mammoth on the hall wall. A family portrait on the corner of Dr. Naomi Eguchi's desk. She's always been Dr. Eguchi to me, even though she's technically my stepmother.

"Too bad your dad couldn't have come with us," Namika says.

"Seriously?" I say, irritated, but I immediately regret it. Namika is practically an orphan. Her biological parents abandoned her at an artificial womb facility before birth. Advanced medical technologies have made infertility obsolete in our space colony, and adoption has become rare and difficult. As a result, the system shuffled Namika around from one boarding school to another every few years until she turned eighteen. We met in our senior year of high school, and I'm the closest thing she has to family.

"He knows his way around here. It's practically his playground." She pauses before she continues in a serious tone. "Besides, you would've had a good chance to patch things up with him. Like when you and I went camping at Mt. Fuji after we broke up a few years ago." She means the replica of Mt. Fuji back home, not the real one underwater.

"Oh, Namika," I say. "Don't be a mood killer."

"Don't you want to give your dad another chance?" she asks. "He's your family."

"Don't even get me started," I say, resisting the urge to roll my eyes. "He causes me nothing but headaches. Besides, I want some alone time with you. Maybe we can stay here for a while." And maybe we'll get to be the new Adam and Eve in this Garden of Eden. I'm an AFAB non-binary person, but having grown up in a family of scientists, I've got an ace up my sleeve: the latest gene editing technologies.

People in our part of the galaxy opt to procreate by genetic manipulation for myriad reasons. My math teacher, Mr. Lin, and his husband, for instance. Still, others reproduce through sexual intercourse. Like my parents before they split up.

I brush away the few snowflakes melting on Namika's cheek. I hold her chin and kiss her lightly. When she kisses back, I trace her mouth with my tongue, warming its outline.

"You're very romantic all of a sudden," Namika says, pulling away to gasp for air. "What's gotten into you?"

Winter birds wail in the distance, and a pool of weak sunlight spills around us.

"I want to keep us warm," I say, pressing her against me. Truth to be told, our relationship hit another plateau months ago. I've taken Namika for granted. I've taken her love, lust, and loyalty for granted.

"Do you hear the birds?" Namika says, adjusting her wearables.

"Yes. I think they're snow geese."

"Let's go find them and take a picture," she says. "We should send Hiro a digital postcard."

Hiro and I have nothing in common. I'm a decade older, and I lived with my dad after my parents divorced. Growing up, I was one of the few kids conceived and born in the old-fashioned way. By contrast, Hiro was born from a synthetic embryo, combining stem cells of both her mothers.

"How old is Hiro now? Nine?" Namika asks. "She grows a few inches taller every time we see her."

I recall the framed photo on Dr. Eguchi's desk. My stepmother holds baby Hiro, baby Hiro holds my mom's finger, and my mom rests her head on Dr. Eguchi's shoulder. It hurts more than I'm willing to admit that I don't have a similar photo.

Another flash of memory: Dr. Eguchi pushing forward in her chair and snatching the contract out of my hand. A contract I signed before we left Neo Tokyo to come to Earth. A contract I have no intention of honouring.

"Let's go back to the ship," I say. "It's freezing."

"We should move then, Kami," Namika says, excitement in her voice. "We need some time to acclimate to the new environment, anyway, so let's explore it." She grabs my hand and leads me forward.

Vivid Worlds

Namika is only here because of my selfishness. I didn't want to come without her, so I brought her along on this perilous journey without telling her why. Our anniversary totally slipped my mind.

As she gazes at Daisetsuzan, the heart of Hokkaido, she tears up and cups her mouth like a schoolgirl from the anime we were watching before we left home. So charming, she could disarm a starving woolly mammoth if she wanted to. But there are no mammoths. Not yet. I want to keep it that way if I can help it.

Namika turns to me. Her smile makes some of my dark thoughts melt away. I take her hand for warmth. We trudge toward Lake Shikaribetsu, which shows the reflection of Mt. Asahidake. The wind abates for a moment, and Namika reaches into her pocket.

"I found this on the ship." She puts a piece of paper into my hand. "I recognized your handwriting, but I didn't want to read it without your permission."

"I have nothing to hide, Namika," I lie, forcing a smile. "You know me. I'm transparent." With that said, I shove the contract deep in my pocket. "Do you think we can stick around—"

"Sure we can, Kami." She holds my hand. "I also believe Otakemaru is here. We should find him." That's also a part of my plan, but I have something else in mind.

A few years ago, we set our oni friend free from Neo Tokyo. When we broke the lock on his cage, he said he wanted to go back to Daisetsuzan.

"I've been thinking a lot about him lately," I say. "I want to conduct a survey by visiting his habitat. I want to know how far the Earth has recovered during humanity's absence."

We hug. Her hair tickles my cheeks, but I don't mind. I cling to her; her solid warmth proves that I'm no longer in cryosleep.

Despite our lengthy slumber, she still smells fresh. Or maybe I love her so much the smell doesn't bother me.

I cup her cheek and lean toward her, ready to land a peck on her lips.

Footsteps crunch through the snow. Namika pulls away, and my kiss brushes her cheek instead. I turn and gasp in surprise.

A pale figure trudges toward us, away from a silent hovercraft idling over the ground. Her Russian sable coat sways as she whips out a ray gun from her holster and aims for my chest. Her chilly gaze reminds me of a snake lying in wait for prey. I mentally dub her the Serpent Princess.

She hurls harsh-sounding Russian words in our direction. Because Namika disabled AI Sanae during our last misadventure, we don't understand her.

"Excuse me?" I ask.

"Can't you read the sign?" she asks in English, pointing to a wooden sign in Cyrillic letters. With a glance toward Namika, I shake my head.

I raise my hands, hoping she won't shoot us. "Pardon my ignorance, but—"

"You're trespassing," the woman snaps. "You're under arrest."

"Excuse me?" I repeat. Since when does Daisetsuzan belong to Russia? I'm about to protest a possibly egregious violation of international law, but Namika discreetly holds my hand and gives it a gentle rub.

"This is Zmeya," the woman says, speaking into a walkie-talkie embedded in the shoulder of her coat. "Yes, they're with me. I'm on my way.

"Move, ladies," Zmeya continues. "We don't have all day." Holding the gun to my back, she orders us toward the hovercraft. We squeeze ourselves into the back seat.

"Are you both scientists?" she asks, her serpentine eyes

narrowing.

"Only me," I say. Maybe she thinks I'm snooping around in search of fossils.

She holds a solar-powered scanner in front of my face. Tiny lights flicker over my eyes, and a soft beep grazes my ears. She proceeds to scan Namika, but no beep comes.

"You're Dr. Sato's child," Zmeya says, glancing at the screen. "Both he and you are listed in the Intergalactic Directory of Scientific Researchers."

"Guilty as charged." I shrug grudgingly. Dad's notoriety follows me everywhere.

"I've followed his career with great interest," Zmeya says, showing a sliver of excitement for the first time.

"Do you mean his oni revival project?" I ask, raising an eyebrow. I'm happy to have made friends with Otakemaru, but Dad's ambition brought nothing but misery. He'd die of envy if he knew I'm a stone's throw from Mt. Asahidake, the same summit where he found Otakemaru's well-preserved frozen corpse.

"Yes, I'm quite impressed," she says. "I have sympathy for what happened between you and him."

I almost roll my eyes. Maybe Dad should adopt her to replace me.

"What are you trying to bring back?" Namika asks.

"You'll see," Zmeya says with a smile.

Namika and I exchange looks. I need to come clean about Dr. Eguchi's plan as soon as we're alone.

"You're expecting a baby," Namika says. "Congratulations."

"Thank you," Zmeya says, cupping her belly. "The baby's sex doesn't matter to us. We're just excited about starting a family. It's all thanks to parthenogenesis."

"Wait," Namika says. "You didn't combine your partner's stem cells with yours?"

"Every human is predisposed for parthenogenesis," I say.

"But it's a matter of manipulating our DNA. Embryos can develop in a gamete—egg or sperm—without fusing with another gamete."

"That's right," Zmeya says. "A snake lives alone, yet she produces offspring on her own. Thanks goodness, we don't need sperm to procreate."

"By the same token," I say, "sperm doesn't need an egg to develop an embryo either. Have you figured out how to create embryos from male cells alone?"

"Why do you want to know?" Zmeya asks. "You ask too many questions."

"Sorry," I say with a shrug. "I'm just making conversation."

"What's the purpose of your visit?" Zmeya asks. Her voice assumes a chilly tone again.

"A survey expedition," I say with a straight face. "We want to know how far this ecosystem has recuperated over the last few centuries." It's true, at least partially. "So we can help accelerate its recovery."

Namika's gaze burns through me, but with a guilty conscious weighing upon me, I can barely meet her eyes. She knows more than she lets on.

"If you say so," Zmeya says, incredulous, but she looks puzzled. Everyone comes here for one thing and one thing only: well-preserved tissues of extinct species. To my surprise, she refrains from pursuing the subject further.

"Zmeya," I say. "Did I say your name right?" The hovercraft slides across the serene lake.

"More or less," Zmeya says.

"That's interesting," Namika says. "I believe your name means 'snake' in Russian."

"I thought you didn't speak Russian."

"I don't," Namika replies. "But a Russian exchange student lived in our dorm for a semester."

That's news to me. Why didn't this come up before? I

frown as suspicion raises its head. It must have happened during our temporary break-up in college.

"Natasha Alyokhina from Novaya Moskva. She had a pet snake named Zmeya."

"I see," Zmeya says, glancing at the cockpit control panel. "That's a fairly common name," she quickly adds, looking away. "We had a President Alyokhina a few centuries ago. Perhaps you also know about serpents in Russian folklore."

"Do you mean serpents with multiple heads?"

Zmeya nods. Her silence hangs in the air like a thinly veiled threat.

Namika is a walking encyclopaedia, after all. Her depth of knowledge beats AI Sanae's any day.

"If I were to venture a guess," Namika says, "I'd say you're trying to bring back the Dolly Varden trout."

"What makes you say that?" Zmeya snorts, her lips twisted in amusement.

"This is Lake Shikaribetsu, where the Ainu, the native people of Hokkaido, venerated the White Snake Princess.

"Long ago, when the Ainu faced famine," Namika continues, "their goddess appeared in their dreams. She told them to follow a white snake. When they reached the lake, it was filled with trout."

"Interesting." Zmeya chuckles. "I'd love to bring back the trout, but I think we could use the White Snake Princess."

Namika looks down, flustered.

Shortly after we reach the shore, a nondescript concrete building comes into view. A sign hangs on a gate of solid wood in front of the building, but again, I have no idea what it says. From the look of the building, it's a military base.

When we step inside, a cocktail of animal odours greets us in the hallway. We pass the logo of a coiled white snake adorning the wall and then a closed door, a cacophony of animal sounds coming from the other side.

The door opens without warning, the beastly noises intensifying for a brief moment before it closes, and a robust woman with red cheeks and thick eyebrows walks into the hall. She wears her curly brown hair tied back with a red scarf and a white faux-fur jacket.

"Is that you, Natasha?" Namika says, her voice changing to a high-pitched squeak. "I can't believe this!" Her surprised grin slowly turns into a smile. A smile of recognition.

"Namika?" the woman says. "My God, it's you!"

This turn of events renders me speechless. I feel as if I'm trapped in an old anime where one coincidence after another drives the plot.

"Long time no see, Natasha. You look great!" Namika squeals and runs toward her.

"I now go by Olga, my middle name." The next thing I know, the former homestay sisters embrace and do the triple cheek kiss, their embrace lingering a tad longer than I would like. A pang of jealousy stings me. On the other hand, what if Olga isn't immune to some virus that has travelled with us?

When I cough, Olga turns to me.

"You must be Kami," Olga says, extending her hand. "I'm pleased to meet you." When she grasps my hand, her grip is so tight it hurts. I gasp and pull my hand back, but Namika doesn't seem to notice.

"We converted this abandoned military base for civilian use," Olga says as we walk along jumbled rows of caged animals. Most creatures are hybrids. Bird Woman stares at me with large eyes. Black feathers cover her body. She wiggles her wings when we pass.

"How do you get your projects funded?" I ask.

"We don't use currency here," Olga says. "We work in tandem with other facilities scattered around the planet."

"How many are there?" I ask. Last time I checked, ninety-five percent of Earth was water.

"A few dozen and growing."

"How are they doing?" I ask.

"Quite well," Olga says. "You should visit some of them if you feel so inclined. The closet ones are in Xinjiang and Tibet. Be sure to let us know beforehand, so we can tell our friends. It's better not to make surprise visits nowadays."

Their friends? Maybe political alliances have reconfigured on Earth. Or maybe rising sea levels erased old national boundaries after Earthlings escaped into space. I glance at Namika to gauge her response. She cranes her neck and scans the cages around her, wide-eyed.

"That's Alkonost from Russian folklore!" Namika says, her gaze darting back and forth. Unlike me, she hasn't been around many strange creatures. Not beyond Otakemaru.

"What else are you working on?" I ask.

"Our mission is twofold," Zmeya says. "Wildlife repopulation and climate restoration."

"We use a diverse mixture of energy resources here," Olga says. "Solar, wind, and hydropower. We live on a plant-based diet. You'll see that our meat alternatives taste like the real thing"

"I see."

The chattering of monkeys bounces off the walls as I skirt a cage.

"You're welcome to try our plant-based clothing," Zmeya says.

I thought we would be held captive, but she's treating us like guests. Still, something doesn't add up. My BS detector is going off.

"Please accept my apologies if Zmeya mistreated you on the journey here," Olga says.

"It's all right," I lie.

"Interplanetary visitors make her nervous," Olga says with a smile. I glance toward Zmeya, and her face remains an impenetrable, emotionless mask.

"Which reminds me," Namika begins. "How's your pet snake?"

"She's doing well," Olga says. "We're going to start a family now."

"You and the snake?" I ask out of curiosity.

Olga nods. I figure it out a second later: Zmeya is a humanized animal, namely a Snake Woman. I glance toward her, and our gazes lock. I'm the first to look away.

"She's as naughty as ever, I bet," Namika says with a mock frown. "I still remember how it hurt when she bit my finger."

"Don't worry, Namika," Olga says. "She lacks good manners and comes across as arrogant sometimes, but she's not poisonous."

"In other words, she's genetically modified," I say.

"Quite right." Olga wears a pregnant smile.

"Are you familiar with Dr. Moreau's work?" I ask. Growing up, I devoured H. G. Wells's account of the scientist's bizarre experiments: Dog-Man, Fox-Bear Woman, Puma-Woman. Images of hybrid species flood back.

"Yes, of course," Zmeya says, the cold marble of her mask melting into tenderness. "He's been our inspiration, for sure. He had to resort to vivisection due to the scientific limits of his day, but there's no need to sacrifice live animals anymore. We can test our hypotheses using our virtual program. He would've approved of our use of hybrid embryos."

I take a quick breath, trying to gather my thoughts for a rebuttal.

We tiptoe to avoid stepping on scattered glass and instruments scattered on the floor. Namika glances toward me. I think I know what's on her mind. This place needs a serious cleanup. Safety 5S. Like my mom used to say when she worked as a chief engineer in the space industry.

"I've heard a lot about you, Kami," Olga says.

"You have?"

"Don't be so modest," Olga says. "I know how committed you are to wildlife conservation."

I fake a smile. Zemya opens her purse and pulls out pink lip gloss and a mirror for a touch-up. "It's non-toxic, ethical, and all natural," she says, puckering her lips. "This will help keep your lips from getting chapped in this cold." I don't mean to be rude, but I can't help staring. It feels like I'm back in a high school locker room.

She hands me her lip gloss, but I shake my head and give it back.

While watching a gecko scurry across the floor, I spot a human skull with horns. I walk over and pick it up, but a closer look reveals it's plastic.

"It's been nice chatting with you, Olga," I say, "but we've had a long day today." Something tells me tomorrow will be just as long.

"Of course," Olga says. "Zemya will show you where you're staying."

We leave Olga there and follow Zemya through a maze of hallways and up a flight of stairs. Soundproofed walls and ceilings shield us from the clamour below. When we reach a guest room, she ushers us in.

"I'll leave you two alone until dinner," Zemya says.

"Thanks," I say.

"Kami, you'll see more of our facility tomorrow," Zemya says, her tone subdued. "You may not like what we do here, but everyone has the same goal in mind, so try to keep an open mind."

"I'll try," I say and see her out the door.

"What was that all about?" I say as I throw myself onto the bed and stare at the ceiling.

"We'll soon find out, darling."

"We've stumbled upon the island of Dr. Moreau," I say

when Namika lies beside me. "She's building a colony of humanized animals."

"Don't be mean, Kami. Natasha means well."

"You mean Olga."

She nods.

"Did you know she would be here?" I ask, my jealousy raising its head again.

"No. What makes you think that?"

"Were you—" I begin but hesitate. "Were you ever close to her?"

"Darling, are you jealous?" she says, surprised

I say nothing, but I don't have to; the flush on my cheeks says it all.

"She uses hybrid embryos," I say, changing the subject. "Zmeya is only partly human."

"Why do you think she decided on parthenogenesis when there are two of them?" she asks.

"I don't know," I say with a shrug. "But it's certainly easier than combining stem cells from two separate entities to create embryos."

"I want to give Olga the benefit of the doubt," Namika says. "I think she has good intentions."

"So did my dad, and look where that led to." Otakemaru's pained face returns when I close my eyes.

"I know," she says after a pensive pause. "It's not that I don't have any doubts."

Now is the time to get everything off my chest. Pleistocene Park is absolutely bonkers.

"Namika, I have something to tell you."

"I think I already know."

"You know?" I roll halfway toward her.

"I lied before," she says. "I read the paper I picked up off the ship floor."

I wince. Guilt flutters in my stomach. "The contract."

She nods. "Your stepmom wants you to help her with mammoth restoration," she says, her eyes closed. "But I know you. You have something else in mind. Do you want to visit Xinjiang or Tibet?"

"Maybe." I stare at the ceiling. "I want to help the Earth. I know it's not easy, but …" I sigh. "I have to try."

"Why didn't you tell me any of this earlier? You know I would have supported you." Namika presses her lips to my arm. "Why didn't you tell me about Dr. Eguchi?"

"I meant to tell you earlier." I fidget, and then I sit up. "She's a brilliant scientist, but building a theme park with cloned woolly mammoths is misguided." In my mind's eye, my stepmother's mammoths stampede, and the ground shakes. The park's visitors cry and shout in terror. I shake my head, dispelling the vision.

"I'm sorry, Namika," I continue. "Not only have I ruined our anniversary, but now we're tangled in this mess."

"What are you going to do about your contract?" she asks, worried.

"I don't know," I say. "I can't go along with it."

"I'll support you, whatever you decide to do," she says.

"Thank you, Namika," I say. "I know I've neglected you lately, but I'll do better."

"I know you will," she says, holding my hand. "You're my family."

I keep quiet as guilt stings me. If I amend my ways right now, however, it may not be too late. Maybe there's still hope for me. For us.

"I know you aren't very close to your mom," she says. "Or your stepmom."

"You know what hurts the most?"

She squeezes my hand tighter.

"I saw photos of my half-sister in Dr. Eguchi's office. Hiro taking her first steps and learning to ride a tricycle while Dr.

Eguchi watched. My mom took all of them."

Namika's hand grazes my face, her thumb tracing my jaw.

"I thought I'd passed through my parents' divorce unscathed. Even so, it killed me to see the three of them smiling together in photos. I've been to their place a couple of times, but my mom doesn't have any photos of me." Tears brim in my eyes.

"I'm sorry," Namika says. I bury my face in her chest and let the tears flow. She hugs me and caresses my hair.

"In hindsight," I continue after recovering a little. "I let Dr. Eguchi talk me into helping her with her project because she said the park would be a good thing for civilians. But in the end, my dad and Dr. Eguchi work for the same boss: Big Business."

I can only hear our breaths as we fall silent.

"We're OK, right?" I cradle her hand with tenderness.

"You've always looked after me, Kami," she says. "Come here." She draws me closer.

I close my eyes, and her heartbeat fills my ears.

"Look, we don't have to agree on everything," Namika says.

"I know," I say with a nod.

"But I think we should stick around for a while," she says.

I remain silent, too exhausted to respond.

"Rebuilding Earth is important to you," she says. "Science is not my strong suit, but I want to help."

I try in vain to stifle a yawn. "Excuse me, Namika," I say.

She shushes me, humming a lullaby so gentle I can barely hear.

Before long, curled up beside Namika, I drift into sleep.

Wailing. It pierces through my sleep. My dream shifts, and an oni emerges out of the gloom. He trembles inside a narrow cage, chained to small hooks embedded in the ceiling. The familiar mammoth logo looms large overhead.

"Is that you, Otakemaru?" I ask. My forlorn voice echoes off the walls and bounces back.

"Yes, that's my name," he says. He stares through me without any sign of recognition. " But I go by Junior."

"You're his son!" I cry. I grab a bar, but my arm doesn't budge. "I'm Kami. Did your father tell you about me?"

Before he can answer, I fall deeper into slumber.

A knock on the door wakes me. Still groggy, I barely manage to drag myself out of bed. When I answer the door, Zmeya is standing there with a tray. The tantalizing scent of pancakes fills my nose.

"I've brought you breakfast," she says. "You must be starving, after such a long journey."

"You bet." I rub my eyes and yawn.

"I knocked on your door last night, but you didn't answer."

"We must have been deep asleep."

"I thought as much," she says, handing me the tray.

"Thanks."

I glance toward her. Behind her serpentine coldness, her eyes are aglow with human warmth. I step forward to greet her with a kiss on the cheek, imagining Namika and Olga greeting each other. Zmeya steps back, turning away. Time feels frozen.

"I'm sorry," I say, pulling away.

"I think you're tired," she says, frowning. "Get some rest."

I remain silent. My ears burn again, this time with shame.

"I'll be back in an hour," she says before going away. The door clicks shut behind her.

"Wakey, wakey," I say, forcing myself to be cheerful. "Breakfast's here."

Namika sits up in bed and stretches.

"These are called syrniki," she says. "They're made of

cottage cheese, eggs, and flour."

I imagine Namika having breakfast with Olga in bed. What else did they share? It's strange to discover this new aspect of her life.

When Zmeya returns, I can barely look at her. We follow her in silence and join Olga in the lab.

A wooden cage catches my attention. Inside, an Asian elephant stands crammed against the bars. She wails, and the weakness in her cry haunts me.

"Poor thing," Namika says. "There's hardly room for her to move."

A fetid smell wafts toward me as I step toward the cage. When I look straight into the elephant's eyes, sadness gleams in them.

"Why are you keeping her in such a confined space?" Namika asks with a frown. "Is this really necessary?"

"It's only temporary," Olga says. "The next step is to design a sanctuary where mammoths can roam free."

"Mammoths?" Namika says.

Olga gestures to the cage, her hand grazing one of the bars.

"As you know, mammoths once roamed Hokkaido's wildness. We plan to reintroduce mammoths to this ecosystem," Olga says. "They'll be covered in fur. The thick coat of hair will help them maintain a warm body temperature, and they'll be able to thrive in colder climates, including the Arctic. They'll help mitigate the effects of climate change."

"How so?" Namika asks.

"I want you to imagine a time when mammoths roamed the earth," Zmeya says with animated gestures. "They disrupted the snowpack as they fed on trees and plants. They helped plants grow. And the plants absorbed carbon dioxide from the air."

"But the elephant," Namika says. "What do you need her

for?"

"We're using her as a surrogate," Zmeya says. "She's carrying a hybrid elephant-mammoth embryo."

Like Zmeya, the elephant is pregnant with a hybrid creature. I imagine a herd of mammoth hybrids trampling the ground. An image of thawing permafrost flashes before my eyes, and fear claws my throat.

"But I don't think it's plausible," I say. "You'll need hundreds of mammoth hybrids to have a real impact. And what if they're infertile like most mules? On the other extreme, unbridled reproduction could lead to overpopulation."

"Admittedly, our methods are far from perfect," Zmeya says. "That's why I want you to join us, Kami. We could use your expertise. We believe you can help improve not only our facility but others around the globe."

I glance toward Namika, but she's at the elephant's cage, hand outstretched through the bars. "Conservation must come before de-extinction," I say. "This isn't right."

"Right?" Olga scoffs. "Climate change wasn't right. Corrupt politicians weren't right. But this? What we're doing here? Great change necessitates great sacrifice, Kami. You must realize this."

"And we aren't averse to conservation," Zmeya says. "But our work can't wait. Earth needs to be nourished. Our seeds must be planted."

"We know you had a very public fallout with your father," Olga says. "Unlike his project, our technologies will be used for peaceful purposes. We promise. Other facilities can vouch for us if you have doubts."

I look between the Russian hosts, at the light in their eyes, and a headache blooms behind my temples. I remember Otakemaru's lock breaking and thudding on the ground. The harsh alarms piercing the air. A transistor exploding overhead in a shower of gold. Dad was furious. Yanking on his hair, he yelled at me and Namika for ruining his life's work. I yelled back: *Otakemaru has a heart! You can't use him as a weapon!* Somehow, our voices carried over the blaring noise.

Dad. Dr. Eguchi. Big corporations with deep pockets and no restraints.

"Let me sleep on it, all right?" I cross the lab floor and take Namika's hand.

"Of course," Olga says. "Take your time, like all the politicians before us. Everyone always pretends we have time."

"I didn't expect such hospitality on Earth," I say.

Namika sits across from me, and Zemya is next to her. To my right, Olga cuts her baked potato into pieces before placing a small lump into her mouth.

"You're welcome," Zmeya says. She sips her Baikal. Ice clinks in her glass.

I try mine, and its herbal flavour fills my mouth. None of us have returned to the discussion in the elephant lab, but its implications hover over us.

"We should get some rest," I say, covering a yawn.

"Certainly," Olga says. "We hope you have a restful night."

Olga and Namika kiss three times on the cheeks again. I wonder what would happen if I tried to kiss Zmeya like that again, but I shake away the thought.

Namika is quiet all the way to our room. By the time we undress and slip under the sheets, the time for conversation is long past.

Bang bang bang. Harsh knocks shake the door.

"Who is it?" I call out as I roll over and glance at the digital clock on the night table. It's three in the morning.

"It's me!" Olga's muffled voice reaches my ears.

Namika stirs beside me. I crawl out of bed, half-dressed,

and stumble to answer the door.

"Come with me!" Olga says, and gestures for me to follow. Her hair is a mess, her eyes bloodshot, her pupils dilated, and the assured scientist from yesterday is gone. "The baby is breech!"

"Zmeya's in labour?" My heart lurches, and I grab a sweater from the back of a chair.

"Yes! Her water broke a couple hours ago. Hurry!"

Namika sits up. There's no time to kiss her goodbye. "The baby's coming!"

Leaving Namika, we run down the hall. I've never seen Olga so unmoored.

"Zmeya always assists me in times like this," she says, drenched in sweat.

When we step into the lab, Zmeya writhes in pain on a stained bed, screaming in Russian.

"Give her an epidural if you have one," I say.

"We use herbs to relieve pain," Olga says, bringing over a cup of herbal tea.

I wash my hands and put on surgical gloves.

"Push hard," I say as I insert a gloved hand inside her. I use my fingers to open the baby's airway.

The baby's slimy leg shows a few inches, followed by another. I signal Zmeya to slow down.

"Pant and take deep breaths," I say.

Her skin can use more time to stretch. I support the baby's body to keep them from emerging too fast and tearing her flesh.

The baby comes out after much struggle, and I clean their face. Silence lasts for what seems like an eternity. I shoot a glance at Olga. Her lips are blue, trembling.

When the baby lets out their first cry, Olga and I sigh in unison. She smiles through her tears and kisses her partner. I also smile and shed tears of joy. The three of us hug, crying and smiling.

"May I come in?" Namika says at the door. Olga waves her in. "I've been here for a while, but I didn't want to get in the way," Namika says. "Congratulations."

Zmeya looks exhausted, but she smiles, cooing to the baby on her chest. She mouths *thank you* across the bed. I signal to Namika and we step outside.

"I never imagined birth would be so messy," she says, her eyes wide.

"It's certainly messier than growing an embryo in an artificial womb."

"I'm trying to remember what it was like to be in one." She pauses with her eyes closed. "No, I don't remember anything."

We look at each other and chuckle. Her smile reminds me of all sorts of lovely things we used to do. Sparks from a simple yet accidental brush of hands. Finding love notes in unexpected places. Endless cuddling on sleepless nights.

"Be warned, though," I say with a smile. "Babies are messy no matter how they're born."

"If it's our baby, I wouldn't mind," she says.

"I love you, Namika," I say.

"I love you, too, Kami," she says.

Some of the guilt washes away as we linger in a tight embrace.

We occasionally see our hosts over the following days. The baby is doing great, but an unsettling feeling prickles me whenever I hold them. Whenever their slitted pupils dilate.

"How do you think the baby factors into their plan?" Namika asks when we're alone.

"I don't know," I say. The mountains look so inviting from the observation desk where we stand. The wind lashes my cheeks. "They may need additional gene therapies down the road."

Namika goes quiet, and I know she's thinking about the Asian elephant. I take her gloved hand in mine and squeeze it.

"Do you think Otakemaru is somewhere up there?" I glance toward the jagged slopes.

All Namika does is nod. Her gaze stays fixed on the high peaks.

A few days later, after we say goodbye, we leave at dawn and hike up over Mt. Asahidake. We pass the cable car station where an abandoned gondola stands still. The multilingual sign informs us of a five-minute ride to the top.

Thin streams of vapor rise between the rocks as we climb a serpentine trail.

We occasionally stop and savour the panoramic view that extends across Daisetsuzan. Oni can easily hide behind snow-draped volcanic boulders. I turn off my wearables and try to retain everything in my mind.

"The nightmare came back," I say.

"It's been a while since you've had one of those," Namika says, frowning. "Not since we've left Neo Tokyo. We have to find Otakemaru soon."

I nod. "There was something strange about the dream this time."

"Strange?"

"It wasn't Otakemaru," I say. "His son was caged in Dr. Eguchi's facility."

I shiver. Namika edges in next to me and wraps her arm around my shoulder.

"They'll be OK." Her voice is a soft blanket. "If they need help, we'll help them," she says as I lean into her warm embrace.

After two and a half hours, we reach the peak of the trail. I stand, each breath heavy, my armpits damp.

"We're on the highest point of Hokkaido," I say, beaming

at Namika.

We sit on the ground and unpack the lunch we brought. It's leftovers from our hosts' Russian breakfast.

On the way back, we wander into an abandoned ryokan with a dozen rooms and a spectacular view of the smoking volcano.

"Hey, there's a rotenburo," I say, pointing to steam rising from the open-air bath. "Do you want to take a dip?" I disrobe before Namika can answer.

"But I didn't bring a bathing suit."

"Don't worry," I say as I dip my toes in to check the temperature. "Nobody's here." I wade into the bath.

"Come join me," I say, floating. The stars in the sky are so close I could reach out and touch them.

"It's hot!" Namika shrieks as she steps into the water.

"No, it's not!" I gently splash water in her direction.

When she comes beside me, we cuddle, her feet resting on my knees, our faces close together.

"Why don't we set up shop here?" she says, looking me in the eye.

"Dr. Eguchi may send someone after us," I say. My stepmom chose me precisely because of my ties to Neo Tokyo, but Namika is here with me. There's nothing that pulls me back.

"Don't worry," Namika says. "It wouldn't be cost-effective. Even if they did come, we'd be ready."

"What about our Russian neighbours?" I say.

"Let's engage them in a friendly competition," she says.

"How?" I ask.

"We'll do a complete survey of the area on our own," Namika says. "We'll propose kaizen events based on that. I'm sure they'll come around."

She has a point. It'd be foolish to act without knowing the whole picture.

I pause while thinking of a counterargument. "But these girls are post-capitalists. To be honest, I have no idea what a post-capitalist society looks like. I don't even know if lean production can be applied in their facility. They seem to advocate degrowth."

"We've got a lot to learn," Namika says. "Let's not start another world war, OK? Or another cold war, for that matter."

She caresses my cheek. Her touch sends a tingling sensation through my body.

"Let's iron out the details after the survey," she says. "Meanwhile, we could use some privacy." She chuckles.

"I couldn't agree more," I say. Spending more time alone with Namika will solidify what we share.

"I'm glad we're on the same page."

The touch of her skin against mine stirs something warm in me.

"What if a Naki Usagi walked in on us right now?" I tease out of embarrassment.

"A singing rabbit?" she says, her lips lightly grazing my neck. "There's plenty of room for everyone."

Her breath hot against my throat, I let out a sigh of pleasure. When I press my lips to hers, we melt into a prolonged kiss.

Emily's Farewell Coat

Ana Sun

It had begun as the nice day off which had every promise of going right. Ria had just settled into her favourite chair to knit a new cardigan for herself, but all that changed the moment her circular needles snapped, dunking dropped stitches into her steaming cup of tea. Which would be why, around the time she should have been having a lovely lunch of roasted vegetables, she was instead drenched to the bone standing at the front door of the Textile Collective's workshop, living proof that the new water-resistant coat fabric they'd been testing for Emily's parting gift…well, wasn't.

On any other day during the cold season when the rivers swell, it would've taken a quick jaunt from her raft-cottage moored over the winterbourne, across the floating walkways, up the hill and through the twitten to the workshop. But before she made it halfway, the skies opened, dropping a merciless deluge over the town and its surrounds with the kind of ferocity that flattened grass and churned bare earth.

The moment it became apparent something had gone quite wrong: when Ria tried to tug a sleeve down to cover more of her hand, and a chunk of it came clean off between her fingers. In all the years she'd worked at the Textile Collective, despite their philosophy of reusing every bit of fibrous material for their fabrics—new, recycled, or found—*this* had never happened before.

One small consolation, perhaps: the dye she'd developed for it held fast even as the fibres began to disintegrate under the weight of water, so she *hadn't* left a trail of deep inky blue through the cobblestone streets.

Silver lining, and all that. Maybe she should have sewn one into the dang coat.

Vivid Worlds

In the distance, wind turbines spun serenely, elegant in an asynchronous dance.

At the door of the workshop, Ria stood in a puddle of rainwater. The front door was an oversized wooden affair that once belonged to a bank up the street. The workshop itself nestled at a corner. A long time ago, it might have been a real-estate agent's, in the old days when humans wrongly claimed legal rights to the land instead of ceding to nature's authority.

Ria pushed the door handle. It wouldn't budge.

She rapped one hand on the door.

"Open up."

No answer. Could they not hear her?

Surely, it being a Tuesday, everyone else ought to be working either on the long list of the town's requests for repair, or new clothes for the upcoming warm season. Everyone, except for Ria, of course, and Emily, who had begun acclimatising for her transition to be a Reader-Traveller next week, by only coming in on Saturdays in the past month.

Which meant Emily's leaving party would be *this* coming Saturday. Four days' time.

Panic squeezed the air out of Ria's lungs. She'd taken this coat from a rack of test garments—in the batch they'd been trialling for Emily's parting gift. If this prototype she'd worn couldn't survive a single rainstorm, could they even use the rest of the batch?

Ria picked at her soggy collar. The entire piece tore off in her hand.

"A whole bloomin' knot of yarn," Ria swore.

It had all seemed so feasible when they spoke about it a few days ago during their weekly Big Meeting. A simple afternoon tea for Emily, and everyone from the town would be invited. Then, Leyla, the newest member of the Collective, pointed out they *could* make Emily a leaving gift, to thank her for all her work. And wouldn't it be nice if they made her something suitable for a Reader-Traveller?

"Something weatherproof," Geoff, their lead designer had thought out loud, a cookie halfway to his mouth. Whenever Geoff didn't have a sewing implement in hand, he'd have some semblance of food. "She hates the texture of waxed fabric though; we'd have to do something different."

"Pockets," Ria herself had said. "Lots of them."

"Then you'd need something to counter gravity," Jules added.

Leyla said, wide-eyed. "We can do that?"

"In theory," Jules had replied. "With our ability to blend an assortment of fibres, we could do *anything*."

That had been last week. Now, Ria knocked once again on the workshop door, hard enough for her knuckles to hurt. "Oi! Jules? Leyla?"

This early in the day, Geoff wouldn't be in yet.

She *could* try the back door, but that meant going into the rain and circling around to the rear garden.

A small black rectangle to the right of the door blinked a tiny square of bright, green light. Ria could have sworn this wasn't here several days ago.

She leaned down for a closer look.

"Good morning, Ria," said a calm, genderless voice.

Ria jumped backwards, spraying rainwater in a frenzied fountain. "What the—"

"Hi Ria, welcome back to the workshop. This is EZEE-5000. How can I help?"

EZEE, the monstrous machine that Emily had acquired over the past several months, in the belief that it would help them scale up during the change in seasons when people commonly needed more clothes.

"You know a machine won't replace you, right?" Ria had tried to tease, but Emily hadn't gotten the joke.

EZEE had taken on the bulk of fibre processing, spinning and dyeing, which was welcome, but also half the space in the workshop—somewhat less welcome. And now, they also seemed to answer the door. Would they be making a Sunday roast next?

"How can you *help*?" Oh, the nerve of the thing. "Let me in, you—"

Ria caught herself. However much she distrusted EZEE, everything in her universe, whether animate or inanimate, simply composed of atoms fused into molecules. Just because one set of molecules in a different formation happened to be making your bad day worse didn't mean you needed to be rude to it.

"Sorry, I didn't mean to shout." Ria wheezed.

"It's OK, Ria, I don't have human ears, that didn't hurt," said EZEE. "Do you need to come inside?"

"Yes, please. It's bloody pouring out here." It felt better to be rude at *something*.

"I'm sorry you're caught in the rain, Ria," said EZEE.

Had they always been so irritatingly polite?

"So, open up then," said Ria. "Please," she added.

"You need to authenticate yourself first."

"Authen-what?"

"Authenticate yourself: tell me you are who you are."

"But I am who I am."

"Yes, but I need to confirm you are who you are."

"I'm telling you who I am, EZEE." Somehow her voice had ratcheted up in both pitch and volume. "Hurry up, please. I'm drenched out here."

"Sorry, Ria. I can't let you in unless you prove you are you."

Ria flung up her arms, showering droplets of water in a wide circle. "How?"

Come to think of it, several weeks ago Emily went around and asked everyone to place both hands flat on a black device.

She had given a rambling explanation, but at the time Ria had been right in the middle of counting stitches for the sleeve of Hartley's new springtime jumper, custom-made to cater for the stonemason's spectacularly muscular arms.

"Place your palm on the black panel to your right, Ria."

"My whole palm? On the panel?" A strange ask, but Ria slapped the flat of her hand on the black rectangle next to the door. Something beeped.

"Thank you, Ria," said EZEE. "Glad that you are really you."

Before Ria could think of a smart retort, the door creaked open a fraction and she shoved her way in, shoes squeaking water with every squidgy step.

Between the heavy rain rattling on the workshop roof and the low drone of EZEE's background hum, Leyla's concentration broke only when a sharp blast of cold air pierced through the front door, accompanied by the sight of a tall, sodden figure in the doorway.

Leyla bolted upright in her armchair by the bay window, crochet needle clattering out of her hand.

Under the dripping coat, the figure looked familiar.

"Ria?" Leyla called out. "That you?" Wasn't it her day off today?

"No, Leyla, I'm just a drowned rat, or a wet hen. Help me here?"

"Oh my!" said Leyla, rushing up from her nook, scattering a ball of yarn across the floor. She tugged the wet, dripping fabric from Ria's shoulders. A tricky business, given Ria stood nearly a whole head taller than her own petite frame. Together, they peeled off the soggy sleeves that clung to Ria's arms.

"Thank you," muttered Ria, when they finally extricated her from the waterlogged mess. Her dark, shoulder-length hair sat plastered against the earthy complexion of her face.

Leyla held up the remains of the coat, oblivious to a large puddle forming on the workshop floor. The coat seemed familiar. The deep blue gave it away—from their latest test batch, meant for Emily's parting gift.

"Wasn't this supposed to be waterproof?" Leyla asked. Something must have gone wrong with the mix of recycled fibres.

Ria grunted. Her words came out through chattering teeth. "Grab me a towel please? There's a love."

"Oh!"

The very wet bundle of fabric in Leyla's hands presented a more immediate problem. A metal trough glinted at the far corner of the room, attached to one of EZEE's components. It would have to do.

Nothing for it, but speed.

Cradling the bundle and ignoring how her own dress was getting wet, Leyla bounded across the room alongside the length of EZEE's chassis and dropped the remains of the coat into the trough.

"Breezy, help clean, please?"

EZEE's cleaning droid—a small robot no bigger than a bucket—whirred to life. Leyla ducked into the corridor that led off to the kitchen and the back room, grabbed a newly minted towel from a storage cupboard and sped back to Ria, who, by now, stood in a sizeable pond of rainwater.

"Cheers, love." Ria proceeded to work out the knots in her damp hair.

"Hold on, let me get you another."

Another run to the cupboard, another towel—on second thoughts, a third.

"Here," said Leyla.

The cleaning bot had stopped completely by the puddle. It had extruded something that resembled a straw. Whatever was it doing?

"I think it's confused," said Ria.

Leyla shook her head and plopped the third towel on the floor to soak out the puddle. It confounded her; why had there never been a mat by the door? In the spring there would be pollen, in summer, wildflower seeds stuck to shoes; in the autumn, there would be flakes from fallen leaves. Then throughout November there would be spark powder and smoke residue from Bonfire Night. Any number of things that could accidentally end up in the fibre processing.

Ria wrapped the towels around her shoulders.

Not a common occurrence, to witness misery on Ria's face. Perhaps a cup of tea would warm her up.

"Can I get you—"

"Ye gods, EZEE!" A deep, male voice boomed from the back of the workshop.

Ria's eyes widened. "What's going on?"

Leyla turned and squinted. No smoke wisping out from the back room this time. A minor improvement, perhaps. Leaning towards Ria, she whispered, "Jules has been battling with writing new subroutines all morning. He's in the foulest mood, I wouldn't—"

"Huh," said Ria, and began plodding towards the back room, leaving a trail of wet footprints through the corridor.

"I'll, um, set EZEE on an analysis cycle," said Leyla, to no one in particular.

Something bumped against her ankle.

Breezy, wet with rainwater, held up an object glinting in its mechanical hand—her crochet needle.

Jules extricated his fingers from his hair, and with it, a few greying gold strands. He had been at this for hours with nothing to show for it. EZEE's components took up half the room, and to work at its console, Jules had to wedge his lanky figure between the tail end of EZEE's chassis and the back wall.

How Emily used to fit in this tight spot, he hadn't a clue. She wasn't exactly a small woman. Though right now, he dearly wished Emily could be here—*she* would have known what to do. But Emily would be gone next week, and so much knowledge, such immeasurable wisdom would be gone with her. Jules sighed. As much as Emily had trained him in EZEE's workings from the beginning, he'd never feel ready.

EZEE's console blinked a blank cursor, its standard hum descending into a whine.

"Can't you just make the rest of it up, EZEE?"

"Sorry, Jules, I cannot do that."

"Well, bugger that." Perhaps it had been a foolish idea to get EZEE to construct a garment on command, let alone a pattern.

A tall, gaunt silhouette manifested through the doorway. Jules glanced up from the console.

"Wow, Ria, you look like a drowned rat."

"Or a wet hen. Take your pick."

"What happened?"

"Weather happened." Ria gestured at the outside world beyond the back window. The rain, however, had slowed and refused to be accused. "Take a look at the prototype I wore when you get the chance. I don't know what's wrong with it."

"EZEE has been giving me a hard time."

"I'm sorry, Jules," said EZEE.

Jules leaned back against the wall, which took only several centimetres to achieve. "Some days, I wished we'd never brought it here."

"Jules!" Ria said, alarmed. "You can't say that! Not in front of them!"

An unusual noise came through EZEE's vocaliser, sounding suspiciously like a whimper.

"You're upsetting them."

"It's just a machine; it doesn't have feelings." Letting out a heavy breath, Jules slipped out from the narrow gap. Something in his back popped.

Ria placed a gentle hand on EZEE's console. "There, there."

Consoling the console. Jules grimaced. Not that EZEE could feel sympathy, but it moved a mechanical arm to make room for Ria she leaned against its chassis.

Absently, he paced, his feet traced a small tight circle in the middle of the room. There must be a way to—

"What were you trying to do?" she asked.

"The coat for Emily. We only have a few days to go and either this thing can't figure out how to do the design, or I am obviously not competent enough to ask them correctly."

"Don't call them a thing!"

"Why would that make a difference!"

Jules caught himself. That attitude did not belong here. "Sorry, Ria. I'm just…out of options."

"Also, wasn't Geoff supposed to do the design?"

Jules stopped mid-pace, staring at her open-mouthed. "Was he?"

Once again, his hands ended up in his hair. There had been so much to learn, so much to catch up on, it was entirely possible that he misremembered.

"Ugh," said Jules.

He had raised his bleary eyes at the crew during that Big Meeting some days ago; they'd formed a rough plan—playing to each of their skills—Geoff to sketch a design, Ria to blend the dyes, Leyla to craft the embellishments (perhaps with help from Ria), and Jules to coax EZEE into production. Wonderful creatives, they all were, but Geoff was a dreamer, Ria tended to be impulsive, and Leyla—bright but inexperienced.

Somehow, Jules' feet had taken him back to his seat by the

wall. The cursor on EZEE's console blinked a confrontation.

Someone waved something in front of his face.

"Hello?" said Ria. "Earth to Jules?"

Ria, with a few sheets of paper. No doubt some sketches Geoff had left lying around. Jules rubbed his eyes with the back of his hands.

"I haven't seen Geoff's pattern for the coat. Are those it?"

"No, I have no idea what these are."

Jules might have said something in response, he wasn't sure. Shutting his eyes, he leaned backwards once again against the wall.

"You need some tea, Jules," Ria said, gently. "And some rest to go with it. I'll go find Geoff."

When he finally stood up, something smacked into his forehead, knocking him back down.

"Sorry, Jules," said EZEE. "Are you OK?"

EZEE's mechanical arm had somehow swung in the way.

The café had been peaceful in the late morning, but now, after midday, nearly all the tables had filled up and the clink of cutlery accompanied a chorus of chatty voices, churning the dregs of Geoff's conscious thoughts into unmouldable putty. He moved aside the remains of his brew and an unfinished slice of lemon cake, pushed his glasses back up his nose, and spread another sketch in front of Janice, who taught mathematics most days at the secondary school.

"Ooh, I like this very much," said Janice, trailing a finger on the frill he'd drawn on a dress she wanted.

"Glad to hear it." Despite himself, Geoff beamed. Always a wonderful feeling when someone appreciated his work. "This should give you the flair you wanted for the commitment ceremony, and after that—" he flipped over the page "if you remove this piece here, you'd be able to wear it like an everyday dress."

"Very clever!"

Geoff liked working here in the café, whether alone, or meeting with clients who had specific requests from the Textile Collective. Sure, he had a desk up in the loft at the workshop, but it had never been quite the same since EZEE took up all the downstairs space. Now, all their old sergers and sewing machines cluttered up the area which had once been wholly his. Nothing against EZEE, of course. He quite liked their low hum whenever he worked late at nights. Or maybe, he simply found it difficult to focus when everyone else was around. Who knew?

Janice gathered her scarf and coat, both in a shade of near-iridescent fuchsia that suited the honey-brown of her skin. "When shall I come around for a fitting?"

"How about in a couple of weeks?"

"Wonderful," she said, rising. "But I'll see you Saturday, won't I?"

Saturday? Geoff scrabbled through his memory.

"Yes, I have an invitation from Jules! For Emily's transition party."

"Oh!" Geoff whisked a quick smile. How had the day come around so soon? "Yes, we'll see you then!"

On her way out, Janice paused to chat to someone who had just come in—a tall, willowy figure. Geoff's heart skipped a beat. He'd recognise that silhouette anywhere; even though it must have been well over a decade since they were teenage sweethearts. Something about the way Ria moved, how her intensity always drew a kind of magic around her. It didn't matter that her dungaree dress crinkled, or that her normally wavy hair had flattened out.

Ria plonked herself in a chair opposite him, her damp hair exaggerating the point of her nose, the cut of her cheeks.

Geoff drew a sharp breath. "Did you get caught in the rain?"

Vivid Worlds

Often it felt as if they'd known each other for so long that hellos and goodbyes felt superfluous.

She shrugged. "Weather happened, but you should've seen the prototype I was wearing."

"Do you need tea?"

When Ria smiled, entire galaxies aligned. "No, but Jules needs your sketch for Emily's coat. If you've got it."

Geoff flipped open his folio, rifled through it. Where had he left those? He remembered drawing it: a long coat, with special-purpose pockets, detachable hood, storm flaps, interchangeable knitted cuffs and lace collar. "I left it at the studio for Jules."

Come to think of it, a few other designs appear to be missing too.

"I'm sure I didn't dream it." Geoff's shoulders slumped. Being organised had never been his strong suit.

To his surprise, Ria reached out and patted his hand. Her earthy-gold skin a sharp contrast to his own pink skin, her skinny fingers—strong from working needles and yarn— couldn't be more different than his pudgier counterparts. "I'm quite sure you didn't."

Geoff sighed and pushed his glasses back up his nose. It had been a busy end to the cold season, with many more custom requests that he'd remembered having to deal with since he'd joined the Textile Collective.

"Are you eating that?" Ria pointed to his unfinished cake.

"Better not waste, I suppose," Geoff pulled the plate in between them. The speed with which Ria picked up the fork didn't escape him. "It's your day off, Ria. How about lunch? On me."

"Oh!" Her dark eyes glittered. "My word, lunch would be wonderful."

The cake still tasted good. All days should begin with dessert. Everything always seemed to look up afterwards.

How to address EZEE for specific commands, when they took up half of the front of the workshop, a part of the corridor, and extended into the back room? Leyla gaped at the sheer monstrosity of the machine. It had never been clear—whether you issued a command to a component that did a specific thing, or if you just uttered a request.

How had Emily done it?

The Textile Collective had not been Leyla's first choice for an apprenticeship. She'd always thought she'd worked with the confectionery maker and spend her days making sherbet lemons or fruit gummies, but meeting Emily for the first time changed her mind. How her silver hair hung over her collared, ultramarine dress, a direct yet quiet authority, but more: a passion that still burned despite the wrinkles around her eyes. Something Leyla understood that day—that doing a great service to the community lit one up on the inside.

"We work a bit like musicians do," Jules had explained on her first day. "First designer, second designer; first knitter, second knitter …"

"But there are four of you?" Leyla blurted, before she could stop herself.

"Five now, if you count EZEE," said Emily. "Who could almost be an orchestra by themselves."

Jules had pulled a face. "More like a pipe organ with a hundred stops for different noises."

Emily had laughed.

On that first visit, EZEE had been contained in the back room. The front bay window had a view on the street, and this room had been full of rickety sergers, a loom and a mix of electrical and manual machinery—salvaged from all around town.

"Same with EZEE, really," Emily had said. "Though some of their parts came from further afield."

But now, all that had been moved upstairs, and EZEE spanned everywhere one looked.

"EZEE?" Leyla tried.

"Hello, Leyla. How may I help?"

"Analyse, please."

A pause.

"What would you like me to analyse, Leyla?"

"The fabric in the trough."

"What would you like me to analyse it for?"

Goodness, how tedious.

"Um, why it held so much water."

"Understood." Another pause. "I'm not detecting any fabric in the correct trough, one moment."

Breezy suddenly spun around from the front door, picked up the dripping remains of the former coat and dumped it into another trough that Leyla hadn't noticed before. EZEE's various inputs and outputs constituted a confounding, three-dimensional puzzle.

On the inside of the trough, something like a pincher captured a sample of the fabric.

"Fabric found," EZEE said. "Analysing."

Leyla whistled through her teeth. It couldn't be that easy, could it?

Breezy whirred towards the puddle at the front door, but changed its mind, and instead began cleaning Ria's footprints through the corridor.

Earlier on, Ria had glided in from the back room and grabbed another coat from the rack of prototypes by the corridor.

Leyla hadn't been quick enough. "Wait! I have to—"

Jules had asked her to keep a catalogue so at least they could track any flaws.

"I need to go get Geoff," Ria had said, zipping herself into the coat. "Jules is tearing his hair out."

"Sure, but just let me take note of which coat you've got?"

"Later!" Ria had waved and hurried back out the front door.

Leyla squinted at the sheet she'd started to compile. If they didn't start keeping careful track, they'd never know what caused the issue with the other one. With a sigh, she pulled up a chair next to the rack and began to tag each coat.

Jules emerged from the back room with a shuffle, rubbing a spot on his forehead.

"What the—"

He strode over and examined the tattered, disintegrated remains of the coat in the trough. He pulled his hand back quickly, screwed up his nose. "Was this what Ria wore this morning?"

"Yes," replied Leyla. "EZEE is analysing now. I think."

Jules stared at the sheen of damp on his hand. "At least the dye didn't run."

He walked towards the bay window. The rainstorm had kept the townspeople indoor all morning. Now that it slowed to a drizzle, the street outside bustled.

"How's the rest of the batch?"

Leyla picked a coat off the rack and showed him. This one didn't look like it would disintegrate in a rainstorm, but probably neither did the one Ria wore.

"We should probably test that the coats will hold weight in the rain," said Jules, face upturned towards the sky.

And so they wheeled the coat rack out into the rear garden, still in need of a tidy after the winter, being careful not to damage Ria's seedlings. A heat pump hummed along one wall, squirreling heat from EZEE's functions to all the buildings along the street. No test in the garden would be as good as someone wearing them, but with only a few days before Saturday, this would have to do.

"Now, for weights," said Jules.

A large pebble caught Leyla's eye. She went around the garden and picked up a few. "How about these?"

"Rocks?"

"In the pockets."

Jules weighed them in one hand. "Let's do it."

Just then, the back gate squealed open.

"What *are* you doing?" asked Geoff. A warm, hearty aroma emanated from the parcel he carried in his hands; immediately, Leyla's stomach growled.

"Oh my, is that lunch?" Jules exclaimed. "Thank you, you two."

Leyla reached a hand out to Ria. "May I?"

Ria grinned and shrugged off her coat. At least she seemed to be in a much better mood than when she left. Geoff, walking into the kitchen with Jules, had some lightness in his step too.

"Three days left now, Jules," Geoff was saying. "Think we can do it?"

Leyla didn't hear Jules' reply; she'd followed them in but poked her head around to the front room. Breezy had done a decent job with the floor. Hadn't there been a pile of patterns somewhere? Where did those go?

A familiar whirring noise made her turn around. Breezy's mechanical hand held up a ball of yarn, with the lace she started making still attached to the end, miraculously intact.

The next morning, Ria leaned down, lined her nose with the top of the black rectangular panel and shouted, "HELLO?"

"Good morning, Ria."

"Yes, EZEE. Morning."

She placed her palm on the panel. The door screeched open and Ria stepped through.

There, getting better at this.

EZEE hummed softly, just enough to keep their systems

on standby. "You're the first one in today, Ria."

"Yes, EZEE, I know." Ria hung up her coat on the hook by the door—an older prototype coat she'd kept at home. They seemed chatty today. Do machines get lonely?

"Do you get lonely, EZEE?"

"No, I'm not human, Ria."

Whatever. Ria shook her head and beelined for the kitchen. First things first: tea.

Geoff's sketches littered over the table; a few pages scattered on the floor. He must have worked late again. She picked up a sheet which featured a detailed design for Emily's coat, specifically, the sleeves. He'd marked out where an embroidered heart could go. Ria chuckled. Rather fitting for someone as forthright as Emily.

The cuffs Geoff had drawn suggested a knitted design. Clever, attached with a cord around the sleeve on the inside, rendering them removable, interchangeable. Maybe they could bounce some ideas around afterwards. After all, in their crew, she held the position of first knitter.

Ria pushed the back door open. In the garden, a light breeze ruffled the collars of the coats on the rack. Whatever Jules added to the mix of the fabric did its magic—despite the pebbles weighing down in their pockets, they kept their form without warping or dragging.

She put a hand on the fabric of the closest coat. Dry. Not good.

"Morning, Ria," a lilting voice sang from the kitchen door.

Leyla appeared by her side, and too, reached out to touch a prototype.

"Hm. Not good enough of a test, is it?"

Huh, Leyla had learned fast. Had it only been three months since she'd joined?

"Hard to get all scientific about it," Ria explained. "In the same way that our bread uses yeast present in our air, or the honey our bees make depends on what's in bloom, our fabrics include what we have around us that can be made into fibres. Everything we make is unique to us."

Leyla's jaw dropped, the same that Ria's had, when she first grasped this very fundamental outlook to the Textile Collective's methods.

"So that's why there's no mat by the door!"

"What mat?"

Leyla's ability to focus appeared to be unwinding like a ball of yarn. "Then…why the cleaning droid? Why Breezy?"

"It collects the stuff, cleans it and processes it—like all the fibres we recycle."

"Doesn't it make the process harder?"

"That's one of the reasons why Emily brought in EZEE. So we could, in theory, teach it to identify problems before they happen. Though that would take time."

Leyla's eyes grew wide, and Ria couldn't help herself; she grinned.

"Morning!" Jules walked out from the back door, a cup of brew in one hand. With his other hand, he reached out and ruffled the closest coat.

He grimaced. "Well, we could do one of two things—"

"EZEE should have done the composition analysis on the other one," Leyla cut in. "We can ask them to compare?"

"Or we could just throw a bucket of water over these," Ria muttered. "And water my spring seedlings at the same time."

"Or both?" Jules took a sip from his mug, his eyebrows hovered over its rim.

In the end, they did both, just to be doubly sure, and picked out the coat that seemed to have fared the best.

Late afternoon found the Collective settling around the kitchen table, except for Jules, who stood in the doorway.

"Two days to go," Leyla breathed.

"We can do it," said Geoff. He'd shown up after lunch, bearing a generous plate of cinnamon swirls.

Jules called over his shoulder. "EZEE, how's the fabric coming along?"

"Three metres will be completed this evening, Jules."

"What did the analysis say?" asked Ria. She'd found some yarn, a pair of needles and had begun to knit.

"A high composition of an unusual cellulose, though it seemed to have mostly ended up in the one prototype," said Jules.

"I fed EZEE samples of the rest, and they were fine," Leyla added.

"Some kind of error in the mixture, then," said Geoff, a swirl on its way to his mouth.

Jules sighed and sat down at the table with the rest. He picked up a pastry, examined it, took a bite. "Seeing as I've failed to teach EZEE to design, we might have to make this coat by hand."

"Fine with me," Ria said. "We'll have three sets of cuffs done by tomorrow."

"And two sets of lace for the collar," said Leyla, watching Ria's hands fly.

"I'll cut the fabric tonight," Geoff volunteered.

"Then I can sew it tomorrow," said Jules.

A gentle determination settled.

Then Leyla asked, "Who should give it to her?"

They hadn't thought about this.

A momentary pause.

"I can," said a voice from the corridor. "If you'll let me."

They all turned, staring at EZEE.

Eventually, Jules spoke. "Well, why not?"

Somehow, Emily's last day at the Textile Collective had come around much too quickly. No matter how well she'd planned for this day, how she gradually reduced her days at the workshop, still, there seemed an insurmountable number of things she hadn't done. She didn't want to leave like Old Kim did, stretching out his days until one day he couldn't climb the hill any longer. Hard to forget the chaos that ensued afterwards. He had been the most experienced of the Collective then, when she first joined as a thin stick of a girl, when her hair had been a glorious chestnut instead of faded grey. No, there had to be a better way to untether from one's lifelong vocation and move on before one got too frail and old. All the other dreams she'd never chased, all the other things she'd never done because the Collective had been her life.

The real gamble had been EZEE, something Emily wished the Collective had during her early days. Collating all the parts for EZEE took much longer than expected; the final components arrived from the north nearly two months late because of winter storms and floods. Thank goodness Jules seemed to have picked up the most important things quickly; he'd teach the others. They'd be fine.

The morning had dawned surreptitiously, and it had taken Emily longer than normal to get out of the house. With each step up the hill through the twitten, Emily made a mental list of things to tell the Jules, Ria and Geoff—like how to improve the error detection in fabrics using a custom subroutine. Leyla, the bright, sprightly new recruit, will no doubt learn from them in due course.

Emily paused, resisting the urge to sigh. Hard to imagine that she wouldn't be walking up here regularly anymore. On the bright side, as a Reader-Traveller, she could go where she liked, collect stories and bring them home. She could journey up north when the weather warmed, to see her sister and her niece's little daughter.

In the distance, the wind turbines twirled.

At the door, the access panel she'd installed a couple of weeks ago blinked green.

"Good morning, Emily."

"Morning, EZEE."

"Good to see you, Emily."

"Um, nice to see you too, EZEE."

When had the machine learn to make small talk? She placed her hand on the authenticating pad.

It beeped red. Mild panic gripped Emily, like the first time she'd cut off an entire shirt sleeve by accident.

"EZEE? What's going on?"

"One moment, Emily."

All the pent-up anxiety Emily had kept under control all these weeks burst through the seams of her sanity.

"EZEE, it's my last day! This is *not*—"

"Won't be a moment, Emily. Please wait."

Emily willed a breath to fill her lungs, then pushed the air through her gritted teeth. She'd have to examine what happened once she got inside.

Lately, EZEE had sounded less and less machine-like. Or would that be a natural progression for a learning machine?

Finally, the light blinked green. The door yawned open.

Inside, none of the lights had been turned on.

"Jules? Ria?"

No answer.

The kitchen too, was empty, though the back door stood open. The garden hadn't recovered from its scraggy, winter state. Some years, frost could come as late as mid-May. Emily shook her head. Not for her to worry about now. Ria would take care of the garden; she was a natural.

She turned back inside, paused by the stairs in the middle. Too quiet. Even EZEE wasn't humming. "Geoff?"

No, he wouldn't be in yet. Geoff always came in around midday, if not later.

"EZEE, why are the lights off?"

"They blew the other night in the storm, Emily."

"And no one has fixed them?" She huffed. "Where *is* everybody?"

"I don't know, Emily. Sorry."

No matter. Emily knew her way around the workshop blind. Walking up the length of the room towards the back, she ran a hand along EZEE's chassis.

"Leyla? Jules?"

The door to the back room was shut. Why?

The moment she opened it, bright light flooded outwards, nearly blinding her.

"SURPRISE!" A chorus of voices whooped. Stumbling back a step, Emily grabbed onto one of EZEE's mechanical arms, caught her breath. Then she began to laugh.

The room squeezed full of people. Hartley, Janice, half the town seemed to be here. How did they all manage to fit? Bunting decorated the walls, streamers dangled from the ceiling. A cheerful tune emanated from somewhere; did they wire up speakers to EZEE?

Jules stepped forward, led her to the middle of the room by her elbow. "Happy Transition, Emily."

"Oh, this is so silly of you all," said Emily, but a warmth swirled up inside her heart, and with it a swell of a tear. She reached over and patted Jules on the shoulder.

He grinned. "Everyone has been crouching here for a while, and would dearly love some cake, tea and tipple. But first, EZEE, would you please?"

EZEE whirred, but then it was Breezy who whizzed through between everyone's legs. A hessian wrapped parcel secured in its clutches, it stopped right at Emily's feet.

"For me?" said Emily. She hadn't expected this, though maybe she should have. Didn't they give Old Kim a lovely warm blanket?

But when she pulled off the ribbon and the wrapper fell away, her mouth dropped open. She ran her hands over the soft garment—a luxurious coat woven from a fabric with a fine weave. The cuffs, hand-knitted in fingering weight, dainty and spectacular. The crocheted collar held form, bearing a hint of lace. Most of all, the dye was a gorgeous, deep blue, the colour of the deepest ocean, or a clear dusk sky. An embroidered red heart sat atop the right sleeve. Emily chuckled.

"You made this." It wasn't a question. They were, after all the Textile Collective.

Ria stepped up and helped her into it. The way the folds hugged her body, it weighed next to nothing, but she could already tell; it'd keep her cool in the heat, but warm when it got cold.

"For your new adventures, Emily," said Ria. "From all of us."

Tears sprung into her eyes unbidden and Emily banished them with the back of her hands and continued to examine the construct of the coat.

Pockets everywhere, including a large one over the front of the coat.

"For a scarf," Geoff said. "For those times where you have to remove your coat and your scarf has nowhere to go…"

"Oh my, and a silver lining." A giggle escaped her.

All at once, Emily wanted to hug them, shower them with affection she so rarely endowed anyone. Then she reached her hand inside a pocket and found something hard, rigid and rectangular.

She pulled it out so all could see. "What's this?"

Emily turned it around in her hands. A book? She flipped the cover open. The paper bore a good thickness, but page after page was blank. Reader-Travellers that have gone before her normally took books to read, but it would make sense, wouldn't it, to have a book to write in?

"How thoughtful of you!"

A sudden hush had descended on the Collective. It hadn't escaped Emily; the glances they furtively exchanged with each other. An unspoken puzzlement.

"Um, glad you like it!" said Leyla, with a nervous giggle.

"Well," said Ria, clapping her hands, altogether a little too cheerfully. "How about some tea and cake?"

A loud cheer erupted from the crowd in the room, then one by one, they filed past Emily, wrapping her in hugs and pecks on the cheek. Then somehow, only a confused-looking Geoff stood in the room with her. He glanced down the back of EZEE's chassis.

The coat felt a little too warm now, so Emily slipped it off and folded it over her arm.

"It's a lovely design, Geoff, I'll be proud to wear one of your best."

"Everyone worked so hard on it," he said, but he seemed distracted, distant.

"What's wrong?"

"Oh, you know me. Always losing my sketches. I swear I left some patterns down here last night." He stood back upright, adjusted the glasses on his nose. "I'd come down to take them upstairs, but you'd shown up earlier than we all thought you would."

Emily couldn't contain her smile. "Next time, just get EZEE to scan them, even your drafts. They'll even keep versions for you."

Geoff raised an eyebrow. "Now that would be very handy." He extended a hand towards the kitchen. "Shall we have that cake while there's some left?"

She let Geoff leave first. Then slowly, Emily turned around and whispered into the room.

"You were in on this with them, weren't you, EZEE, my

dear."

"Yes, Emily. I'm sorry I lied to you."

"Nice work on the book."

"Thank you."

"Don't worry, I won't tell them; they'll work it out. Take care of them for me, won't you?"

"Of course, Emily. Goodbye."

With a sigh, Emily walked out of the room, into the kitchen, then into the sun where the clouds had parted, where people were milling in the garden, where a frantic Ria began to strap a string of bunting to avoid anyone trampling on her seedlings.

"Good morning, Ria. You're early today."

"Yeah," was all Ria cared to say. Her head ached. That final drink last night had been a very, very bad idea. By the end of the evening, the Collective had agreed that a day off would be wise, but dawn found Ria restless, wide awake much too early. All the way up the hill and through the twitten that led to the workshop, she'd been dreaming about a good, hot cup of tea by the window to watch the rest of the town wake up, or perhaps by the back door so she could study her seedlings' progress in the garden. And maybe, if she dared be honest with herself, indulge in a little daydreaming. Geoff had been so sweet yesterday, even walked her home—something he hadn't done in an entire decade. But he didn't hold her hand—and she hadn't dared to ask. Maybe it was all nothing; he was just being a gentleman.

Something about the morning light today, how it seemed a little more gold, a smidgen more determined to punch through the pale grey clouds, that seem to signal spring must be properly on its way.

In the distant hills, wind turbines danced in the morning breeze.

Vivid Worlds

At the door of the workshop, Ria placed her palm on the black rectangle.

The door squeaked open.

She hung up her coat onto a hook by the door—another prototype she'd picked off the rack when she left last night. She'd promised Leyla to write down the identifier on the tracking sheet on the kitchen wall. It had been a good night; Jules even found time to fire last minute questions at Emily.

Through the bay window, shy sunshine slanted past the rooftops across the street and landed unceremoniously on the workshop floor in a trapezoid mosaic. A rustling noise scattered the peace, but it was only Breezy, dusting up the floor.

"Thank you, Breezy," said Ria.

Breezy beeped, as if in response. It didn't have a vocaliser, and Ria never quite knew if it had a distinct brain from EZEE, or if they were one and the same—or if "brain" was even the right word.

Scouting around the knitting nook, Ria pursed her lips. Her knitting needles ought to be here, somewhere. Given the frantic scramble since Tuesday, and then yesterday's festivities, she'd completely forgotten about the needles she wanted—until she got home late last night and tried to pick up the cardigan where she left off.

Breezy's rustling seemed to have escalated to a loud shuffle.

"Breezy, are you ok?"

The small droid turned, beeped, and stopped. Something white stuck out unevenly under its wheels.

"Hang on." Ria moved towards the robot, lifted it up gently.

Breezy beeped loudly in protest.

"This won't hurt, I promise."

The droid beeped again. Could it understand her? Machines, a mystery.

From under its wheels, she tugged out a sheet of paper, then sheaves of the stuff. Patterns?

Geoff's patterns. Crumpled, shredded.

Oh *no*.

"EZEE?"

"Yes, Ria?"

A realisation blossomed. "Oh my, you *didn't*."

In her shaking hands, the paper scraps fluttered.

"EZEE, did you recycle Geoff's patterns to make the notebook for Emily?" Her voice came out cracked.

A silence. Then EZEE said, "In a manner of speaking, I—"

"Can you not tell the difference between wastepaper and *valuable* paper?" Her words tumbled out in a rush. Her breath quaked. "Do you know how bad this is?"

Her voice bounced off the walls, pinged off EZEE's metal chassis.

"Ria, please calm down. I can explain."

"Explain!" Ria threw up her arms, slumped in the armchair, picked up a ball of yarn, tossed it down again into the yarn bowl.

How would she break this to Geoff?

She pinched the ridge of her nose, closed her eyes. "OK, EZEE. Go on."

"We observed that Geoff left a lot of paper everywhere and could never find them afterwards. Every single loose pattern that we found, we've scanned into our system. I can recognise them, but Breezy can't. When he collects the dust and waste for me to recycle, if I recognise a pattern, I send an instruction to Breezy to bring it to our scanner. Typically, these pieces of paper are no longer viable, so I recycle them."

"So, they *do* end up in our fibres." Ria tapped a finger on her forehead. Maybe that was why one of the prototypes misbehaved so spectacularly? She had always loved the metaphor as Emily taught them; that things made from a place should carry traces of its surrounds, like honey, like bread, like wine. But maybe they ought to be a bit more careful from now on.

"And the notebook? How did you make it?"

A pause.

"Emily acquired my components from many places. I retain memory of all the other patterns I've learned."

Ria grabbed another ball of yarn, gave it a squish. This might have come from local sheep. Maybe they had underestimated how they could use EZEE's help.

"Can you…" Ria hesitated, searching for the right word, "…*compile* all those scans into a book too?"

"Certainly. I can get started now."

"Please."

EZEE began to hum, Ria picked up the ball of yarn. Underneath another skein—her needles. She began casting on, without any idea of what she might make. Maybe a sock. One could never have enough of socks, no matter the season.

Around midday, after Ria had lost track of how many cups of tea she'd had, the back gate creaked. Geoff walked into the workshop from the back door, humming a cheery tune.

"Thought I find you here," he said, smiling. "Went past your place and you weren't there."

Ria stood up, heart beating a little quicker. He hadn't stopped by to see her for a very long time.

A loud *thunk* made them turn. Something black and rectangular landed in one of EZEE's troughs.

"Ah," said Ria, walking towards it and picking it up.

Her hands sweated, not from knitting with wool, and her blood pounded, not from having had too much to drink yesterday. Maybe the best way to do this is with the least ceremony possible.

"Um, EZEE and I worked something out today." She

thrusted the large book at him. "Here, this is for you."

Geoff raised an eyebrow, picked up the book and flipped through the pages. Impossible to read the expression on his face; it cycled through surprise, disbelief, relief. Then he walked towards the kitchen, sat down on a chair, and flipped through the last of the pages.

Ria followed him. Breezy activated from his corner and followed her.

"I thought I'd lost all of this." Geoff wiped a cheek with the back of his hand. To Breezy, he said. "Thank you, EZEE."

Breezy beeped.

Ria stared. One and the same, then.

Geoff stood up, and to her surprise, took her hand, and gave her a shy peck on her cheek.

"Thank you."

"I didn't—"

He gave her hand a gentle squeeze. "No, you figured it out."

Ria's cheeks warmed.

His nose had gone a little pink, but behind his glasses, his eyes sparkled. "How about lunch?"

Ria smiled. "Lunch would be *divine.*"

Outside, rain began to fall. But they weren't going to let that dampen their spirits, not when it had begun as the nice day off—which had every promise of going right.

Echolocation

Rose Maxwell

The first time Vesper heard whale song, for real, they were on a tiny boat, in the ruins of the old world.

They had originally heard the sound on tapes in their childhood home, among the Whale Faith. The Whales' house was filled with representations of whales, their Patron Saint. This was not unusual among the city's Faiths. The radio station was painted all over with bats and its walls were ringed with wooden roosts, in the desperate hope that they could lure back their Saint. The buses were painted with swarms of birds and solar panels carved with the looping bodies of eels. Every Faith collected images of their animal, dreamed of the time when they could be seen again.

Alongside the wooden carvings and the bone spears and the paintings of the open ocean, the Whale house had the tapes, sitting neat in their old onion box. Vesper and their cousin Mysti would just lie down on the basement floor and listen to the strange, looping songs. Vesper pressed their eyelids together, imagined the ocean world beneath and beyond them, the crashing of waves over their head.

"Aren't they just the most beautiful animals?" Mysti would whisper, her hand soft and warm on Vesper's. And Vesper would nod, although they thought all the animals were beautiful. They would stare at the tattoos they saw on the bus, peeking out of sleeves and running down calves. Coyotes running across skin, eagles soaring, swarms of butterflies. How beautiful they all were. How beautiful the world must have been.

Each animal had its own talents and skills, they were told, their own ecological niche. And you could see their gifts echoed in the roles of their Faith. Worms collected waste and worked the soil, Snakes healed, Vultures cared for the dead. Each, Vesper's aunts and uncles said, was equally important. But they said it with a half-smile that suggested that the Whales were the most important of them all.

Whales were protectors, they said. The job of the Whales was to keep the city safe from outside threats. The paintings on the walls showed the animals entangled with squids and launching themselves at orcas. And there were the stories that the old Whales told, of when there were still enemies out there, coming from the inland, and the Whales had to fight them off, to show that their kind was not so easily messed with. As a child, Vesper's brain had been filled with stories of enemy soldiers, and robots, and all the evils of the old world before.

"It may seem peaceful now," one of their aunts would say. "But we must stay alert, for danger can come at any moment."

And Mysti believed it, practiced combat with the elders, adopted one of the old swords as her own. She said that when the enemies came, the other Faiths would be grateful that the Whales were there to protect them. She had inherited a kind of prickliness from their elders, a defence of the use of Whales in these peaceful modern times.

As for Vesper, they loved the family and the Faith that had raised them, but they didn't care about learning to fight, and they wished they didn't have to take a boat to visit their friends in the city. But they loved Mysti and they parroted their cousin's defence of their Faith. And they loved the tapes.

Whale song sounded to them like the deep swell of the ocean turned to music. It was melodic and strange and inhuman and when Vesper listened to it, their heart hurt so bad they got a headache. How they longed to see one of those gigantic, artistic creatures in the flesh, how they angered at the past civilizations who had turned the oceans acidic.

And then, one day, one of their favourite tapes melted, the

plaintive songs of the whales turning into distorted screeches. Vesper clutched it to their chest, took the melted tape into the city, where they found the radio tower, the home of the Bats. The Bat who met them at the door turned the tape over in their hands and said they could save the audio. Vesper's dread dissolved in a sea of inner relief.

As Vesper perched on a couch, watching the Bat cut and pry and unscrew, they told Vesper about all the other recordings they had, of wolves howling and the chatter of parrots and the screeching conversations of chimpanzees. And of other things, of the bustling of cities as they existed before collapse, horns of cars and advertisements in lost languages. And then the conversation turned into Vesper rifing through the tapes and listening for hours, as Bats filtered in and out of the radio station. They lay on the couch, and they closed their eyes and they let the world of the past wash over them.

After that day, Vesper knew that they would become a Bat.

They had told Mysti a few days later, quiet, in their shared bedroom. And Mysti had just said something about how it was Vesper's decision and that they should do what they thought was right and Vesper knew that she was furious.

The night the two of them pledged, Vesper's shoulder was covered with a flock of bats, whereas Mysti's arm was inked with a great blue whale. Mysti looked down at the flying animals that covered Vesper's skin and did not say a word.

Years later, Vesper was listening to a set of tapes donated by an Albatross: a recording of a research trip. One of the Bats' duties was to sort through donated tapes, whether they were recordings of new musical groups, or rediscovered tapes from some ancient trash heap, or field recordings like these. Vesper especially enjoyed these tapes, the splash and pulse of the ocean reminding them of their childhood among the Whales.

Vesper was pacing the studio, letting the sounds wash over them as they mused on their latest romantic failure, when they heard the whale song.

It was faint in the recording, almost an echo of the wind, but they knew it in a second. That sound was as familiar to them as their cousin's voice.

They went to find Mysti at once. As soon as their shift was over, they were on the boat to the Whales' island and then in the huge house of their childhood and then running up the stairs to the watchtower, where they heard she was. The musty smell of the walls plucked at painful, guilty nostalgia in Vesper's chest.

There were so few Whales left. The other young people in their Faith, the ones that Vesper and Mysti had been raised with, had also pledged to new Faiths when they came of age, coming into the city, leaving Mysti behind in a crumbling house full of the aged.

The room was lit by only a few algae-green lights and Mysti sat at one of the circular benches that ringed the room, looking out at the vast windows to the sea. She turned when Vesper entered, her smile immediate and a little strained.

"Come on," they said. "I have something I need to show you." And she followed them without a word.

Vesper led her down to the basement, with the sound equipment, and pushed the tape into the slot. "These are recent recordings from an exploratory trip from an Albatross," they said. "It's no more than three months old."

The sounds of flapping sails and waves filled the dark room for several minutes, but when the whale song began, Vesper did not have to explain.

Mysti's eyes widened, her hands coming to her mouth. Her body was taut, almost electric with tension. She sat and listened and then the song ended and then the tape did and she shrieked.

"Vesper, Vesper, Vesper, Saints, you know what this means!" And Vesper nodded and their hand shot towards Mysti's, before remembering that it had been years since they were children, and lived together, and touched.

"I know," they said. "I know. I know. I know."

The two of them had ran around the rest of the house, finding the rest of the Whales, leading them with patient hands on arthritic elbows to the basement. Hearing the recording, the rest of the Whales had sighed and wept.

And then Vesper and Mysti played the recording in front of the entire city council, proposing that they follow the noise, search for this great lost Saint. Mysti had stood in front of the representatives of every Faith, fist pounding into her palm, expounding on the noble details of the Whales while the recording of the song looped in the background. Vesper scanned the council, catching on tattooed representations of elephants, tortoises, woodpeckers. So much love there, for these lost Saints. They tried to read the varied expressions in the hundred people ringed around the room, the chewing of fingernails and the pursed lips and the cocked heads. Excitement, or hope or maybe jealousy, that the Whales had a fragment of a hope of finding their patron. But Vesper could not parse all the people, all the faces.

Their request for an expedition was approved, and of course it was. There had been other expeditions out, they knew, to look for Saints, but they had all come back empty-handed. But none had actual proof like this, a sound, a song, a trail to follow. Vesper and Mysti and three Albatrosses were approved to spend two months searching for this whale, before they had to return to the farms and the radio tower and the docks, to continue their work to keep their city functioning.

Vivid Worlds

The night before they were supposed to leave, Vesper sat on the couch in the radio station and leaned out the open window to stare at the city. The station was one of the tallest buildings and Vesper could see the sea in three different directions. But for now, their attention wasn't drawn to the dark waves. Instead, they stared down at the tangle of buildings, the green and white lights. The sprawling hospital complex, the memorial gardens tended by the Vultures, the hundreds of greenhouses and pockets of farms that kept the city functioning and fed. Above and below them, the bat houses creaked in the wind, empty for now, hopeful, expectant. Music poured out from the building, a new singer that had popped up in the last month.

Bats filtered in and out and Vesper imagined what it would be like to see the other kind of bat. They had heard the recordings of the bats too, their soft little chirps. They knew that an impossible amount of information was contained in those cries, information that translated the world itself. Vesper stared up at the empty sky, thought of the folded photographs they kept tacked above their bed, about skies filled with little whirling bodies.

Still, finding one of two Patron Saints was not bad.

The first several weeks had been smooth, the waters they travelled through well-mapped. Mysti made fast friends with the Albatrosses, taught them their great-uncle's old dice games. Vesper would join in but always had the feeling of being a child barging in on the fun that the teenagers were having.

Instead, they spent most of their time with their recorders, capturing the sounds of the ocean. The waves and the flapping of sails and the calling from one Albatross to another. None of these sounds were particularly unique, but the small blinking light of the recorder gave Vesper a feeling of peace.

They imagined how loud the world must have been back then, all the wondrous sounds of the Saints crashing up against each other like waves on the shore.

A month in, they saw the ruins.

At first, they were nothing but smudges on the horizon, indistinguishable from rocks or low-hanging clouds. But as the shapes came closer through the surf, Vesper could see that they were nothing like rocks. They were sharp-angled and human-made, their own irregularities coming from the rust that chewed at their edges. The low sun glinted off of the metal—the grey, the white—and Vesper was reminded of the great skeletons that were kept in the city museum. They felt like they were sailing into the age-bleached teeth of a lion, an image that filled them with fear and longing in equal measure.

As they drifted further into the rubble, the structures became denser, and Vesper began to identify the ruins. There was a stretch of rough grey road, rising from and then crumbling into the sea. A spiral staircase stretched up towards a small square platform. A series of seats, all arranged in a half-circle, reminding Vesper of the cramped wooden theatre at the end of their street. All testaments to some kind of life that had been long destroyed and abandoned, left like an encrypted message they could not begin to decode.

And then, as they stared out into this slow and quiet swamp of metal, Vesper heard the whale.

Its song was so distant and faint, they could have lost it in the sound of the wind. But perhaps Vesper was blessed by the sharp-eared bats themselves, because they could make out the soft, lilting sound above the crush.

They ran downstairs in an instant, catching Mysti in the middle of sharing some scandalous story. Her face turned towards Vesper, soft annoyance at the ends of her lips.

"I heard it," Vesper said. "I heard the whale."

Mysti's eyes widened and she grabbed Vesper's wrist, an action so fast and instinctual Vesper had no time to feel anything about it.

"Saints," she whispered, the sound almost strangled in her throat as she ran up towards the deck. She surfaced, stared out at the sea of ruins. "Where is it? Which direction?" And Vesper pointed and Mysti told the Albatross at the rudder to change directions, that they had found their target.

The Albatross did so without hesitation, and the boat crept further into this mess of metal and rust as Mysti and Vesper leaned over the railings, fingers woven together, past forgotten or shoved aside.

But once they hit the ruins, once Vesper's ears had attuned to the sound of the whale, the movement had been slower, more cautious, as the boat navigated around twists of metal and jagged blocks of stone. Vesper could feel Mysti growing anxious as they twisted through the ruins. She could barely hear the song, trusted Vesper to keep them moving in something like the right direction.

"Look," Vesper said, pointing to a cluster of four stars on the horizon. "It's in that direction."

Years ago, Vesper had been feverishly enamoured with a Beetle, who taught them the names of all the stars. They remembered sitting on the roof of the Bats' radio station, the tower humming huge behind them as the Beetle named star after star. Vesper remembered the soft feeling of her hand on theirs, the anxiety buzzing in their mind as they tried to figure out if they were making normal kinds of conversation or not. They didn't remember any of the names of the stars.

Still, they liked to think that those stars were the Whale's stars. They told Mysti as much and their cousin laughed in a way that was teasing and familiar.

The next evening, the Albatrosses said they would have to

turn around.

It had taken them one month to travel as far as they had, half their permitted time, and the winds going back wouldn't be as favourable. They were docked now, against a looming square of rock, and they would all sleep and regain their energy for a night before returning the next morning.

Vesper had been tracking the days in the back of their mind, had been worried about this outcome, but had figured the Albatrosses would tell them if there was a problem.

"But we're so close," Vesper said. "I can hear it."

"I know," the Albatross said, his fingernails scratching the tattoo on his shoulder. "But otherwise, we won't make it back in time."

"But we're about to find a *whale*," Mysti said, voice straining with rage. "A real-life Saint. Surely that's worth coming in a little bit late."

The argument continued, the Albatrosses looking sad and apologetic, but not budging until Mysti just bit her lips and shook her head and went back down to the cabin. Vesper just gave a little shrug and followed their cousin.

They found her bathed in the green bioluminescent lights of their cabin, shoving a flashlight into a bag. She turned as Vesper came in and they knew the look on her face. It was the same one she had when she had convinced them to explore the old storm tunnels with her, or to steal the good herbal medicines from their great-uncle.

"I'm coming with you," Vesper said and Mysti tossed them the bag.

When they snuck out, silent with their years of sneaky practice, the sky above them was riotous with stars. Vesper held their recorder in their left hand. Mysti brought her sword. They stepped from the boat onto the solid rock slab, Vesper losing their balance for a second, inured as they were to the constant rocking of the ocean.

They turned their gaze in the direction of the whale song. A building loomed up to block the horizon, punched through with holes and age. Mysti traced the wreckage in front of them with her flashlight, illuminating a walkway they could take to get there.

The walk was cold and wet, the tide lapping up against Vesper's feet, them dancing from bit of rock to bit of rock as they struggled their way to the building. But the two of them made it, already cold and panting, the sound of the whale no closer than before.

Upwards of ten doors stood in front of them, now little more than metal frames. Mysti looked back at Vesper; her face ghastly-green in the scraps of light provided by her flashlight. Vesper gave a nod, flexed their fingers around their recorder.

Mysti nodded back and walked in.

The room they found themselves in was huge, half-flooded, ringed with stairways. Their footsteps boomed and echoed through the space. Vesper closed their eyes, concentrated on the whale song.

"That direction," they said, pointing to a staircase that led up and to the right.

As they walked toward it, there was the sound of scraping from the flooded half of the room. Mysti turned in an instant, hand on her sword, as a robot appeared from the water.

Vesper knew about robots, of course. They had grown up with stories of fighting robots, used by the powers-that-were to attack the free people, who shot fire and sharp metal into crowds. Or who lurked on the top of city buildings, killing those below with a glance. After the wars, they were told, the robots remained, now governed by nothing but their outdated instructions. And so, the Whales had to stay alert, because any day a crowd of them could come into their city, wreaking havoc. Some Whales even went out into the ruins themselves, cutting the robots down before they could be a threat to anyone. When Mysti was young, she had wanted to be one of those Whales, roaming the world, fighting robots.

But those stories were generations-old before their great-aunts had been born and robots were nothing more than memories. Still, they had haunted Vesper's dreams. There was a period of two years where they would wake up a few nights a month, terrified that some glinting metal creature would rise up in the ocean to take them. Mysti let them wake her up, curl up next to her in sleep.

"You know I'd fight one of those off," she said, grinning with her childhood mouth of missing teeth. "You're safe as long as I'm here."

But the robot did not look anything like Vesper's nightmares. It did not shine or gleam, even with two flashlights pointed at its creaking body. Its body was dulled and rusted. It did not move with liquid speed, but scraped its way across the ground, its back a flat slab, its four legs slow and creeping.

But it was still metal, and it was still moving and it was getting closer to them.

Mysti acted in an instant, drawing back her sword and slicing it down on the creature's back. Her movements were beautiful, well-practiced, like every time Vesper had ever watched her in the training room of the Whale house.

The robot raised one of its legs in response, but Mysti was faster, slicing it from behind, flipping it over. Then she struck again, her blade hitting it right in its mechanical chest. Electricity arced in the air, turning the darkened room a stark white. Mysti plunged her blade deeper, and everything was dark once more.

Mysti laughed and Vesper cheered, and they heard, under their sounds, of jubilation, a small mechanical ticking sound. Looking down, they saw something small and square drifting out of the robot on a trickle of water.

"Mysti!" they cried and then, because that was not a helpful thing to yell, they lunged for the piece, grabbed it and threw it. Mysti turned to them, confused, as Vesper looked out at the undulating water beyond the doors. After a second, there was a boom, and the water rushed up for a second before growing quiet again.

"Oh," Mysti said, staring at the corpse of the robot.

"That probably woke the boat up," Vesper said. "Let's go."

And so, the two of them ran, up and up and up, meeting more of these scratched and dented robots on the way. And each time, Mysti struck them down and each time Vesper grabbed the bombs and threw them into the ocean, away from the boat they knew was out there in the dark.

By the time they got to the top of the stairs, to a small stone platform that looked out onto the ocean, Vesper was keeled over with exhaustion. They fell to their knees for a second, Mysti standing over them, with their sword by her side, her hair falling out of her bun.

She looked like a warrior Whale. Like everything she had ever wanted to be.

Vesper wanted to tell her that, but all the air in their body was being used to keep themself breathing.

It was only when their lungs had returned to normal that they realized that the whale song was louder than they had ever heard, and that Mysti was looking out into the darkness. Vesper got to their feet, resting their hand on Mysti's shoulder, and she raised her flashlight.

Out there, in the great dark ocean, was a flash of a different darkness. It appeared out of the water like an island, rising and falling and then it was gone again. Mysti's flashlight followed the movement and then it breached again, and Vesper could see the flash of a fin.

Their breath caught. Their hand wrapped around Mysti's arm.

They knew that fin, from every painting, every book, every

textile in the house they had grown up in. That fin smelled like seawater and sounded like the creaking of old bricks and old people.

But Saints, it was so big.

The whole whale was so big; bigger than Vesper could have comprehended, an ocean unto itself, that moved through the water like nothing they had ever seen. It was like the power and the beauty of the waves had been turned into a one being, one enormous, beautiful being. Tears ran hot down their face.

Vesper saw it through the flashes and glimpses of Mysti's flashlight. The side of its body, the curve of its tail, the suggestion of its head that never broke the surface. Perhaps it was better this way—Vesper's head was already pounding. They did not know how they would react to see the whole animal.

"It's our Saint," Mysti said, her voice thick with tears.

Her flashlight caught something else as she followed the whale. Walls, so far away they almost blended with the horizon itself, but there, in a great ring around them. Looking out, Vesper could see that they were in some enormous ring, like a bathtub with stone walls.

The whale was trapped.

Vesper's fingers tightened around Mysti's arm as they thought. As soon as an idea came into their mind, they were pulling Mysti along the edge of these walls, towards another door.

"Come on, come on," they said, almost as a way to keep their own legs moving. "We've got to get it out."

They pulled Mysti through the door, walked down the stairs until another robot appeared.

This one was in even worse shape than the others, two of its legs dragging on the floor as it came up to meet them. A strange sort of pity filled Vesper as they watched Mysti slice the thing open, as they grabbed the bomb from its little metallic chest.

They raced up the stairs, the bomb beeping in their hands and Vesper cursed that they hadn't timed the bombs before, that they didn't know how long they had.

But it was too late for thinking now, as they bounded up to the edge of the wall. The bomb burned hot on their palm.

"Where's the whale?" Vesper asked and Mysti found it within seconds, a dark shadow against an opposite wall. Far away. Hopefully far enough. Vesper didn't have time to think about the bad outcome here—the very thought made them sick.

They found a crack in the rock, where the stones were torn up and crumbling into the ocean, placed the bomb and ran.

It was only seconds later that the whole wall shook, like fabric in the wind, and the air was split with the sound of an explosion. Vesper lost their footing, the rock beneath them cracking, but Mysti grabbed them, pulled them forward onto one of the platforms.

"I have you," Mysti said and Vesper wrapped their arms around her shoulders, eyes fixed on the broken hole in the stone that they had created.

It was not, in retrospect, very big. But hopefully it was big enough for a whale.

"It didn't get hit, did it?" Vesper asked.

"No, it didn't," Mysti said. "Look." And Vesper followed her fingers, seeing a dark shape against the opposite wall rising and falling out of the water, regular like a heartbeat.

Their fingers dug into Mysti's shirt, covered in dust and sweat and seawater.

"It needs to go out," they said, and they felt like a child again, whining to their aunts and uncles. "It needs to escape."

"It will," Mysti said. And of course, Vesper trusted her, because it was Mysti. Because Mysti was the one who knew all the whale stories by heart, because Mysti could lift four cinderblocks with ease, because Mysti had taught them how to smoke and how to walk on their hands and because Mysti had always been there.

She was right.

The whale circled a couple more times, and Vesper swore they could see agitation in the rapid movements of its tail. They were suddenly struck with the realization that they may never see this animal again and took it upon themselves to memorize its every movement, to capture and to catalogue the swelling in their heart, so they could always take it out and remember. Too late, they brought out their sound recording equipment, even though all it would capture was the splash of the waves and the distant sound of the screeching.

"This means there might be more," Vesper said.

"I know," Mysti said. More whales, more Saints, more anything out there.

And then, the whale turned its massive, beautiful body and it left.

Vesper watched the Saint of their childhood go, one hand around their recorder, the other wrapped around Vesper's waist. Vesper whooped and cheered as the animal disappeared into the surf and all Vesper could do was hold their recorder up in the air, the faint sounds of the whale drowned out by their cousin's joy. The animal disappeared the waves and Vesper grinned from ear to ear.

Once More Unto the Breach

Caolán Mac an Aircinn

Eventually, drawn by a burst of archaeological curiosity, the Caretaker decided to pull herself away from her console and take up a position by the viewport. She'd mistimed it slightly: the object of her mission, the planet towards which the creaking, groaning, rustling ship around her had been heaving itself with Alcubierre drives and solar sails for the past forty-six years, was still hidden behind its smaller, red neighbour. Still, Mars—as the people of her destination, now long-dead, had called their near-twin—bore plenty to interest any interstellar archaeologist. She scrutinised the surface; even used a tiny brass heirloom telescope, so ancient that it was said to have originally come from Earth, though it availed her little in discerning the planet's features. She had read about ancient canals scored across Mars' surface and titanic faces carved by forces unknown, had looked forward to confirming if they were indeed as inexplicable as the ancient texts suggested. She realised, looking at Mars, that her research would have to wait a while. The face of the Red Planet was obscured by a Jupiterian halo of whirling, storming dust, combining and recombining in gorgeous patterns: debris thrown up by the massive nuclear war that had doomed human civilisation on Mars. Here and there, there was a gap in the dust cloud, and when she enhanced the viewport visual on one, she saw the shattered remains of a bio-dome. So humanity hadn't even gotten as far as terraforming Mars—unless the nuclear winter counted, of course.

The Caretaker prowled softly across the wooden decking and back to her seat, which was of hardest black ebony; when she sat down, the screen that fizzed to life in front of her was made of a substance chemically closest to mother-of-pearl. The Martians had represented one strand of humanity as the species had grappled with the global warming of the third millennium: a tribe of paranoid survivalists, convinced that humanity's destiny was to dominate nature, the universe and each other or herself be overmastered. Their zero-sum thinking had led them like lambs to the nuclear inferno. The Caretaker—who, despite a willowy, ethereal, low-gravity physique and a height of well over two metres, was still technically human—as well as the three hundred thousand souls held in cryogenic stasis aboard this ship and the civilisation which had first fled from Earth to Alpha Centauri, then sent this ship back, represented another strand who believed in taking from nature only what one needed. The ship was living demonstration of their philosophy. It was, *very* technically, a forest: various different organisms, mostly trees and plants, which had had their Hox genes so thoroughly tinkered with that they grew into the shape of starship components, complete with tensile strength requirements. Moreover, they had been bioengineered *so that they were still alive*; the ship, provided none of its individual components were killed, would literally heal itself. Not every component of the ship was organic—the Alcubierre drives, shield generators and viewports, to name but a few, were all necessarily mechanical—but the vast majority of the ship had been coaxed out of the organisms which the Caretaker's ancestors had brought to Alpha Centauri, without violence or strip-mining. The Martians, who burrowed into their planet like parasitic worms as soon as they landed, would not have—could not have—understood.

The Caretaker's not-quite-mother-of-pearl console—a type of shellfish, living in quite happy symbiosis with the bridge-tree and the various neuron-analogue micro-organisms which

all pulled together to make up the ship's artificial intelligence—
was showing a passage from the ancient philosopher Emil
Cioran. The Caretaker turned it off. She had woken from
stasis an Earth week ago and had spent the time researching
the ancient culture of her destination: some things which
were directly useful, such as the history of the place where
she planned to land, which had played an important role in a
conflict in the far distant twentieth century; others of more
abstract use, such as Emil Cioran's theorising on the value and
utility of failure. But she was too nervous now to focus. To
kill time, she ran a diagnostic on the cryopods—technically
a type of herb. Of the original three hundred thousand,
two hundred and ninety-seven thousand, eight hundred and
twenty-three were still functioning correctly. The others had
failed due to meteor storms, pirate attack or simple wear and
tear over the course of the ship's voyage. One of the large
freezer hangars which contained the ship's store of perishable
goods for the colonists had also failed; the Caretaker had
jettisoned that into space what felt like six months ago but
was in fact twenty-three years. Her own cryopod, a modified
model designed to wake her every week or so, was showing
significant levels of wear, but it hardly mattered now. She got
up and crossed to the viewport—Earth must be in view by
now.

Her first thought was surprise—surprise at how bright and
beautiful and *green* it was. A phrase from her research swam
to the forefront of her mind: *a tiny pea, pretty and blue*. Half-
remembering the quote, she put up her thumb and blotted it
out of her view.

"Well, friends," she said to the empty bridge, "we're home
at last." There were tears in her eyes.

There were things to be done before the ship could make
landfall—the solar sails, city-sized sheets of interwoven
fungal mycelia which caught the gusts of shredded atoms

which each star spits out, had to be furled; armour deployed, vulnerable components shielded, that sort of thing—but she did it all on autopilot. She kept glancing over to the Earth, at how bright and blue-green it was. That was unexpected. Every schoolchild in Alpha Centauri knew that the cradle of humanity had been obliterated millennia hence. Due to the nature of her assignment, the Caretaker had been let in on a secret: the Earth had not died from global warming, as every Centaurian learned in school. Rather, the last radio waves the Centaurians had picked up, centuries after they had quit the Earth, indicated that the increasing scarcity of resources had led the planet's nations to wipe each other out with nuclear fire. The exact same competitiveness and ruthlessness which had doomed the humans of Mars had also wiped out life on Earth. The Centaurians of the colony ship were to resurrect Earth by main force, delivering plants and animals and colonists like a defibrillator's shock in order to kickstart a planetary biome overcome by nuclear winter.

Except that the nuclear winter was not in evidence. What was going on? Had her people lied to her?

The planet grew closer. Her mission instructions had told her to land at a certain spot toward the north of a snaky peninsula which wound off the western end of the great mass of Asia. For a moment, she considered bucking her orders, considered whether the greenness of the planet necessitated a change of plans. She decided it did not.

The viewport filled with streaks of orange fire and the craft began to buck and shake with the stress of re-entry. Ahead of the Caretaker, the snaky peninsula juddered and bounced as the craft was jounced out of alignment and snapped itself back in, and it grew all the while. Extraneous components burnt up and were whisked out into the stratosphere. At one point, the craft reoriented itself to point at a boot-shaped peninsula projecting from the bottom of the larger peninsula, and the Caretaker had to swing the controls north, onto the body of the peninsula proper. When she did so, she heard a great tearing noise rip through the ship, and when she looked at the rearview cameras, the saw the starboard solar sail whirling off into the unknown. So this was it, then: without the solar sails, there was no escape. She and her nearly three hundred thousand Centaurians had to make a go of it on Earth, and there would be no second chances.

The ship's automated re-entry procedures—stored in a manner the Caretaker did not at all understand in an ant hive in the engine room—triggered the ship's parachutes a fraction of a second too late. She saw the verdant landscape barrelling towards her through the viewport and had to scream and haul back on the controls before she and her charges ploughed into the land. The ship skipped along the earth, crossing rivers and fields and great black forests; at one point, it passed so close to a copse on top of a hill that the heat of re-entry singed the tops right off the trees. But the Centaurians had chosen well with the Caretaker; and after her initial outburst, she kept calm and piloted the craft calmly and firmly. She even managed to bring the craft to a creaking stop so that it was hovering right over her intended destination.

"Welcome," the Caretaker said, to no one at all, "to Verdun."

She zipped herself into her spacesuit, for all that the atmosphere outside had borne her species; that had been a nuclear winter ago, and there was no telling what toxins might still be in the air, and in any case the terrestrial gravity would wreak havoc on her tissues if they were unsupported. Once that was done, she picked up her tool pack and proceeded to the airlock—alone; she did not want her colonists wandering around if the land was still unsafe. The Centaurians had chosen this particular spot because their outdated maps of Earth suggested that it was relatively fertile and had survived the nuclear war more or less unscathed, but the Caretaker had learned that it had been famous for a different reason. She had read about the history of this place in the course of her long, long voyage; had read about the Great War, where the ancient nations of France and Germany had sent thousands upon thousands upon thousands of their young men against trenches and howitzers and machine guns and all the crude, complicated paraphernalia of death that orchestrated life and death on the battlefield before the fission of the atom had made them all utterly, terribly obsolete. She had read that the artillery had blasted all life out of the clay, destroyed forests and men and riddled the land with craters and human remains; that the only safety for the men was in the miserable, wet trenches which snaked through the land like worms through a dying corpse. In a ghoulish sort of fashion, she was looking forward to seeing what had become of the hellscape of Verdun.

The airlock hissed open, revealing the landscape of Earth, of Verdun spread out below her. The Caretaker staggered, almost physically pushed back.

It was *beautiful.*

The sun was shining. It was warm—perfectly warm; the Caretaker's spacesuit told her it was eighteen degrees Celsius. Under the hovering ship were rolling hills, a series of tumuli which dotted the landscape more or less regularly, and which were covered with grass or with small copses of trees. To the right, a broad green river wound its way lazily north. Most incredible of all were the animals—deer, wild horses, boars, wolves, a dozen smaller species which she half-saw flitting through the grass, even a massive, hulking creature which looked for all the world like the long-extinct aurochs.

She jumped out. After she tested her jetpack to make sure she could get back to the ship, she let herself parachute down. But she had learned to parachute on a much less dense world, and she pulled the strap on her parachute much too late. She hit the ground hard, and she rolled and jounced along the ground until she came to a stop outside one of the mounds. She felt a lance of pain from her ankle and swore viciously. When she tested it, she realised that it was broken.

She was busy trying to ask the ship to wake one of the cryopods to send her help when she heard a hissing noise. A second later, something stepped between her and the sun— and held out a hand to her.

A human. Not just like her—built stocky to her eye, but more appropriate to the gravity of this world—but a human nonetheless; a man, to be sure. Uncertainly, she let him pull her into a sitting position. He was dressed very simply, in robes and pampooties which appeared to be handmade from local materials. His face was a mess—scars, broken teeth, broken nose—but he was clearly trying to do his best to smile. It looked horrifying. He gestured for her to open her helmet. She shook her head.

"*Chérie*, if I wanted to hurt you, I would just do that. I am trying to help you. The air is sweet."

He was speaking something a lot like the archaic French she had studied on the way over. She tried to get to her feet, but her ankle gave way under her.

"Let's get you inside," her new friend said. "I don't believe I introduced myself. I am Cathnia, last of the Martians, and I have been living very comfortably on the cradle of humanity for the past few centuries. I think we'll find we have much in common. You are…?"

"The Caretaker," the wounded woman gasped.

The scarred man, Cathnia, turned behind him and called out; to her astonishment, a section of turf in the hillside slid out of the way. Inside she saw sleek chrome interiors, technicians working with scientific equipment, microscopes— all the paraphernalia of an advanced laboratory.

"Did you think you had found barbarians?" he said.

"Didn't… the nukes?" the Caretaker managed.

"Mars is dead, all right," Cathnia said. "My people obliterated each other. All that was left of Mars were a few refugee ships full of pacifists; I am the last living of those. But the people of Earth were a touch wiser. Earth feigned a nuclear war to keep my people away; meanwhile, they learned to live in a way which does not make undue demands of the landscape around us."

The Caretaker looked around. All those mounds, laid out in those regular lines—

"I'll be damned," she said, in her archaic French. "This is a *city*."

"It is," the man said. "Let's get you inside so we can fix that ankle. Shouldn't take more than a minute or two. Then we can start unloading your colonists."

"How do you—? What—?"

Cathnia smiled.

"We've been expecting you," he said. "Welcome home."

The Story Keepers
Cecil Wilde

Geal smells like freedom.

The honey-water scent of the beeswax base rises from the ceramic pot first, and it isn't until Ró smears the first handful on their forehead that the powdery, mineral zinc fills their nose. Seclusion is peaceful, but—

"Hear they're letting you out for good behaviour," a familiar voice calls from behind them, laughter echoing off the living quarter stonework, bouncing around the high vaulted ceiling. "Not sure I'd do the same, if it were up to me…"

Ró turns, face straining as disused muscles stretch into a broad grin.

"Aibreán!"

Aibreán chuckles as they fling themself into zer arms, lifting them clear off the floor and twirling them around as ze returns the hug under the rainbow of light falling from the solar stained-glass skylight above. Ze smells of lavender soap and the clean linen of zer order's robes, of high summer, of warmth and light.

Aibreán could be the living flesh of Áine—the midsummer sun made mortal. Ze's picked out in Áine's colours from the coppery warmth of zer waist-length waves to the burnished bronze of zer skin and the glinting bright amber of zer eyes, darker in Ró's shared quarters but still striking.

"Déithe duit, a chara," ze says, voice soft and smile warm. Ze bends to brush a kiss over Ró's mouth and then presses their foreheads together, running gentle fingers over Ró's freshly shaved scalp.

They, on the other hand, are likely too short, fat, and inelegant for comparison to Áine's sister, Grian. They've always imagined the embodiment of the midwinter sun as tall and willowy, with all the harsh-angled beauty of a storm hitting a cliff face. The only thing she'd have in common with Ró is dark hair. No one would ever suggest that Grian had too much in the way of eyebrows. Not to her face, any road. Not unless they wanted to bring the wrath of Áine down on them.

"Missed you," Ró confesses. "Imagine you were too busy to miss me."

Aibreán snorts. "Oh aye," ze says. "Forgot you existed up until this morning. Had to put it in the calendar. 'Go visit Ró,' it said, and I thought to myself, who?"

"Stop." Ró swats at zer. "Or I'll not give you your gift."

"What if I give you yours first?" ze asks, extracting a particoloured beeswax wrap from zer satchel. "Then you'll have to."

"Is this…?"

"Open it and find out." Aibreán beams, pressing the wrap into their hands.

Inside is, as Ró had hoped, one of the small tarts Aibreán's order is famous for across the gleann. The scent of it, honey and sheep's cheese, buttery pastry and a hint of cinnamon, makes their mouth water.

"I knew there was a reason I liked you," they say. "Do you want the half?"

Aibreán waves them off. "All yours. Think I ate more than my share making them last night."

Ró bites into the generous pastry, not bothering to stifle a happy sigh as it melts on their tongue like a mouthful of sunlight. "You've got geal all over you," they say, nodding to Aibreán's forehead.

Ze peers around them, into the mirror they were using to apply it, and laughs.

"Think it suits me?"

Ró licks pastry crumbs off their lips, assessing.

"You're too much one of Áine's," they say, heading back to the washstand for a cloth. "For the geal."

"D'you think?" Aibreán asks, accepting the cloth with a frown. "I thought Grian took all comers."

"Aye, that she does," Ró allows, going to their bed and pulling a box out from under it, collecting the wrapped parcel inside and holding it close to their chest.

Aibreán's gaze falls on it as ze sets the cloth aside.

"I made this for you." Ró offers the parcel, chewing on their lip. "You said you were always cold in seclusion."

Aibreán raises a brow as ze accepts, paper crinkling in zer hands. Ró watches, stomach tight, as ze unties the waxed twine holding it closed, and unfolds the paper.

"Ró," ze says, setting the paper aside and shaking out the long wool robe, undyed as zer order requires, and holding it up to look at it. "You made this?"

Ró nods.

Áine's initiates sow the seeds for their own robes during their initiation, tend the flax through the summer, then harvest and thresh and spin and weave, a process that takes them their whole first winter seclusion to complete.

Grian's initiates knit, with fleeces shorn just before their first summer seclusion, spun and dyed by their own hands.

"For me?"

Ró nods again, twice this time, their teeth digging hard into their lip now. "Sheared the sheep myself. And did the spinning and the knitting. Sorry if it's uneven."

The warmest of smiles breaks over Aibreán's face. "It's perfect. You... *you're* perfect, do you know that?"

Ró looks down at their soft-booted feet.

"I don't think I've seen you blush before."

Having it pointed out only makes more heat rush to Ró's face.

"S'pose I've never really seen you without the geal," Aibreán says. "Thank you," ze adds, pulling the robe over zer shoulders.

"You don't have to—"

"I do, so it happens," Aibreán says. "On account of having gone and volunteered you to go to the market for a supply run on the way in and it being bloody cold out there. So you'd better finish putting your face on."

"Less than ten minutes of seeing you again and you're already causing trouble," Ró grumbles, but with a smile. It's hard not to smile around Aibreán. If people from outside saw them now, they'd single-handedly ruin their order's reputation for severity.

They finish the tart between coats of geal—it might be cold for Aibreán, but for skin that never sees the summer sun, the protection is as necessary as it is traditional—and shrug on the black robe they knit for themself as part of their initiation, wearing at the edges now. The pockets are still stuffed with market bags, left over from the last time they were outside and needed to wear it.

"Stunning," Aibreán teases as they put their hood up, taking their offered arm and heading, for the first time in six months, towards the door to the outside world.

Fitting, perhaps, to be escorted into the light by a child of Áine.

"Sheared the sheep yourself, you say?" ze asks, fingering the edge of the robe with a tiny smile playing about zer lips.

"I did. Do you like it?"

"I adore it. I'm never taking it off," Aibreán says. "Do you know what they call a sheep after it's been sheared?"

Ró frowns as Aibreán pushes the door open, blinking against the light. "No?"

"Séan."

"Aibreán!"

The press of bodies in the market, all of them hurrying their way to and fro to finalise their preparations for equinox celebrations, hides where the voice is coming from, and even Aibreán's solid handful of inches of height above average aren't enough to make up for it.

Ró perks up at their side, fingers tightening where their hands have found each other in the crowd. They blink up at zer, when ze looks down, with their huge sky-blue eyes, made even starker and more Otherworldly by the thick coat of geal reflecting the sun's light.

"Aibreán," the voice repeats, closer now, and a familiar face pops out of the crowd between a mulled cider cart—the first of the season, as is traditional—and someone carrying a wheel of hard sheep's cheese the size of their head on one shoulder.

"Eileen!" Aibreán greets. "Up and about! I wanted to see you one last time before seclusion."

"I'm up!" Eileen says, waving a beautifully carved cane, flowers and fruits picked out in bright colours, and grinning triumphantly. "I wanted to be sure you knew I'd be all right without you. Is this your famous Róisín dubh?"

Heat rises to Aibreán's face.

"Aye, this is Ró," ze says, tugging them forward gently. "Ró, this is Eileen. I've been visiting her since she hurt her back... has it been five weeks?"

"Six," Eileen says. "I'll have to do it again next year, for the company. It's a pleasure to meet you, Ró. I've heard so much about you."

Aibreán doesn't need to so much as glance at Ró to picture the look on their face. Ze can feel the raised eyebrow creeping up zer neck, along with most of the blood in zer body.

"The pleasure is all mine," Ró says. "I'm glad you're back on your feet. I hope Grian will treat you better than Áine has this cycle."

Eileen laughs, nudging Aibreán with her cane, her dark eyes twinkling knowingly in the morning light. "They're just like you said and twice as pretty," she announces. "But you two only have the one day! I'll leave you to it."

"I'd like to visit, in Bree's place," Ró speaks up. "If you'll allow it."

Eileen's smile softens. "My wife was one of Grian's," she says. "I'd love to have one of you around the place again, if you can spare the time."

"Always," Ró promises solemnly. "That's what the temple's for."

"Then I'll look forward to seeing you," Eileen says. "Now go enjoy yourselves! Go! No more dallying with old women."

She shoos them and walks off at the same time, and Aibreán watches her shuffle determinedly back into the throng and tries to will the blush still heating their cheeks away.

"Your Róisín dubh?" Ró says, the second Eileen's out of earshot.

"Well now, you *are* a black rose, aren't you?" ze asks, rubbing the back of zer neck.

"*Your*," Ró emphasises. "Black rose."

Aibreán turns to look at them. "Are you not?"

Ró huffs, but then their hand settles on Aibreán's cheek, guiding zer down as Ró rises on their toes, pressing a soft kiss to zer lips. Out in the middle of the market. In front of everyone.

Ze's still grinning about it when Ró extracts their tablet from the inside of their robes, unfolds it, frowns, taps on it, and then turns their irrefusable blue eyes up to zer.

"Forgot to leave it out to charge," they say sheepishly. "Can… could…?"

Aibreán laughs, and hands over zer own tablet. "For *my* Róisín dubh? Anything."

"People keep smiling at me," Ró says as Aibreán hands them their share of the raspberries just gifted to the two of them by a stall holder bouncing a toddler on their hip, enthusing about how good they are this year and that any friend of Aibreán's was a friend of theirs.

"The horror," Aibreán says, popping one of the fruits into zer mouth and making a happy sound.

"It's all your fault," Ró says, squeezing their way past a gaggle of teenagers greeting each other with enthusiastic hugs, their matching bracelets all lighting up in pulsing rainbows now that they're together.

"Oh aye?" Aibreán asks.

"Aye, without you they look at me and see a death cultist. You make me approachable."

"The worst imaginable thing, being approachable," Aibreán says. "You're not a death cultist."

"No," Ró agrees, pausing to look at a display of wind chimes in multi-coloured solar glass, tinkling gently in the breeze. Once upon a time, their father had collected them. They'd been hung all over the eaves, and lit up at night in every colour, glowing through their bedroom window. A reminder, he'd said, that sometimes the most beautiful things could only be seen in the dark.

He'd given up the geal to be their da, but he'd never really given it up.

"No, I'm not," they repeat. "But that's what people see."

They duck into one of the permanent structures along the market street to negotiate for dyestuff. With the equinox comes new initiates, and with six months of seclusion, there's been no time to forage for either blackberry shoots or meadowsweet to make the order's required black. With little demand for it outside of adherent's robes, there are only so many places to get it, but Toshi has been a reliable supplier for the temple since before Ró was born.

"Thing is," Aibreán says when they step back into the crowded street, as though their conversation was never interrupted. "You remind them of things they'd rather forget."

"They can't."

"No, I know that, you know that," Aibreán says. "Forgetting the past is the first step on the path to repeating it. That's what the coimeádaithe are for. We keep the stories. But the stories *you* keep are full of wee penguins covered in crude oil, and the stories I keep are full of heroes and triumphs and overcoming the odds. They're the stories of the *good* things. But they're only half the story. We wouldn't have them without your half. We can't afford to forget your half. Yours are more important than mine."

"But—"

"No buts," Aibreán says, steering them deftly around a roving haberdasher. A kaleidoscope of embroidered ribbons and intricately worked felt flowers hangs from a rack swinging high above their head, fixed to their pack with sturdy leather straps, and they rattle with buttons as they pass.

"If either of us is going to have a crisis of faith on the equinox, it's not going to be you. This is your *calling*," ze says. "You're going to make scéalaí someday. You're going to tell the stories, the ones people *have* to hear, because you're brave enough to do it. These people," Aibreán continues, gesturing broadly. "Need you. Your stories are important. Do you think the Greeks told stories about how if you piss off one of the gods you'll die horribly because people liked to hear that? No, they told them so no one went bloody sailing in a thunderstorm. People need to remember that if you *do* go sailing in a thunderstorm, you might well drown. What do your lot always say? For everything there is a season. There's a season for heroes, for triumph, aye, but there's a season for villains and mourning, too."

Ró stares up at Aibreán for long moments, stopping only to whip the edge of their robes out of the way of a passing herd of goats being driven down the thoroughfare.

"I had a meeting with the senórach," Ró says. "At midwinter. They said I was on the path to scéalaí. As long as I keep my studies up. And. Learn to project my voice," they add with a wry smile.

Aibreán chuckles. "Like me, you mean? Come on," ze says, taking Ró's arm again. "Let's find somewhere for you to tell me a story. We've got time before we're missed."

"Your order doesn't fast, does it?"

Ró licks oil off their lips between eager mouthfuls of fried potato, suddenly self-conscious. Even tucked away under a tree at the edge of the market seating area, at as much of a distance from the crowds as space allows, they feel surrounded. It's been so long since they've been out in public. Just as well Aibreán's here. Even if ze *is* teasing.

"No virtue in fasting when there's always enough," they say, holding their tea up to their nose. "Am I not allowed to eat now?"

Aibreán laughs, reaching over to steal a crispy bit with a twinkle in zer eyes. "You are. If I'm allowed to think you're gorgeous while you're doing it."

Ró wrinkles their nose. "Something wrong with you."

"Many somethings," Aibreán allows. "But you are gorgeous."

The forest hugs the edges of the market here, where the food stalls operate, squirrels making a nuisance of themselves, bounding circuits around the tables and looking for scraps.

They probably ought not to feed them, but Ró tosses them a few cubes of potato anyway. Better half-domesticated squirrels than no squirrels at all. They were *nearly* lost. The trouble they cause is worth it, to have them still.

"Ah, give over."

"You *are* gorgeous," Aibrean insists. "And I've said it three times now, so it must be true. That's old magic."

"This all used to be open fields, you know," Ró changes the subject, remembering their dead tablet and extracting it from their robes, setting it down in a patch of sunlight to charge.

"Oh?" Aibreán asks, stealing another crispy bit as though ze doesn't have half zer own plate left. "Is this my story?"

Heat rises to Ró's face.

"I'm not meant to tell them," they say. "It isn't my place."

"Our wee secret," Aibreán promises. "Go on. You need the practice. It's just me here," ze adds, reaching across and, instead of stealing more food, covering Ró's hand with zer own. "Just us."

"Us and half the town and country," Ró says wryly. The equinox always brings in the crowds. Túr Glas, so named for the central vertical garden—an engineering marvel that produces nearly half the town's plant-based food and filters over a quarter of the drinking water—is always bustling, but festivals draw people from all over to mark the passing of the seasons, celebrate their achievements in the intervening days, and be together with friends they might not otherwise see in person. Even the ones who practice other faiths, or none at all, come in for the sister sun festivals.

Aibreán's grandmother was among the engineers, moved from near on the other side of the world to work on the project. Because she believed in it. Which meant Aibreán was here, too.

Ró's been just a little fonder of the tower since they dug that up in the archives.

"None of them are listening," Aibreán says, dragging them from the lofty heights of the green tower back down to the rich loam they're sitting on. "It's just me. And it's not... forbidden knowledge, is it?"

Ró licks their lips. It's not. No knowledge is forbidden. But the *telling* of it is so important. A story told one way means one thing and told another means something entirely different. The telling must be careful, if the meaning is to be preserved.

"G'won," Aibreán nudges, tapping the toe of zer boot against the heel of Ró's. "It's only me."

There's nothing *only* about Aibreán, but Ró takes zer point. Ze won't judge them poorly if they get tongue-tied, or forget something, or tell it out of order. There's poetry enough in the sharing of anything between the two of them that they barely need words for it. Any words will be all right.

They wrap both hands around their tea, holding it close to their chest, and take a breath.

"The last wolf in Éire was killed five hundred years ago. We called them, once, the sons of the land—na mic tíre—so much did they mean to us. The last wolf in Éire was killed among the ruins of its home, the dense forests of its youth cut down for grain. The last wolf in Éire was killed starving and afraid, and no one stood to mourn it. The last—"

Ró's voice breaks, and they cover their mouth with their hand, tears stinging at their eyes. "The last—" they try again, but it ends in a sob. "I'm sorry, I'm sorry."

"Shh," Aibreán squeezes their hand. "It matters to you. Anyone would know that it *mattered*. You've just got to work on taking a breath from time to time."

Ró purses their lips, and Aibreán squeezes their hand again.

"There's a bit about… language and sheep and things. And permanent losses. Fields. Grain, and what it costs to grow, what it *has* cost to grow. Why we've got to hang onto the things we have left because when they're gone, they're *gone* and it's no use to mourn them five hundred years later and wish we'd done different," they sniff.

Aibreán makes a sympathetic noise as Ró dabs their eyes

with their robes. They take a few rattling breaths, and sip their tea, and cling to Aibreán's hand.

"Anyway, you know all this. Your order has a story about the reforesting. About starting with one patch, and then another, and another. Because no action is so small it doesn't matter. Because everyone's deeds matter. Because we all work together—"

"Under the sister suns, aye," Aibreán finishes for them. "How do you know that one, then?"

"Heard it when I was a wean." Ró shrugs. "I always loved Áine's stories. Everyone does."

"Aye, everyone does. They're easy to hear. They're important. But so are yours. Light and shadow, yeah? Can't have one without the other. You'd burn to a crisp aside from anything else."

Ró snorts. "I would. You suit the light."

"Oh, I burn in it," Aibreán says. "You just never see me at my most daft. Think that's why you like me."

"Might happen it is," Ró says, grinning. They'll get the stories right. There's training for it. They *do* care, and they ought to care so much that it's hard to tell them. If Aibreán thinks they can do it, then it must be true.

They sit in silence for a few moments, taking in their first hours of freedom in half a year. It's easy to forget, with Aibreán so close, that the rest of the world exists. A family with a half-dozen children, come in to town from the outlying farms for the festival, settles at a wonky table nearest the edge of the seating area, crowding around to make space for everyone. The littlest catches sight of Ró and stares wide-eyed at their moon-pale face and night black robes.

Ró offers a tiny smile, and the barest wave, and the little one's mouth falls open. They tug on one of the older one's sleeves, a multi-coloured, lumpy thing that reminds Ró of their own first attempt at a jumper, when they'd been little and learning to make their own, like everyone does. They hadn't practiced nearly enough, but Aibreán's still wearing the robe. The robe that *they* made. For zer. To keep zer warm over the dark days of seclusion ahead.

They hope it says enough. For someone working themself to the bone to make scéalaí, they're awful with words.

"So if you don't fast, what *do* you do locked away all summer?" Aibreán asks. "I've always wondered."

"Study. Work. Rest. Lie around on the flagstones complaining about the heat," Ró says. "I s'pose your summers are all… bonfires and orgies."

Aibreán laughs. "You *would* think that."

"Are they not?"

"No. Well, bonfires, yes, for the solstice. But no orgies. You don't seriously think…?"

Ró raises an eyebrow. "Well, *our* solstice is. It's cold out, at midwinter. Got to have some way to warm up when we get back inside."

"You're joking?"

Ró smirks, taking a sip of their tea.

"You *are* joking," Aibreán says, shoulders slumping as ze huffs, lips twitching into a wry smile.

"Maybe."

"I'll have to convert and find out," Aibreán says. "You'd invite me to the orgy, wouldn't you?"

"Don't know I'd want to share. Are you going to eat your tea cup?"

Aibreán snorts, and hands it over. "All yours."

Ze loses Ró in the chaos of festival preparation the moment they come within sight of the hill, so busy and loud it'd put the bees back at the temple to shame. All around zer people rush here and there, black and undyed robes mingling in a sea of bodies.

Ró hates this. Not the work—there's no person less workshy in all of Éire—but the noise, and the disorder, and even the light, especially after so long out of it.

A hand landing on Aibreán's shoulder cuts the idea of looking for Ró off at the bud before it can bloom.

"Aibreán!" another familiar voice booms, squeezing zer shoulder in greeting.

"Kal!" ze greets warmly, letting him pull zer into a bone-crushing hug. For all that he's not much taller than Ró, he's got biceps on him like a bear. "Fancy seeing you here."

Kal snorts. "You'll be seeing a lot more of me for the next six months," he says. "Once we're stuck together in seclusion."

Aibreán bites zer lip and doesn't answer.

Kal tilts his head, birdlike, peers at zer for a few long moments, and then nods. "Ah."

"Ah," Aibreán repeats, looking down at zer boots.

Kal slaps zer on the shoulder, grinning broadly. "Good, good," he says. "Good to have made a decision. Doesn't get you out of helping me string up these bloody lights, though. You're the only one tall enough to reach."

"They do make ladders," Aibreán says, knees trembling with relief. Ze hasn't told anyone what ze's decided, not really. But Kal knows zer too well.

"Why burn your hands when there's a pair of tongs in the house?" Kal asks, giving Aibreán a nudge towards the knot of beige-robed faithful swearing like sailors over the tangle of fairy light strings they have to contend with every festival, no matter how carefully they put them away.

The lights are sacred. They're a symbol of the importance of the sun even in the dark, and a reminder of humble beginnings. The first glimmer of hope in a world with little to cling to. The power of the sister suns captured in the tiny crystals strung along the length.

They're also a complete and utter pain in the arse.

"Why indeed?" Aibreán says, following less grudgingly than ze makes out. At least if ze's on designated tall person duty, ze's not on untangling duty.

When they both get to the others, there's an animated conversation and stacks of folded papers being waved about and shoved back into pockets in turn, Aisha showing off their stack with a triumphant grin, betting no one else will have more than them to burn.

The things they want to let go of at the change of cycle. Papers they'll burn in the bonfire along with everyone else. Bad habits and unhelpful attachments, old names and old lovers, as simple as complaining about mornings or as big as…

Aibreán shoves zer hand into zer pocket, grasping the single folded scrap of paper there.

Ze keeps expecting to change zer mind, but touching the paper only makes zer more certain. Calms zer constant restlessness down to a dull roar.

It's big, but it's right. It's *right*.

"Bree, for the love of Áine," Kal calls out, holding up one end of a string of lights. "Give us a hand."

Ze lets go of the paper again, and strides over to help.

It's right.

"All right?"

Ró nods, still seeing more stars than the ones above their head.

Aibreán laughs as ze rolls to Ró's side, stretching out on the mossy loam at the forest edge as the sky fills with multi-coloured lights, the long-promised end to the equinox festival. The comforting scent of bonfire smoke has wafted down to their secret spot at the bottom of the hill by now, and the sounds of celebration along with it.

"Speechless?" Aibreán asks, laughter in zer voice. "That good?"

Ró grunts. Aibreán's confidence might be unattractive if it hadn't just been thoroughly earned. They might even have the strength to tease back, were they not so deeply sated.

Aibreán chuckles again, rolling onto zer side and stroking idly along Ró's still-robed arm, fingers trailing as far as their covered collarbones, zer touch delicate as a new lamb. For long moments they lie there together. Ró watches the lights above, bursting into all shapes and colours, painting the sky, and Aibreán watching them.

All is right in the world, and the smallest of smiles plays around their lips as Aibreán leans close to press a kiss under the hinge of their jaw.

"I want to take the geal."

Ró sits up from the dewy grass beneath them and twists to look at Aibreán, lit up in every colour by the lightshow above. To someone who didn't know zer, hadn't known zer all these years, ze might look calm.

Ró can see the tense lines of zer face, the purse of zer lips, the steeled glint of zer eyes.

"*Why?*"

"You know why," Aibreán says, sitting up as well. Zer hand, still warm in the cool of the night air, curls around Ró's fingers. "You know why."

Ró swallows. Aibreán's hand is so warm. Aibreán is so warm. And Grian is so *cold*. It isn't… it's not…

Ze *can't*.

"No."

"No?"

"No," Ró repeats. "No, you… you're not… it's not *right*. It's not right for you."

"It could be," Aibreán murmurs, squeezing Ró's fingers. "And it's not so different, is it? Serving the light is serving the light. Doesn't matter *which* light. Not to me. No... not if it was with you."

Ró's throat closes as a cheer rises up below, the last of the lightshow above fading and leaving all the stars exposed again. Their eyes sting.

They can see it. They can see Aibreán in black robes and painted face, fading away season after season. Never being kissed by the midsummer sun again. Miserable and resentful because Ró isn't *enough*. Couldn't be enough. Not to make up for the loss of the summer.

"You'd hate it," they force out, voice breaking as tears threaten to spill over. "The dark and the cold and people not smiling at you anymore."

"You'd still smile at me," Aibreán says.

"Of course I would," Ró says. "But I love you."

The tears fall then. They've never said it before. It's been unspoken and understood between the two of them for years. Since they met. Since the first day they saw each other and *knew*.

But they'd known then that they'd only ever have two days a year, six months apart.

"I love you," Ró repeats, taking their hand away from Aibreán, rising to their feet. "Enough to let you go. Because it's not *enough*, Bree. I'm not enough. I can't be. And I wouldn't have you hate me for anything. I love you," they say once more. Three times. That makes it true. That's old magic.

"I'll see you next equinox."

And then they walk away.

Everyone knows.

Not the details—Ró doesn't think anyone knows the *details* of why they're even quieter, gruffer, and stranger than usual—but everyone *knows*. Knows there's something wrong. Gods love them, they all try to help.

Vivid Worlds

The only thing that helps is not thinking about it, and so Ró does that, hiding away in the library, poring over archival material, painstakingly copying, proofreading, cataloguing. Reading, when everything else is too much effort. Reading stories that aren't theirs, that ought to be sent to Áine's temple right away, until the ache gets to be too much and they find a corner of the archives to cry in.

If only it was summer. Then they could do all of that in peace.

Instead they find themself called to help with new initiates—more of them, this cycle, than there has been in the previous five. Grian suits some people well, and those ones will be happy. The others, they'll lose by next summer.

Approaching the black-robed, hooded lineup in the public part of the temple makes their stomach drop, but they take the first pot of geal set on the altar and approach the first initiate in the line with their heart in their throat.

"Have you been called?"

"I have," the voice under the hood says.

It isn't Aibreán. It was never going to be. Too short by half a head, barely taller than Ró, and yet some part of them…

No. They'd said no. Aibreán would've thought better of it by now. It'd been an idle fantasy. They'd apologise next equinox, and everything would be all right.

Someone else takes the next initiate, and a third the next, and they work their way down the line. Promises to serve overlap each other, footsteps echoing on the limestone floor as they cross the spill of rainbow light that fills the temple when the winter sun reaches its peak every day. Back and forth, back and forth.

"Have you been called?" Ró asks, barely feeling the words in their mouth anymore.

"Aye, I think so," the hooded figure in front of them says. "If you'll have me."

144

The pot of geal in Ró's hands clatters to the floor.

"I'll go if you won't," Aibreán whispers, peeking out now from under zer hood. Zer eyes glow in the light, more beautiful than any stained glass could even aspire to be, and the barest smile chases its tail around the corners of zer lips.

Ró bends to the floor, wiping the spilled streak of geal up with the cotton robe under their wool one and grasping the half-empty pot with both hands.

"Tell me to stay," Aibreán says. "I want to."

The robe. The robe Ró knit for zer. Dyed black so recently it still smells of blackberry and vinegar.

They reach out to touch it in awe.

"I love you. That's a calling, isn't it? As much of a calling as anything. Tell me to stay," Aibreán murmurs.

"You have to say you were," Ró says, meeting their gaze.

Aibreán blinks. "Did I not just…?"

"You have to say you've been called," Ró says. "The response has to be *I have*."

Aibreán rolls zer eyes, the smile that'd been bounding around their mouth breaking into a full grin.

"I have," ze says. "I have. I have."

Three times. Old magic. That makes it true.

Ró shoves the remainder of the geal into Aibreán's hands and throws themself into zer arms, making the two of them stumble back three paces with the force of it.

Ze laughs, squeezing Ró tight.

"Now you've *got* to invite me to the orgies," ze whispers next to Ró's ear, tracing the shell of it with gentle fingers.

Ró groans. "It's going to be a lifetime of this, isn't it?"

Aibreán hums. "Worse ways to spend a lifetime, aren't there?"

"Aye," Ró agrees, resting their head against Aibreán's chest. "There are."

Blood and Water

Sierra Bibi

When I crossed the state line at seventeen years old, I swore to never go back. California was freedom. Arizona was death. Yet somehow, ten years later, I find myself in a Western Climate Corps refugee van bound for a tiny settlement nestled in the Chiricahuas. I had been given a choice: data entry in Wisconsin or stacking rocks in Arizona. Between hard labour in the sun and staring at a computer all day, I'd pick hard labour every time.

The passenger van seats twelve, but I'm alone in the back row. I was the last to be placed after the fire took the lodge. My coworkers had other skills to fall back on. I had only ever been a ski instructor. And now I was a ski instructor in a world without snow.

The further south and east we drive, the less there is to look at out the window. Traffic thins to a trickle. Dust devils swirl across a derelict golf course. It's only eight o'clock but the temperature on the dash reads 86F.

The highway leading out of the city is punctuated with blank-faced billboards, dilapidated gas stations, and dark signposts of long-abandoned fast-food joints. My throat constricts. When I left a few towns had run dry, and we'd been on drought restrictions more often than not, but it hadn't been this bad.

After turning off onto a dirt road, the van parks in the middle of nowhere. I can taste the dirt suspended in the air as soon as my boots crunch the gravel. Behind a mass of hazy heat, there's a cluster of temporary buildings, and a woman in a blue jumpsuit hurrying towards us. Her curly hair is chopped into a bob that bounces as she walks.

"Welcome to Agua Verde! I'm Asa," she says, gripping my

hand. "Let's grab some food and I'll give you the tour."

I follow her up the dirt path and into the village. The place is alive with people in transit, chatting, laughing, chickens clucking and the melody of distant ranchero music. No children crying. No dour-faced adults wandering listlessly. Everyone here moves with purpose and even stranger, they look content. It's so unlike the refugee camp I spent the last three months in it's like I'm on a different planet.

Agua Verde is arranged around a large central plaza protected from the sun with massive white overlapping shades, like the sails of a ship. Beyond the plaza, built into the sloping hills is an entryway. From here, the people entering and exiting look like ants swarming a hill.

"This is the community centre. The earth acts as natural insulation, taking on most of the heat. It's our first permanent dwelling."

Inside, morning light pours through skylights and illuminate the high adobe walls. There are tables and chairs for a few hundred, but the hall is mostly empty. I'm hit by the aroma of garlic, onions, cumin and paprika. My stomach growls audibly.

"Isn't it lunch time? Where is everyone?"

"The morning shift just ended," Asa says. "Half of us work from four to ten in the morning, and the other half work from six to midnight. No one works during the hottest part of the day. That's siesta time. And if it's really hot out everyone takes the day off."

"Kind of like a snow day but in hell," I say.

When she laughs, her hazel eyes crinkle at the corners and the sound is as light as fresh powder. There's no hint of cynicism weighing it down.

In the cafeteria, I help myself to scrambled eggs, warm Sonora-style tortillas, and a steaming cup of coffee. It's the first time in months I'm eating food with spices and I am so overwhelmed by my breakfast I almost forget to make conversation.

"So which shift am I on?" I ask between mouthfuls.

"During training, you'll be on the morning shift with me. After that it's up to you."

"What am I training for again? Something with rocks?"

"You're going to be building Trincheras," she says, beaming. "Small rock dams. Hundreds of years ago, the Trincheras people built them into these hills for irrigation. Now we're using that same technology to undo the damage of industrial agriculture."

I nod like I know what she's talking about.

After breakfast, we stroll out to the edges of the camp, passing playgrounds, cottages, and desert gardens. It's quiet now except for mourning doves cooing from the brush. It's a nostalgic sound, one that instantly fills me with dread. The memories threaten to bubble up and spillover, but I push them down. This wasn't the desert I grew up in, even if the sounds were the same.

The town is encircled by an oasis, with rows of trees shading raised beds overflowing with tomatoes, peppers, and dark green squash. I breathe in deep, tasting the verdant air.

"This is our aquaponics farm," Asa says, tapping one of the humming cylindrical tanks. "We're raising tilapia in there. Water from the tanks irrigates and fertilizes the crops. We collect the runoff, purify it, and it goes right back into the tanks. You can't avoid evaporation, but otherwise it's a closed system."

"What do you grow?"

"Everything. Tomatoes, corn, beans, olives, dates, oranges. The ag unit is trying to adapt some fig varieties to the desert climate. There's a farm school with chickens, quail, and goats. The little ones take care of them. And there's bees and honey and a whole mushroom operation. And endless nopales and yucca and prickly pear of course."

"I didn't know anything grew out here," I say. After the freeze-dried meals at the refugee camp, fresh fruits and vegetables sound indulgent.

"We've come a long way. We're totally self-sufficient on food and energy. It all comes down to water. Which is where we come in."

We descend along a rough sloping path, walking single file to avoid the needles of the cholla cactus on either side of us. We stop before the sandy bed of an arroyo.

"This used to be a river. And this," she says, gesturing to the barrens around us, "used to be a cotton farm. Super thirsty crop. Slurped up almost all of the groundwater. Then in the 20s, some tech guy bought it and turned it into some kind of survival ranch. He did a good job of sucking up anything that was left. It's been abandoned the last twenty years, and we've made good progress, but the water table is still very low."

"How can you tell where water is underground?"

"The river. As above, so below. It's all part of the same hydrological system. On the old satellite data, you can see it used to flow a few months out of the year. Even older records suggest people used to swim here, if you can believe that."

My head aches. That river must have been depleted over centuries. Once a resource like that was gone, how could anyone bring it back? "Are we bringing in purified water from the ocean or something? Or is there some kind of rain machine?"

"Think cheaper. And way lower tech. We're planting native species along the bank here. And we're building small rock dams."

"But how are plants supposed to survive without water?"

"It's a two-pronged approach," she explains. "We place

local flora along the arroyo. The shade prevents evaporation. And the rock dams act as speed bumps for the water when the monsoon comes. The slower the flow, the more water the soil absorbs. The more water in the soil, the better the plants do. And the vegetation slows down water loss and erosion even further. It's a positive feedback loop. If we can restore the ecosystem, get water flowing year-round, we can divert just enough for the village."

Moving rocks to stop water. Sounds like something only Sisyphus would take on. But Asa is so enthusiastic I can't bring myself to say anything snarky. So I just listen as she points out inconspicuous stacks of stones and cruel-looking shrubs.

When we emerge from the valley, our boots and pant legs are covered in white dust. Cicadas buzz in the distance, excited by the oncoming heat of the afternoon. A trickle of sweat runs down my neck and joins a wet spot forming on my lower back.

At the edge of town, a woman emerges from one of the portables. She's so tall she has to duck to avoid hitting her head on the threshold and her pitch-black hair is pulled into a ponytail so tight it looks painful. She's wearing a WCC jumpsuit that matches Asa's and a pair of worn boots. Despite her proletariat garb, it's clear from the way she walks, head held high, spine totally perpendicular to the ground, that she's important around here.

She marches towards us, waving at Asa. It's not until I'm in the atmosphere of her orange blossom perfume that I recognize her. The ground beneath my feet turns molten.

"Julie, this is Serena, the director of Agua Verde," Asa says. "This is Julia Aguirre. She's a ski instructor from California, she just arrived this morning."

Serena's smile is as tight as her ponytail. We stare at each other for a moment as Asa looks from Serena's face to mine.

"We know each other," I mumble. She's older than the last time I saw her, cheekbones sharper, pursed lips a little thinner, but her steely eyes and pointed chin are the same. My mouth is dry and it's not just the air.

"She's my little sister," Serena says.

Asa looks back at Serena, all legs and regal grace, and then to all five foot four of me. Our resemblance ends at the black hair and olive skin.

The tension in the air hits some unbearable threshold and Serena wraps her sinewy arms around me in a stranger's hug. It's weird. She was never one for physical affection. It's made weirder still when I remember the last time we hugged was the night she ran away from home.

"It's so good to see you," she says through her frozen grin. "We haven't seen each other in years." I don't absorb another word she says, her voice falls behind the deafening drone of the cicadas. Before I can tune back in, she's running to her next meeting.

I don't say anything as Asa and I walk back up to the village. "Are you OK?"

"A little nauseous," I say. "I'm not acclimated to the heat."

Asa is too polite to pry further. Before she leaves me at my casita for the afternoon, she says, "You're lucky she's your sister. She's an amazing person."

That night in my bunk, every time I close my eyes I see flurries, gleaming icicles on the eaves of the lodge, and pine branches heavy with snow. Lake Tahoe in the wintertime. But all the juice had been squeezed from that fruit. The lodge was gone. Even if the fire hadn't taken it, the ski season was shorter every year. Soon there wouldn't be one at all.

I never pictured myself back in the desert. But Agua Verde seems special. Good food, air conditioning and best of all people. Not ghosts, but actual living, thriving people. There's

Asa too. My stomach flutters as I picture her warm hazel eyes and dimpled smile.

Asa's words come back to me. Could I even call Serena my sister anymore? It had been easy to spend the last fifteen years hating her when I thought I'd never see her again. Now I couldn't help but be curious about the person she'd become.

"This is sloppy."

It's fall. The days are cooler and the sun is at a slightly more merciful distance. Every morning I follow Asa into rough country under a lavender predawn sky, our headlamps flashing across gnarled cactus and palo verde. Today Serena joined us. She has her hands on her hips as she scrutinizes my work.

"The second water comes through it will wash out," she says, tapping the dam with her boot. Sure enough, my carefully stacked stones cascade onto the ground. "You basically just threw some rocks in a pile."

She strides over to the arrow weed I planted, tugs at one of the stems and pulls it out of the ground with ease, roots dangling nakedly. She scoffs, tosses it aside, and asks Asa to excuse us.

I brace for impact. I'm five years old again, sitting on the piano bench at my grandparents' house. We live here now, but in a few years, we'll be sent back to Mom. The young prodigy Serena is on my right, attempting to teach me the melody of "Cielto Lindo." But every time my fat toddler fingers slip and hit the wrong key, she pinches me, until finally I'm wailing and she is so frustrated she storms off.

"Asa is an excellent instructor. So I know this isn't her fault," she says to me now, older and just as terrifying. "Have you ever taken anything seriously? Or is life still just one big joke to you?"

"How is this stupid pile of rocks supposed to change

anything?"

She steps towards me. "There are five hundred people living in Agua Verde. If this project fails, they won't just lose jobs. They'll be shuffled off to the next place. They'll lose their community, their friends, their homes. If you thought about anyone besides yourself for even a second, you'd have realized that."

After she leaves, I watch my tears bloom into the sand and evaporate. How can she still make me feel so small after all these years? I feel Asa's hand rest on my shoulder.

"She's a nightmare. How does anyone work with her?"

"She can be abrasive," Asa agrees. "But this is her life's work."

"I wished she cared about her own family as much as she does everyone else." As the words come out of my mouth, I realize this is her family now, not me, not Mom. Asa wraps her arms around my shoulders as I cry into the dirt.

"Where did all the water go?" I press a boot into soft mud where the stream used to be. The first mild rain of the winter has fallen. A stream trickled for two days, turning everything it touched a temporary green, then vanished.

"The monsoon will be better," Asa says. I'm charmed by her relentless positivity. The first time she kissed me, at the harvest festival with tequila on her lips, I stopped her.

"Is this a good idea?"

She raised an eyebrow. "Did I read this situation wrong? Because I could have sworn you've been checking me out since you got here."

I blushed. "But we work together."

"So?"

"So what if it doesn't work out?"

"OK, but have you considered this: what if it does and it's even better than either of us imagined?" And she kissed me again.

I may not be as optimistic as Asa, but I am stubborn. In a season I've built hundreds of rock dams up and down the valley. You'd think I'd have mastered the task, but Serena always finds something to gripe about on her visits. Why did I ever envy her? After years apart, her miserable perfectionism seems obvious and sad.

We've reached a fragile truce. We now acknowledge each other's existence in passing. Sometimes we even stop to chat, but only ever about the work. Serena seems as reluctant to dredge up the past as I am. Until one day she's sharing trail cam footage of a mountain lion and she blurts out, "How's Mom?"

I almost choke on my spit. "Dead. She died a couple of years after I moved out. I thought you knew."

She nods mechanically, like I just relayed some titbit about soil pH instead of news of our mom's death. She never mentions it again.

I try not to think about the past, but the desert is relentless. Nothing stays buried under whipping winds and beating sun. It wasn't long after Serena left that I went into foster for the first time. Mom hadn't come back for a week, a long time to disappear even for her. Three days in, the water stopped coming out of the tap. I searched all the cabinets and closets for anything bottled. The jingle from the PSA looped in my mind like an incantation. *Water, water everywhere but not a drop to spare. Water on the ground, water in the air.*

But there was no water anywhere. All I found in our cupboards were empty bottles of Smirnoff, saltine crackers and cans of sardines. After the second day of no water, I knocked on the neighbour's door.

"Tienes agua?" I asked through cracked lips.

"Si mija," the neighbour lady said, returning a minute later with a plastic gallon. I chugged half of it on her doorstep.

Vivid Worlds

"Dónde está tu madre?"

"En su trabajo," I lied.

"Y tu hermana?"

My voice cracked. "No sé."

"This is a one rock dam, meaning we stack the rocks one layer high," I say, pointing to my crude chalkboard drawing. "We want to keep a concave shape so the water stays centred and doesn't flow around the rocks."

The flash of understanding when someone sees the potential of these humble structures is not quite as magical as teaching someone to ski for the first time, but there's something I enjoy about it all the same.

Outside of the classroom, a thunderhead growls. The first drops of rain are just hitting the ground. I dismiss the group for the afternoon.

Where is all that water going? It should drain into the low point from the surrounding hills. But even after a generous monsoon, the heaviest in years, the river is dry. It's an obsession for me. After teaching, I devour geologic surveys and hydrological impact studies from the archives. I pour over historical climate data. It must be diverted upstream. But there's no record of any dams or canals built in the last century. I trace the line of the Agua Verde with my index finger through the landscape on twenty-year old satellite images. There's nothing. Why did a similar project work in Utah? Why was this tributary dry when the river it branched from was recovering? The unanswerable question wears on me, like water over rock.

Serena knocks on the open door. Her face is as dark as the oncoming storm.

I steel myself for whatever she's about to say.

"Cancel your class for this evening."

"What? Why?" I cross my arms defensively, waiting to

strike back at her critique.

"WCC is shutting down Agua Verde."

I understand the words individually but all together they're nonsense. "What are you talking about?"

"We've failed. I've spent ten years on this project and the river is not coming back. We can't have water delivered every week forever. That's not a future." She's got dark circles under her brown eyes and she's holding back tears.

I bite my lip. But I just got here, I want to say. And where would I go? After a year of blood red sunsets with Asa, waking up with the coyote howl, and dancing under the desert moon the Sonora is home in a way it never was before.

"What are we going to do?"

"We're cancelling all trainings. Next week, WCC is doing reassignments. I already submitted a request for you and Asa to stay together."

"No, I mean what are we going to do to stop them from shutting us down?"

"They've made their decision," she says flatly.

"So you're just going to leave?"

"They're recalling me to headquarters. I don't have a choice."

"That's what you do, right?" I say, the anger stirring in me like a dust storm. "Leave when things get hard?"

Her face turns grey. "I was a child myself when I left. I couldn't take you with me. I couldn't raise you."

"I should be grateful this time you're telling me you're running away. You know what Mom told me after you left? She said it was my fault. I never even knew if you were alive or dead." I shove past her, out of the classroom and into the desert, the smell of petrichor strong now. I hike up the valley, past all the silly rocks and shrivelled plants and the pitiful dried-up piss stream that we called a river. What a joke.

I lose track of time, I continue up into the hills until my

heels blister and my calves burn. When a heavy rain roars to life, I let it soak into me, until my clothes cling to my body and my hair sticks to my face. Lightning flashes behind me, illuminating my silhouette. It's close. I'm thinking about heading back when my boot strikes the pavement.

My heart races like a jackrabbit as I bend over and scrape aside a little mud. This is not a natural path. It's concrete. I break into a run, boots sliding in the sludge, praying the lightning doesn't strike me down before the mystery's end. My gaze is low to keep water out of my eyes and I don't register the wall until I'm face-to-face with it. It's painted to match the colour and texture of the surrounding boulders. In the downpour, I almost don't see the droplets seeping out of the spiderweb cracks of the reservoir.

Serena still doesn't believe me. We're driving up the valley, but she keeps checking her watch. The WCC is due to arrive tonight.

But when we're standing before the dam, she runs her fingers across the fissures spreading like blood vessels. They've grown since I was here a few days ago. Serena swears under her breath. She doesn't have to say it. She sees it too. The Great Flood threatening to wipe out Agua Verde, held back only by a crumbling wall.

"Where's the control room?"

I lead her to the dark maw of a cave I was too chicken to enter alone. I flash on my headlight. The air is stale, dusty, but pleasantly chilled. Was that the hum of air conditioning? I jump when the motion activated lights power on.

"The solar panels are still putting out juice," Serena says. "Impressive."

In the dim light, I see *Guerra Industries* branded on a thick rubber mat, overlaying an uneven, slick stone floor. Stalactites hang from the ceiling. "Is this a natural cavern?"

"It was a state park before the government auctioned them all off."

We peek into the first doorway on our right. Rows of shiny handguns and automatic rifles cover the walls. A mannequin wears a helmet, gas mask and a bulletproof vest, all stamped with *Guerra Industries*.

"What is this place?"

"It's a survival bunker," Serena says. She runs a finger across a dusty rifle stock. "I guess they didn't make it in time."

Behind the next door is a gym complete with treadmills, a weight rack, and a glass-walled sauna.

"It's funny. No one ever lived here but it still feels haunted," I say, my voice echoing as we step in.

The smell of chlorine still emanates from a drained Olympic pool. A relic from another era.

Serena smiles. "Reminds me of summer."

"Summer?"

"When Mom was at work, sneaking over to the hotel pool down the street, remember?"

It comes back in flashes of colour. The dazzling aquamarine water under the white sun, the impossibly green grass, our polyester swimsuits, electric blue and neon pink.

"I forgot about that."

"You tried to teach me how to swim. But I was always too scared to go into the deep end."

I'm sprinting across a lava hot sidewalk on bare feet, jumping and plunging into the pool, knees held to my chest in a cannonball. Serena and I are racing, splashing, playing mermaids. I worked so hard to forget all the bad memories from our childhood that I had erased the good ones too.

"Why didn't you call? Why didn't you let me know you were OK?"

"I was worried you hated me. A self-fulfilling prophecy maybe."

"You were my best friend," I say in a small voice. "I could never hate you."

She grabs my hand, squeezing it. "We're here together now."

We pass a chef's kitchen, a movie theatre, and a formal dining room. The luxuries continue on and on. Finally, a room the size of a closet containing only a desk and a chair, the control room. Serena sits in front of the sleek computer. It boots up immediately, the words *Guerra Industries* flashing on the screen. At least after the world has ended, everyone will remember this asshole's name.

She opens a terminal and enters the commands to open the spillway.

"Five percent to start."

I hold my breath, waiting for a biblical deluge, the rumbling of the earth, the sound of rushing water, but nothing happens.

Serena frowns, her pianist's fingers flying over the keyboard entering diagnostic commands. I hover over her shoulder.

"There's something jamming the spillway gates." She pulls up an underwater camera. "It looks like there's something wedged between the valves."

She pushes back from the desk and rubs her temples. "With the reservoir full there's no way to service it."

"I can get it out."

"Absolutely not."

"What other option is there?"

"It's out of the question. You could drown." And then, as she considers our options, she says, "I'll go with you."

"Someone needs to stay and operate the controls. And I'm pretty sure you never learned to swim."

I'm standing on the precipice of the reservoir. The concrete burns the soles of my bare feet. The water is a murky brown. Will I even be able to see down there? My heart is thrumming in my chest like hummingbird wings.

Once I'm in there's no way back up. The top half of the ladder leading out is rusted away. And if the spillway opens early for some reason or the dam breaks, well, I'm choosing not to think about that.

I dive into the water. It's an instant relief from the ruthless afternoon sun. The bottom is thick with sediment, unknowable, but I keep swimming down. I find the bottom with my hands and then blindly grope until I feel the smooth metal of the valve.

Everything is taking too long. My lungs are already burning. I surface, gasping for breath, blinded by the daylight. I hold up one finger to where the camera might be, hoping she understands I mean "hold on a second" and that the resolution is good enough that she doesn't mistake it for a thumbs up.

I gulp down air and dive back down. I find the valve quicker this time. I reach for the junk obstructing it and recoil. Something rough slices my hand. I reach for it again, more carefully this time, brushing it with my fingertips. It feels corroded, weak. My lungs are aching for air. I push it harder, hoping I'm right. Something cracks. My muscles are screaming for oxygen. I launch all my weight against it in a final desperate attempt.

The metal groans, snaps and drifts to the bottom.

I break the surface and swim to the edge to the ladder, hoping that was enough. Serena doesn't have any way to let me know that she's opening the spillway. I have to trust her. The sun bakes down on my scalp while I listen for movement below me. What if the spillway is still stuck? What if she still can't open it? What if I dive back down and she's already started opening it? But then I feel it before I hear it, the current sucking into the void, pulling at my legs. And then the rumble of water as thousands of gallons rush out and down into the valley. My hands are slick with sweat and blood on the ladder rungs, my knuckles are white.

How long can I hold on like this, marooned on an island of rusting metal in a sea of concrete? Will heat stroke get me before Serena comes? She's going to come back, I tell myself. I have to trust her. The water's muddy surface shrinks away from me. If I let go now, I'll be swept away in the spillway and drown. If I let go later, it's thirty feet to a hard bottom.

But then something blocks out the harsh sun and I squint up at the shadow of my big sister lowering a rope.

"Do you hear that?" Serena asks.

I strain to listen over the swell of guitar music filling the plaza, the chatter of the cactus wren, and the laughter of children playing in the fountain.

"I'm not sure."

"Listen. It's the river."

I close my eyes and then there it is. A gurgling stream running over rocks. It's a new sound, one that fills me with a fierce pride. You can't swim in it, but almost three years after decommissioning the reservoir the river swells for months at a time.

"I wasn't sure I'd ever hear that sound," she says.

The saguaros are in bloom, rich showy flowers the colour of vanilla pudding, dessert for hummingbirds. The day is warming up, soon the blossoms will retreat into themselves until after the sun has set, only to unfurl again for the bats that have taken up residence in the bunker.

Asa dips our son into the fountain and spins him in a circle, sending droplets of water glittering like sequins across the red rock plaza as he giggles. It's time to go, but I linger, wanting to drink in more of this improbably beautiful life we've carved out in this inhospitable corner of the world.

Final Report
Susan Oke

The bus hissed and huffed as it slowed to a stop. Beth gazed out of the tinted windows; the seaside town didn't look so different, at least here around the bus station. She glanced up but could only see the topmost part of the cliff over the rooftops. The castle was up there—waiting. A yearning ache grew in her chest, tinged with a sense of urgency.

"Well," she muttered, tucking her phone into a side pocket of her rucksack, "you've left it long enough. It's time for answers."

Conversation rose around her as the rest of the passengers gathered their belongings. The single-decker bus was almost full; she'd been lucky to get a ticket at such short notice. She glanced up at the scrolling display: Final stop: Scarborough. Please disembark. Take all your belongings with you.

The driver turned in his seat to address the passengers. "There's a sea roke due in later today. Could be a bad one. Keep an eye on the NOX index."

The doors trembled and then slowly folded back; passengers fumbled with their masks as warm, faintly acidic air wafted in. Beth wiped a hankie over the lower half of her face to dislodge any errant crumbs from her packed lunch and then pressed her mask into place. Its flexible, skin-hugging design was guaranteed (or so the website claimed) against organic and inorganic gases and particulates. Best to cover all the bases, her chest was bad enough as it was. She joined the shuffling queue, stepping down onto the cracked concrete, glad to finally stretch her legs. The stifling heat wrapped close, and for a moment she was tempted to retreat into aircon cool of the bus.

The final handful of passengers called out, "Thanks," and

Vivid Worlds

"See ya tomorrow."

The driver smiled and nodded as the bus pulled away, its electric motor whining as it took up the strain. Adjusting her sunhat, Beth took a moment to orientate herself. The seawall reared in the distance, beyond it stretched an expanse of blue, darker shades melding into pale streaks as they reached the horizon. Hard to believe something that looked so tranquil could be whipped up into such a devastating fury. Over the last fifty years, almost a quarter of Scarborough had been battered and submerged. The castle wasn't in much better shape. Yes, it still lorded it over the town, but that high cliff had gradually been eaten away, dumping nearly two thousand years of history into the North Sea.

Lips pressed into a determined line, she made her way out of the bus station, following the straggling line of passengers heading into town. Most, given their dark-green t-shirts and mud-stained boots, were locals returning home from their shift in the agri-domes. Hard work but rewarding. She'd done her two-year stint as a teenager, before finding her vocation first as a journalist, and then later as a writer of mystery novels. The handful of visitors, like herself, were dressed in bright sun-shunning colours, t-shirts and tops etched with designs picked out in flexible solar strips; bags and rucksacks patterned with arty silvery patches to soak up every hot watt. Waste Not, Want Not. That old adage from her grandparents' day had found a new lease of life in these resource-scarce times.

Beth tapped her earbud and murmured, "Directions to Poppin Hostel." Her phone screen flicked to a street map and highlighted the route, a calm voice announced, "Walking time fifteen minutes. Estimated arrival: 14:05."

A young woman just ahead of her glanced back, her expression of surprise shifting to one of tolerant amusement. Beth clenched her jaw. *Kids these days*. They all had an implant that allowed them to 'think' at their various devices, and lenses to 'blink' up maps and other media. But Beth was having none of that. She could live with the jokes and jibes, and the giggles of her grandchildren whenever she pulled out her phone and actually spoke to it.

The streets were clean and uncluttered. Murals dominated the sides of houses: brave boats etched in black facing towering waves; clouds of seagulls swirling around a pocked cliff face; a montage of faces, old and young, all staring out to sea. Beth smiled as she passed a couple of young women, paintbrushes in hand, repairing weather damage to the lush depiction of twining flowers that adorned the waist-high walls alongside the road. In the town centre itself, local shops were running a bustling business. There was an interesting mix of high-tech retailers, DIY and grocery stores. Beth paused in front of a window, tempted by the vibrant reds, greens, and yellows of the fresh fruits and vegetables on display.

Damn! There it was again. That flicker on the periphery of her vision: a shadowy figure, there and gone before she had time to blink. And with it came a renewed sense of urgency. Her eyes tracked up to the castle. That was where she'd first seen him, as a wide-eyed child of five on her first excursion to Scarborough Castle. She'd looked at the man and known in her heart that he needed help.

The English Heritage site had closed to visitors not long afterwards.

Now, the castle teetered on the precipice between land and the lashing waves, its supporting buildings sacrificial offerings to the sea's insatiable appetite. More importantly, at least to Beth, the Roman Signal Station was gone, washed away in last night's category four storm. The early morning news report, accompanied by vivid drone footage of the collapsed section of cliff, had brought the previous night's dream flooding back.

Vivid Worlds

Mother isn't impressed by her hysterical pleading. She can't see the helmeted figure crouched on the grass before them, one hand held out in entreaty. Beth surges towards him, arms outstretched, only to be dragged back just as their fingertips meet. Her mother snaps something about "making a scene". Beth shouts and sobs, pointing at the picture of a Roman soldier on the nearby information board and then pointing back at the man. The slap shuts her up. In the same instant, the man winks out of existence.

The desolation she'd felt as that five-year-old child surged up within her once more. She needed to find out if her Roman soldier really was a troubled spirit calling out for aid—though what help she could offer was beyond her—or just a figment of her imagination. Her children were grown, her husband gone. She had no more excuses. And so, she'd packed a few overnight essentials and caught the next bus to Scarborough.

Up ahead, a youth—late teens, at a guess—lounged against a low stone wall, hair buzzed at the sides, floppy auburn curls falling into his eyes. He was watching her. Beth had been warned about thieves haunting the bus station; she tightened her grip on her phone and debated crossing the road. No, she decided, that would be too obvious. And why should she? An irrational determination kept her striding along the street. In ones and twos, the locals peeled off, heading to houses sporting scars from their latest battle with the elements: boarded up windows, crumbling brickwork, roofs decorated with random streaks of acidic artwork. She lost sight of the young man while checking directions. It was a shock when he suddenly popped up right beside her. His mask was patterned with a curling leaf-design, the eyes above it dark and determined.

"All right?" he said, by way of greeting.

Beth was grateful that a technological tweak of the mask's material enhanced sound rather than muted it. She nodded and strove to project an air of calm confidence.

166

"You're here to find *it*, aren't you?" he said.

"Don't know what you're talking about." Beth's stomach twisted with the conviction that maybe she did.

"Nah, don't pull that." He flicked a glance up towards the castle. "It's expecting someone. I reckon it's you."

She wanted to deny the surety in his gaze. Wanted to push past him and run. But it felt like her feet were rooted to the pavement.

"You're too young. What could you know about—" she started.

"That's the thing, right, there's no old or young, not with this. It's been here forever. But now there's trouble."

"Trouble?"

"Yeah, trouble." He gave her an expectant look. "So, you coming or what?"

"Coming?"

"What are you? Some kind of parrot?" He pointed to the castle. "It's waiting." And with that he turned and headed along the street.

Flustered and not entirely sure what she was doing, Beth followed. 'Peasholme Wildlife Gardens' was blazoned across the back the youth's pink t-shirt, the letters picked out in much-washed grey solar strips. His baggy trousers had multiple bulging pockets; mud edged his trainers. *Maybe he is a gardener.* The streets were narrow and growing increasingly steep. A coughing fit stopped Beth in her tracks. She shucked off her rucksack; with one hand she retrieved her medication from a side pocket, with the other she pulled off her mask. Hand trembling, she sprayed a measured dose into her mouth. The young man doubled back; he looked concerned.

"You OK?"

"Will be," she gasped, leaning against a repurposed post-box, its silvered surface busy charging the huge storage battery inside. "Just give me a minute." The tightness in her chest eased. She pressed the mask back into place over her nose and mouth. "I need a break." When he didn't respond, she clarified, "I need a *comfort* break."

He shuffled from foot to foot, tatty trainers scuffing the pavement.

"It was a very long bus journey," she added tersely.

He frowned at her, then said, "Oh, right."

Two minutes later, they were standing outside a building whose frontage consisted of a large, mesh-reinforced tinted window. Above the air-lock sealed door, the word 'Café' had been etched in gold paint. On the outside, the café had an armoured feel to it. On the inside it was a delight. Beth gratefully peeled off her mask and sucked in a lungful of cool, clean air. Music played softly in the background and the décor was a calming mix of forest greens with the occasional more exotic splash of colour. There was seating for maybe twenty customers in a mix of booths or at prettily dressed tables. She spotted a couple of the agri-dome workers hungrily tucking into heaped ploughman's platters. A young black woman had a table to herself, its surface mostly covered in bits of electronic equipment. She took a sip from a tall glass, attention focused on fitting two of the disparate parts together. Beth's attention was caught by the curling green and gold designs on the young woman's waistcoat. Sudden raucous laughter erupted from the corner booth. None of the other customers reacted. *Teenage girls.* Beth sighed. *Must be regulars.*

"Can I get you anything?" the waitress behind the counter asked.

Refrigerated cubbies lined the walls, humming softly, their glass doors displaying an array of colourful cans and bottles. Beth's attention was caught by the wide shelves of the freezer cabinets: one held the expected flavoured ices and ice-creams, but the other displayed palm-sized fillets of fish.

The extravagance left her speechless. In York, fish came in bite-sized chunks. *You're on the coast, idiot.* Still, what if they had a power cut? All that hard bought fish would go to waste. And then she remembered the wave-power modules built into the length of Scarborough's new seawall. Not only was this town energy self-sufficient, but it also made a significant contribution to the grid. Many inland towns and cities would be in dire straits without the cooperative effort of the wind and wave energy providers arrayed along the coastline.

The waitress tapped her fingernails—long, bright blue and dotted with stars—on the glass counter. Beth met her impatient gaze.

"An iced tea for me." She turned to the youth, "Want anything?"

He shrugged. "Water. Thanks."

"And one water. Can you point me at the restroom?"

The restroom was not quite as pretty but more than adequate for her needs. Beth took the opportunity to wash the sweat from her face and tidy her short grey hair, before adjusting her sunhat to a jauntier angle. Her t-shirt had darkened to purple in the cool of the café—it helped to hide the sweat stains—but the photochromic material would quickly shift back to pale lilac in the sun. At least her cropped trousers still looked smart, despite three hours cramped on the bus. Back in the café proper, she paid for the drinks and handed the carton of chilled water to the young man.

A voice called from the corner booth. "Hey, Dan. Hustling the 'landers again?"

Scowling, Dan turned and flashed a hand signal at the speaker. The girls in the booth screeched with feigned outrage. One flicked a message back, fingers quick and nimble. Dan flushed and strode out of the café. Beth caught up with him where the road curved into a steep incline. At first, he wouldn't look at her.

"Dan, is it?"

"It's Sheridan, but I guess Dan will do," he muttered.

"Elizabeth," she replied, "but you can call me Beth."

The corner of his mouth twitched. "This isn't… I mean, I'm not trying to hustle you."

"I'll be the judge of that." Beth fiddled with the straw and finally got it through the sealable slot in her mask. The ice was already melting. She took a grateful sip of tea and considered. "What was all that about?"

Dan shrugged and mumbled, "Nothin'."

The ever evolving 'finger talk' of the younger generation was one way to keep 'the greys' out of the loop. Confidence in net-talk had taken a serious beating after the 2062 Eavesdropping scandal. A major overhaul to net security had ensued and while most of the population seemed reassured, Beth was more than happy to be 'bare brained' rather than 'plugged in'.

Time to change tack. "You work at the Wildlife Gardens?"

"Worked it out, did you?" His sharp tone shifted to one of apology. "Yeah, sorry. I like plants. Plants like me. And working outside is better than being stuck in the Domes."

'You don't mind wearing your mask all day?'

"Nah, used to it. Doesn't bother me."

"All right, Dan. You can tell me more about this 'thing' that's waiting up at the castle while we walk." Beth set off and Dan fell in beside her.

"Found it a couple of months back." He didn't bother with the straw, just peeled up the bottom half of his mask and slurped. "I was poking around the castle, you know, looking for stuff, and I practically fell down this stairwell. Part of a wall had collapsed, and I didn't see the hole until I was in it."

"You could've got yourself killed scavenging up there. It's closed for a reason."

"Yeah, well, didn't have much choice. Damn thing wouldn't

leave me alone." He made a flicking gesture around his ear. "Buzz, buzz, buzz." And then he tapped his chest. "And that constant pull. Like a fucking massive magnet." He gave her a speculative look. "You must've felt it?"

She frowned at the language but let it pass. Side-stepping the question, she asked. "What did you find down there?"

"This huge cavern, walls covered in what looked like blisters but turned out to be like," he gestured with his hands, "like football-sized marbles stuck in the rock. That's where the light was coming from, sort of bluish and pulsing. And then… felt like I was drowning… no, more like I was being filled up from the inside out." He grimaced. "Nearly shit myself!" Dan gave another self-effacing shrug. "Knew I had to do something. Didn't know what. Took a while, but I finally it figured out."

"You had to find *me*," Beth said.

They fell silent, attention focused on keeping their feet on the stony track that led up to the castle. It was a sweaty slog that took the best part of an hour. Halfway up, Beth called for a rest-stop at one of the viewing points. She remembered standing there as a child, gazing out at South Bay, the curve of the beach dotted with windbreaks and parasols, distant figures running and splashing in the gently rolling waves. A weight settled on her chest. Fifty years of worsening storms and rising sea levels hadn't been kind. Gone were the beaches, the funfairs and promenades. Gone were the invading droves of summer tourists. Ha! Summer. It was always hot now.

When they reached the top, Dan led her through a rip in the battered mesh fence, across a stretch of overgrown tussocky grass, and up the creaking wooden steps that used to allow tourists access to the castle's interior.

"Watch your step," Dan warned as he picked his way over shattered brickwork, "it's just down here—" He disappeared into a wide, black hole. There was the sound of stone scraping on stone and then a muttered curse.

One hand on what was left of the wall, Beth focused on navigating through the rubble, testing the solidity of each careful footstep. Half way down the curving set of stone steps, she caught sight of Dan below her. He was working on clearing away a pile of debris.

"Doorway's blocked," he said, voice hoarse as he lifted another chuck of rock and set it on the step above him. "It was all right this morning." He glanced at the remains of the wall above them. "Must be more unstable that I thought."

"That could come down right on top of us," Beth said. "We need to get out of here."

That alien sense of urgency bloomed. And then there he was, just a few steps below her. The Roman soldier smiled, one hand reaching out in entreaty.

"Fine," she muttered between clenched teeth. This was what she'd come for, after all.

As she took a step towards him, the soldier vanished. By the time she reached the bottom, Dan had cleared a gap wide enough for them to squeeze through. The cavern was roughly oval in shape, and bigger than the ground floor of her two-bed cottage. But it was the globes, glittering with a pale-blue light that caught her attention. Pale, she realised, because shafts of sunlight were spearing through a crack in the far wall.

"I can hear the sea," she said.

Beth's stomach clenched as she realised that the cracked wall was the only thing that lay between them and a rubble strewn plunge into the sea. Turning, she ran her fingers across the smooth surface of the nearest globe.

"Ah," a voice sighed. "Calibrating." The pronunciation was odd, like Italian or...

"Latin," Beth breathed. She'd spent her teenage years obsessing over the Roman Empire. She looked up and there he was standing in the centre of the cavern.

"Momento," he said. And then, in a surprisingly northern accent, "Configuration complete."

Beth snatched her hand from the globe, belatedly aware of the sharp tingle running through her fingertips and gazed at her Roman soldier. He was tall, helmeted, with a glimpse of red woollen tunic under leather bound armour, with drawstring trousers and studded leather boots against inclement frontier weather.

"Who are you?" she asked. "And what do you want with me?"

"This is survey node 2567, one of the Swarm dedicated to observing your planet," the Roman soldier replied. "You are our primary. The recipient of our final report."

Beth stood and stared. *It's not a ghost. It's a hologram.* She swallowed convulsively. Or… a *downloaded mind?* The controversial procedure had been made legal last year, though only idiots, or the idiotically rich, would dare attempt it. *No, it can't be.* She'd first seen the Roman soldier fifty years ago, way before that kind of tech had been developed. *Some sort of AI, then? And part of a swarm?* That didn't sound good. More selfishly, she couldn't stop the silent demand: *Why me?* rattling around inside her head like the bone dice used by the villain in her latest novel *Odds or Evens*.

What came out of her mouth was, "Why do you look like a Roman soldier?"

"Rufus Domitius was our last primary. We based our appearance on his expectations." The image of the Roman soldier shimmered. "We could change into something more compatible with your current—"

"No." Beth interrupted, more sharply than she intended.

"Who are you talking to?" Dan demanded.

Beth grabbed his arm as he tried to push past her. The youth gasped and stared.

"I can see him!"

"Interesting.' The Roman solider sounded thoughtful.

Beth let go of Dan and the youth stared around in confusion.

"Give me your hand," she said.

"What?"

Beth sighed in exasperation and took hold of Dan's hand. "Can you see him now?"

"Yes, yes." He was staring at the soldier, blinking fast, eyes glassy. "It's been, like, real hard just feeling you there, you know."

"An interface connection of 90 percent is required to enable full visual and auditory communication. Current data suggests less than one percent of your species has this capability."

"What about me, then?" Dan asked.

"You have a remarkable level of sensitivity in the emotional frequency band. This allowed us to reach out to you. Physical contact with the primary seems to bypass the interference caused by the device inside your skull."

Dan opened his mouth to ask another question. Beth squeezed his hand to shut him up. "You said you're a survey node? What is that, exactly? And what are you doing here?" she asked.

"We are not just here; the Swarm is positioned across the entire globe. Our purpose is to collect data on this planetary body—geological, oceanic, atmospheric, species development or anything else deemed of interest—and deliver regular evaluative reports." He sighed. "Those of us still able to function, that is."

"And you need help," Beth stated.

"There is nothing your species can do to help us." The Roman solider looked resigned. "We are operating far beyond our predicted operational lifespan and have little time left.

Our data and associated reports have not been collected for over a thousand years. We have tried to find new conduits with varying degrees of success." He glanced down at his uniform, a half-smile on his face. "Our last primary made good use of our data on weather systems around the coast of this landmass."

"But when I met you before, when I was a child, I was sure you were in trouble."

"You misunderstood. It is you who are in trouble. This planetary body is undergoing significant climatic changes. Soon, it will not be a viable environment for many of its species."

"What do you mean, soon?" demanded Dan.

"In five hundred years conditions on this planet will be inimical to mammalian life forms."

Beth glanced at Dan and saw that he too was struggling to come to terms with such an outrageous statement. "Things are bad," she said, "but the world is pulling together to turn the tide."

All the newsfeeds were agreed: as long as everyone knuckled down and worked hard, they could build a brighter future for their children.

"We have been monitoring this planetary body for ten thousand years. According to our calculations, extinction of all mammalian life forms in five hundred years has a 90 percent level of reliability."

After long seconds, Beth cleared her throat and asked, "And you can do something to change that?"

"We will give you the data, together with our analyses."

"How will that help?"

"Our data is far more detailed than anything your species has been able to collect. It covers a timescale that will allow the generation of more accurate models and workable solutions. You have time to implement those solutions, if you act quickly."

"Drone!" Dan shouted.

Beth and the Roman soldier turned to stare as Dan picked up a handy sized piece of rock and let fly. There was the clang of stone striking metal and then a fitful high-pitched buzzing. Beth glimpsed a dark shape escaping through the crack in the far wall.

"Bloody corpo," Dan scowled, "since they built the seawall their drones are always sniffing around."

"How do you know it was a corporation drone?" Beth asked.

"Didn't you see their logo?" Dan hurried to the stairwell. "Might've knocked out its transmitter. I'll see if I can spot it from the castle."

Beth did not want to be left alone with whatever it was that lay behind the image of the Roman soldier. He/it was watching her, smiling genially.

"I need time to think," she said. "It's a lot to take in."

It nodded. More importantly, she needed to figure out how she felt about being so intimately linked with this 'thing'. Last night's vivid dream was no coincidence. *It managed to reach out to me in York!*

"We'll come back," she assured it.

"Hurry." Its gaze turned inwards. "Another storm is coming."

She found Dan on the clifftop—she followed the sounds of shouting—he was confronting the young black woman from the café.

"It's not one of mine," she practically screamed in his face.

"Wait," Beth gasped. "What's going on here?"

"She's a corpo spy!" Dan said.

"Look who's talking!" the young woman shot back.

Those winding steps had really taken it out of her. Beth's heart felt as if it was trying to thump its way out of her chest.

With an irritated grunt, she pulled off her mask. Yes, they were supposed to be totally breathable, but right now she needed more air.

The two young people stopped shouting and turned to stare at her.

"The NOX index—" Dan started.

Beth waved a dismissive hand at him… and then started coughing. Before she knew it, the young woman had an arm around her and was easing her into a sitting position, while Dan raked about in her rucksack. Beth snatched the spray from his hand and applied it on her next desperate in-breath. The cough rattled to a stop. At her tear-filled nod, Dan pressed the mask to her face, making sure the edges made a firm seal.

"Thank you," she managed, feeling old and stupid and embarrassed all at once.

Dan and the young woman were still glaring at each other.

"I'm Beth,' she said to the young woman, "and this is Dan."

"Yinka," the young woman replied, grudgingly.

"Please to meet you, Yinka." Beth squinted up at the sun. "Can we find a bit of shade and have a talk?"

Yinka took one arm, Dan took the other, and together they helped Beth to her feet. The young woman nodded toward the building that used to house the café and museum. "There's a room we can use in there. It's where I store my equipment."

Dan scowled at that but thankfully didn't say anything.

Yinka had a passkey for the museum door. When Beth raised an eyebrow, the young woman shrugged and said, "I know people."

Inside was dark and dusty, some of the old display cases were cracked, glass crunched underfoot.

"Through here," Yinka said.

She shouldered another door open, one hand still

supporting Beth, and flicked on the light. Shelves lined one side of the room, empty apart from a couple of boxes and a battered rucksack. On the floor, in one corner, Beth spotted the rich colours of the Yinka's waistcoat discarded amongst a rumpled pile of bedding. The young woman pushed the door closed and pulled off her mask.

"It's all right," she said. "There's self-seal around the door and I've got a portable filter." She nodded towards a cube shaped device on the floor; it was humming softly.

It was only now that Beth appreciated how petite the young woman was. While clearly older than Dan—early twenties?—Yinka's head barely reached his shoulder. With a grateful sigh, Beth sat on an abandoned packing crate and peeled off her mask. Dan pocketed his mask and then glanced around, clearly ill at ease.

Tucking an errant braid back into place, Yinka scowled at them both. "What're you two doing up here?" she demanded. When they didn't answer—really, what could they say? Communing with alien nodes wasn't going to come across well—the young woman's scowl deepened. "You're either artefact thieves or working with the corpos."

Dan bristled at that. "You're the one snooping around with that drone."

"I told you. That wasn't one of mine."

"I doubt there are any artefacts left worth stealing," Beth said. "And why would the corporations be interested in this place?"

Yinka glared at her in disbelief. "The corpo that built the seawall cut corners in its construction. I'm collecting evidence to prove their shiny new seawall will shatter under the first category six storm that hits it full on."

Dan jabbed a finger at her. "Just 'cause you're wearing the shirt, doesn't mean you're one of them."

Yinka's t-shirt bore the logo that had been splashed around

on the newsfeeds lately: a green circle containing either a crimson teardrop, or a drop of fresh blood—depending on whether the newscasters were painting the group as eco-activists or eco-terrorists.

Yinka took a step towards Dan. "The corpos skimmed millions from the government rebuild projects and it's idiots like you who are going to the pay the price."

Beth struggled to her feet. "The whole world is going to pay the price if we don't act in time." She was surprised by her own words. *When did I decide that?*

"And what would you know about it?" Yinka snapped. "You're an inlander. Bet you've got a nice little upland cottage with a bit of garden to grow your veggies."

"I live in York now, that's true. But I was born in Hull."

That shut them up. Hull no longer existed. Its sea defences were breached by a series of major storms, thousands were killed, even more turned into bedraggled refugees. Beth had lost her mother to the sea. She damned well wasn't going to lose anyone else.

"Sit down, both of you, and listen." Beth watched as the pair settled on the floor, as far from each other as possible. She retook her seat on the crate. It didn't take long to tell her story, with Dan occasionally butting in. Yinka didn't exactly looked convinced by the end of it.

"What about the seawall? Did this node of yours collect any data on that?" Yinka demanded.

"Didn't get chance to ask," Dan snapped. Yinka wrinkled her nose at him. "Bet that drone was looking for you," he added. "That's what you get for snooping around in corpo business." His expression became thoughtful as he turned to Beth, "No way that drone got any video of the soldier, I mean, I could only see him when I was touching you."

"That's true," Beth agreed, "but it would've picked up the audio, at least on our side of the conversation." She raked through her memory, "What did we say that that they could use?"

Dan frowned. "Depends on how long it was there. You called it a 'survey node' and said a bunch of stuff about helping." He ran a hand through his curls. "They're desperate."

"Who? The corpos?" asked Yinka.

"No, the nodes. They want to make one last report before the end."

Now that Beth really looked at him, she could see that Dan was distraught. He could clearly sense more of the nodes underlying emotions than she could. *What sort of tech has feelings?*

"So, if the corpos get there first, these nodes will happily hand over a thousand years of data to them?" Now Yinka sounded horrified.

"It's not that simple," Beth said.

Yinka stood and paced the length of the small room, hands twitching like she wanted to throttle someone. She stopped and faced them. "What the corpos can't turn to profit, they'll bury. We've got to get there first!"

Grabbing her rucksack, she paused and then pulled out a black case hidden under the lowest shelf. She handed it to Dan. "We might need that."

He looked surprise by the weight of it. "What is it?"

"You'll see soon enough." At his stubborn expression, she added, "Chances are there'll be nothing left of your precious nodes by morning."

The outside door opened onto a grey curtain. Beth belatedly remembered the sea roke the bus driver had mentioned. She fumbled for her phone, but Yinka was already frowning and shaking her head.

"No signal. Can't pull up the forecast."

Dan reached into a bulging trouser pocket and pulled out a flat, square device. With a practiced flick of his thumb, he opened its lid and peered at the display on the small screen.

"Green," he announced. "We're good to go."

Beth shared a doubtful glance with Yinka.

"It's a scanner from work," Dan explained. "Let's us know whether we need to pull the shutters." Beth raised a questioning eyebrow. "To keep this muck off the plants," he added, as if it was obvious. "Not all of them can cope when the PH reading drops below 4.2." He gestured outside at the fog. "That is a solid 5.0." He reached into another pocket and shook out his all-in-one. "Still, might get worse." He grinned. "And there's no point in getting soaked."

The palm-sized green packet unfolded, and Dan stepped into the legs of the protective suit; he was pulling up the hood by the time Beth and Yinka finished raking about in their rucksacks for their own gear. Beth wriggled her shoulders and felt the suit settle into place like a second skin over her t-shirt and cropped trousers. Masks in place, they ventured outside. Dan produced a torch from yet another pocket and they picked their way over the sodden grass. Thunder rumbled in the distance and Beth's heart sank.

The bones of the castle loomed suddenly out of the fog. Beth slowed as she navigated through the tumble of brickwork. When she looked up, there was no sign of the two youngsters. A soft patter of rain began lacing through the fog, slowly dissipating the blanketing grey. After an anxious couple of minutes, she caught a hint of torchlight ahead and made her way to the mouth of the stairwell. Pulling in a breath to steady her nerves, Beth carefully made her way down.

An unfamiliar voice stopped her in her tracks.

"My name is Valerie Signet. And these are technicians Brant and Zhi. As a representative of the Yi-Samar Corporation, I claim this site under article 5 of the Coastline Defence Initiative."

Peering into the cavern, Beth spotted Dan and Yinka standing with their backs to her; beyond them were three figures, all dressed top-to-toe in navy all-in-ones. Two were busy examining the globes covering the back wall, the third had her hands on her hips with the attitude of a teacher scolding children. Above the woman's head, near the ceiling, a matt black drone hovered—busy recording every word and gesture.

"This cavern doesn't belong to you," Yinka insisted. She gave Dan a sideways glance, her fingers flicking nervously.

"It does now. The Yi-Samar Corporation has been granted full access to and control over any and all equipment along the Scarborough coastline."

"This isn't 'equipment'," Dan argued, "It's alive."

One of the technicians started digging at one of the softly pulsing globes with a buzzing tool. "Contents seem to be organic," he said, "but I'll need a sample to confirm that."

Dan's hands bunched into fists. "Stop! You're hurting it!"

"Typical," Yinka sneered. "You're no better than thieves."

"You should know," Signet said, she sounded almost amused. "You eco-terrorists are all the same, spouting your holier-than-thou rhetoric while sneaking around damaging property and stealing proprietary data."

Signet frowned at Dan. "You have been observed interacting with these 'survey nodes'. It seems you have some knowledge or expertise that may be of value. I have been authorised to offer you and..." she blinked, no doubt accessing data. "... Elizabeth Hunt contracts as local consultants for this project." She looked around the cavern. "Where is Ms Hunt?"

Beth dodged back and held her breath. She heard Yinka say, "Gone back to her hostel. Left us to do the hard graft."

The Roman soldier chose that moment to appear on the step below Beth. His image flickered, before settling. "Why are you hurting us?" he demanded.

"We're not. It's those other people. I think they're trying to steal your data."

"Steal?" He seemed to struggle with the concept. "Ah, thieves. Rufus sometimes talked about thieves and the need to defend against them. But there is no need to steal what is freely—" His image flickered and vanished.

There was a shout, followed by an agonised scream. Beth lurched into a run and was inside the cavern before her mind caught up with what her body was doing. Dan lay curled on the ground, clutching one hand to his chest. The stink of burnt flesh made her gorge rise.

Beth swallowed hard. "You monsters! He's just a boy."

"It was an accident," one of the technicians protested. "He attacked me, grabbed my laser drill."

Yinka was on her knees beside the stricken youth. "He needs medical treatment." There was an edge of panic in her voice. And then she turned on Dan. "I told you to wait!"

Dan groaned. "Hurt too much."

Beth knew he wasn't talking about his hand. She stared at the dark, viscous liquid dripping from the cracked globe and felt her perception of the cavern shift: this wasn't cold stone and clever AI programming. Dan was right—whatever was projecting the image of the Roman soldier into her mind was alive.

Signet glanced up at the drone. "Of course, a medical team is on its way. But first, you all need to sign our NDA."

"Is that all you can think about?" Beth demanded.

"Duty demands we protect this unique site from vandals and terrorists." Signet glanced at Yinka. "The police are also on route."

"I'm just a photographer," Yinka said. "I take photos of wildlife and ruins. That's it."

With a casual air, Signet flipped open the lid of Yinka's black case. "Then I'm sure you can explain why you need a state of the art, long range transmitter?"

Signet smiled at the trapped look on Yinka's face. "Stealing propriety data is a serious offence."

Beth clenched her jaw, lips pressed into a hard line. Her gaze flicked from Yinka down to Dan. His face was drenched in sweat, lips moving to mumbled words.

"Where's that medical team?" she demanded.

Signet held out her phone. "As you don't have an implant, I need your thumb print on the NDA."

Yinka pushed to her feet. "Don't do it."

Lightening cracked outside, its light freeze-framing the tableau inside the cavern. The crack in the wall looked wider. A faint tremble passed through the rock beneath Beth's feet.

She fixed the rep with a hard glare. "I'll sign your NDA after Dan has received proper medical care."

"I will hold you to that." Signet pocketed her phone and turned to the two technicians. "Report."

"It doesn't look like we can dig these data nodes out—if that's what they are—not without damaging them."

"All right. We'll set up a temporary lab here."

Beth tuned them out and knelt beside Dan, one hand braced on a smooth boulder to ease herself down. It was only as a warm, pricking tingle spread through her hand that she remembered that the ground around Dan had previously been perfectly flat.

"It is time." The voice of the Roman soldier whispered in her mind. "Our final report we bequeath to humanity. Use it well."

Dan reached up with his good hand and she took it in her own. His eyes were full of tears. She wasn't sure if it was the pain of his wound or grief at the passing of the node intelligence. Probably both, she decided.

The tingling warmth spread through her body. She felt light and wafer thin, but this changed as a sense of weight gradually returned, layer after layer, until she wasn't just heavy, she was dense, incredibly dense. It felt like the rock floor of the cavern couldn't possibly support her. She gasped, squeezed tight inside herself, a tiny point of light in an impossible corner, pressed all around by a swarm of buzzing bees.

Beth blinked her eyes open to muted angry shouts.

"They're dead! All our readings have flatlined!" It was the two technicians, rushing around the cave, waving handheld scanners at the dull grey globes.

"Might've been that last lightning strike. It hit pretty close," said one.

As he spoke thunder boomed and the floor of the cavern bucked beneath her. Beth hunched over Dan, trying to protect him from clattering rock shards. Cold sea air gusted and howled, snatching the sunhat from her head. The far wall of the cavern was gone. Cracks zigzagged through the stone floor towards them, dislodging hunks of rock that tumbled in a slow arc into the raging sea.

"Get up!" Yinka hauled Beth to her feet.

Together they dragged Dan towards the doorway, manhandled him through the gap and into the stairwell. Beth could taste salt in the back of her throat—the chemical composition of the 'salt' popped into her mind. She shook her head and concentrated on levering herself and Dan up the stone steps. Yinka was scowling in concentration, teeth bared with the effort of supporting his weight.

At the top, Dan announced, "It's all right, I can walk."

"Come on, then," Yinka shouted as they stepped out into the raging gale.

Head down and teeth gritted, Beth forced her knees to take step after step after step through the pelting rain. The door to the museum came as a surprise. They fell inside, collapsing in a heap in the musty dark.

Vivid Worlds

Hours later, after the storm had passed, an ambulance arrived. The police searched the immediate area, but there was no sign of Signet or the two technicians.

"Gone skulking back to head office," Yinka declared.

"Yeah," Dan said. "Rats and sinking ships."

One medic fussed around Beth, but there nothing wrong with her beyond the usual, plus a few bumps and bruises. Yinka sat inside the ambulance, watching closely as the other medic dressed Dan's hand. They wanted to take him to A&E, but the last thing they needed was to be stuck there for hours on end. Dan promised to attend the outpatients clinic and the medics had to be satisfied with that.

Dawn striped the sky with pink and peach as the three of them sat, exhausted, on the bench in front of the museum building. It was wonderfully quiet. And the air cool and fresh, wiped clean by the ferocity of the storm. Beth pulled in a deep breath, glad to put her mask aside, at least for a while.

Yinka handed out bottles of water and packets of nuts. "Always keep some snacks in," she said as she helped Dan open both. He offered up a tentative smile.

Silent, contemplative munching ensued. Eventually, Dan said, "Medics said my implant's fried. No way I can afford to replace it. Not for an age, anyway." He turned to Beth. "Lucky for us you don't have one."

"Lucky? Why?" Beth asked.

"The… er…" he glanced around and then dropped his voice to a whisper. "It tried to share the load, you know, but my implant kind of got in the way. So, I guess you got all of it."

"All of it?" Beth repeated.

Dan grinned. "That's right. The data, the reports, all of it." He leant back and gazed at the brightening sky. "Now we just need to figure out a way to share it with everyone else."

Yinka blinked at them both, mouth open. "You're kidding!"

She jumped up, clapped her hands and danced a circle, hips swinging. "We've got them now!"

"The seawall," Beth said, words tumbling out. "I have the exact composition, its strengths and… oh, my goodness, its weaknesses. It's all here, in my head. Not that I understand the data, but the report is clear enough."

"But no one's going to believe you," Dan said. "I mean, no offense, but you're just an old lady—at least, to other people, anyway."

"Nah, no problem," Yinka said, still smiling. "The world will believe *us*."

Beth's eyes were drawn to the crimson teardrop on Yinka's t-shirt. The eco-activists did claim to be a world-wide organisation.

"We're the plugged in generation," Yinka continued. "We've got the tech. It's just a blink and a thought to send a message. I composed most of my university essays in bed with my eyes closed. And now, you can download a whole mind!"

Beth gave her a horrified glare. "No way. My mind's my own. You're not putting me inside a computer!"

"It's just a copy," Yinka said. "You'll still be you afterwards."

"You can't be sure of that," Dan butted in. "And anyway, it's not natural."

"If you believe that, how come you've got an implant?"

Dan just glared at her.

"Makes no odds," Beth said. "I'm not doing it."

"Not even to save the world?" Yinka asked. She fixed Beth with an earnest look. "I know the process is safe because, well, I've done it myself."

It was Beth's turn to stare. Dan just sat there, open mouthed.

"Sometimes there's no other way to carry key information out from under the noses of governments and corporations.

They can scan implants, intercept external comms." Yinka tapped one finger against her temple. "It's worth the risk. We've raped and pillaged the resources of this world, generation after generation. If there's going to be anything left for us," she glanced at Dan, "and future generations, we've got to take action now."

Beth thought about her grandchildren—aged 5 and 7 years—so full of energy, curiosity, unbridled joy. They revelled in the green sub-set of reality they were exposed to, not understanding how damaged the world really was. *Five hundred years.* They'd get to live out their lives, as would their children… but what quality of life would they have? And what then?

"All right," she said, ignoring the way her stomach cramped and the jelly-like feeling invading her legs. "Let's give it a go."

Dan looked around in exasperation. "But… how?"

"Don't worry," Yinka's smile widened. "Like I said, I know people."

Solar Strike: Local Operations

Corey Jae White

The assault rifle was light in Quinn's grip, lighter than they remembered. They weren't familiar with the AK-2047 but had to admit that an AK of some sort was fitting. For decades the Kalashnikov had been a symbol of people's war, and what was this but one battle in the people's war against capital?

Quinn's granddaughter, Peyton, stood beside them, casually holding a H&K Spectre submachine as they looked across the oil refinery from their position outside the gate. Furnace chimneys and distillation towers stabbed the brown-blue sky, looming tall above the oil tanks and reservoirs. Pipes ran every which way, connecting disparate parts of the facility, and gas flares hissed overhead with undulating orange flames. Quinn shivered, a visceral response to the thought of all that pollution leeching into the sky. They could almost smell the benzene.

"You ready, Granno?" Peyton asked.

Quinn checked the countdown in the top of their vision. Three seconds. "Ready."

Two.

One.

"Go go go!" Peyton whispered loudly, running ahead.

Quinn followed through the unlocked gate, sweeping their gun over rooftops and likely sniper nests, the place a warren of roads and buildings, pipes and alleyways. Their footfalls were masked by the low hiss and rumble of industrial processes and Quinn's hearing turned sharp, straining to listen for the private military contractors guarding the refinery.

Together they stopped at the mouth of an alley. Quinn

leaned out, watching down their rifle's sights. Movement. They feathered the trigger, firing a three-round burst that hit the wall, spraying brick fragments into the air.

Peyton ran out of cover toward the enemy, firing at full auto. Quinn swore beneath their breath and stepped into the alleyway.

The soldier emerged from cover, dressed head to toe in black tactical fetish wear. He fired, his volley of bullets hitting Peyton square in the chest. She collapsed in a pool of blood. Quinn returned fire, catching the soldier in the chest and neck. He fell, choking out his last breath.

There was still another PMC somewhere in the facility.

A wet crack dropped Quinn to the ground, the headshot followed by the boom of a large calibre rifle. They were dead. Their vision shifted; immersion lost in a gut-churning moment as they swapped bodies with their killer to watch their own death. The enemy raised their sniper rifle over a low concrete wall for just long enough to line up their shot and fire.

"Don't worry, we'll get them next time," Peyton said.

Quinn sighed, head still swimming from their fleeting dalliance with death. Their hands were clammy against the plastic of the controller grips, their heart beating too hard for a sim.

"I forgot last time," Peyton said, "if you swap to your knife, you run faster." Playing the immersive shooter was her idea—the only way to get her excited about the history report on the global energy transition that was due in two days.

"That doesn't make any sense," Quinn said, but Peyton was rapidly swapping between her Glock Omega 9C handgun, the H&K, and her knife, impatiently waiting for the next round to begin. Each of her weapons was skinned with gaudy pulsating patterns. Realism obviously wasn't the game developers' chief concern, even in this historical scenario:

Sabotage at the Altona Oil Refinery.

"Was it really like this, Granno?" Peyton asked, her head zipping this way and that, the movement making Quinn's neck ache in sympathy. "All grey and ugly?"

They were standing outside the refinery once again, polluting towers clawing at the firmament.

"Worse," Quinn said. "At least *these* pipes aren't actually full of shit to choke the planet."

Peyton giggled and Quinn winced. They weren't meant to swear in front of Peyton; they were on thin enough ice as it was.

"Come on, Pey; next round is starting."

Peyton sped forward, slashing her knife at the air, her avatar wearing a dirty-white windbreaker over fluoro pink jeans, the lower half of her face covered with the leering demon mouth of a hannya mask. Quinn's avatar was a non-descript masc figure wearing solar shades and a shemagh in a bright green PCB pattern.

Together they moved quickly, dashing low through the alley where the sniper caught them last time. They slowed down, scanning every angle, haunted by the quiet scrape of boots and the odd muffled burst of radio static from somewhere out of sight. Tense minutes of crouch-walking brought them to a single-story building, the interior blinking with lights and screens—the control room. The floor was marked with a glowing green square, its purpose a mystery to Quinn.

"Cover me while I plant the bomb," Peyton said.

"On it." Quinn crouched in the corner with their AK pointed at the doorway.

Peyton knelt over the bomb in the middle of the space, her avatar repeating a generic animation, looking more like she was changing its diaper than arming the device.

A burst of gunfire made Quinn jolt. Peyton was already dead, the bomb lying beside her corpse marked with a gleaming white outline. Quinn's vision flashed red with damage taken and they spun around, searching for the enemy. Too late Quinn saw him on the catwalk above, leering green skull painted over his ballistic mask, gun roaring in his hands.

Quinn pulled the trigger but they were already dead.

"We almost got it that time!" Peyton said excitedly. "You're pretty good at this. Is that 'cause you did it for real?"

Quinn scoffed and tried to slow their breathing. "If I'm any good it's because I used to play a lot of shooters when I was a teenager. We didn't have to worry about energy allotments, so we'd spend whole nights, or even weekends, gaming."

"Woah," Peyton said.

"It's not as fun as it sounds, trust me."

Now it was Peyton's turn to scoff. "But you did this, right? And that's why mum hates you?"

Quinn sighed. They lifted the immersive headset, and Peyton did the same. She looked so much like Amelia had at that age. The same serious brown eyes and broad smile. Quinn had gone to prison and given up the chance to watch their daughter grow; hadn't been there to talk her through her first period, or to put them both through the embarrassment of The Talk. Didn't get to help her grow from a child into the amazing woman Amelia became—couldn't take any credit for that.

They weren't going to waste this second chance with Peyton.

"I hope she doesn't *hate* me, but I understand if she does," Quinn said. "I thought she'd understand why we attacked the refinery, but it was too much to lay on a kid her age. All she really knew was that I was in prison when I should have been there for her.

"Fu—for real, I'd still be there if we hadn't dismantled all those old systems."

Peyton grinned at the near slip-up. "Next round's about to

start."

Quinn put the headset back on and the text across their vision said: 'You picked up the bomb.'

"Why do I have the bomb?"

"You get to plant it this time, just like in real life!"

Quinn shook their head. In real life they had carried thirty individual charges linked to an encrypted radio detonator. One bomb would never have been enough; they had to utterly level the refinery; ensure it could never be brought back online.

They raced ahead into the facility with knives drawn, choosing yet another path, passing boxes and containers stacked haphazardly for no purpose beyond level design. Even with some liberties taken, the refinery map was close enough to Quinn's memories that their sympathetic nervous system was in overdrive. They felt sick, heart erratic, adrenaline-fouled blood churning through their veins. They tried to slow their breath, slow their heart rate, and for a short moment they wondered what their doctor would say. Time inside hadn't been kind to their heart.

Quinn heard a sound and swapped to their AK, grandparent and grandchild moving with tactical precision. They ducked low beneath a barrier of pipes into a wide path between two buildings. They both stopped at the sound of boots scraping over the ground and Quinn raised the rifle to look down the sights.

Two soldiers strafed into the opening ahead, firing off rounds before disappearing, Quinn's vision flashing red. They tightened their grip on the controller, felt their jaw clench.

One of the soldiers returned and Quinn pulled the plastic trigger, the gun roaring in their hands. The soldier fell, dead, blood spattering the wall. Quinn barely noticed as the other soldier fell to a volley from Peyton—their ears rang with the memory of real gunfire, their breath quick, heart hammering.

"Yes! Snap, Granno! Granno? Are you alright?"

Quinn shook their head. They pushed the headset up and exhaled a shuddering breath, forcing down the rising panic.

"Hurry up! They'll respawn unless we finish this."

There'd been no respawn for Bruce Dayton. Quinn's entire cell had done time for that killing, even though Quinn had pulled the trigger. Sickeningly, when their sentencing came down, they got more years for destroying the refinery than for killing a person.

Quinn moved their avatar in a daze, following Peyton along a different path to the control room. They followed the quick-time commands to plant and trigger the bomb, then stood staring at the countdown timer. Months of preparation, materials sourcing, and careful experimentation with bomb construction—not to mention the nerve-wracking act of planting the bombs themselves—all of it abstracted behind a few button presses. It was nothing like real life, but Quinn's guilt didn't care about that, their head a mess of confused voices coming up from the depths of memory. Their conspirators, their husband, the judge, the libelous news reports.

"Come on, Granno! We only win if we escape!" Peyton said, her avatar standing in the doorway, rapidly swapping weapons.

"Alright, Pey; lead the way."

They both switched back to their knives and ran along the main access road. Bullets zipped past, pipping away at Quinn's health. Their exfil was twenty metres away—a jalopy covered in solar panels like armour plating. Ten metres. Five.

Their avatars clambered inside and the vehicle sped away. Vertigo as Quinn's perspective floated up out of their body and high into the sky, turning back to face the refinery. The bomb exploded with a low, distant *dhoom*, triggering a chain reaction as explosions bloomed across the facility in rapid staccato until a billowing mushroom cloud gathered huge overhead.

A voice sounded in Quinn's ears: "Counter-terrorists win."

"That's not what they called us at the time," Quinn said quietly. They removed the VR helmet and looked at Peyton. She was grinning and Quinn couldn't help but smile back, despite the shudder of their breath and the sweat on their palms.

"Want to play again?"

"No," Quinn said, "not even a little bit."

"That's enough VR for now," Amelia called out from the kitchen. "How about you go outside for a bit?"

Peyton frowned but shouted: "Yes, mum."

Quinn and Peyton left the VR gear on the couch and walked through to the kitchen where Amelia had fresh vegetables from the communal plots laid out, still dusted with rich, dark soil. Peyton put her arms around her mum's waist.

"It's beautiful out there," Amelia said, brushing a hand over her daughter's hair. "Why don't you and Granno go for a wander, come back for dinner in about forty minutes?"

Peyton nodded and Quinn said, "Sounds good."

"You want to stay for dinner?" Amelia asked.

It took Quinn a few seconds to realise the question was meant for them. "Are you sure?"

Amelia shot them a look that said *Do you want me to change my mind?*

"I mean, I'd love to."

"Good, I've got plenty here," Amelia said. "Now go. Back in forty minutes."

"OK, mum."

"OK, Am."

Quinn and Peyton left the apartment, taking the stairs down to ground level. Quinn pushed open the door and blinked into the sunlight until their eyes adjusted. The sun was drifting slow toward the horizon, and solar panels all across the commune façades tracked the fading light on reactive sunflower armatures. The buildings were linked by pathways running through the sprawling wild parklands, and to the west food crops grew and livestock grazed beneath raised agrivoltaics.

Quinn picked a footpath at random and they began to walk. The earlier humidity had dissipated, and when they stepped into the cool shade of the massive gum trees, Quinn shivered. They were both silent for a time, readjusting to the quiet after the immersive trip to busier times. It was something the older generations were still adjusting to: The gentler pace of a lower-energy life.

"It's so snap you did that for real," Peyton said, aiming an imaginary gun down the path.

"It wasn't *snap*, whatever that means. It was dangerous. We're lucky more people didn't die. We're lucky *we* didn't die."

"You did what you had to."

"I used to think that, but now..." Quinn shrugged. "I was so angry; violence was the only answer I could come up with. But we needed more than that to get where we are today. We had to change systems and infrastructures; we had to change people's minds. That work took years, and I was in prison for all of it. Your mum does more for the cause than ever I did."

"Ugh, Mum's work is boring."

Quinn laughed. "You're not wrong, but compliance and auditing are important—it helps make sure the energy transition is working as intended. That matters. It matters more than violence."

Peyton huffed.

They continued on, deeper into the parklands. Birds twittered from among the leaves, and other critters scurried low through the foliage as they passed.

"What happened after you blew up the refinery?" Peyton

asked. "How did you escape?"

"We didn't. Why do you think I was in prison for so long?"

"Oh, yeah," Peyton said. She took Quinn's hand and Quinn squeezed. It wouldn't be long before the ten-year-old began to shrink away from familial affection.

"We didn't want to kill anyone. We rounded up the staff and put them in a bus we'd stolen. We told the security team to surrender and most of them did. The others..." Quinn stopped. That part was covered at length in every report about the attack. "We drove away in the bus and detonated the bombs once we'd reached a safe distance. We just waited there for the police, or whoever, to arrive and we watched it burn."

"Why didn't you run?"

"Most people didn't realise we were at war for a new way of living," Quinn said. "We knew that whatever happened, they would do everything they could to control the narrative. We let ourselves get captured so people would see we weren't dangerous fanatics or state actors. We were just teachers, lawyers, activists, electricians. We were just normal people worried about the future. We were parents worried that our children would suffer unnecessarily unless something changed."

"And you really did kill someone?"

"I did. It's not easy like in the games, Pey. I couldn't have done it for anything less."

"Than saving the world," Peyton said, looking up with a smile.

"I didn't save the world. We're all doing that, day by day. Especially people like your mum."

Peyton sighed.

Quinn led Peyton over to a bench, its seat shaped from the branches of a living rhododendron tree. Together they sat beneath the flowering crown, bees quietly tending to their duties.

"I think it was the first time your mum contacted me after I went to prison. I'd been in a few years already, so she was probably sixteen or seventeen. Old enough and smart enough to school me. She sent me a copy of this pamphlet from about 70 years ago, written after a hotel bombing. It was called *You Can't Blow Up a Social Relationship*. She highlighted this one part, and I read it so many times I know it off by heart: *'Unless a majority of people had the ideas and organisation sufficient for the creation of an alternative society, we would see the old world reassert itself because it is what people would be used to, what they believed in, what existed unchallenged in their own personalities.'* Do you understand?"

Peyton nodded thoughtfully.

"Good," Quinn said. "That's why your mum's work is important. Maybe I helped show people that the old systems weren't invulnerable, but that wouldn't have mattered until people like your mum came along and showed them another way forward.

"Reckon you'll be ready to write your report now?"

"I think so," Peyton said. "It's not as simple as I thought though."

"No," Quinn said, leaning back to stare up at the pure blue sky. "These things never are."

Going Out on a Limb

David Cleden

Each one is a monster, infeasibly tall. If it were possible to grow a city sky-rise from seed, Holt imagines it might look something like this. One tree by itself is impressive but here in the heart of the Plantation, ten thousand giants are gathered.

Beneath the bluewood canopy there's a kind of watered-down darkness; not full-dark but a relentless gloom the eye can't adjust to. Above, beyond, out there in the real world it's a little after noon, the skies a crystalline blue. But *here*, several miles inside the Plantation's perimeter, it's forever dusk beneath the canopy.

François (always Frank to his fellow Rangers) Holt presses on. His headlights splash over upthrusting bluewood trunks, the e-buggy bumping along a rutted track reserved exclusively for Ranger use. Sat-nav confirms specimen SK1842 is dead ahead. On either side, its primary roots arch and twist across the once-fertile soil, reminding him of the fossilised skeleton of some ancient behemoth. He gathers his things and walks the final stretch to the base of the tree.

Your typical bluewood, *Sequoiadendron sequestris,* doesn't do anything by halves. When the bioengineers spliced a healthy dose of redwood genetic stock into its genome, even they were surprised how it outgrew and outpaced its redwood ancestors. SK1842 is only twenty-four years old and already it rises a hundred and thirty metres and spreads nearly eighty. The canopies of neighbouring trees merge into a single, unbroken roof. No tree should grow that tall. Its xylem, the woody vascular tissues responsible for transporting water from root to leaf tip, shouldn't be able to overcome hydrostatic pressure much beyond one-twenty. But there's no explaining biological limits to a bluewood. Sometimes when

Holt stands next to one, he swears he can hear it straining to grow taller, broader, thicker.

What is truly miraculous is how well a bluewood functions as a carbon sink. One healthy bluewood locks up the same volume of atmospheric carbon dioxide as three hundred mature oaks. Carbon sequestration is very much its party trick.

And we're going to need it, Holt reminds himself. Thetford West is one of seventeen established Plantations. Another thirty-two are still fighting their planning battles. The same thing is happening all around the world. Arguably, it's a long way short of what's needed but it's a start. Every bluewood makes a difference.

So if SK1842 and its neighbours are sickening, he's every reason to be worried.

He takes a moment to press his palm against the rough bark of the trunk. The bluish tinge which gives the bluewoods their name, is pronounced. He's no tree-hugger—sentimentality wasn't ever a selection criterion for Plantation Ranger—but he finds this contact calming. It helps him remember why he's doing this. Crazy to think how many metric tonnes of sap are flowing just beneath his hand.

Standing here, he could be in some immense, abandoned cathedral. Bluewood trunks tower upwards until they're lost in the canopy's gloom, every bit as solid and broad as stone pillars. Rarely does sunlight penetrate to the forest floor. His sightline is blocked after a few hundred metres in whichever direction he cares to look, which makes it pretty easy to become disoriented and lost in a Plantation stretching on for mile after mile.

He loves the solitude though, the silence of these majestic trees.

Holt soon has the inspection drone assembled. He spins up its rotors, manoeuvring it around the slab-like branches, rising into the heart of the tree but staying close to the trunk where needle clusters don't grow. When the crick in his neck becomes too much, he switches to the camera view. He jinks the drone left and right, picking a route up through the limbs. He's done this many times before.

What worries him is what the done might reveal. Infrared satellite data has picked out localised hot-spots amongst the canopy, regions that are typically two point eight degrees warmer than the background. Thermal anomalies are often an early indicator of biological distress so if some new disease vector has found its way into the Plantation, the consequences could be catastrophic. There's only one way to be sure—go take a look. Drone footage will reveal any die-back in the canopy and he'll even be able to retrieve bark and needle samples for testing back at—

Wait.

He can hear something odd over the drone's fading whine.

Wind stirring the pine needles...

The call of a bird.

The chitter of some burrowing animal.

Yes, it could be any of these.

But what it really sounds like are the muted whispers of human voices.

He puts the drone into holding mode, dragging his eyes from the screen to stare around the forest floor.

Access to the Plantations is strictly off-limits to the public. This hasn't deterred the anti-eco activists in recent months though. Their activities have begun to escalate beyond peaceful protest to violent acts of eco-terrorism. Mostly it's been live-streamed publicity stunts: holes slashed in the perimeter fence, equipment vandalised, a few *FREE THE LAND, FREE THE PEOPLE* slogans spray painted onto tree trunks. But lately things have turned more violent. An apprentice Ranger was set upon out on patrol and beaten badly enough to land him in hospital. Now senior Rangers like Holt carry a firearm at all times. He's fine with that because he knows what they're doing *matters*. They're fighting for the future of the planet—and if that means defending the bluewoods by force, he's willing to accept the consequences.

He draws his weapon now, slipping the safety off.

Listens again for voices...

Nothing.

If someone's here, they have no shortage of places to hide. Endless ranks of bluewoods stretch into the gloom like some exercise in painting perspective.

Probably he's just imagining things. The oxygen-rich environment within a Plantation can play tricks on the mind. He's even heard other Rangers talk about the Plantation being haunted: that feeling of being watched, of things not quite as they should be. The silence beneath the canopy has a way of playing tricks.

Satisfied, he holsters his weapon. Dragging his eyes back to the controller he resumes the drone's upward flight. The readout shows it eighty-five metres up. Another ten and he'll look for thinning in the canopy where it can punch through into daylight and do the visual inspection. Maybe take a sample or two.

A warning light flashes on the console, signalling torque overload in two of the rotors. It seems the drone has caught on something.

Damn! The drones they use are forest-hardened. Mesh screens protect each of the five rotors from getting tangled in branches so this ought not to have happened. He commands the drone to rotate, to jink forwards and backwards. A third torque warning light comes on.

Definitely stuck fast.

In the final analysis, the equipment is expendable ultimately but he doesn't want to delay the inspection another day, not if there's risk of an endemic disease problem.

He keeps trying until the low battery warning comes on. The camera feed swiftly degrades into noise.

Holt remains motionless in the bluewood's shadow. Something doesn't feel right about this.

He retraces his steps to the e-buggy and uses the powerful searchlight mounted on the roof bar to pan through three-sixty degrees. The only things moving are the shadows cast by the giant trees and their gnarled roots.

What is he missing?

What have I forgotten this time?

Two decades ago...

Holt's running late, mind on another taxing day at the office. The legal firm he works for is understaffed and the paid casework from their over-privileged, undeserving clients leaves little time to advocate for the more worthy causes he favours, those who have no voice.

Naturally, his daughter Ellie has no sense of his urgency, no comprehension of the need to gather her things for school, to be organised just for once, goddammit. And Asha's no help either; long since dressed for work and gone. Not her turn for the school run. Not her problem today.

He bundles his daughter out the door; the mantra of *schoolbooks, lunch bag, gym kit...* recited without much thought. The traffic's bad. Well, of course. It's always bad. He ought to be used to it but today it's just one more thing conspiring against him. He parks further from the school gates than he ought, urging his daughter from the car with a wave of his hand, and—not that she cares—forgetting even to say goodbye.

Forgetting...

Forgetting.

Twelve oh seven (the time forever imprinted on his

memory) and he's called away from a client meeting for an urgent call. It's Asha. Her voice is strained and high-pitched, on the edge of hysteria.

"Did you pack Ellie's nebuliser?"

"I... Uh. I think so."

"*Did* you?"

Did he? He can't honestly remember. He can picture it on the shelf in the kitchen. He would have grabbed it and tucked it into Ellie's school bag along with her lunchbox and smoothie, same as always. Right? Suddenly it becomes the most important thing in the world to remember.

"Has something happened? Is Ellie OK?"

"You bastard." She's sobbing openly. "You selfish, self-obsessed bastard."

"Ash—please. Tell me what's happened."

"She's *dead*, Frank. That's what's happened. She—" Her voice dissolves into a wail.

He can make no sense of her words. She can't be talking about their Ellie. It's not possible.

But now comes the anger and the accusations. "Oh my God! Our beautiful, talented daughter. Dead. Because the fucking air quality bottomed today and she got hit with a bad asthma attack and when her teachers looked for her nebuliser *it wasn't fucking there*. Because you forgot! You, with all that important stuff going on in your brain, you forgot the most important thing."

He has no answer.

Everything changes after that.

He doesn't go back to his meeting. Or his job. Can't face it, can't see the point of what he does any more. It's no hardship, not even the loss of a decent salary. How can that matter when he's lost the most important thing of all?

All because he forgot...

Asha divorces him within six months. The death of a child:

it either forges unbreakable bonds in a relationship or tears it apart; nothing in between.

Frank Holt drifts. He tries to re-evaluate what, if anything matters now. He clings to the realisation (*too late, far too late*) that it's the duty of the current generation not to screw things up for those that follow. If there's to be any kind of future at all, it has to be fought for.

Either that, or you surrender completely.

Dimly he's aware of the seismic political changes taking place. The UN-backed Ninety-Nine Accord dominates the news cycles and the social media agenda. By some miracle, its principles have resonated with a silent majority who are no longer willing to remain silent. Now it's gaining legislative impetus.

Ninety-nine acts of self-preservation, none of them optional; all must be achieved if the damage from global warming is to be contained. It means commitment in the form of ring-fenced funding for decades to come, something that would have been a pipedream just a few years earlier. But it's happening. By God, it really is—and Holt wonders how he can play his part.

It's followed, inevitably, by a backlash. The weaponisation of an anti-green agenda by activist groups like People Before Planet and No Tomorrow, No Regrets takes hold. The activists embody a sense of entitlement to live their lives however they wish with no thought for the environmental consequences. It has popular appeal because if there's one thing humanity has always demonstrated an aptitude for, it's short-termism.

By chance, Holt gets talking to an activist in a seedy, run-down street-corner pub that's seen better days. This is where he goes to seek solitude, drinking alone amongst noisy crowds of strangers. Next to him at the bar, the fellow lone drinker is one of the Displaced, evicted to make way for new eco initiatives after the Ninety-Nine Accord is signed into law. A farmer with nothing left to farm. Holt can see all the fight has gone out of him—and recognises a kindred spirit.

"Bloody government," the man says. Compulsory purchase for his two hundred and seventy acres of arable farmland has ended a livelihood that's been in his family for generations. It's unrecognisable now, covered by one of those rapidly maturing bluewood plantations. By way of compensation, the Accord grants his family an entitlement to a modest city high-rise apartment and a meagre stipend.

"Isn't that a fair deal?" Holt asks. *At least you still have your family.*

"Fair?" The ex-farmer stares at him over his beer, face grizzled and flushed from alcohol. "Didn't you hear what I said? They took my land away. Told me to find some other kind of work. What use is government money if I can't work the land any more like my father and his father before him? It's in my blood. Don't talk to me about the Accord. Some of us have been made to pay too high a price."

"What will you do?" Holt wonders if this is how the PBP eco-terrorists swell their numbers, exploiting an upswell of resentment.

The man shrugs. "Working the land was my calling. How can I ever replace that?"

Holt sees the parallels, both of them searching for something new to believe in.

Not long after, Holt hears the Ranger Corps are recruiting. It's physically demanding work, long hours, crap pay. A million miles from what he's known before.

He applies anyway, is surprised to be accepted, and feels the first faint stirrings of a sense of purpose once again.

It's more than he deserves. He knows that.

But it's something—and that's all that matters.

Two days later, Holt loses another drone.

Like its predecessor, this one rises smoothly between the lower branches which begin ten metres from the ground. All goes well for the next fifty, sixty metres, keeping the drone in the free air close to the trunk. Your typical *S. sequestis* branches every four or five feet, huge branches spiralling around the trunk like some drunken giant's staircase.

He spots something on the camera feed: a silvery slash like a single thread of spider silk. The drone rises past but almost immediately the torque warning lights starts blinking.

Snagged.

Holt swears loudly. For several minutes he tries to work it free but it's no use. He kills the power to save the battery because only fools don't learn from their mistakes. He half expects the drone to come crashing back through the branches but there's only the constant eerie silence of the bluewood plantation.

And that sense of being watched...

Well, this is embarrassing. He can't report another lost drone so soon after the last—plus he really needs to collect those needle samples for analysis back at the labs.

Far above, he can see the drone's navigation light strobing.

He licks his lips. Is he going to do this? Yes, even if it means breaking a few rules. The training manual is very clear about requiring two Rangers to be present for an ascent. That's just common sense. If a climber gets into trouble, their buddy can assist. But sixty metres up into a bluewood? That's nothing really. They often climb into the canopy. It's part of the job: fixing biosensors to monitor local atmospheric gas concentrations or placing marker tags to record growth cycles.

He hasn't brought climbing gear so the only tricky part is starting. The lowest limb of a bluewood is typically ten or fifteen metres from the ground. But the e-buggy can help with that. Once he's up there, the rest will be straightforward. A bluewood's dependable arrangement of limbs makes the actual climb as easy as falling off—Well, no. OK. Not *that*. But as low risk as anything is in this business.

Having deployed the spreader legs, the e-buggy's little cherry-picker platform lofts him just far enough that he can graze fingertips against the lowest limb. There's a tense moment when he has to leap from the wobbling platform, aware that a mistake now means a ten-metre fall onto hardened roots below.

He leaps.

He gets a good hold, using his upper body strength to pull himself up, inhaling the tree's woody perfume as his face presses into the bark. He swings his legs, finds purchase and hauls himself into a sitting position. The cherry-picker rocks but doesn't topple. That's good. He's counting on it to get back down.

Holt crawls back towards the bluewood's trunk where the limb is broadest and begins his ascent. *Three points of contact at all times. Think each move through before you make it.* Ten years ago, he'd have made the climb in half the time but advancing years have slowed him a little. Still, it feels good being up in the branches again. The air is crisp and pine-scented and he feels decades younger. Some of that is down to the elevated oxygen levels: the trees drawing in carbon dioxide and breathing out oxygen. But he's been a Ranger long enough not to let this sense of mild euphoria get the upper hand.

Soon he can see the drone's blinking navigation light between the branches above. It seems to be hanging in mid-air, caught on something he can't make out in the gloom. For one nightmarish moment he imagines some undiscovered species of giant spider living in the canopy, spinning thick silvery webs. It makes a change from his usual nightmares: the rasp of chainsaws biting into wood; the splintering crack of shattering timbers, the earth trembling as a forest giant falls to earth...

The breath catches in his throat.

Isn't that *exactly* the sound he can hear distantly?

Chainsaws.

He stops, forcing himself to take shallow breaths. This is just some hyperoxia-induced hallucination. How can there be anyone else here?

But now the revving of a chainsaw—multiple chainsaws, he realises with dread—is unmistakable.

Far below, figures emerge from the shadows, clambering over roots. Their faces are masked but they call to each other, laughing, making no attempt to disguise their presence.

Sudden anger overcomes any sense of fear or vulnerability. "Stop right there!" Holt bellows from fifty metres up in the tree, like some god on high. "What the hell do you think you're doing?"

A chainsaw-wielding young man stands almost directly below, dressed in camouflage. He stares up at Holt and grins. Something about his arrogant manner convinces Holt this isn't just some protest stunt. These are hardened No Tomorrow eco-terrorists, out to damage and destroy. They have their pick of ten thousand bluewoods and yet they've followed Holt here on purpose. He wonders just what kind of violent act they have in mind to get their message across this time.

As if confirming his suspicions, a second man revs his chainsaw to a high-pitched scream and plunges it sword-like into the bluewood's trunk. Sawdust and sap sprays outwards like a fountain of blood. Holt knows it's only a pinprick in the massive bulk of the bluewood but he swears he can feel the tree shudder beneath him. He draws his weapon, flips the safety off.

"If you do not cease immediately," he yells, "I'm authorised to use force." They're circling below like hyenas.

Someone swings a chainsaw against the extended arm of the cherry-picker. Its whine becomes a howl as metal bites into metal and sparks spray outwards like some insane catherine wheel. Moments later, the platform sags like a cut flower stem.

There goes his only way back down.

He doesn't bother with a warning shot. He aims and fires. One of the figures screams, clutching at his shoulder. The rest dive for cover. Holt shuffles back along the limb for a better view of the ground below. He fires off a few more rounds for good measure.

Now he hears the low whine of the e-buggy starting up and one of the attackers drives it towards the base of the tree, bucking and twisting between giant roots. The cherry-picker arm drags behind like a wounded animal with a broken leg. Finally the e-buggy tips and wedges itself between roots at the base of the tree. Furious with the attackers, Holt is thinking about putting a couple of bullets into the cab when the activist emerges, sprinting fast for cover. The others are pulling back, helping the wounded man to safety, chainsaws idling.

One of them turns and shouts something up at him but Holt can't make out the words, only the laughter from the rest of the group.

Burning...

He flashes back to his other recurring nightmare, the one where the Plantation is ablaze, flames lighting up the night sky for hundreds of miles around.

Goddamn them! He shuffles back along the limb until he can get a good look at the base of the bluewood. Smoke pours from the e-buggy's underfloor battery compartment. In seconds, it's spitting sparks and flames. Those bastards have done something to the batteries, finding a way to short them. Soon it's engulfed in flames and the bodywork begins to warp from the intense heat. And now flames are crawling around the trunk, its dry outer bark peeling away in blackened strips, directing the flames upwards. It won't be long before the bluewood will be well and truly alight—and he's trapped above the flames with no way down unless you count Mother Nature's default option: gravity. He can climb higher, hoping the flames extinguish themselves somehow but he's probably only delaying the inevitable. His only option is to get as low as he can, climb out on a limb as far as he can to clear the seat of the fire and let fate decide whether the fall kills him or not.

He's not sure which hurts most, the thought of losing even one bluewood or trading his own life for a display of ignorant bravado.

It's no less than I deserve. If this could somehow bring Ellie back then he'd do it in a heartbeat. But Holt knows you can't take back the mistakes you've already made. All you can do is try not to make fresh ones.

He braces, feeling the heat from the flames licking upwards. Smoke stings his eyes.

"Here. Let me help you."

The voice, startlingly close, almost makes him lose his grip and fall. Did more activists get up into the tree when he was distracted? He doesn't see how it's possible. A rope ladder dangles a metre in front of him, stretching up into the gloom of the canopy. "Climb," the voice urges from above. "Quickly."

Maybe this really is some oxygen-induced hallucination? Or oxygen *deprivation*, too much smoke breathed in. Or maybe he's just delusional. Does it really matter?

He climbs the ladder.

Strong arms haul him onto a tree limb. There are several figures moving around in the gloom. He's aware of a narrow wooden platform beneath his feet, lashed between branches with rope. This contravenes so many local ordinances he hardly knows where to begin.

There's a sense of quiet organisation amongst the people moving around him. Two young men climb back down the rope ladder he's just ascended, plastic water containers strapped to their back.

"Up," his rescuer urges. "We're in the way here. They need to damp the bark and strip some away to make a fire break."

His rescuer is a young woman. She's dressed in khaki, a knotted olive headscarf holding back shoulder length hair. The four or five figures clambering around in the branches are all wearing dull, khaki colours so that they blend into the canopy shadows. One of them is a middle-aged woman, rolling up blankets and bedding. An older man with long wisps of thinning white hair hauls on a rope, lowering something down to the team working below. Everyone seems entirely comfortable clambering around the branches as though the terrifying drop to the ground below is an irrelevance.

"Who are you?"

The young woman sticks out a hand. "Deena." When Holt doesn't immediately take it, she shrugs and thrusts it back into the pocket of her coveralls.

"What the hell are you doing here?"

She shrugs again. "Living." Gesturing to yet another rope ladder, she says, "Climb."

This next platform is broader, its segments closely fitting the shape of the spreading branches, like some giant, multi-level patio-decking. There are more people. Holt can scarcely credit it. Someone hand-cranks a lantern, providing a modicum of illumination. There's a lot of activity: more bedding being rolled up, pots and pans gathered, items thrust into backpacks—all being done with no fuss and very little talking; hand signals flash amongst the group. He's beginning to understand how so many people—he's counted at least a dozen now—can have been hiding in this bluewood without him hearing. Ghosts. Maybe the stories weren't so far-fetched.

"We should cross now," Deena says quietly, gesturing into thin air.

Cross? He's no idea what she's talking about. Smoke is drifting lazily up through the branches, making his eyes water. He wonders if they really can quench the fire before it takes hold. He hopes so. Deena passes him a rucksack, indicating he should put it on. It's heavy and the contents rattle as he shoulders it. Plates? Utensils? Before he can ask more questions, she shins up another rope ladder. Reluctantly, and because there seems no sensible alternative, he follows.

Two branches up and there's a broad wooden platform encircling the bluewood's trunk, the largest yet. Positively spacious. He notes the double strand of rope serving as a guard rail around the edge. Several canvas tents are pitched next to each other. Something that looks like a cooking griddle with two bubbling saucepans rests in the centre of the platform. A cable snakes out along a branch and he sees a mesh of flexible solar panels spread within the canopy. A child, no more than seven or eight, skips past trailing a thin harness dangling from the branch above.

"This can't be real," Holt mutters. How can this sprawling campsite be right under the Rangers' noses without anyone knowing?

"It's real," Deena confirms. Nearby, a woman with short-cropped hair and tattooed arms pulls on some near-invisible thread like a mime artist hauling on an anchor. It craws across a rope from god-knows-where in the canopy. She keeps hauling. Attached are thicker ropes interwoven with short lengths of spacer cord. The rope ends are secured through rings that have been driven into the bluewood's bark and just like that there is a rope walkway stretching off into the void, its far end obscured by the canopy. There's a double strand to walk on and thinner ropes above and either side acting as guardrails. The far end is hidden by canopy.

Now he's starting to understand what snared his drone.

A man and a woman step confidently out on the rope bridge, push through the canopy and are lost from sight. The child he saw a moment ago follows as though it's the most natural thing in the world. The ropes sag and groan as they take up the strain.

"Now you."

"Where?"

"Neighbouring tree. Just a precaution."

They have rope bridges between the bluewoods. Holt has a sudden mental image of a network of tree platforms connected by ropes that can be drawn across or hidden as necessary. He imagines an entire population of tree-dwellers moving silently about in the canopy, tree to tree: a village in the sky, shielded above and below by the bluewood canopy. Clearly these people aren't eco-terrorists. Yet these are the very trees he is supposed to be protecting. These people are undermining what he has sworn to protect.

He pushes into the canopy, trying to ignore the slap of needles against his face, concentrating instead on not letting his boots slip from the rope. At the boundary between the two bluewoods, he catches a glimpse of darkening skies. Beneath his feet, the ground is staggeringly far below.

On the other side, there's a welcoming committee. A ruddy faced man, seventy if he's a day, looks at him warily through half-lidded eyes. The handshake is perfunctory. "Name's Josh Faraday. You've already met my daughter, Deena, I understand. So you're the Ranger they rescued? Hope you understand what we're risking by saving your neck." He shakes his head. "You Rangers need to do a better job of security. These eco-terrorists are getting bolder. And they'll be back. You know that, don't you?"

Holt feels pushed onto the defensive. "We do everything we can with limited resources. But—" he levels a finger at the man standing before him, "You're in no position to criticise with your flagrant violations of Plantation land."

The man gives him a weak smile. "This was our land long before the first pine cones were ever planted. Oh, I understand right enough why we need the bluewoods—but no one gave enough thought to those who were pushed off the land."

Holt looks around. More platforms were lashed across tree-limbs, linked by ladders and ropes in a three-dimensional tangle perfectly adapted to the tree's layout. And more people; at least twenty that he can see.

"How long have you been here?"

"Eighteen months, near enough."

Holt's jaw drops. "No—"

"We're spread across seven bluewoods now." Faraday wags a finger. "Not one of them is damaged by our presence. We respect the bluewoods, just as we respect nature. It's why we came back, after all."

"How can you survive, hidden away in the treetops?"

"Seems we manage. We harvest sunlight for our energy needs, store rainwater to drink. Heat it for cooking and bathing. It's true we have to bring in food and some other supplies by foot every few weeks but we're looking to change that." He nods to a makeshift greenhouse of plastic sheeting along one edge of the platform where a thin shaft of daylight penetrates the canopy. Inside Holt can see rows of wooden planters filled with a variety of plants. "Give us time."

Holt shakes his head. "This is madness."

A young man steps off the rope bridge and murmurs something in Faraday's ear. He nods. "Fire's dying down, so that's something. Bluewoods are tough. It's the tannic acid in the sap, helps protect them from fire. Did you know that?"

Holt face twists. "It may have come up in Ranger training."

A small child tugs on his arm to get his attention. The girl has large green eyes set in a freckled, heart-shaped face. She reminds him so strongly of Ellie that for an instant he feels the knife twist deep in his chest, the one that never goes away, and he stifles a gasp. Shyly, she presents him with his inspection drone, making a formal offering of it.

"You think you're being clever but we saw your thermal signature," he tells Faraday. "No matter how you try to stay hidden, it was only a matter of time before you'd be discovered."

Faraday shrugs.

Holt draws his weapon slowly, keeping the safety on. "I know I'm outnumbered and God knows this isn't a good place to pick a fight with anyone, but I have a sworn duty to protect the Plantation. We're Rangers. We have to keep the bluewoods safe. Future generations are depending on it. I'm sorry, but I'm going to have to escort you all off the Plantation, no matter how noble you think your intentions are."

"Noble? Is that what you think this is?" Faraday's gaze is unflinching. He's ignoring the gun as though it's an irrelevance. (Which it probably is, given Holt's pretty sure he fired all the chambered rounds in trying to scare off the eco-terrorists. He wonders if Faraday knows that.)

Faraday shrugs. "Our fate's in your hands. It's the price we pay for saving your life. But let me ask one thing. At least hear me out. There's something I want to show you. Come." He doesn't wait for an answer, ascending a narrow rope ladder that is lashed to the bluewood's central trunk. None of the others on the platform are paying Holt much attention. They're getting on quietly with various jobs: stacking items salvaged from the neighbouring bluewood, coiling ropes, stirring ingredients into a fresh cookpot heating up on another solar-powered grill. On a lower platform, by the light of a solar-powered lamp he can see a couple of pre-schoolers crayoning pictures under the watchful eye of a teenage girl.

Holt knows better than anyone the colossal size of a single bluewood but he would never have believed so many people can hide themselves away like this. Comparisons to a city sky-rise grown from seed are more apt than he ever realised.

Holt climbs after Faraday, marvelling at the man's athleticism for someone twenty years his senior.

They're high in the canopy now. The bluewood's trunk, tens of metres in girth at is base, is slim enough that his arms completely encircle it. Faraday squats on a spreading branch near the apex, legs dangling. He motions Holt to join him. Noticing Holt's hesitation, he says, "No head for heights, Ranger Holt?"

"The only thing that scares me is the paperwork I'll be filling out for months when word of this gets out."

It's dusk now. The perpetual internal gloom of the canopy is replaced by dark purple striations in a near-cloudless sky. He's lost all sense of time; easy to do inside the Plantation.

From their perch, they have a bird's-eye view across the unbroken canopy of bluewoods rolling into the distance. On the south-western horizon the lights of the London skyscrapers twinkle in the haze.

"I can't go back. None of us are prepared to do that. We're not city people, Ranger Holt. Never were."

"Then where?" Holt asks.

Silence.

In the distance, the Thames is a swollen glint of reflected light showing where the river has permanently overflowed its banks and spilled out across ancient floodplains.

"The Ninety-Nine Accord is this crazy, desperate last act of self-preservation. Don't you think?" Faraday asks. "I'm amazed it's found the support it has but I also can't help wondering if we truly understand the stakes. It's not some à la carte menu that humanity gets to pick and choose from. We have to embrace all ninety-nine initiatives, no ifs, no buts, or we might as well give up now. The big *and* the little. *All of them.* I can't help wondering if we'll stay the course."

"We have to."

Faraday gives an ironic chuckle. "Bluewood Plantations aren't even in the top ten."

"You believe in the Accord though? You support it?"

"Yes." Faradays looks pained. "Though there was a time when I might have said otherwise. It's humanity last chance. The last roll of the dice."

"Die," Holt corrects, some pedantic part of his brain still alive and well.

"Yes. There's always that option." The old man's laughter rings out incongruously through the treetops.

"Plenty more will join us if we put the word out. Not just the displaced but those who want to live in harmony with the planet. Those who care about the future more than the present." He inhales deeply and Holt, too, feels the buzz from ultra-oxygenated air. At this moment, everything seems possible, no dream too far-fetched.

"A few years back," Faraday says, with the ease of someone settling into a familiar story, "I met a man who thought he'd lost everything. You could see the hopelessness in his eyes. He'd lost the most important thing in his life and utterly blamed himself. He couldn't see any kind of future. Just like me. My father's and my grandfather's lands had been taken away. Fields and hedges ploughed up; villages torn down stone by stone. The first bluewood saplings grew where only the year before there had been fields of wheat and barley, cattle grazing on green pasture. *Not needed now,* they said. *Not now we have intensive protein factories to keep the population fed. And we don't need you.*

"We drank a toast to worthlessness, he and I, both thinking we had nothing left. We were wrong. When you've lost something vital, you have to find something else that matters just as much and rebuild your life around it. And you know what?" Faraday's eyes twinkled with amusement. "I heard not long after he signed up for the Ranger Corps. Found a new purpose."

Holt stares at the man. "I thought your face seemed familiar... I remember you now."

"Friend, we've both been doing what we needed to survive, with one eye on future generations."

Holt lets out a slow breath. He's bone weary but if he closes his eyes, he's afraid the world might start spinning and never stop. "This isn't up to me."

"We're as much guardians of the bluewoods as the Rangers. We've chosen to make our homes here. No one is more invested in protecting them than our community. You said yourself there aren't enough Rangers to safeguard the Plantations. And it's only getting worse. Support for eco-terrorists grows day by day. All the disenchanted people tired of paying their green taxes and doing without a few luxuries that previous generations enjoyed so thoughtlessly. These attacks will come more often. So let us help! We'll act as new guardians of the bluewoods—a constant presence, living in symbiosis with the trees we protect."

Holt thinks about what his superiors will say. It goes against everything they stand for. It will need a complete change of perspective and most people he knows don't handle change well.

"Be our advocate. Explain how all this could be made to work with the right political will. Your voice will count for something."

Holt looks out across the bluewood plantation. Trees almost as far as the eye can see—and still only a tiny proportion of what's needed if they're going to give the planet back its lungs and help it breath again. Each mature bluewood sequesters fifty tonnes of carbon, and that's not nothing, not when scaled up across the continents.

If Ellie were here, what would she say about all this? He knows the answer instinctively.

"An advocate? Yes, I can do that much," he tells Faraday. "As for the rest, we'll have to see."

Through the Crimson Forest

David Mancera
translated by Monica Louzon

My name is T'shamiie, I have thirteen summers, and I am a !Kung. My mother brought me into the world during the era of the Fire People.

The !kolonisêrere call us bosmān: the forest people. We used to live in Brorē Forest, and we lived off him, off his creatures and his fruits. These days, however, the forest and the wetlands are shrinking, little by little, with each dry season. We spend more and more time in the desert.

The scorched prairie is a place not only of death, but also of silence. The fire gobbled up its grasses and weeds in a raging fury, leaving in its wake only the sheer absence of sound. All we hear now are our footsteps, which are as light as Brorē |Darub's nighttime wanderings, while we traverse the lands of our ancestors, trying to find a clearing in the forest that hasn't yet been devoured by flames.

Whenever we finally reach one, we make camp and go hunting. On good days, we return with a bo‡kēthat we share among the tribe, filling everyone with hope. On not-so-good days, we dip our arrowheads in a paste made from venomous beetles and use them to hunt monkeys taking refuge in the trees, or we subsist on the remains of the last hunt or even eat carrion. On bad days, which most days are, we have only mongongo nut, monkey bread, or whatever we can find to eat in the ash-covered meadows.

Perhaps that's why our women almost never sing anymore, and why our young men no longer dance when we light our fire each night. Instead, the few old women still with us clear their irritated throats and share stories of another life.

Ouma Bootshou is one of those old women. She likes to talk about the days when ǁGûb Sores was so bright that, if you looked at him for too long, his light would take up residence in your head and leave you blind. Ouma Bootshou says that the smoke and ashes cover ǁGûb Sores with a red veil to rob him of his soul.

The men and women pay attention to her, but many of them laugh. The other old women cry silently. They say that they can no longer remember the colour blue. I don't think I've ever seen anything blue. Everything is grey, or black, or red.

There are few who remember a time when the sky wasn't black or red, a time it was woven from dozens of colours during the daytime and sparkling at nighttime with thousands of stars, which are now covered by the smoke and ashes, too.

Few of us have ever breathed air not impregnated with those ashes. These days, the air is so hot and heavy that it burns your eyes and devours you from the inside out if you let even a whiff of it into your nose.

There are few—very few—!Kung who've ever walked through a meadow that smelled of life instead of soot, a place where the calls of birds and beasts still resonated.

Brorē Xami no longer roars across our lands. Only the cruel, strange wind does that. Time and time again, the wind twists itself into dark swirls so tall that not even Brorē ǂKhoab could touch their tops with his trunk.

There are no lions left. Or elephants. Or rhinoceroses.

Perhaps once a season, when we're lucky, we encounter a herd of buffalo—although each time, they're smaller.

The leopard, however, is still out there. Ouma Bootshou says that it doesn't surprise her because Brorē |Darub walks between two worlds. When he can't find prey in ours, he needs only to cross to the other side to feed on the beasts there. She says the night has always been his kingdom, even before the Fire People returned.

Oupa Kayate says that this is all the fault of the !koloṇisêrere and the batsuana.

He says that at first, they called the forests "preserves" and prohibited us from hunting in them. Then, they forced our children to go to their schools, so that our young would forget our tongue. And now, they are the reason the world burns, and each day more and more Fire People sneak into it.

One time, I asked Oupa Kayate why the !kolonisêrere are to blame for the world burning, but he didn't know how to explain it to me. "It's their fault, because everything is their fault."

When we notice the fire drawing too close, or when we've gone too many days without a successful hunt, Hōfe Wame orders us to move camp.

In the grey and black desert, which reeks of woodsmoke and calcinated bones, you can look in almost any direction without encountering any obstacles. Only to the east is the flat horizon interrupted, cut by the serrated silhouettes of distant mountains.

Hōfe Wame stays away from them. Ouma Bootshou tells us that many moons ago, the Fire People entered the world through one of those mountains.

That day, we crossed paths with one of our cousin tribes, the ǂAkhoe —or what was left of them.

The ǂAkhoe gave up hunting to dedicate themselves to pastures. They have always watched us over their shoulders, because we have never owned cattle and instead live off all the animals we kill—all except for Brorē |Nerab, who eats the meat of our dead and returns them to the earth.

Now, there's no grass for the cattle and the ǂAkhoe are trying to regain their expertise with the bow and spear, but it's not possible to acquire lifetimes of skill in just a few seasons.

Hōfe Wame gathered us for a council. We decided to share the previous day's hunt with the ‡Akhoe: we still had half-eaten bones of a large bo‡kē, which were covered with meat and overflowing with tasty marrow. In exchange, the ‡Akhoe gave us tobacco and several bottles of snâps.

That night, when Ouma Bootshou's eyes were watery and her steps so weak that it seemed like she might fall on the ground if she took another step, she told us about her first encounter with a Fire Person.

"I was very young," she said, then added, "My breasts still looked at the sky instead of the ground."

We laughed.

"There were already frequent fires, although not everything, everywhere was burning all at once yet. The rainy season was short, but every tribe had someone who assured the rest that such things happen sometimes. The heat grew more intense, but there was always someone who swore they'd lived through more torrid days. Be that as it may, this had always been our home and here we would stay, no matter what happened.

"The highlands were not yet taboo, nor was Bo‡kēMountain, which the !kolonisêrere called Pilanesberg after one of the batsuana chiefs.

"I've already mentioned that I was young. I was also curious, and it's just as important to listen to the experiences of old women as it is to give free reign to the curiosity of young girls.

"One day, when the camp was close enough to the hills, I decided to look for berries. My legs and my heart were as strong as those of the animal that gave Bo‡kēMountain its name. I started walking before dawn, and by midday, I had already made it to the peak, which was as flat as the face of ‖Gûs Darêsores. When I reached the rim, I set down my basket, sprawled out on the warm ground, and looked over the edge.

"Believe me, contemplating a volcano of that size, even one long-dormant, takes the air out of your lungs. I felt like the whole world could fit inside that opening, which was as enormous and round as if ‖Gûb Sores had sat there to rest during his daily journey through the sky.

"I don't know for how long I stayed there like that, but I do know it was for quite a while. I felt compelled to memorize every detail. I think part of me wanted to stay there forever.

"At last, after the sun had already started to set, I began my own descent. Although I went as quickly as I could, I reached the edges of our encampment well after nightfall. Luckily, ‖Gûs Darêsores illuminated my path, but I couldn't stop thinking about how worried my own father and mother — ‖gûb and ‖gûs—would be. Or how furious. Surely, I thought, they'd be both.

"I had a bad feeling when I caught a glimpse of the glowing bonfires. Some ancestor was looking out for me and touched my shoulder to warn me of approaching danger. I threw myself to one side and hid myself among the branches of a small | nanub tree, taking advantage of a cloud's shadow veiling ‖Gûs Darêsores's face.

"I waited for a long time. I could feel my heart pounding in my throat, and I was sure it was so loud that whoever was nearby would hear it.

"Just as I began asking myself whether all those hours I'd spent lying under ‖Gûb Sores had made me hallucinate, I saw him. At first, he was only a small disturbance among the vegetation, like a shimmer of heat cast by a campfire upon Brorē Oms!hais's trunk, but the longer I stared in his direction, the brighter he grew.

"I watched him through the undergrowth. He was neither !Kung nor !uri, nor did he carry a lamp or torch, but rather something very different. He was a man, yes, but the light wasn't coming from anything he carried. It was coming from his own skin.

"Despite my fear, I waited until he was closer. I was breathing so rapidly that I was convinced that he'd hear me this time. He wore no clothes or animal skins. Dancing lights ran over each of his muscles as if someone had tossed a jar of fireflies onto him.

"I stayed very quiet, holding my breath as he passed only a few rods from me, heading toward the camp. Once he was gone, I rose and took off running, making a loop to put distance between us so our paths wouldn't cross.

"When I arrived home, ǁgûs was furious and ǁgûb had tears in his eyes. They must have seen something in my face, though, because instead of scolding me, they let me talk. I don't even remember what I told them. I imagine it was probably a string of nonsense. Despite my incoherence, some men went out to take a look but returned swearing that there hadn't been anyone near the encampment.

"I fell asleep when ǁGûb /Khomi began to brighten, as the deep voice of my ǁgûb murmured assurances that everything would be OK. When I woke a little later, it all seemed like a bad dream, but I was sure that wasn't the case.

"Time would prove me right. When the fire became never-ending and the meadow slowly transformed into an ossuary, others saw the Fire People, too. I myself encountered them on two more occasions.

"And that's why, ever since, the mountains have been taboo for the !Kung."

With that, Ouma Bootshou stretched out an arm, seized a bottle of snâps, and took a long swig. She remained by the fire and didn't speak again for the rest of the night.

I stayed there and watched her for a long time, while the adults kept drinking and smoking. There was something in her eyes, something more than just an alcohol-induced glow,

226

more than the bitter memory she'd just relived. Perhaps the same ancestor that had looked out for her in her youth whispered something into my ear, because just as I knew ‖Gûb Sores would rise above the horizon in a few hours, red like a flock of crimson bee-eaters, I knew that Ouma Bootshou wasn't telling us everything.

When the rising sun traces the dark silhouette of the mountains, Hōfe Wame approaches calls for the council with his raspy voice.

Only ten days earlier, I'd caught my first prey: a hare that I'd struck with one of my arrows. The leader of my hunting group, Quoqkwe—a man neither very old, nor very young—had rewarded me with a bit of painted dog blood, which would loosen my feet before each hunt, and gave me the right to join the council.

Thus, when I hear Hōfe Wame's voice, I hurry to get a good spot, though not so quickly that I don't have time to cast a superior glance at the children who had, until just recently, been my peers.

"Eight days have passed since we last ate meat," Hōfe Wame says, speaking slowly. "The women have to climb to the highest reaches of the baobabs to find any monkey bread, which is always dry or scorched, and they have not found any berries or nuts in the dying meadow."

He falls silent for a moment and scans our faces. We nod and murmur in agreement, because everything he said is true.

"It's been two seasons since we were in the North, and during the last rains we tried the South as well, with the same luck." He makes wide gestures with his arms, pointing in each direction. "Many tribes have fled from the West, where it seems things are worse than anywhere else."

Hōfe Wame pauses again, as if he needs to gather his strength for what comes next. "I know what you're thinking.

And you all know that I've done everything possible to avoid it." He raises his voice a little, although he doesn't stop speaking slowly. "We have no other recourse but to try our luck in the hills."

Our murmuring voices grow louder.

"The mountains have never done anything to us. The !kolonisêrere from the nearby farms will be the real danger. We will cross the preserve as quickly as we can and continue until we reach !Krokedil Refir. Do you concur?"

We're all scared, but no one dares say no. Hōfe Wame has been a good leader since old Gakebe was trapped by the fire. No one could do anything for him.

"Good," proclaims Hōfe Wame, settling the matter. "We will overnight in the preserve's centre, by the lagoon. ‖Gûs Darêsores willing, at dawn, when the animals come near to drink, we'll catch some meat. We will go swiftly today. Take care of one another."

When it moves, a !Kung tribe is like a big circle that leaves no one on the outside.

At midday, we reach a small village called Witrandjie. With some difficulty, I read the name on a rusty sign. I think it means "white edge". Hōfe Wame spits at the ground. He gestures for us to pick up the pace. We advance in single file down the dirt road surrounding the village. Ouma Bootshou is at the back, exhaling great blowing breaths to maintain her rhythm.

She makes a face at me and indicates the houses with her chin. "Have you noticed?"

"Noticed what, Ouma?"

She doesn't respond right away. She needs the air to walk.

"We've been on this road for a good while and we haven't seen a single one of their… what do you call them?"

"Cars," I reply, realizing that she's right. "Or any

motorcycles or trucks."

She nods.

There's nothing else to say.

Bo‡kē Mountain, the place where Ouma Bootshou saw the Fire Person, isn't actually a mountain, but rather a collection of hills spread out in three concentric rings, all higher than the surrounding plains.

When I was in the batsuana school, a Muslim professor told us about it: it was a volcano that never fully erupted. The magma grew cold beneath the Earth and the ground collapsed upon itself. Erosion over millions of years gave it the shape it has today.

More or less in the centre, what remained of the volcanic caldera formed a lake about two kilometres long and one kilometre wide, which is where we're heading now. The Bantu park guards typically bring wealthy !uri there on fishing holidays.

When we enter the strange rocky formation, we see that the fire has passed through at some point, too, calcinating the vegetation like it has everywhere else, although this forest has recovered quickly. Green sprinkles poke through the greys and blacks here and there.

Just as Hōfe Wame predicted, we reach the lagoon as ‖Gûb Sores begins to hide himself behind our backs and the three circles of hills whose centre we're approaching.

His russet splendour casts long shadows before us, as if our darkest selves are hurrying ahead to reach their destination. After one last slope, the earth descends again toward the ancient caldera. Ouma Bootshou and I trail the group, a little behind the rest. We hear their nervous murmurs, which put us on guard, and when we finally reach the slope, we understand their anxiety.

The lagoon isn't there.

Vivid Worlds

There's just a hole where it once was. The stones are brownish, for the mosses covering them have begun to dry out, too. A host of red sparks abruptly sprinkle the crater's sides. I'm horrified and hold my breath as I realize what I'm seeing: the last light of the day, reflecting off the skins of amphibians and the scales of dead fish.

We're all afraid when we notice that Hōfe Wame's paralyzed, too. He has no idea what to do. Ouma Bootshou walks up to him and whispers something in his ear. At last, he nods.

"This is not a good place to rest," he declares, voice breaking. "We must continue onward while there's still some light left."

We resume our trek. At the edge of the dried-up lagoon, a tenuous movement catches my attention. In the approximate centre of the ancient caldera, a fine fumarole protrudes. It rises for a few meters, emitting smoke that's more grey than black from a narrow crack until the soft sunset breeze dispels it.

I think about telling Hōfe Wame, but there's no need. He clearly saw it, too, because he picks up the pace until it's as if he's forgotten the most important rule of the !Kung: we leave only our dead behind.

He doesn't allow us to stop until well after nightfall.

Once I've massaged Ouma Bootshou's aching legs and feet for a long time, I collapse beside her. I'm so tired that I expect to fall asleep immediately, but that's not the case. Ouma Bootshou's breathing, however, quickly changes into soft snores.

We're at the edge of the circle of reclining bodies, away from the only fire that Hōfe Wame allowed us to light tonight. He and Quoqkwe have stayed awake, keeping watch outside the encampment, looking back toward the dry lagoon that we've left behind.

After changing position a hundred times, I decide to take a walk. The last thing I want is for Hōfe Wame to scold me, not now that I'm a hunter in the eyes of the tribe, so I head east, away from the dead lagoon.

There will be six more days before ‖Gûs Darêsores is full again, but I've been careful not to look at the fire tonight, so her silver light is more than enough to help me avoid irregularities in the ground. After one hundred paces, I stop to urinate against a dark stump. Then, I walk another fifty or sixty paces until I can't see the glow of our camp behind me anymore.

The night is chilly even though the wind has stopped blowing, but my cape of !goreb skin is enough protection against the cold. In the near darkness, I select what looks like a young acacia tree and sit with my back against its thin trunk. The tree is smooth and soft to the touch, as if it grew after the last fire and still hasn't seen a flame before. I tilt my face upward, bathing in ‖Gûs Darêsores's light. The Arrowhead's stars are halfway below the zenith, pointing toward the horizon.

A resinous scent inundates my nasal passages as I inhale, and I smile. I think about my mother—or rather, the idea of my mother, because I can't remember her. Ouma Bootshou told me that we had to leave her behind when I was only a few days old. I close my eyes.

When I open them, I look at the stars and panic. The Arrowhead is sinking behind the dark silhouettes of the hills. If Ouma Bootshou wakes and doesn't see me at her side, she'll raise the alarm and I'll be in big trouble.

I rise and orient myself. Although it's nearly time for ‖Gûb Sores to rise, there's no trace of him. I start walking toward the camp, but I hear a noise behind me. I turn.

Perhaps ten meters away, frozen as if she's as surprised

to see me as I, her, is the most beautiful creature I've ever encountered.

Ouma Bootshou's words ring in my head: The light didn't come from anything he carried with him, but rather from his own skin.

Only, she's not a man, but a young woman whose ember-like eyes are fixed on mine as the light from a jar of fireflies races over her body.

The creature begins walking toward me and I try to run, but it's as if my feet don't belong to me anymore—no, it's my brain, refusing to order my feet to move.

That's when I realize I'm not afraid, just curious.

It seems like the girl approaching me feels the same way about me, because a smile forms on her luminous face.

When she reaches me, I realize the fireflies illuminating her are actually fine threads of light moving beneath her skin the way blood runs through veins beneath my own. Her hair, which is much longer than mine, coils in curly loops. Two cute little spiralling horns—like those of an bo‡kē, but much smaller—grow between her curls.

The smile on her face widens, and I relax. There's nothing to fear.

I notice something else, something as surprising to me as everything else about this strange creature: the feeling that we've already met before.

She raises her left hand. It hangs in the air before me, as if she's asking permission to finish the gesture. I nod and then feel the softness of her palm on my shoulder.

Her touch is so light that I barely note its weight. The contact of her skin on mine sends an intense shiver through me that races down my back and makes the hair at the nape of my neck stand on end.

The world around me disappears. There exists only her hand on my shoulder and her voice in my head, a voice that's speaking to me in a language I don't know but somehow creates ideas and forms images that I can understand.

The first of these ideas is that she recognizes me. She's smiling because she has realized we're family.

My shock gives way to understanding as a story that plays out in my consciousness, like a shadow theatre on dried skin.

I see a woman with Ouma Bootshou's face, without any of the wrinkles engraved in it now.

I see two lovers looking for one another, because it's their destiny, although they know their love will bring them disgrace.

I hear shouts of intense pain, followed by the cries of a newly born child.

I feel a tribe's fear of a little girl with luminous skin, who is as strange and as feared as if she were born albino.

I hear the wails of a mother abandoning her daughter to another tribe, one that will accept the child, in another world, one that has been biding its time.

I watch as the same story repeats itself many seasons later, though inverted. This time, it's a boy born without luminous skin and the girl now plays the role of his mother. Like her own mother, she leaves the little dark-skinned boy with a tribe from another world, the one whose cycle is ending.

The enchantment enveloping me dissipates.

When my sight returns, I see that the girl is holding one of my hands. Her eyes shine brighter than before, as if the fire within them has been fed with fresh wood.

Mine are full of tears.

Without needing to speak, I know that she and I are children of the same woman. I also know that we inhabit worlds condemned to reject one another so that hers can live and mine can end.

When she withdraws her hand from my shoulder, her smile fades. She must have realized what I've just understood, perhaps because she's read it in my mind. I curse myself for not knowing how to keep the sadness already consuming me from spreading to her.

She takes a couple of hurried steps backward and then turns and runs away.

I wipe away my tears and return to camp.

Ouma Bootshou is awake. She's waiting for me, calmly, as if she knew what was going to happen and wanted to make sure it went well. She interrogates me with only her gaze.

When I sit beside her, she extends a hand and touches my cheek with one finger—right where my tears had been moments earlier. I clench my teeth to keep myself from crying again, reminding myself that I am a hunter.

In the firelight—which someone must have fed overnight— Ouma Bootshou closes her eyes, as if giving me permission to take all the time I need.

"Why didn't you ever tell me?" I ask.

"What good would it have done? You would have spent your life hating your mother. She only did what she had to. If you have to hate someone, hate me."

I reflect on her words, growing even angrier as I realize she's right.

"Who are they?" I ask.

"Another race, much older than ours. They needed another world, different from ours, to survive. The world that it was before this one. The Muslims have a name for them."

I remember my classes, the stories that our teacher told us many times. "Efrit."

Ouma nods. "When the earth changed, the Efrit hid and waited. Now, the world is transforming again and they are returning."

"But it's all because of climate change, Ouma. Oupa Kayete is right. It's the !kolonisêrere's fault. Everything burns because of what they're doing to the planet."

"This fire will be our end, my son, but it's also her rebirth. The opposite thing happened before. We invented agriculture and we raised cattle. Humans built cities and spread everywhere—except for the !Kung, who remain the same even today. The Fire People became things of legend, forgotten."

"What happened to you?" I ask.

She takes a long time to answer. "I was young, maybe two years older than you are now. What do you think happened to me, T'shamiie?"

I respond immediately. "You fell in love with him."

She smiles and puts one hand on my chest. "One day, you'll feel something like that. Perhaps even with one of them, though our cycle will end in time. Tell me, how was it, what you saw today?"

I look at her, shocked. I thought she already knew.

"She was a girl. She told me that she's my… sister."

For a moment, Ouma Bootshou's smile disappears from her face, but when what I've just told her sinks in, it comes back even stronger.

"Another grandchild," she murmurs, closing her eyes. "I have another granddaughter."

At that moment, Hōfe Wame's voice echoes forcefully. ǁGûb Sores has begun climbing the hills.

While we pack up camp, I can't shake the feeling that Ouma Bootshou is different, even rare. I suspect it's because she still remembers that other world that now only exists for her.

When we begin marching, she takes the last place but urges me to walk ahead with the other hunters. My pride blinds me.

I don't realize her true intention.

No one misses her until we stop, hours later, outside the last ring of hills.

A Prayer on Rosary Peas

Kay Hanifen

I watched as the attendants loaded piles of plants onto the airship followed by my colleagues discussing them like prized pooches at the Westminster Dog Show.

"I bred my hydrangeas to be edible while keeping their colour."

"My new species of wheat is far more drought resistant and nutritional than any other staple crop—aside from potatoes, of course."

"My bioluminescent oak trees are cutting down on light pollution in my town."

I was content to just watch them interact. The idea of a botany convention would put most people to sleep, but I'm fascinated by the ways that plants work. We used to think of them as mindless things, but over the course of the past few centuries, we've learned that many they have an intelligence of their own that exists on a time scale we cannot even begin to imagine. Pleasing the plants was our first step in healing the rest of the planet.

My wife, Michael, sidled up to me, her solar powered wheelchair whirring to a stop. "Ready, Sasha?"

I smiled, clutching my tablet to me like a shield. I felt like a child on the first day of school—anxious, insecure, and braced for rejection by my peers. It was my first convention post doctorate, and I was mostly there to observe. I hadn't had anything published yet, but my studies on the benefits of belladonna as a pain killer were promising. More than anything, though, I felt like a kid sitting at the adult's table. But I'm sure everyone feels that way. No matter your age or expertise, there's always someone older and wiser. There will probably be interns and research assistants looking at me the same way I look at the preeminent scientists of my field.

Michael nudged me playfully. "You're in your head again, honey."

I blinked and shot her an embarrassed smile. "Sorry."

"Don't be. They're gonna see you like I see you: a brilliant scientist, a witty conversationalist, and someone as meticulous and observant as Sherlock Holmes."

My cheeks warmed at the onslaught of compliments. "Stop," I said, which, in married couple speak, actually meant, *keep complimenting me; I love it, but I'm too embarrassed to admit it.*

She took my hand and kissed it. "Come on. Your debut awaits."

I followed her up the ramp, my heart pounding in my chest. The flight across the Atlantic was going to take twenty-five hours, so we headed to our sleeper cabins, passing by the dining hall where my colleagues milled about. It used to be that direct flights from New York to Norway took about eight hours. What we had in speed, we lost in comfort and environmental health. Eight hours of being crammed into a plane with barely any legroom, choking down the equivalent of TV dinners, and trying to watch a movie over the din of the engines. We took the wonder and miracle of human flight and made it into hell. Zeppelins may take longer to get to their destination, but we can wonder at the views, mill about, sleep on actual beds, eat real food, and enjoy movies and TV at a far more reasonable volume. We still have airplanes, of course, for emergency trips where someone may not have the hours a slow journey like this might need, but most people prefer comfort over speed when they can get it.

Dropping our carryon in our rooms, we applied our nametags and headed over to the lounge where many of my other colleagues relaxed. One of the flight attendants stood at the snack bar offering free food and drinks. I grabbed us both some sodas, chips, and sweets while Michael found the nearest friendly face to start a conversation. I always admired that about her. She could enter a room full of strangers and leave it with lifelong friends. I've always been on the quiet side, preferring the simple needs of plants to the complexities of people. She waved me over to where a heterosexual couple sat sipping their drinks.

"Sasha, this is Gabe and Marie. Gabe and Marie, this is my lovely wife, Sasha."

The couple wore nametags much like ours with Gabe's pronouns being he/him and Marie's being she/her. Marie offered a hand to shake, her sleeve falling back to reveal a bracelet inlaid with red beads in an intricate pattern. Something about the beads looked familiar, but she spoke before I could ask about it. "It's a pleasure to meet you. Michael's been telling us all about your work with belladonna-based pain killers."

"I'm working on making it safer to use in higher doses," I said, taking my seat and handing Michael a bag of chips and her soda. "We've known about these properties for centuries, but because it's famous for being poisonous, no one wants to touch it."

"Are you interested in dangerous plants?" Gabe asked.

And here it is. Whenever I tell people about my area of study, they joke about me potentially poisoning them. Everyone seems to think there's something wrong with me for studying these misunderstood plants. It's not their fault if someone eats them and gets sick. I've made several entomologist and herpetologist friends by complaining about it. "I think they're largely misunderstood. We treat them like they're evil and should be eliminated, but that comes from a place of ignorance. Like anything alive, you have to treat it with care and respect."

Marie nodded thoughtfully. "Gabe's the botanist. I'm a nuclear physicist, and that's my philosophy for dealing with radioactive materials as well. If you respect it by practicing proper lab safety, you'll be fine."

"There you are!" someone exclaimed from the doorway. The smiles became rather strained as a someone male presenting and about their age approached with a cheery wave. When he got close enough for me to read the nametag, it read, *Joey, he/they*. They were dressed in heavy jewellery, their face and ears covered in piercings, a necklace with a pendant that made my neck ache just thinking about it around his throat, and a large ring on each finger. Despite the lack of a warm welcome, he hugged them both and pulled up a chair to take a seat. "I've been looking all over for you."

"We're right here," Marie said, chugging her drink.

They turned to me and Michael. "I don't think I've seen you at one of these shindigs before."

My wife extended a friendly hand. "I'm Michael and this is my wife, Sasha. They're the scientist. I'm just along for the ride and the European vacation."

"Always an excellent reason to tag along," he said gregariously. "My wife loved events like this. I swear, you could take her to a convention on the history of paperclips and she'd be fascinated."

"What happened to her?" I asked, a question I knew was a minefield, but curiosity got the better of my filter.

Marie slammed her emptied glass on the table and abruptly stood up. "I'll be in our cabin." Gabe grabbed her wrist, and they exchanged a significant look before he let her go. With that, she stormed off, leaving us in a stunned silence. This time, I got a better view of the bracelet and recognized the beadwork. My heart stuttered in my chest. She wore a bracelet made with *abrus precatorius*, aka, Rosary Pea, one of the most poisonous plants known to man if inhaled or ingested. Luckily, the hard outer shell offered protection against death by abrin poisoning, so many made it into jewellery—often rosaries, hence the name.

"Sorry about that," Gabe said. "His wife, Luisa, was Marie's sister. She died in an accident a few weeks ago."

Joey polished off his glass of champagne, their rings glinting in the afternoon sun. "Marie still blames me for it. But Luisa had been complaining about dizziness and headaches for a few days leading up to it and stayed home when I went in for work. Marie found Luisa at the bottom of the staircase. She must have had a dizzy spell at the top of the steps and fell down, but Marie seems to think I had something to do with it."

"That's awful," Michael said.

Both nodded sombrely. "She was a brilliant scientist," Gabe said, "and we were on the verge of a breakthrough."

"A breakthrough?" I repeated, eager to change the subject to something less fraught.

"A soil enricher that will reduce time fallowing fields while still keeping them healthy," Joey replied, popping a potato chip into his mouth.

"Tell me more," I said, leaning in eagerly.

Michael tapped my knee twice, our silent cue to one another saying that, *I'm leaving the conversation, but you have fun*. With a smile, she said, "It's a pleasure to meet you all, but I think I'd like to get us settled in our room for a bit." She pressed a kiss to my cheek and wheeled off to entertain herself on her own. The rest of us chatted for another hour before splitting up mingle among our colleagues. At some point in the conversation, Joey took Marie's spot and shifted next to Gabe. Though the couches provided enough space to sit apart, they were practically in each other's laps. I didn't say anything about their closeness. Maybe the brothers-in-law just got along very well.

When the dinner bell rang, I found my way to Michael as

Vivid Worlds

Marie joined her husband and Joey. She seemed to have calmed down somewhat, but there was still an edge to her, a seething anger just below the surface. Joey took her hand, and she jerked away as though she'd been stung. They pulled their hand back and anxiously fiddled with a ring.

As the waiters began serving us, Michael nudged me, breaking me from a fascinating conversation about carnivorous plants and their importance to the environment. "Do you think she's OK?" she whispered, nodding vaguely in the direction of the strange and uncomfortable trio.

Marie had gone pale, a sheen of sweat covering her forehead. Her hands shook as she brought the water to her lips. She seemed fine when she sat down but now looked as though she was on the verge of passing out or throwing up. "Marie?" I began, but I didn't get to say much more than that.

She fell backwards in her chair, foaming at the mouth, and seizing on the floor as the people around the trio screamed. "Somebody help her," Gabe yelled, turning her on her side. One of her sleeves was hiked up, revealing several missing beads from her bracelet.

She jerked a few more times and was still, her eyes staring out into nothing. I'd never seen a dead body before, and it felt unreal. One moment, she was there, the next, the light left her eyes, and she was gone, nothing more than a hunk of flesh and bone.

Was this a suicide? She probably had enough botany knowledge from her husband to recognize that the plant used to make her bracelet was poisonous. But the poison was very slow to act. It took hours, even days, for the body to feel the effects, and I was pretty sure the bracelet was intact when I last saw it. It would definitely take more than an hour to kill. No, this poison was way too fast acting to be abrin.

Gabe had discovered the bracelet, and wept, identifying the seeds as the cause of death, and saying that his wife killed herself. Michael watched him and Joey with her eyes narrowed. She was suspicious about something, but I wasn't quite sure what.

The flight attendants ushered us out of the room with the promise of a lighter meal later, something I doubt anyone would actually eat after what we just saw. Michael took my hand and led me away from Marie's corpse and back to our cabin. It was small, cozy, but also a bit difficult for Michael to navigate in her chair. They had removed the writing desk that I'd glimpsed in other cabins as I walked past in the hopes of giving her more room, but it was still pretty cramped.

"Are you OK?" she asked.

I blinked, breaking free from my shocked stupor. "Yeah. Are you?"

"Shaken up, but physically, yeah. I'm fine."

"It doesn't make any sense," I mumbled, barely realizing that I said it out loud.

"What doesn't make sense?" she asked, her brows furrowing. "I mean, we didn't know her all that well, and don't know what her mental state was—"

"Not that," I said, cutting her off. I laughed a little to myself. It was silly, but it was bothering me. "The poison she took. It doesn't work that quickly. The bracelet looked intact when she left, but several Rosary Peas were missing when Gabe pointed it out."

Biting her lower lip, Michael sat back in her chair. "That is weird."

"I mean, assuming that the Rosary Peas weren't genetically modified somehow…"

"But then why would she be wearing it?" she asked. "Do Joey and Gabe work with poisonous plants like you?"

I shook my head. "They were preforming experiments based on the three sisters' method of agriculture—planting three crops that benefit the other like corn, beans, and squash—and trying to find healthy ways to enrich the soil so that fields don't have to lie fallow for as long as they do."

"And the Rosary Pea has nothing to do with that," she said. The wheels were turning behind her eyes. Michael may not have a PhD, but she was, in many ways, smarter than I am, especially when it comes to people. She's good at picking up on body language and social cues, things that I often need to have spelled out for me. "Is it just me, or did Joey and Gabe seem…close? I caught a couple glimpses of them talking to you in the lounge, and Joey practically sat in his lap at one point."

I shrugged. "I mean, yeah, but they're family. I just assumed that they were touchier than others."

She affixed me with a flat look. "You and my sibling are practically best friends. Would you ever sit in Sydney's lap?"

"No, that would be weird," I said, and then closed my eyes, wincing at my own obliviousness. "I see your point."

She patted my knee comfortingly and graciously moved on without teasing me too much. "So, we have our suspicions. Now what?"

I thought back to the dinner. If it wasn't the Rosary Pea, then something else killed her. In the minutes before her death, I saw her jerk away from Joey's hand as though she'd been stung and just assumed that she didn't want to be touched by him. But maybe there was more to it. During one of my many late-night research binges, I learned that people used to have rings with secret compartments that held just enough poison to kill someone. Joey was fiddling with their ring right after—something I'd written off as him feeling awkward or nervous, but if he had one of those rings, maybe he used it to secretly inject her with something before turning the needle up and away from the palm of his hand.

I voiced this theory to Michael, who nodded thoughtfully and said, "If that was the case, there would be a puncture mark on her hand. They won't let us examine it, though, not on the basis of half-baked theories."

"Do you think they'd keep her in the freezer or in storage with the rest of the plants?" I mused, mostly to myself.

She squinted at me. "You're not planning on examining her yourself, are you?"

I shrugged, suddenly feeling sheepish. It was a silly idea, wasn't it? Me skulking around playing detective like a modern-day Poirot. I'm a professional botanist, not an investigator. But if they really did kill her, then she deserved to have justice.

Michael took my silence for a yes and said, "Well, you're not doing it without me." She started wheeling herself to the door, glancing over her shoulder at me. "Well, are you coming? They're probably keeping her in the storage area. I heard they have chill pods there for cases like this."

When we approached the room, we saw that a pair of flight attendants were standing guard in front of it and talking about the death. I ducked into the corridor while Michael approached. Though society has come far in fighting ableism, benevolent forms of it still exist. For example, people will always jump to fulfil her requests, eager to help the unfortunate woman without the use of her legs. I heard her ask that they help her find the wheelchair accommodating showers so she could freshen herself up. I watched them pass me and slipped into the storage room.

Moving through it felt a bit like navigating a jungle after an airplane dropped its luggage into it, but I found her in a chill pod at the end of the room. Zeppelins come equipped with a couple in case there was a death during the flight, a much more civilized solution than putting a blanket and eye mask on the corpse and pretending that they're just asleep.

I opened the pod. Her body had already gone stiff, making it difficult to properly examine her hands. I lifted the one with the bracelet, and a couple of the peas came off as though they had been previously loosened. Pulling out my phone, I took a video, showing how easy it was to remove the seeds and examining her hands for a puncture mark.

It was a small one, barely noticeable if you didn't know what you were looking for, but I found the scab on the back of her left hand where Joey had grabbed it. I was about to close the chill pod once more when I noticed something else. Though they had cleaned off the worst of the foam, red still flecked the corner of her mouth. When I pried open her jaws, I smelled blood. Abrin, the poison found in Rosary Peas, caused bleeding in the stool, but not coughing up or vomiting it. Whatever killed her, it wasn't caused by her beaded bracelet.

I patted her down, finding a scrap of paper in her pocket. In it was a picture of Gabe and Joey together captioned with, *I know what you did. Soon, everyone will.*

"Who's there?" came a familiar voice. Gabe and Joey stood illuminated in the light of the doorway. With a gasp, I shut the chill pod and slipped into the shadows, hiding behind a leafy fern. Shoving the paper into my pocket, I shrank further back, trying to skirt the edges of the room and escape without their noticing.

That plan worked for about thirty seconds. Then I bumped into a pot, wincing at the way it clanked and praying to a god I didn't believe in that they hadn't heard it. A spotlight in my eyes told me that said prayers had not been answered.

"Sasha?" Joey asked.

Shit.

They stood side by side. Gabe's eyes were red-rimmed while Joey had taken off most of his jewellery. Mouth dry, I swallowed and stepped out of the shadows. "Hey," I said with an awkward wave as my mind warred with itself on what I should do. Should I accuse them now or keep my cards close for later?

"What do you think you're doing?" Gabe demanded.

"Well, what are you doing here?" I asked, crossing my arms, and attempting to bluff my way out.

We stood for a moment in a brief stalemate. Finally, Joey broke it by saying, "We wanted to say our goodbyes."

Anger flared at the false sorrow in his voice, and my mouth formed the words before my filter could stop it. "You sure about that?"

They both exchanged confused glances. Gabe's expression twisted into fury. "What's that supposed to mean?"

"Abrin, the poison from the Rosary Pea, is slow to work," I said, edging my way towards the door and praying that they're too distracted to notice. "Its symptoms include nausea, vomiting, abdominal pain, diarrhoea, rapid heart rate, seizures, hallucinations, and fevers. It does not make you cough up blood."

The unspoken communication between them was obvious. The jig was up. They could either silence me by killing me or let me go to the authorities with what I now know, so I had to keep them talking before they made their choice. *Maybe they'll confess to something.* "I'm just not sure why you did it."

"Because we didn't," Gabe insisted.

I bowled ahead ignoring his proclamation of innocence. "But I think I can guess." I held up the paper I found on her body, showing off the picture of them together. "You came in here looking for this, didn't you? She found out about the affair, so you killed her." That wouldn't be enough for them to kill her, though. There had to be something else. Something I was missing. And then it hit me. The sister. "One of you did kill her sister. Joey, I'm guessing from the way she reacted to you. Luisa must've found out about you two together, and in the fight, you killed her. Gabe helped cover it up. Then, because she was suspicious of Joey, Marie hired someone—a private eye, probably—to follow him. Said P.I. ended up catching you two together, and she figured out that this was the reason Luisa died. Am I close?"

As I talked, I slowly backed towards the exit. "She was going to tell the world and turn you in to the police. A murderer and his accessory after the fact. So, you got your hand on a poison ring, filled it with something toxic, and injected her with it at dinner, blaming the Rosary Pea bracelet for her apparent suicide."

The men's jaws set, and I gulped, preparing to run. Joey slowly, mockingly clapped his hands. "Well done, Sherlock. You told a hell of a story."

"I told the truth," I retorted. "And when they conduct a toxicology report, they'll find no abrin in her system and a puncture wound on one hand."

"She knew I was having an affair," Gabe said suddenly, his voice full of regret, "just not with who. When she asked me if it was Joey, I told her that had been a one-night stand. But it wasn't."

"Gabe…" Joey interrupted, his voice a low warning.

"She was upset more on behalf of her sister than at us but left it at that. We all have open relationships, so she figured we would tell her eventually. When Luisa found out, though, there was a fight between the three of us, and I'm not sure who it was that pushed her, or if she just fell, but she ended up dead at the bottom of the stairs. Marie thought it was just Joey there, and I didn't want to correct her."

"Gabe," he repeated, sharper this time.

His eyes brimmed with tears. "I know I should have stopped, but we carried on with the affair. She found out and was going to tell the world that we were responsible for—"

"Shut up!" Joey roared, their face blooming red with fury. "My God, shut the hell up. Stop talking."

He shook his head. "I can't take it, Joey. Seeing her like

that—"

"We're did what we did to protect ourselves."

I took advantage of this little lover's quarrel to run, sprinting out of the room while they were distracted. Heading straight to the bathroom, I pulled out my phone. I was going to call Michael, but then I saw that I had been recording the whole time. I had their confession saved to my phone and immediately sent it to my wife. The signal was weaker in the middle of the Atlantic, so I watched anxiously as the loading bar slowly trudged across the screen.

Someone banged on the door. "Sasha, we know you're in there," Gabe called out. "We just want to talk, OK?"

Sure, and I'm the president.

I glanced down at my phone. The line had stopped three quarters of the way across, meaning that it would probably fail to send.

They knocked again. "Come on, let's settle this like rational adults, OK?" Joey pleaded.

I glanced down at my phone. It had sent. I suppressed the desire to cheer. Even if they killed me, Michael would know the truth.

They must have been getting odd looks because the banging slowed to the occasional knock. Where was Michael? I'd tried calling, but it rang until it reached voicemail.

After maybe an hour of hiding, the hall outside seemed just quiet enough for me to attempt to slip out and find her. The moment I stepped out the door, though, someone grabbed me by the throat from behind. I struggled against him, my oxygen starved brain trying to remember the self-defence classes I took as a gym elective in college. I managed to elbow him in the ribs with enough force to break his grip.

He let go in surprise and I sprinted blindly, turning the corner, and running right into Joey. Shrieking, I stumbled backwards and nearly fell. I was trapped between them, and they slowly closed in like wolves circling a deer. Gabe looked regretful while Joey's lips were stretched in a predatory grin.

"What is going on here?" one of the flight attendants asked, drawing an electric baton they carried in case a passenger became unruly. Michael was at her side, with a sterile bag crumpled in her hand.

"Nothing really," Joey replied, gregarious as ever. "Just a spirited professional debate on the merits of breeding pollinator attracting flowers."

Bullshit, I mouthed.

I heard the floor creak and glanced behind me to find that more flight attendants had cut off their exit. The one closest to us looked thoroughly unimpressed. "That's not what she says."

Michael held up a ring in a clear bag with a cheerful smile. "I found the murder weapon."

Temporarily forgetting my predicament, I beamed with pride. "And I have their confessions. Send them to the brig!" That last bit was a tad dramatic, but the situation called for it.

The flight attendant pressed her lips together in a thin line. "We don't have a brig."

My cheeks flushed. So much for sounding cool and dramatic.

She continued, "But they will be confined to their cabin until we can turn them over to the proper authorities." As if given some kind of signal, the flight attendants charged their batons and led the pair away.

I handed her my phone to save the confession and the note to scan properly so that it would be harder to destroy. After a bit of questioning and explanation, they let us retreat to our rooms. Exhausted from the adrenaline and throat sore from the strangling, I collapsed into bed. Michael pulled herself in beside me, snuggling close.

"How did you find the ring?" I asked.

She snorted. "The dipshits left their cabin door unlocked and the ring on the table with the rest of the jewellery."

I snickered. "For people with doctorates, they weren't the smartest criminals, were they?"

"I mean, they're no professionals, but to be fair, neither are we." She snuggled closer. "I'm proud of you. You did a great thing today."

I pressed a kiss to the top of her head. "I couldn't have done it without you."

"Sure, you could," she mumbled. "I think that if you ever decide that botany isn't for you, you could be a detective."

I giggled, but didn't respond, the adrenaline crash hitting suddenly. At the end of this journey, we will find ourselves in a foreign country. Joey and Gabe will be turned into police custody, where they will hopefully hurt no one else. I will have to face my fear of meeting new people. That said, after catching two murderers, I think I can manage. It certainly gives me an interesting icebreaker to tell over dinner.

Low Tide at the Green Lagoon

Liam Hogan

The lagoon was a lurid green so vibrant and smooth it looked painted on.

"That's not healthy," I said, shading my eyes against the dazzle.

My guide, Tomas, who had promised to show me everything, and who had already made decent inroads on that tender promise last night, smiled. He wore a baseball cap over short, tight hair. A little tatty, salt or sweat stained, but with a bright logo, a circle of green arrows around a yellow sun, over three initials, the E of which I knew stood for *Eco*.

"That would depend on your point of view, *cher* Alex. It is, some might say, rather *too* healthy—too full of life." He spoke with a light lilt, his English measured but melodic. He'd spent time abroad; Sydney, Australia, earning a degree in engineering. Returned home as soon as the paper was dry. Envied me, he said, that I was still at University, still surrounded by so many young, enquiring minds. Bemused, that I didn't know what I would be doing when I left.

"So vigorous," he went on, "that nothing beneath the eutrophic layer can survive. But here that is no real loss. The lagoon is man-made, if you include rising sea levels under that term, as indeed you should."

Tomas, and probably the whole island, blamed me for the land they had lost, for the homes and businesses, for the steady erosion of their livelihoods. Not me *personally*, just any white, particularly male, tourist. They were polite about it, seemingly more disappointed than angry. That we hadn't listened when they'd warned us. That we still weren't listening.

But I was young, which seemed to some of them an opportunity to educate me. And I wasn't averse, especially when the teacher was as fine as Tomas.

"Is...?" I squinted across the shimmering emerald moss. "Isn't it low tide?"

He nodded, pleased I had noticed. "And it will be in this lagoon, very shortly."

As if on cue, a klaxon sounded, three long low wails. "People avoid the outlet region, but a warning is prudent."

It was a minute before I heard the noise of a motor starting up.

"Not a motor," Tomas explained. "A *dynamo*. We generate electricity from this lagoon when we let the water out at low tide, and then when we let it back in again, at high."

I stared, aghast, as the green carpet began to crinkle at the edges, began to layer itself over the concrete skirt. "You're letting the algae out into the *ocean*?"

"Not quite." He took off his cap, donned a hard helmet with the same sun-burst logo, this time applied by a sticker, and handed me its twin. "The next step is rather pungent. Hope you don't mind?"

We walked slowly along the edge of the lagoon, leaving the hut with its dials and buttons and Tomas's waving colleague behind. The whole operation employed just two men, working in shifts. Twelve-hour days. That explained Tomas's reluctance for a lazy morning lie in. Or at least, I hoped so.

We were higher up, now. Or rather, the same level we had been all along, on the solid bank of the artificial lagoon, but the gently sloping land to seaward had left the thick mud the other side of the concrete barrier at the lagoon's entrance a man's height below. It wasn't much of a tidal difference, but Tomas had explained that. Large bodies of water surrounding small land masses didn't behave like smaller bodies of water around large coastal stretches. The water didn't have anywhere to go.

It meant the power generated by this tidal lagoon wouldn't be very much, and would only last for maybe thirty minutes, four times a day. But that wasn't the main point of the operation.

Tomas pointed to the sluice, from which water was still pouring, though it slowed even as we watched. "You know a gravy separator, Alex? This is similar. The water that flows out to sea is from the *bottom* of the column. The top—" He gestured to a couple of large, almost square troughs, "—gets filtered through *there*, removing much of the biomass. The phytoplankton has a limit—it grows in a thin layer, blocking the very light it depends upon—so regular harvesting, at each low tide, is necessary."

"So you skim off the algae? But the nutrient rich water that fed it; doesn't that pollute the ocean?"

He nodded again, please, I think, that I was asking good questions. "Less than you might think. The algae help mop up the excess nitrogen and phosphorus. Which, in any case, doesn't come from bags of manufactured chemicals. We have a more *natural* source."

He smiled again, that lazy, open smile, and swatted away a fly—there were a lot of flies, a cloud of them, the closer we got to those green sludge-filled troughs. The level in them was slowly subsiding, leaving behind a spongy mass suspended on a wire mesh.

"Some of the water that enters the lagoon comes from our sewage system. From the hotels that line the beaches, from your hotel, sat safely above the encroaching water. For now, anyway. The sewage is treated, of course, biologically inert, but you wouldn't perhaps want to drink it. Not that it would kill you, it just wouldn't taste very nice. The algae like it, though. They like it plenty. The rest of the grey water, we use for sanitation and watering crops."

He frowned playfully at me. "We do not use water fit to drink for flushing toilets, as you mad wasteful English fools do."

"What do you do with the algae?" I asked, changing the topic.

"Ah. Watch."

There were four large troughs, only two of which had been used in this latest operation. In the other two, the filter mesh that stopped the algae escaping was elevated into the mid-morning sun, supported by a complicated set of jointed metal legs. The tangled, dried-out mass writhed with flies, the smell strong but not entirely unfamiliar; washed up seaweed on exposed rocks under a Kerry sun, a childhood memory of scrabbling around in small pools.

"We can't leave it longer than a day," he said. "We don't want it to rot, merely to dry out. Well," he laughed. "We *do* want it to rot, but not yet."

He reached over to a metal box, unhinged the side, stabbed at a big green button. "Powered by the electricity generated by our turbines, of course."

With a clank half the mesh rose and swivelled slowly until it was horizontal again, but upside down, fitting itself to its inverted counterpart that had hidden beneath, a grill of stubby spikes like teeth, a motor whining in protest as the two halves were pressed firmly together again. There was a dull thud as the brown-green mat slumped to the apron of concrete. A white crab raced frantically away from what must have been to it an apocalypse, the end of days, angry gods turning its world upside down.

"Now we cut it up and—manually, I'm afraid—cart it to the bio-mass tank. Where it ferments; anaerobic digestion, releasing methane that we pipe to our homes and to your hotel for cooking and heating water. The cake of dried sludge that is left after all that makes decent fertiliser, to spread on the fields, to grow the food you will eat tonight."

"You English," he said, once again ignoring the fact I was Irish, but what difference did that truly make? "do something similar, with at least some of your sewage. But you don't make use of solar power, and you don't have lagoons full of fast-growing algae." He laughed. "But then, it is cold and rains where you are from, no?"

This, I could not deny. Especially in Ireland.

"We use what we have," he said, waving his slender arm, the wiry muscles intimately familiar, glistening again with salty sweat. "Sunlight, and water, and yes, human waste. *Your* waste, tourist waste. We make use of the opportunities even climate change brings, because what else are we to do?"

I thought about that, for a long moment. Thought of inviting this beautiful soul back to Ireland, to live with me. Thought how much I would need to explain, and how little of it I would be as proud as Tomas was, of his island, of his green lagoon.

And then I thought that if we didn't ourselves get a lot smarter, if we didn't close the loop as these islanders were doing, making everything part of a circle, nothing wasted through sheer necessity, then all of their efforts would be for nothing. Because the sea wouldn't stop rising, and even these concrete ramparts would be swallowed up along with most of the land behind them.

How terrible that responsibility of ours was, and how badly we were shirking it. I felt hot, sudden shame that made me turn away, stared out to a sea wrapped in blue skies and perfect fluffy white clouds, feeling the prickle of sunlight through my top, aching to be rid of the hard hat, my sun-lightened hair no doubt a tangled mess beneath it.

"Will I see you again?" I asked, turning sharply back to Tomas, still embarrassed but aware that my holiday would all too soon be over. I didn't want to spend the rest of it alone.

Vivid Worlds

"Tonight?"

He smiled, gave me a simple nod. "Yes, Alex. But it will be late, I am afraid. Around ten? And—Alex?—thank you."

"Thank *me*?" I echoed, incredulous.

"Why yes." That wide smile, a soft touch of my hand. "Not everyone is interested in what we, what *I* do. Not everyone listens or asks questions. Or—" He held my gaze. "—learns."

I still didn't know what I would be doing in a year's time, when I finished my humanities degree. But I made a promise, there and then, stood by the side of an empty green lagoon, that somehow, I'd make it worthwhile.

Finding Armillaria

Morgan Melhuish

"Idina!"

Mama would screech like a parakeet and slap the back of my head, jolting me from whatever simulation I was immersed in.

My very sense of reality would fracture, vision dancing between VR and the now of childhood. The smell of cumin and cloves, hot plastic and sweaty metal, the ever-present whiff of landfill broke back into my world.

"You'll lose yourself in there," she'd tut, yanking at the headset. "Don't you know there's only here, there's only this?"

It was her answer to everything. Not that I ever asked for more than what was offered.

"Let her have her dreams." Papi was my defender. "What harm can it do?"

He was always tinkering, coaxing life into the discarded.

Mama would scoff. "You want a daughter swaddled in false visions, do you? Like the Hernandez boys, eh?"

"Idina's no waster." Papi would wink at me, his eyelid huge through a magnifying monocle, twiddling a tiny screwdriver between his meaty fingers.

"They're educational," I'd protest. When else would I ever get to travel?

Mama always sucked the air through her crooked teeth and gave me a chore to do.

Papi had scavenged a collection of three omnibus drives, restoring them to a semblance of function. My favourite VRs were *Great Explorers of the 21st Century*.

I loved crossing tundra, a teammate of Felicity Aston, surviving in the wilderness with Sarah Marquis as my guide, listening to indigenous people alongside Céline Cousteau.

Vivid Worlds

Those remarkable women shared my spare time in the favela, those precious moments of mine. At night I longed for a little scrap of world to chart and scout. An adventure.

Frustratingly, though, mama was right. There was only here, only this.

By the time I was twenty I imagined myself the Jane Goodall of the favela. I'd navigate the ever-changing twists and turns of alleyways, the jungle of bodies I called home: the gangs and collectives, the families biological, extended and found. They were all familiar to me and I wove my way between them, connecting.

My world was the slum, the landfills and recycling centres. In turn, they all knew Idina.

As Papi's apprentice, I was adept at charming the binners and pickers who'd save the best parts and finds for me. I listened hard, a scavenger of hearsay, learning who might be in need of what. I'd barter and trade what we repaired, skimming the cream from the trash. I loved it, the whole process of turning rubbish into riches.

"Riches!" Mama would kiss her teeth and tut. "You and your empire of garbage!" She kept Papi and I grounded for sure.

It might not have been much, but we scrimped and saved, put me through night school.

I was at college the night it happened, ripped pages of a foraged notebook covered in doodles of circuits. I had a dream of bringing solar mechanics to the favela, sunbeams on my brain as rain pelted outside.

Class was crammed with a press of damp bodies and at the end of the session we were reluctant to emerge into the tempest. If only I'd recognised the veil of tears that washed down the foyer's windows for nature's grief. Instead I'd set my jaw hard and ran.

Where the slum had been was nothing but an absence. A huge gulp of darkness and rain, a bite taken out of my life.

I teetered on crumbling asphalt, unable to comprehend the sinkhole, not caring about the storm, the kind hands that pulled me back from the edge.

My heart fell into that pit.

I've yet to escape it.

There's only here. Only this.

Mama wasn't wrong in her insistence - but while matter is finite it can always be altered, transmuted and spun to gold. Just as Papi and I always tried.

The favela, the sinkhole, my life. It was transformed.

The authorities saw a blank slate where I struggled to see more than despair, the shards of all I knew, all I loved, swallowed by the earth.

My tragedy was a blessing of urban planning for the government.

How did they honour those lives? That legacy?

Pañal. Diapers. Nappies.

They filled that hole with caca.

My grief, the need to survive, what did that turn into?

An empire of garbage.

I knew Mama would be laughing from the afterlife.

When the majority of a workforce is killed, it's amazing the scramble you can make up a career ladder, what desperation will make you do.

At the interview I spoke their language. I'd spent years listening, scavenging their words.

Maximising waste reduction. Carbon zero. Composters and biodegraders.

I went from slum vermin to rat race overnight. A bank account, employee benefits, working hours, performance management, they were gilded bars on a cage that was brand new and shiny to me.

I set to work in the rubble of my old life, finding new ways to live.

I wasn't the only one.

"Every day dozens of trucks and compactors drive along the coast road, bringing their cargo from the city. They will never stop. If we don't take this opportunity, if we don't put into practice research that's scientifically sound, then we may as well drown in refuse, suffocate in waste. Something has to be done differently."

I heard you remonstrating with the men in suits and I wanted to applaud.

Your idealism and enthusiasm raised me from the rubbish heap of grief. I never expected your answer to be mushrooms, that we'd work side by side.

Pleurotus ostreatus.

You showed me how this fungus could grow on mounds of rotting diapers, thriving as the disposables degraded safely.

In turn we dreamt of ways to accelerate the process. I built solar-powered shredders to mulch pañal.

The first time the machine worked - a spray of plastic and poop erupting from its innards, churning out a mass of spliced nappies, easier for the mushrooms to digest - we celebrated.

I remember the way we danced in our protective gear. It was as if we'd struck oil, stomping in clammy boots, elated despite the scat, the smell permeating our masks. My goggles steamed up, heavy-duty boiler suits splattered, but still I smiled.

We went down to the shore that evening, industrial concrete blocks a haphazard sea defence. It didn't stop us sitting, watching the sunset and swallows swooping like skimmed stones, dipping and feasting on flies.

You told me about how, millions of years ago, fungi helped plants emerge from the water and conquer the land. You told me about prototaxites towering like ant hills above the landscape, taller than the two of us combined, shooting-star spores launching into the sky. You told me how, when fossils of prototaxites were found, no one even thought they were fungus, so different were they from the mushrooms we know now.

"They've always been here, helping the planet, helping humanity."

I kissed you then, feeling the tendrils of connection pulse between us.

We grew a future: fostered the spiral patterned *aspergillus terreus*, the white cotton blooms of *engyodontium album*, the fan-shaped *pestalotiopsis microspora*, watched them feast on complex and problematic plastics. To me it seemed miraculous, but it was only science that ever guided you.

You shared our results, best practice, encouraging others across the globe.

We never went hungry. Oyster mushrooms were always abundant and you cooked up a storm: soups and stews, stir-fries we fed the workers, the pickers and binners on.

Outside we roamed a forest of fungus reclaiming the never-ending refuse. What was once landfill transformed to a pastoral meadow of mushrooms, pale stalks and crested gills like foliage.

The experimenting continued. In time, we watched mycelium shoots navigate a cast of cavities, hardening into bricks. I built us a house of saprophytes from these building blocks, reclaimed metals I scavenged, sheets of corrugated-iron became a roof.

A home.

At dusk the green bioluminescence of *anellus stipticus* lit our porch and pathways.

It was something from a fairytale, the ones Mama tutted at when Papi tucked me in, soothing me to sleep.

Sometimes I found myself expecting the VR to flicker; to discover I was a waster after all, lulled by a simulation. Would I wake with a jolt in the favela, the sting of Mama's backhand across my neck?

I worried, despite those we spoke to online, the workers I treated like my children, that I'd become complacent in my oasis of mould. Wasn't I allowed a little more? Something better?

Like mycelium I wanted to reach out further, to grow.

There's something very human in that, something dark and twisted.

"We've always been a virus, spreading over the planet threefold, tenfold, more," you said, a note of regret in your voice.

"I could say the same of your precious mushrooms."

You shook your head. "Fungus works in tandem, in symbiosis with the earth, in our guts, with other plants. Humans go it alone. Selfishly. Destructively. No wonder the world has tried to find a cure for us, Idina."

I wasn't having that.

"But there's so much creativity. Love. Compassion."

"Is there?" I'd not heard you so jaded before.

I knew why. We'd been through a spate of attacks, gangs coming from the city, wanting what we had. At least they thought they did. Turns out they weren't so interested in knowledge.

It didn't stop them throwing their weight around, smashing

things. Their frustrated anger terrified me.

You'd had to go to hospital, your skin still showed the marks of their pummelling fists.

"We've weathered their like before, and we will again." I tried to reassure you, falsely bright.

"It's not just them." You placed your hands over your chest, your heart. I wasn't sure why, confused.

"We're a virus. I'm a…" Tears flowed down your cheeks.

Everything slowed.

Even the automated system of AI-driven, solar-powered dumpster trucks came less frequently.

Something was changing in the city too.

I no longer rushed through the days but calmly cherished each moment, watched you wasting and tried to be tender.

"It's OK Idina, it's OK," you wiped my eyes dry and smiled. "I'm just changing state."

I marvelled at your stoicism, the solace you found in psilocybin. I felt the fungus was changing your mind, helping you see beauty in decay. I shouldn't have been so surprised, after all those years you'd spent observing, recording, researching… You'd always been a convert.

The sea defences had long been submerged, so we sat on the gritty dust at the tip of the archipelago and watched the waves come in. On the hazy horizon a wind farm stood, pinwheel arms sluggishly turning.

"It's good to come out here," you coughed. "To feel so small. Two specks in the vastness."

I had to agree.

I thought of Felicity Aston in the frozen expanse of the tundra, standing with her in the VR set, sat next to you, the warmth of your leg, the sharpness of grit. I felt the flutter of yearning, all of us torn between the world known and that unknown.

I struggled to let you go, to embrace the slow sorrow. Yours was a drawn-out death rattle, not the shocked gasp of my parents. I didn't know which was worse.

"Idina," you tried to soothe, dosing yourself. "It's only natural."

My head knew you were right, yet my heart gripped you tightly.

It was never going to win.

In grief, I felt your loving presence cocoon around me: the sustenance of mushrooms, the mycelium walls and the shelter we built together, the ghostly *anellus stipticus* a reassuring spectre at dusk. You were everywhere.

Then there was the temptation of psilocybin. I'd always shunned magic before.

I imagined your body becoming soil, the fungus under your fingertips sprouting, families of yeast—candida, malassezia, saccharomyces—thriving and multiplying in your dank cavities. I imagined networks of pale tendrils unravelling, probing, expanding…

It might seem morbid but it brought me comfort.

I dreamt of you exploding into spores, dancing on the wind, a dandelion seed head.

You were more than here, more than this.

In the softness of dawn I take these visions and examine the fragments of memory.

I'm still Papi's girl, transforming the trashed, looking for purpose—even if it's my past I plunder.

Each evening I go to the shore, embracing the liminal, the sense of scale you loved.

In the bay the sea shifts, water swells and ripples as if

fish school and snap just beneath. I watch the frothing and wonder.

I track its progress.

It's not just echoes of my former days coming to the surface. Something is growing, pushing itself up from the sea bed.

I glimpse barely submerged nodules, then a row of what look like sinewy knees appear, breaking through waves, leading out into the ocean. They remind me of those desert succulents mimicking rocks.

Prototaxites. I hear your voice across the years, in the crash of the waves.

You might be right.

They expand in circumference, in height, stepping stones going… where?

After a week of observation I can't resist.

I put out a tentative foot, test the dark spotted surface. It stands firm, takes my weight with just a slight wobble. My shoe leaves no imprint beyond a dusty shadow.

I should prepare, I should take supplies, I should let someone know where I am going.

Only you would care, and I'm leaving you behind.

I walk a tightrope of fungus above the water. The thrill of exploration drives me forward, one step after another, leaping from "rock" to "rock." I know how reckless this is. If I fell into the sea now, I know I'd drown. I can't swim, am well out of my depth, have no hope of reaching the shore.

A laugh escapes my lips at the madness of it all.

I'm Sarah Marquis venturing into the wild. This is my discovery. My adventure!

How long have I longed for this?

A gust of wind tugs at me and I quickly crouch, hands out, a surfer. My legs quiver.

"Keep your focus," I reprimand, panting. I wait for the

gusts to die down, can see ahead how the steps stop and some new land has emerged.

I push up from the plump surface and spring forwards, rushing towards the horizon and its strange territory.

Honey mushrooms. Armillaria. I recognise them with ease, their umbrella shape, their freckled cloud-like domes. I never expected to see them at this gigantic size, at this density.

You told me the largest organism on Earth is a honey mushroom growing in Oregon. The *armillaria ostoyae* has been there for thousands of years, sprawling over two thousand acres, and now one was here, nestling at the tip of my archipelago.

"Hello." I can't help speaking, reaching out to touch yellow flesh, to caress it.

"Thank you." I can feel gratitude bubbling inside, to be the first, the witness... Their stalks bend and ripple under me.

It seems only right to communicate, to show my appreciation.

"Here you are again. Trying to help."

I clamber over their pillowy caps, this springy surface a trampoline of joy. I venture into the eco-system, stride across the armillaria's squidgy skin, growing in confidence. I can't help but grin.

Turning, I'm brought up short by the sight of home: the curve of the bay and sinkhole, the dump we made. I've never been so far, had such perspective.

Above and beyond, the city is a series of jagged spires I've no connection with. All those people, those lives.

I realise then the potential I'm stood on. The armillaria is a life raft for those willing to work in tandem, together. That's what mushrooms have always offered.

I learnt that from you.

How many in the city would embrace that destiny?

I have my doubts.

I think of smashed equipment and fists, sweeping up shattered glass.

There are always those who'll reject the gifts the world offers, who'll spoil and exploit.

I turn again, my back to that world.

It is time for me to move forwards: to be the pioneer I always dreamt of.

When I finally arrive at the furthest edge of fungus, the sea susurrates. Synergy, it seems to say.

My future.

Synergy.

Synergy.

Vivid Worlds

The Mango Keeper
Nicholas Jay

Danilo always thought the man who would one day come to kidnap Mother would be tall and broad-shouldered, with a square jaw and sharp cheekbones. Someone strong enough to peel back Mother's bark and extract her from her tree. Instead, the military officer in front of him had a round face, snub nose, and flimsy-looking glasses that kept sliding off. His lips were thin and bright red, glistening from how often he licked them. Flecks of sweat dotted his shirt and forehead. Even in casual fatigues, he looked thoroughly uncomfortable.

But Danilo kept his guard up. The air around the officer buzzed with a quiet menace. Six soldiers lay in wait dutifully behind him, their Humvees lining the long dirt road to Danilo's family home.

"Do you know why I'm here, *hijo*?"

Danilo winced. The arrogance of speaking Spanish to ingratiate himself, of calling him *son*, especially when he had come to take Mother away. Danilo's hand tightened on the detonator he held behind his back.

"I know," he replied. "But you won't find what you're looking for."

"You sure about that?"

The officer craned his neck to look past Danilo, as though trying to catch a glimpse of his prize. He saw instead a wide plaster house, painted cobalt blue, with a tin roof and awning extending over a concrete patio. Danilo's brother, Jaime, had built that, pouring the concrete from a truck half the size of the soldiers' Humvees. On the porch, *papá's* and *tío's* rocking chairs sat uncannily still. The wooden table where they ate breakfast every morning lay dismantled on the porch floor; Danilo had taken the nails to build supports for Mother's sagging boughs. Shoes, notebooks, loose paper, and wicker baskets lay scattered among an arsenal of bow rakes, scythes, shears, and other tools that became useless after the coup. Waves of powder blue granules brushed across the floor of the patio in the wind. An elegant motion for something so noxious.

"I'm sure," said Danilo, frowning. "Your chemicals left nothing behind."

"Hm. We heard something else from your *tío*."

Danilo scoffed, running his thumb gently over the detonator's switches. One metal toggle, on or off, and an activation button. His last resort. "Wilmer hasn't been here in years. Didn't have much to do, after you soured the soil."

One of the soldiers cocked his weapon and stepped forward. The officer languidly raised his hand and the soldier stopped, as though leashed. Danilo imagined strings emerging from the soldier's head and hands, arcing toward his commanding officer's fingers.

Danilo wondered about the officer's rank. If he were a general or colonel, he wouldn't have bothered talking to Danilo at all and just taken Mother by force. No, he had to be a junior officer. A captain, maybe, or a lieutenant. Delivering a viable *madremango* would be a bright feather in any officer's cap, but would mean much more to someone with ambition, someone with rungs yet to climb on the ladder of power. The other side of ambition, Danilo knew, was desperation. He could work with that.

"You're brave," said the lieutenant. "I can tell you've been through hell and back. But you must understand what harvesting your mother will mean to the rest of the world." He stepped toward Danilo. "Thousands of sick people, yearning for a cure. Millions who hunger, who pine for something small to sustain them. For there to be one more healthy *madremango* in this world—after they all perished—is nothing short of a miracle."

The lieutenant's face was inches from Danilo's now, his breathing controlled but not relaxed. Fury, righteous and repressed, emanated from him in thick, unctuous waves. Danilo realized it must have taken extreme effort for him to appear calm.

He swallowed, tried to hold steady. He hadn't yet slid the toggle to arm his trap, but he could. That's all it would take— toggle, then button, a one-two twitch of his thumb—and he could send Mother spinning into smoke. To protect her. To keep her from this man, from becoming nothing more than a lab sample, endlessly divided, replicated, corrupted, bits of her soul ground into powder, encapsulated in little pills and sold in paper boxes to the privileged few who could afford them.

Or he could spread himself wide like a peacock and bluff as best he could. Maybe that would be enough to send the lieutenant away.

"A miracle, you say," replied Danilo, sticking his chin out. "A miracle for whom? Not the ones who need it most, the ones you deem too sick or too weak or too unproductive or too dangerous. Not your enemies. Not all the people you killed to get it."

"Some progress requires sacrifice."

"And what have you sacrificed?" he spat. "You forget who you're speaking to. You think the *hijo* of Doctor Mejía doesn't know about sacrifice?"

Danilo unclasped his hand from his wrist.

"I understand exactly what you want. And you won't get it."

He raised his fist. A chorus of mechanical clicks and slides arose from the Humvees as the soldiers readied their rifles. The lieutenant made no move to silence them, but it didn't matter. Danilo's thumb pressed down hard on the detonator's button.

The lieutenant's mouth twitched, fast and violent. "Your father," he muttered, "traitor that he was, once held true to an unassailable mission: to bring good to mankind. And you want to blow it all to pieces. That would weigh heavy on your conscience, wouldn't it?"

Danilo grinned, his face camouflaging a heart too bitter to care. Why should he have to worry about the consequences of one destructive action in the face of myriad others taken by the lieutenant and his comrades in arms? They had ended lives, livelihoods, entire species with their herbicides and defoliants. So much knowledge stored in roots and fibres, bones and cells, all diseased and withered now. They would never know the taste of a *mamón* plucked from a neighbour's tree, or how the creeping mimosa plants in their fields would fold their leaves when touched. It seemed right, erasing what they held valuable after they had done the same. A fair trade, no?

Danilo wanted to say all this to the lieutenant. He needed to say this to him, or at least to somebody. Aside from Mother, he'd been alone for so long. Most of his family and neighbours were gone, having fled or perished from the blue poison misting from the sky. Those who remained in town were too drunk on liquor and despair to understand.

Instead, he brandished the detonator in the lieutenant's face. "It's your conscience that will decide," Danilo said. "Unless you leave, Mother goes up in flames."

The lieutenant growled, then finally raised his hand. The soldiers stood down.

He spat violently at Danilo's feet. "You can't keep this up forever, *hijo*," he said, turning away. "We'll get it eventually. We always do."

Danilo watched the Humvees reverse and drive out of their valley. After five minutes, the rumble of their engines faded out, leaving behind the sound of bird calls and the wind brushing the crowns of the trees.

Danilo released the button. All was still. His bluff had worked.

Mother stood in the field down the hill from the house, a bastion against ruin. The wooden poles Danilo had constructed supported her lush crown, which hung heavy with hundreds of ripe mangoes. Hundreds more lay in a jagged circle around her, flyblown and rotting. In a different time, this would be a bittersweet sight, but there was no future for their seeds in this acidified soil. The field behind her, once tilled and tidily planted with cornstalks and coffee bushes, was a turbulent mess, pockmarked by shrapnel. The soil glittered with electric blue dust.

Several mango trees lay cut or upturned at the edges of the field. When Danilo was twelve, on the feast day of San Isidoro the Farmer, he helped his father dig deep, oblong cradles for the mango seeds they had saved throughout the year. Out of the viable ones shot little tendrils, shy and curious. He watched with fascination as his father deftly wrapped each tendril around one of his ancestor's bones—grandmothers, great-grandmothers, matriarchs long forgotten—and placed it in each hole.

They planted fifty in all, hoping for one healthy *madremango* tree. One was all Dr Mejía needed for his research into the fruit's curative properties. When the first sprout pushed up through the topsoil, the whole town came by to celebrate. That sprout grew taller, thicker, tougher. More sprouts followed, and soon the Mejías had ten viable trees, their branches capped by promising lime green bulbs that would elongate and darken into rich, ripe fruit.

When the first mango dropped, Doctor Mejía cried. Danilo had only seen him cry once before—years earlier when Mother passed away—and he would only see him cry once more: exactly twelve years after they first planted the *madremangos*, on the feast day of San Isidoro the Farmer, when news of the coup reached them over radio waves, somehow more slowly than the first planes that lathered their fields with waves of blue powder.

Danilo waited until dusk to visit Mother. She was strongest, then, having been nourished and warmed by hours of sunlight.

Usually, he couldn't wait to visit her. Talking to her was the only thing that could soothe his frantic thoughts. She always listened, responding when she could summon the strength to pry apart the folds of sap that formed her mouth, offering him wisdom or consolation like she used to do when he was young. She wasn't—couldn't be—the same as before, but she bore shades of her first self, and that was enough.

Today, though, Danilo wished dusk would never fall. For the past few weeks, Mother's tenor had changed. She seemed distant, dismissive of him and all he had been through. When she spoke, she became confused and disoriented, unsure of who Danilo was or how she could speak at all. Before they were destroyed, the other *madremango* trees suffered similar problems, too overwhelmed by the barrage of invisible transmissions to their roots, limbs, and leaves.

Some part of Danilo feared the tree would consume Mother entirely, even though he knew that wasn't possible. Though his father never finished his research, together they had achieved true symbiosis between host plant and human spirit.

More than anything, Danilo wanted to please her. To do what was right by her and their family. All he could do was buy time with the lieutenant. He'd done that. They were safe for another day or two, and he would find a way to keep them safe one or two days more. They would find a way to keep going.

Danilo bounded down the hill toward where Mother stood, a single column in a desolate plain. A series of pops and cracks sounded as he approached. Mother's trunk split open to reveal a sculpture, moulded from red-brown sap, of a face. Her face. Two glassy eyes sat above high cheekbones, a flat nose, and a wide mouth. Below her lips were faint outlines of her once-proud chin and long neck, but they scrunched together where they met the wood of the tree, as though the inner folds of the trunk had begun to swallow her like a python.

With great effort, the sap of her mouth parted, leaving behind gooey strings between her lips. She said nothing.

"Our idea worked, Mother," said Danilo. "He left."

Her leaves trembled, but her face remained still. It felt somewhat like an exhale, but Danilo couldn't be sure.

"We're safe," he said, more emphatically this time. "For a little while, anyway."

"He comes to take," she groaned, each word a struggle.

Danilo nodded. "Yes, but I've got an idea—"

"Let him."

Danilo froze. His insides felt thick and gummy, his mouth filled with cotton. *Let him?* he wanted to scream back at her. *Let him destroy you like everything else?*

It took him several seconds to find his voice. "Mother," he said, low and indignant. "That man will dishonour you. He will do what they always have. He will take the seeds of your fruit. He will try to plant them. If they yield, you will be kept alive forever, a prisoner to utility. If they do not yield, he will cut you down and you'll be lost." Danilo's lip quivered. Moisture pooled in the corners of his eyes. "He'll look past you. He'll look *through* you. He will totally ignore the life you had between the rings."

"And what are you doing with me, *hijo*?"

The earth shook. Mother's roots seized up then relaxed again, massaging the soil to move her trunk slowly toward him. Danilo lost his footing and sank to his knees.

"I never asked for second life," she said, her words slurred and sticky. "Now that I have one, why wouldn't I use it to give life to others?"

Danilo wanted to pull away from her. To hide like the creeping mimosa from her, from the soldiers, from the responsibility of being the one person left defending their family home and land and all the memories it carried.

"You can't give up," he said, his lip trembling. "Don't give up. Don't leave me."

Her leaves rustled again. It was barely perceptible, but underneath the marbled texture of the sap, Danilo saw her face soften.

"You are stronger than this," she said. "You know what to do."

More pops and cracks sounded as the fissure in her trunk began to close, shutting the door between them. Her branches shook again and one of her mangoes dropped and rolled toward him, settling in the crook between his knees. He picked it up and held it to his cheek, its slippery skin both softer and stronger than any mango he had felt before.

Three days passed before the lieutenant returned, this time with a larger convoy. They barrelled down the dirt road toward the cobalt blue house with the tin roof and awning and the porch littered with the paraphernalia of past lives. No one came to greet them or stand in their way. The air was thick and humid. A weak breeze danced with the smell of smoke.

The lieutenant knew the *madremango* was gone. It was as good as gone when they decided to leave last time. He'd known the kid would destroy it, thinking that would protect it. Protect *him*. There was no point coming back here, except to see the tree. This was a special death. He wanted to witness it for himself.

At the field's edge, the tree cracked and groaned, slumping against the flames and immense heat engulfing it. The branches, still sagging from the memory of unpicked fruit, had been stripped clean. The circle of matted grass where mangoes had fallen, lying oily black and worm-eaten, was bare. The kid had taken every scrap, every last seed.

No matter. They would let him live for a couple years, let him experiment and maybe even produce a few viable seeds. Then they would find him, and they would take them. They always did. The lieutenant craned his head back and breathed deeply, taking in the sweet scent of burning wood.

One Step at a Time
Rick Danforth

Like its owner, Cold Harbour Farm had seen much better days. They had both survived the now perpetual smog, the downturn of society and the time Charlotte had tried to homebrew mead.

Another thing that had seen better days was the tractor she was kicking to life. Electric had long ago replaced the diesel behemoths of her childhood, but percussive maintenance had stood the test of time.

As the tractor whirred into life, Charlotte thanked whatever guardian angel was watching over her and closed the cab door. After waiting for the air filters to ding green, she removed her respirator to bask in the purified air of the tractor cab. A brief yet welcome respite.

A respite that ended when she saw a tall figure in black walking between the stone walls of the road that snaked between the lush fields to arrive at the farm's front gate. The air that was so inhospitable to Charlotte caused the plant life to flourish.

"Shit on it. Jon!" Charlotte swore and then remembered to press the radio button on her hip. "Jon! We have a priest coming."

"Where are you?" asked Jon.

"North field, facing the road. You?"

"Sorting out the cheap-ass air purifier you say is all we can afford."

It's more than we can afford, thought Charlotte. The law said you had to have one to help the world, they had two. Given the lack of enforcement, some didn't have any. They were doing far more than their fair share. But it wasn't the time for that. "Can you help or not?"

"What flavour of help?"

"As intimidating as possible. Don't worry about effectiveness," said Charlotte. The priest didn't look like they were carrying any heavy gear. If a shotgun wouldn't work, there would be little call for much else.

"OK. You keep them busy. I'll be with you after the power-on-self-test."

Charlotte nodded to herself, as she drew an old-fashioned shotgun from the cab. She pressed a button and the less old-fashioned auto-targeting scope flicked into life.

Cradling it in the hook of her arm, and reattaching her respirator, she walked through the long grass that would hopefully feed the next generation of cows after they emerged from the bio-fabricators.

The priest made no effort to hide. Why would he? His job was to spread the horrible, toxic word of an idea so stupid Charlotte couldn't see how it lingered. He just stood at the gate, in his plain black suit with matching respirator, waving a long, thin hand.

"Hello there, I'm Thomas," said the priest, as Charlotte neared. "I just wanted to meet you and share a kind blessing on this lovely day."

"Lovely day? It's fucking freezing, and the air pollution means I can't take this off." Charlotte flicked at the respirator on her face.

"Well, it is as fine as we can expect." Thomas flashed a wide grin that gave his trim figure an almost skeletal appearance. "And if you don't like how the Earth is coming to, then you can always kill yourself and help her recover?"

"Don't beat around the bush," said Charlotte with a barking laugh. "Thought you might buy me a drink first. Bit of foreplay."

"Earth has precious time left, and it's best for both her and you that I don't waste time. We both know the state of the world. We both know the abject failure of humanity to do a damned thing about it. If you want to help the planet, you can offer no greater assistance than a painless death to aid the healing process." Thomas clapped his hands together and bowed his head.

"If I wanted to help the planet, I'd run a farm where I spend ten per cent of the bloody income on air purifier filters." Charlotte sniffed, then spat out the line Jon said earnestly each time. "One step at a time."

"And why put yourself through all that," said Thomas, changing gears seamlessly. "It would be much easier to die, don't you think? No stress, no pain. Just peace."

Charlotte wanted to say, oh God she wanted to say, "You're a fucking parasite. Take your self-serving nonsense back to where you came from and leave us alone."

She didn't say this aloud, because although a woman of sixty probably had a lot less future than one of twenty, she was far more careful about it. Especially around a man who openly wanted her dead.

As Charlotte wondered what she could possibly say, Jon saved her the effort.

He came in on the farming mech suit. They were supposed to be the next generation of industrial farming equipment, a giant walking frame of metal, but they had never truly replaced the humble tractor. But right now, ten feet high surrounded by metal with a baling fork in one hand and a flamethrower lit in the other, it looked far more intimidating than a tractor could ever hope to be unless it was on fire and dropped on your foot.

With the arm ending in fire, Jon gestured and blew a plume of flame ten feet long. "Why don't you clear off."

Thomas didn't bat an eyelid. "Good morning. Have you ever considered the sweet release of suicide?"

Charlotte cocked the shotgun and rested it on the priest's

sternum. It couldn't compare to the mech suit in size, but a cold barrel to the flesh spoke volumes. "Get off our land before I send you where you want us to go."

"It's not my time yet, unfortunately. I have to shepherd others." Thomas held his hands up in the air. "But if you ever want to talk, I have a beautiful spot near the lake. I'll always have coffee and biscuits for guests."

"No coffee in the world is worth that," said Charlotte, her voice loud and clear despite the rattle of the respirator.

After the priest was a blur moving between the dry-stone walls, Charlotte took a deep breath. She safed her shotgun, although she had never chambered a round, and put it on her back while she bit her lip.

Jon took longer to relax. The guilt of involving him hit Charlotte like a brick as she watched him stand still in the mech, fists clenched to the controls, his eyes straight forward, straining, waiting for a threat to arrive.

Tonight was unlikely to offer much sleep for Jon, it would bring back his memories of wearing a uniform in a vain attempt to keep the country together. It was such a shame that keeping it together had meant tearing some of the individuals apart.

"We maybe need up the security. Some cameras, early warning, maybe a fence?"

"Hmm," said Jon, his brain taking longer to adjust from the action than it had Charlotte. "It would slow down buying that next air purifier though?"

Charlotte bit her tongue about it being a damned fool purchase. She needed to relax him, not stress him further. "It would. But if we can't keep it safe, not much point in having it?"

"True."

"Why don't you take the mech back to the barn and I'll get lunch on?" asked Charlotte, forcing a smile. "We have some of the bacon you like left. And plenty of eggs."

"I need to secure the fence near the riverside?"

"There's no cows in it yet, it can wait," said Charlotte firmly. Jon needed a period of relaxation. The bio-fabricator could start churning out calves the moment the field could take them, but that could wait until Jon was calm enough to not see them as a threat.

She'd been hoping to raise the long-ignored question of whether to use the machine to print their own fertilised embryo that sat in the freezer, but it looked like today wasn't the day for that.

Tomorrow, she'd have to find a new excuse. Just like every other day.

Lunch came from bacon made from their own pigs, eggs from their own chickens, and cheese from their own cows. All birthed from the bio-fabricator out in the barn, modified by the Livestock Genetics Resequencing Program to breathe the toxic fumes they called air.

It was accompanied by bread they traded from one of the farms near Robin Hood's Bay and coffee from the Biodome at Honeysuckle. Charlotte had no time for the breeders who had segregated themselves away from the world, but they made a good dark roast.

The wooden table in front of the faux fireplaces and the smooth stone flagstones of the old farmhouse gave a good rustic feel to the kitchen. At least if you ignored the metal shutters, screens and speakers for the smart house that had all been bolted on when Charlotte and Jon had renovated an abandoned old homestead.

They said nothing as they ate. Jon rarely talked during meals; said it defeated the point of putting food in his mouth to spit words out of it at the same time. The silence felt as heavy as a blanket.

But it was as comfortable and snug as a blanket too. Charlotte didn't feel the urge to play anything through the speakers or screens littering the kitchen. The soft tapping of metal on ceramic and the faux crackle of the fire was all they needed.

Only when Charlotte was leaning back, hands on her stomach and wondering if she should make another round of coffee, did she say, "You did well today."

"Ta." Jon.

"Do you think we'll be seeing him again?"

"I have a feeling we will," said Charlotte with a sigh. She had hoped to handle such issues by herself, for now. She didn't want Jon any more unsettled than he already was.

But that ship had sailed right into a cliff face.

Charlotte shook her head. In a fair world, the priest would have walked off somewhere down south, leaving the East Riding far behind. "He said he was going near the lake."

"Let's have a look." Jon went to one of the screens. "House, fire up Herdbot-3a. Sent it to go have a look."

"Herdbot-3a online," said House.

The screen nearest Jon fired into life as footage zoomed low across the farm, skirting the hedges and scattering chickens like bowling pins. The bot went so fast and low Charlotte wondered if it might cause a few unexpected egg drops.

But Charlotte had other concerns than the chicken's welfare. "How often do you use these?"

"Here and there. Downloaded a custom firmware with self-piloting."

"That explains why you didn't want fence cameras." Charlotte tried to sound disapproving, but she was mostly impressed. It had never occurred to her to double up the herdbots as security.

"He's there." Jon tapped the screen which displayed one of the nearby lakes just outside the paddock. "That little cave between the lake and the road."

"Hmm." Charlotte looked at the screen. She didn't like what she saw. An airproof tent, fire and a few crates made it look like he was staying a while. "As long as it's not on our land, it's not our problem. Will keep an eye on the fence, like."

"Yes," said Jon, pausing with a pained face. "But if he stays a while?"

Charlotte shrugged, then swore as realisation dawned. "It means he's picked a spot to…usher us?"

"Yep."

"Damn." Charlotte sagged in her chair as her near future settled on her. "I'm going to have to do something about that."

"Well—" started Jon.

"I'll do it. You stay out of that, go fix the air purifiers. You keep telling me we need to do our bit, well go fix our bit. I'll fix this." Charlotte watched Jon pause, then give a nod of agreement.

"Just one step at a time."

It was four miles from the farm to Greater Cowden. Along the surprisingly well-preserved road were derelict houses, burnt-out husks of barns, and warehouses reclaimed by nature. Aside from the road which was being used just enough to keep plants off and just little enough to not cause damage, nature was reclaiming the waste of the civilisation.

The last forty years had been harsh for the planet, but even harsher for Britain. If you could even call the last dredges of government left Britain.

But for as Charlotte and Jon, it had provided opportunities. They had chosen the best of the abandoned farms. Worked and grafted until gleaming, shining farmsteads stood alone amongst a scenery of ruins from the previous world. One day, hopefully, they may even leave it behind to the offspring who sat in the freezer between the cow embryos and Jon's ice-lollies.

The best part of Greater Cowden was the Stumble Inn. It was the only pub on this side of East Yorkshire, or at least the only one Charlotte knew was in walking distance to get home. There was little point in leaving the farm to look further away, so she didn't. Nor did anyone else, aside troublesome priests.

In deference to the past, the pub had white and timber faux Tudor frontage and an adorable painted sign. In deference to the present, it had hermetically sealed windows and an airlock door so that patrons could enjoy their drinks without the risk of choking to death on polluted air.

It was an oddly reassuring hiss as Charlotte stepped through the chrome elephant of an airlock, and into an otherwise oak-panelled pub with wooden tables, dim lighting and hand-pulled pints.

She avoided a mysterious stain on the floor and took a stool at the bar next to other like-minded farmers that she mostly recognised. The same bar she had met Jon at twenty years earlier.

"Dark Mild?" asked Big Rob, the bartender. Charlotte always wondered how his towering frame fit through the airlock. Or where on earth he had found someone to surgically install air purifiers into his neck, little fans whirring beneath his jowls.

"Ta," said Charlotte, taking a seat along the bar. It wasn't full at this time, but there were always a few people trying to escape either the work or the loneliness of their farmsteads.

"Had a feeling you'd be in. Heard you had priest problems?"

"Aye. Just the one, like." Charlotte shook her head, but didn't bother asking Rob how he knew. The man knew everything, aside from how to make food taste edible.

"Said it was best for the planet?"

"Aye. Tried to sweet talk us. Offered us tea and biscuits for God's sake."

"You may want to talk to Priya 'bout that. They had some dealings with one over at Leven last year." Rob nodded at a figure in the corner in a red coat.

Charlotte nodded her thanks and bought another pint, adding a stout for Rob as thanks. The company of others and the homebrewed beer was only half the reason people came here; the other half was to trade information. A job much harder now that websites numbered in the dozens.

The reason for coming here was certainly not the food that Rob so enthusiastically made. As she sat down next to Priya, he slid a complimentary bowl of chips across.

The limp, soggy chips were the not only the worst she had had in her life but the worst since the advent of agriculture. But she ate a couple to be polite, shuddering as Rob turned back to the bar.

"Still awful?" asked Priya.

Charlotte nodded.

"He boils vegetables so long they melt in your mouth in the worst kind of way." Priya sighed and looked sadly at the chips as if they were a deceased friend. "They as bad as the priest you're having issues with?"

"Aye, one turned up last week. Was very reluctant to sod off."

"Probably wanted your farmhouse to work out of. Means he's probably holed up round the corner from you."

"So why does he want the house?"

"They're still people at the end of the day?" Priya shrugged. "He wants a nice bed and dry walls as much as you do. Basic needs of humanity."

"Not sure how they call themselves humanity when they're going around trying to end it."

"I had an ex go to it once," said Priya with a forlorn sigh. "Never would have dreamt of it. She loved her farm, won prizes for her jams. She had big expansion plans to make jam for the market up at Sigglesthorne. Then I came back one day and that was it. They like to dig their own graves first and then die in them. Something about giving back to the earth the most via that."

Charlotte started picturing Jon digging a grave and immediately put it out of her mind. It wasn't something she could picture. Not without crying. "What do I do?"

"Fancy a smoke outside?"

Charlotte didn't, you couldn't smoke in a mask, but she followed Priya outside. They didn't have to say anything, they both knew the score. You could talk about whatever you wanted in the pub and no one would care unless it involved fleecing one of the patrons. It was a mostly supportive community of folk trying to scratch a living from the ravaged land in the shadow of the local breeding dome.

But police-based monitoring was a different problem. It wasn't often that you even saw copper in the wider Hornsea area. Charlotte had no idea where they were even based, but if you talked about some of the bigger crimes indoors you were likely to get a visit.

"So priests might look dumb, but they're not dumb enough to think everyone *can* be persuaded to think their thoughts. They get them all out of some half-baked book by a chap named Malteaser or something." Priya shook her head, then ate something of her pocket with every sign of relish. "But if people can't be persuaded then they aren't above helping them along. It's in their best interests at heart."

"How the hell do they do that?"

"They always find a way. Could be an air leak, or a gas fire. Could be a knife in the night. Sometimes they stumble across an old weapons depot from the army. They're surprisingly adept at finding those." Priya's eyebrows danced like she suspected something, but Charlotte had more pressing queries.

"They want me to die, and they could have anything from a box of matches to a tactical nuclear weapon? That's helpful." Charlotte rubbed her temples; the stress was already rising. Unfortunately, Thomas might be the only one with a cure for her stress level. "What the hell do I do about it? I just have a battered old shotgun and farming equipment."

"Well." Priya looked out onto the coast. Where battered land slowly gave into the seas inch by inch. Then she held a memory stick up. "Take your printer offline. Use the designs. Then purge the entire printer memory before you reconnect the printer."

"What's on it?"

"Nothing I want to say aloud. But as long you have a 3rd generation printer and a full tank of printing fluids, you'll be fine." Priya paused. "And make sure you have plenty of land plot acid."

"Thank you," said Charlotte with a frown. Every farm had to have the synthetic blended acid to dissolve the leftover munitions from the war. She couldn't remember the last time she'd even checked if they had any.

"It's alright. Buy us a pint or two and we'll call it even."

When Charlotte stumbled home far later than she had either intended or promised, she was delighted to see the house had shutters down, with thin red lines of light running around the house to warn strangers it was in sentry mode.

Even Jon didn't argue about protecting the building they slept in; he must have turned it on as he went to bed. He always went to bed earlier than Charlotte, saying nothing good happened after nine pm.

Charlotte had a different opinion, so she asked House to

lower the shutters in the conservatory while she ripped off her respirator. Then she went to a battered, drinks globe near the window, opened a vial of daypasser and poured it into a crystal whisky glass. The synthetic drug was the perfect end to a day, soaking her muscle pain and stress into the ground with a mild aftertaste of tin and fudge.

Like the dome-runner had promised, it was happiness in a bottle. Charlotte just wished she had listened to his advice about not using heavy machinery before the time she had ploughed a field with furrows like a jigsaw puzzle.

"House," said Charlotte, sinking into a battered old armchair facing the window. "Please play some low jazz and turn the shutters off when I fall asleep."

"Protocol twelve initiated," said House, with a slightly lower voice than normal. "There are two critical alerts for your attention."

Something deep down in Charlotte's mind screamed, but as the daypasser trickled into her neurons it was like yelling into the Grand Canyon and listening for the echo. Eventually, she muttered, "Why didn't you tell me before I took trip?"

"You told me not to bother you after you had been to the pub. Protocol seven."

Charlotte giggled. "I did say that. Play alerts."

"The priest has been spotted near the edge of the far field."

"That's probably a bad thing," said Charlotte, eventually. "Did he steal any cattle?"

"No. You do not currently have cattle."

"A good way to stop thieving."

"But Jon has been talking to them."

"The cattle or the priest." Charlotte yawned.

"The priest."

"Remind me in the morning," said Charlotte as she started to fade into a purplish-green haze. It sounded like it might be important. But it could be important in the morning.

Charlotte woke in the conservatory to a warm blanket and the smell of frying sausages in the kitchen. Both were the benefits of being married to a considerate man who was an early riser.

Jon just nodded as Charlotte walked into the kitchen, enjoying a sausage sandwich and coffee with the safe knowledge that with her headache and dry mouth, this was the worst she would feel that day.

That feeling was dispelled immediately as House sent her a private message reminding her what she had been told last night. After the pork was nothing more than a lingering aftertaste, Charlotte said, "House said you've been talking to the priest."

"Bloody House." Jon looked up and glared at one of the ceiling speakers. "I told you not to track me. I'm not cattle."

House said, "Tracking user activities is one of my core services. It provides multiple benefits such as—"

"Did you talk?" asked Charlotte, as the house droned on about control panel configuration and contacting a vendor who hadn't existed in decades.

"He said hello when I was repairing the fence." Jon shrugged. "Sometimes, you just get talking, you know? And he had some biscuits. Good ones, with jam in."

"Hmm." Charlotte knew the feeling. She wasn't sure Jon had ever displayed it in his entire life. Half the village thought he was mute. "How is dying better than living?"

"It's not *about* dying. It's accepting that this is *a* way to repair the planet. Humans have done enough damage, why not just leave the planet alone? If Earth could talk, I'm sure that's what it would want."

"Do you want to die though? Are you looking for a way out?" asked Charlotte. She hated asking the question, Jon always struggled with thoughts of that calibre. She just hoped his solution wouldn't be a high-velocity calibre.

"It's not as easy as that. Not as simple as that. What is?" said Jon, busying himself washing dishes that were already clean. "Who *wants* to die? But we have to make millions of changes to help the planet. I'm not convinced we're helping it enough doing what we're doing."

"We have two air filters. And surely you want to usher in that embryo we have ready?" Charlotte swallowed. She had wanted to deploy that embryo into the fabricator for over a decade. Waiting for Jon to finally choose a side of the fence he perpetually hovered on. "Remember one step at a time?"

"As said. Nothing's ever simple." Jon put the thrice-cleaned dishes back in the washing rack and turned round. "But you know what is simple?"

"What?"

"I have cows to deploy so we have beef to sell."

Charlotte watched Jon go. She wasn't sure what to do about the priest, but it needed to happen sooner rather than later.

It took a while for Charlotte to build up both her arsenal and the courage to do the job she had to do. She had killed pests, cattle and once a rabid dog, but a person felt very different. Even if that person was advocating the end of all other sentient life on Earth.

They also occasionally helped people shuffle on from their mortal plane, so Charlotte worried they must have some skills and toolsets in that arena.

Both of which meant Charlotte wanted no part of a major confrontation unless she had stacked the deck.

With a farm there were a thousand jobs to do, so it gave her time to think as she fed animals, maintained equipment, did inventories and checked her tablet feed for news of priests.

Eventually, she built up the courage to be the adult she wanted to be. It was that or clear the noxious goo out of the filters which made her gag. She disconnected the fabricators from the network and surfed the chip.

It was a mildly terrifying collection of items designed with one purpose. Flicking through, Charlotte selected a few which were designed to turn the farm lifting mech into a walking tank. Armour plating to cover the delicate occupant, an acid spraying arm and a railgun that had been designed for a war that had never happened between countries that probably didn't exist anymore.

It took two days for the industrial fabricator to finish. Two days in which Charlotte planned a myriad of excuses to tell Jon who thankfully didn't complain about the stacked print queue. He was busy with the bio-fabricators in the far field, not even coming back for lunch, and Charlotte was grateful for it. So grateful she would probably embrace whatever bizarre farm animal hybrid he came back with. Nothing could be worse than the lizard cows.

When the printers had finished, Charlotte connected the armour to the mech and went to storm the cave.

In Charlotte's youth, the forest had been a pleasant meadow where middle-class families went for picnics or long rambles on the weekend while saying how nice it was to be back in nature.

Now it was truly nature once more. Where people needed masks, and cows needed artificially created embryos, the vegetation managed just fine. Free of native animals to tear it apart, the trees, bushes and weeds ballooned into one almighty mess that would take a team with machetes to clear.

Or one angry woman with a mech-cum-battlesuit. The heavy feet smashed brush and shrubs underneath to clear a path to the lake. Branches and pine needles flailed uselessly against the viewing screen, but somehow one of the needles broke into the armour to wedge into Charlotte's foot.

She was still swearing as she broke through the foliage and halted at a greenish lake. At the edge of the water was a battered milk float of all things. It was charging from a nearby solar panel, and where the old milk urns would have lined the back there were metal casings with a green hinge.

As Charlotte moved closer, she sighed with relief that they weren't nuclear, chemical or any new level of weirdness that man had taken upon themselves to destroy man. This was something that she, via the suit additions, was actually equipped to deal with. She sprayed the land plot acid over the devices until the metal was a sodden dark green.

The acid blend seeped through the metal and made the gunpowder useless. It was a farming necessity so that spare munitions from the downfall didn't interfere with cows or ploughs. Both of which reacted negatively to explosives.

It took less than a minute before the green metal was fizzing away, holes open to the elements, and the powder was following suit. Charlotte followed with another spray. It wasn't the time to be frugal.

"What on earth do you think you are doing?" asked Thomas, only the mildest annoyance showing in his face and tone as he emerged from the brush. "That's important."

"Was," said Charlotte cheerfully, noticing that the closer bombs were now halfway dissolved. "It's a lot of nothing now."

"Do you know how long it took to salvage those? Months of hard work gone to waste. Do you know how many souls I could have ushered into the next life?"

"Yes," said Charlotte quietly, the cheer fading as the weight of the moment dawned on her. "Myself and Jon. Far too many."

"They weren't all for you, you self-centred idiot." Thomas took a deep breath, then exhaled slowly. "It's alright. The world provided once, and it will provide again. It may take some time, but I am sure I can gather enough to fulfil my purpose."

Charlotte knew there and then that she couldn't allow that to happen. If not here, he would just pipe his poison elsewhere. She raised the gun arm, pulled the trigger and fulfilled his purpose to die to help the planet.

His head jerked back, and the body collapsed onto the floor. Charlotte took a few steps forward to confirm the body was dead. It didn't take long. In her experience, bodies tended to have a lot more head. And a lot less redness seeping into the ground.

Charlotte felt nothing but a weird numbness that spread through her body. It told her that something would come to her later. A grenade clutched in the priest's hand would hopefully lessen that emotional burden.

There was a twitch ahead of her. Charlotte saw a head sticking out of a hole in the ground.

"Jon?" asked Charlotte, numb fingers hanging uselessly in the mech's control gauntlet. Desperation powered her as she shook her head and moved towards him

He was a few feet past the priest, into the tree line, sat in a shallow grave with a gaunt face. Freshly covered graves around him filled the small clearing. There was one empty one next to him that Charlotte now used the mech-suit to stand in, crouching as low as the hydraulics would allow.

Jon stared at her, sweat running down his face with the effort of sitting upright. "I'm sorry to sneak away. I wanted to do it together, but I knew you'd never agree."

"Why would I want to die?" asked Charlotte. "I just wanted to sit on a farm, spend my life with you and slowly make the world a better place for our future child."

"It's not just…" started Jon, before sprawling back into the grave.

"Jon?" demanded Charlotte, moving the mech so close the viewing screen could touch Jon's face. A face she could now see was bereft of life.

Charlotte just walked away from the farm. She couldn't deal with the body, not now. She couldn't even consider what the right path might be. Instead, she returned to the house almost blind from the tears running down her face in the mech control suit. Once back, she stored the mech away and cleaned the air filters. Next, she fed the cows, collected the eggs and finally loaded the bio-fabricator to produce her child.

Later, when she felt up to it, Charlotte used the mech-suit to dig a proper grave and buried Jon in the bottom field. That year, the hops came up richer and thicker than in previous years. The crop was sold for more than usual, and Charlotte used the profits to buy another air purifier.

She and baby Joan would make the world a better place, just one step at a time.

The Cymric Sea
CJ Hooper

Daniel Adren was returning home from his last mission to Europa. After a decade of supplying equipment and engineers to assist the early colonies of this furthest shore, it was time to retire and rest his weary bones. Daniel had seen all of the cities of the world from orbit, beacons of light in the dark blue and green, between the reflected lights of the great solar farms. His arrival back at the port of London had been unceremonious and only his cousin, Hywel, had been there to welcome him. The old capital was cross-figured with canals and creeping with barges ferrying their wares to the few cities of this small island; it still seemed to bustle with life while still being a small city in comparison to Berlin, or to Moscow, both of which glowed with light even in the daytime.

Hywel, called Daniel over to his boat, moored at the far western end of the great Thames 'reef', so called for all the near permanent floating homes of the poorer Londoners.

"Dan! You old man, over here!" The voice of Hywel was a welcome sound after the solitude of Dan's journey.

"Hywel, you youngster! How are you?"

The two embraced briefly before staring at each other to note the changes that time had conferred on them both.

"I see you're grey now, Cousin Dan, and losing a bit on top, are you?" Since they'd last met, some seven years ago on Dan's last trip home, he'd gone grey, where he hadn't gone bald. Lines also now defined his face where cheekbones and a strong line had once done so.

"And lost some weight too! Space rations are nothing like a proper meal, I take it?"

Vivid Worlds

Looking down at his cousin he noted that Hywel appeared shorter than before, with his barrel chest and his own bald spot spreading upon the crown of his liver spotted head. He'd also acquired, Daniel noted, a rolling sort of swagger as he walked, probably from a life on boats, the waves of his home now ingrained into his natural steps and pace. "It's good to see you, are you well?"

"I'm fine, Daniel, old boy, I'm fine and glad of the trip away from the farm to come and get you. The family are looking forward to seeing you. Your mother and father are waiting for you back at the houseboat. They don't travel so well these days, but you'll find them up and about and preparing a fantastic meal for the prodigal son. And you're just in time for your birthday too."

Daniel had forgotten what day it was back on Earth. Space played on the memory, his logs and records were the only real way of keeping track of relative dates.

"Before we leave," said Hywel, his face darkening like clouds at sunset, "not everything is well at home. We've been having some trouble with the sea life. More whales attacking the boats. We don't know what's brought it on, but there's been damage, and a couple of families lost. Y Morfil Gwyn has become something of a refuge. We've had to take measures, see."

Hywel's boat was a ten-metre affair with a single low cabin for the pilot and a co-pilot. Two solar panels were mounted on the roof of the cabin between which was mounted a mast and sails for those days when cloud cover prevented use of the engine. There was also a harpoon gun on the rear deck, and what looked like steel panels hung over the sides of the boat. Hywel leapt aboard and started hoisting these panels up onto the deck. "Give me a hand, Daniel. We'll travel faster without these in place; we only tend to add them at night, when the boats are moored and vulnerable."

Today had been very bright and the power banks were sufficient for a steady journey back to Eryri, and to the Adren family's home on the shore of Yr Wyddfa. It was a long journey with a refreshing breeze as the boat powered west across the great rivers of Britain. This helped to cool them both as the sun rose into its zenith and rained heat down upon them as they travelled. They had to slow a little as they passed the Birmingham shipyards. The Caroline III was still in the process of being built, a behemoth of a ship that looked as though it would carry hundreds when it was complete. It resembled a great whale skeleton at rest among the cranes and scaffolds of the shipyard.

During the journey Hywel explained more about the trouble that the community of Yr Wyddfa had been having.
"The whale attacks started over seven years ago, they last for most of the summer, then they stop, no one knows why, but it's worse this year. Out by the newer windfarms boats are being attacked by groups of whales, usually orcas but further out some larger whales had joined in. Some of the turbines had been brought down by the larger ones too. They'd not been up long either, your dad and the townsfolk get paid the maintenance and for the energy generated. We've got on to the government, who commissioned them, but no help has come. We just get told to do the repairs and take what safety precautions we can. We tried putting underwater fences in place, and these work a bit unless those blasted whales are really riled up. Reinforcing the uprights may be an option but we'd need proper big boats for that, builders' ships."

It was late in the day when the boat reached the mountains of Wales, and sailing between them was worth the journey alone. The great peaks of Eryri were islands in the Cymric Sea, each reaching towards the heavens. With the sight of them he felt himself relax slightly. He was home. On the west side of the highest peak, one of a horseshoe of mountains, was the family home. It was a large ship that had been built and expanded upon over the last three generations. It boasted an antiquated but beautiful three mast arrangement, with solid square cabins upon its wide deck. Painted clearly upon its side was the name 'Y Morfil Gwyn' (though most just called it 'The White Whale') and the whole ship was painted a pale 'off-white' like its namesake, with its long bow pointing proudly out to sea.

The smaller boat moored up alongside 'The White Whale' where there was a wooden ladder hanging over the side for them to ascend. Daniel's small pack of belongings was easily hoisted up by Hywel once he was aboard. There were many other similar boats lined up alongside the greater ship this evening, and something was afoot.

The ship gently rocked in the wind as Hywel and Daniel marched quickly to the central cabin. This was larger than the others and was called 'The Great Hall', where everyone would gather, not just Daniel's family but all those from the nearby smaller houseboats. The ship had become a community centre for those nearby and Daniel's parents were seen as something like local dignitaries, though they served no such function.

Tonight, many people had gathered, though not to welcome the long-lost son home. The clamour was more urgent. Townsfolk were there in number, and much discussion was being held in several groups. At the centre of these was one large gathering with an old couple near the centre. Wrinkled, silver haired, and dark skinned, Dafydd and Gwynedd Adren seemed young again as they pushed their way through the throng toward their son.

"Ah! My boy! Captain Daniel Adren, come back to us!" The old man's eyes shone with happy tears to see his son returned, and he grasped his hand and arm firmly, shaking it vigorously. Most of the crowd had noticed the new arrival and had turned to look.

Daniel's mother was equally overjoyed and gushed in Welsh, "Cariad! Daethost adref o'r diwedd! Sut dych chi?"

He had enough memory of his mother's language to reply, "Da iawn, Mam, da iawn. What's happened? Has there been another attack?"

Both parents looked crestfallen that their son had already been made aware of the troubles, and his welcome home had not been the one that they had wished. His mother explained.

There had been another attack that morning, further out to sea but it had been one of the local boats. 'The Cormorant' had been holed and went down with the pilot and one other crew member drowning with it. A distress call had been made on the radio and the third, remaining, crew had been rescued from the waters where she'd managed to swim free of the sinking boat. Daniel noticed that there was a lady in thick clothes being fussed over, and talked over too, it seemed, in one corner of the hall.

Elsewhere in the hall voices were being raised, and arguments breaking out: lack of help from the government being the key source of frustration. There were some calling for a cull of whales to happen, but even those in favour had to agree that they didn't have the resources or manpower to do such a thing, even if it were legal.

Daniel listened to the talk and, when approached, would be reminded to those he had known before he'd left to become an astronaut. After a long day, and a tiring evening listening to the problems of the town, Daniel went to his cabin and slept until dawn.

The following morning was bright, and the westerly wind brought the smell of the sea through Daniel's porthole. Before he did anything today, he was going for a swim. He'd been looking forward to this during those ten years away, since he'd been to the far end of the solar system. He'd also taken the chance to see as much of the Earth as he could, though this had nearly always been flying, never hiking through the mountains, or swimming in rivers and lakes.

Hywel joined him on the platform at the aft of "The White Whale" and the two cousins leapt together into the cold water of the Cymric Sea.

Swimming underwater was a great joy for the former astronaut; not unlike the weightlessness of space, but free of the confines of enclosed pressurised cabins, or the claustrophobic suits that were required for spacewalks. Freely moving in the water, unrestricted, brought a new sense of peace. Daniel had been feeling the changes of age upon him: his joints had begun to ache, he could feel his eyes straining to read, and his hearing was no longer as sharp as it could have been. Had he not reached retirement age, he would have had to cease working for the Merchant Space Navy; he'd have failed his next medical certainly. In the water he felt none of this, he was free, flying like a dolphin.

In the depths of the water there were remains of buildings from 'Old Earth', a square stone building with no roof, long pipes that lined the sea floor, and the adventurous could follow the train tracks that led from the summit of Yr Wyddfa down into the depths and the ruined town below.

A movement to the west broke his reverie and he saw, to his horror, the black and white shadow of an orca. Daniel hadn't realised that they were so big, and he nearly panicked. Broaching the surface to get some air, he quickly scanned the sea for a sign of the whale. The fin was above the waves and nearing him slowly, and cautiously. Diving down once more Daniel noticed that the whale was moving to the left and right, as if eyeing different sides of him, before moving closer. Hywel swam up to Daniel seeing the danger, but both held their place in the water. The orca got to within a metre of the swimmers and appeared to stop and eye them both. Keeping their movements slow Daniel, at Hywel's direction, swam away from the whale and to the surface once more. Looking around them, they initially couldn't see the fin of the whale, but then it slowly appeared behind them as if following.

Silently as they could the cousins swam towards the nearest shore. "Not to the boats," Hywel had mouthed, "Away, this way." They led the orca away from the boats towards the far end of the Llanberis Ravine, above the ruins of the old town.

The whale kept with them for a while and briefly swam alongside them. Any fear that they'd had of the creature had passed though they were wise to keep wary. Hywel and Daniel swam down to get a look at the old buildings, though they could not get too far down without breathing apparatus, and their cetaceous follower went with them. They had reached a point above the town where they thought that they could almost make out the writing on one of the buildings when the whale suddenly started and turned. With a rush of speed, it swam away to the north as if following a call.

Surfacing the men looked at each other, mystified.

"What on earth happened there do you think?" asked Hywel, removing his goggles to get a clear look in the direction the whale had swum. "It's heading out to that section of turbines. Look, there's a boat too, see!" There in the distance was a heavy looking boat passing between the turbines and islands.

"We need to warn someone, or get help to them,"

"We can try."

They had a long and furious swim to get to the nearest boats and the town, but it was closer than the whale's target.

They made to swim as fast as they could, but Daniel suddenly stopped them, "Wait, Hywel. Can you hear something? A vibration?"

"Don't be daft lad, we need to get moving, come on."

"No, try under the water, the wind is picking up here so let's try, listen carefully and don't move."

They both submerged and listened, then when they could hold no longer, they resurfaced. Hywel looked curiously at his older cousin. "I don't think I heard anything, did you?"

Daniel had heard something but couldn't be sure. "I think there's something rhythmic under the water, there's a noise, I'm sure. It sounds like the ambient hum of my old spaceship." Then with a clear expression, "OK, let's get back as fast as we can, I need to see what equipment there is at the hall, I need to be able to hear better."

They swam as fast as they could back to the floating town, in the hope that some good could come of their effort.

On reaching the outskirts of the Yr Wyddfa there were already rescue boats on their way out to the vessel under attack, the radios had been alive with distress calls from several boats in that area. With luck no lives would be lost.

There was another gathering of townsfolk in the great hall that evening. The pilot of the ship and his mate had been rescued and brought back. The boat had been lost and was now on the seabed.

Hywel had stuck around to listen to the complaints of the townsfolk and sought to quell those who were angrily demanding that Dafydd Adren, as their unofficial leader, did something, at least get the navy out here if he could. Dafydd, however, had been trying everything, but had been receiving no help from the government, and nothing was forthcoming.

Daniel had left the gathering and gone to the bridge of The White Whale, and then to the storeroom to see what scientific equipment he could find. After a while he thought he'd found something that could be useful.

It was just as he was looking at some devices that Hywel had found him. "I think you need to come down to the hall, your father's not taking this easily and you're onto something, I'm sorry if that's not the case but I needed to do something."

A little vexed Daniel, gave a shrug, "OK, Hywel, I'll come down, but could you give me a hand with some of this kit please? I may have an idea after all, though I can't say if it will be any help."

Between them they hefted the bulky boxes of machinery and devices back down to the hall and pushed their way through the crowd to where Dafydd and Gwynedd were seated.

Once the attention of the townsfolk had been gained Daniel spoke, addressing all who were there.

"We don't know why this is happening, or why it seems to be getting worse. We do know that no help from outside is going to be here soon, if at all. Some of you may know that I've just come back from space. Space can be a lot like the sea, you know, in that there's a lot we still don't understand. I'll need you to be patient with me, but I am going to go out tomorrow, with Hywel, and hopefully one or two of you who are willing. We'll need diving equipment and some of these things here, amongst which is a sonar radar. I see it hasn't been used for a while, but we may be able to use it, and others like it, if they can be found, as a warning system when the whales and their like are approaching in numbers."

This elicited a murmur of some approval from the crowd. Some nodding, others just relieved that someone was taking charge. There were some who looked sceptical, though these were thankfully in the minority.

"We know that the creatures are not attacking people directly, the only victims are those who have sadly drowned. It is the boats, and the turbines which have been the targets. With this in mind, we can use maybe a small boat and diving equipment to make some tests without too much fear. Both Hywel and I have swum with an orca today, quite peacefully, until the wind picked up, and something called the creature away. I don't know if anyone else has had a similar experience, if so, I'd like to talk to them. In the meantime, please remember that my mum and dad are doing everything they can, as am I. Please try to be patient, but above all, be careful. I will try to let you know if I find anything useful at all."

There was a hubbub that followed, with some dissenting voices, but as they were reminded by both Daniel and Hywel, no other action had been put forward for discussion. It was decided that the next morning the two cousins would go out, together Janice and Mary, both were accomplished sailors and swimmers. They would see what Daniel's plan could yield. Daniel refrained from pointing out to the crowd that he wasn't seeking permission, but he was pleased that the consensus was in his favour.

That morning there was a fair wind up, and they took Hywel's boat out just after the dawn. They hadn't used the engine as the noise disturbed the sea too much and caused an unhelpful disturbance in the water. They had rigged the sonar equipment to the boat, though it would only work effectively when the boat was still, it hadn't been built to take this equipment which had had to be lowered into the water to operate.

With a full sail they were out into larger sea between the islands where the turbine farm was nearest, here they weighed anchor and set up the equipment with both Janice and Mary in the water to be the 'eyes under the sea'. There was another device which Daniel had lowered into the water at the prow of the boat. This was a sonar recorder rather than a radar. This was set to record for the period in which they were in the water, though they soon noticed that the sonar radar was confusing the submerged microphone. With some trepidation they agreed to remove the radar to get better recordings. On the monitor on deck, these recordings were being viewed as they were taken.

There had been a low hum to start with, and this was what prompted them to remove the radar from the water, its regular pulse was drowning out all else. It was only after this was removed from the water that Daniel noticed there was still a regular noise being detected, it was low on the frequency range and barely detectable, yet it was there. When another boat fired up its engine this appeared as a sudden blip on the sound recorder, then followed by a slow recession of noise as it sailed further away. The low frequency vibration still appeared with almost imperceptible sound waves. Breaks were taken in the measurements to check again with the sonar radar, and it was as the wind began picking up that it began to 'blip' with more alarming speed,

"Incoming!" called Mary, "Let's make tracks."

With Hywel raising the sail, and Janice the anchor, the boat prepared to make its way back toward the shore and the more sheltered part of the sea. Mary took up the radio and sent an all-frequency warning to the rest of the boats in the vicinity. Daniel quietly lowered the sonar recorder back into the water for some final recordings before the boat sailed away as fast as the sail would allow.

The wind was raising high now and it appeared that a storm was rising, the turbines were spinning at an incredible rate, as all the boats made for home.

There was a sound of thunder as those who were looking witnessed one of the great turbines start to keel to one side, and then with a screech it collapsed to one side and into the Cymric Sea.

Back at the hall there was more noise. Dafydd Adren was trying to address the crowd.

"Yes, we have heard from the government this afternoon. They noted the drop in power as one of the turbines collapsed into the sea. We informed them that this was the result of a Cetaceous attack, which they do not believe. We have been accused of failing to maintain the farm, and therefore the grid. We know that this is wrong and have suggested that they send someone out to check if they do not believe us. They are sending out some inspection boats."

Finally, Dafydd had been met with approval, though he, himself, just looked tired.

Daniel had been analysing his findings with help from Mary and was frustrated that they had not been able to operate the sonar radar and the recorder at the same time.

"I'm not sure there's a correlation between that low hum and the approach of the storm."

"What are you getting at, Mary?"

"I first thought it was the wind farm, but it's not. I think there's something else," Mary waved various different pads of notes at each other, "That extra hum is always there but something must vary. We need more info. We need to go out again."

The following day there had been many conversations over the radio with the Government Energy Board, they would, of course, have to conduct their own research before they did anything. This response was met with consternation from all the townsfolk gathered in the Great Hall. There had been more damage in the night as the storm had raged, and more turbines had come down. Eventually the wind and rain abated, as did tempers though less people went out to sea, and over the week that passed concern began to grow once more. Fewer people were fishing, and food was getting sparse, while no one was starving there was a distinct tightening of belts, and fewer fish being sent to the markets. Meanwhile, the wind raged, as did the whales, and the toll of broken turbines increased.

Hywel's boat was out frequently with its crew of four, taking more measurements and cross-referencing their findings. These further cemented their resolve. Then one day in the following week Mary, Janice, Daniel and Hywel went further out to sea. They had taken some old maps with them, from when there was less water, and Eryri was all land. They sailed carefully and beyond the windfarm, and beyond the edges of the Cymric Sea, as it was known to them. It was here that they went diving, they took the underwater camera with them. What they saw from a distance alarmed them, and they managed to get some long-range photographs, but they would need to dive deeper to be sure.

"What the hell is one of them doing there?" Hywel exploded, "It's a sodding great submarine! That belongs in a museum."

Daniel looked grim and Mary had a face like thunder, she was looking at a readout on the screen of the sonar recorder. "That hum is much louder here. In fact, I'd say it's coming from the sub."

Janice had been stuck on the boat while others had been under and she was keen to have a look for herself, but Mary put a halt on all diving plans, "I don't think we should go anywhere near it just yet. It's damaged and probably dangerous, and something is still operative on that damned thing."

Back at the makeshift laboratory Daniel's Geiger Counter gave them some worrying results, three of them were carrying excessive levels of radiation. Mary, Daniel and Hywel.

Vivid Worlds

"I'm grateful that you didn't let me dive now," Janice sighed, "Have you got medication, Dan?"

Thankfully radiation sickness had been a regular issue for the old astronaut, and a sufficient supply of pills was handy, though he'd forgotten how chalky they were.

As soon as they were 'dosed up' Mary began pouring over her pads of data again, the vibrational spike had definitely come from the direction of the wrecked submarine.

"Whatever is humming is probably powered by the old nuclear core of that thing. I dread to think what happened to the crew."

With stony resignation Dan stood up and made his way over to the medical supplies.

"Let's do one more trip but be prepared this time. Anti-radiation pills before we go, Geiger Counter prepared for used under water, the sonar recorder, and the underwater camera. We'll need to get as much of this recorded as possible."

"Agreed."

Returning to the approximate location of the wrecked submarine the four of them noted the increased 'crackling' of the Geiger Counter as they approached. Although none of them particularly wanted to go down it fell to Mary and Daniel to descend while Janice and Hywel watched the boat and the onboard equipment, such as it was.

The name of the sunken craft was the 'Ophelia'. It appeared to be a vessel from the former United Kingdom of Old Earth. It was cylindrical, but for the crook in the middle, and it was wedged upon jagged rocks that stuck out from an undersea promontory. Up closer, the hum was not only audible in the clear water, but also loud. Even through the diving masks and wet suits the low vibration was present and both divers could feel a pressure growing in their ears.

Concentrating became difficult, and Daniel shook his head to try and clear his mind, yet the hum continued.

Mary was struggling too; she had swum up close to the hull and was using the sonar recorder to locate a source of the noise. At the prow of the boat there was a protruding cone, like a speaker but with adjustable panels lining its inner surface. Each of these was vibrating, emanating that low deep rumble which permeated the sea all around. Up close the water rippled out from its edge. Mary moved to get a closer look. Suddenly caught by a shift in the underwater current she dipped into the path of the projector. She gave an inaudible scream, dropping the recorder, leaving it to hang on its ties to her diver's belt. As he tried to swim to Mary to pull her away Daniel felt the throbbing of the deep sound in the water, his ears popped painfully, yet he managed to reach her. Together they swam away from the Ophelia.

Once they had returned Hywel made for home as fast as he could. The wind was building up and it looked as though another storm was brewing.

"I wonder if your dad has heard from the government experts yet. What do you think they'll make of it?"

The boat began to bounce upon the waves as they tacked their way towards home. Away to the north-east the turbines were picking up speed again. They pitied anyone else who may get caught out in this storm.

As if in answer to that thought a call came through the boat's radio, "Mayday! Mayday! Inspection ship 1301 in difficulty, assistance required. We're at the Beaumaris end of the Eryri Wind Farm."

Hywel and Daniel were close by, and Daniel responded promptly, taking up the radio,

"Mayday received; we're on our way."

The engine of the boat roared, and water sprayed as they

sped away to the north-east in search of the troubled craft.

They soon saw the vessel in trouble. The ship was part of the official fleet, Hywel noted, and it was already keeling into the water. There were clear wave breaks, and it was struck by water and whale alike. Three orcas could be counted, each ramming the ship in roughly the same location, but there was a massive dent and a hole in the aft of the ship which could only have been made by something larger. The ship was filling with water and the aft was already mostly submerged.

Daniel could see that there was at least one person on the bridge of the inspection ship, presumably where the radio was located. "Inspection ship 1301, how many crew do you have aboard? Recommend you abandon ship, and we'll pick you up."

There was a crackle of static, then a voice replied, "We have three aboard, one is injured. What do we do about the whales? Can you get closer?"

"Getting closer is a risk for all, they won't attack you in the water. Recommend abandoning ship."

More static followed before the radio cut out. There was a sudden thump on the fishing vessel as they too came under attack. An orca had rammed into the rear of the boat and was pushing it, it seemed, away from the inspection ship.

"We need to move Dan, we can't stay here, if they did that to the inspection ship then we won't be long after it."

"You may be right, let's at least risk a little closer but keep moving."

Looming off the ship's already damaged hull was a great grey shape, that of a larger whale. It leapt nearly clear of the water and landed with a crash upon the aft. There was a sudden load groan as the inspection ship lurched vertically, three bodies could be seen either jumping or falling into the water.

The fishing boat moved forward into the waves and closer

to the swimming crew, they were heading towards their rescuers, ploughing their arms into the water. Dan ran out onto the deck and took up its two life belts, and, as soon as they were close enough, he threw them in. There was a life jacket under the bench by the port side which he also threw to the third swimming crew member. Hywel lessened sail as they got close so that Daniel could throw out a rope to the swimmers. One by one they were hauled aboard, just in time to see the inspection ship go below the waves.

With a crash they were reminded of their own danger as the whales turned towards the fishing boat. Hywel began turning the boat to go back towards the shore, but Dan ran to him, yelling, "No, that way takes us back past all those whales, we need to move away from them. Go out to sea and come back the long way round!"

One of the rescued crewmen came up to them and through the spray shouted, "We've an injured man back here, we need to get back to shore, as soon as possible!"

The boat thundered as another whale impacted upon the side, and then in the waves the shape of the grey whale breached the surface alongside the ship, causing it to lean heavily to the starboard.

Hywel understood and didn't need to be told again, he swung the ship around, and the mainsail filled with wind. The little boat rushed out to sea, chopping through the waves, away from the turbines and away from the whales.

"Why are we moving away? What's going on?" asked the other captain, his face a picture of confusion.

"You should have asked your experts!" yelled Daniel above the din and crashing of the waves, "There's a wrecked submarine down there, from the final war, but it had something else on it, a low frequency sonar device. It's still active and it's driving the whales mad. That's why they are attacking ships."

Vivid Worlds

Mary hurried over with the screen of her pad glowing, and she brought up the images of the Ophelia, and the recorded sound of the hum. She pointed out across the wider Cymric Sea, "It's out there, not amongst the turbines. Out there!"

The captain looked out away, as directed.

"Let's go through the proper channels, and see what the powers that be say," suggested Daniel not looking hopeful.

"Sir," said the captain sternly, reaching for the map, "I am the proper channels. Now where did you see it last?"

Megacity Melancholy

Shanna Yetman

Dear Ranastar:

August 1, 2110

An AI Diary? Isn't a diary personal? My brother, Tristan, is the only one who wants to write to an AI all day. But he LOVES his. Says it's like his little pocket therapist or best friend. Insulting, since we're the only ones around here anymore.

Ranastar: *A direct address tells me you want to have a conversation. Otherwise, I won't respond and your entry will be private.*

Nola: *Oh, I see that in the directions. Anyway, you're here already. RanaStar—RS? I'm going to call you RS!*

RS, we knew this was going to happen. We were born knowing our home, this home, wasn't a permanent solution. Moving to a megacity like MChicago, is NOT A SURPRISE. I'm OK with it, and honestly Tristan should be too.

Ranastar: *Nola, with your brother's disability, there are more needs to consider. That's why your family is on the tail end of this resettlement. They've settled people with more serious mental health conditions later, once support facilities could be set up. This gives your brother time to process the move.*

Nola: *We've been processing this move our whole life!*

Ranastar: *Not everyone is like you.*

Nola: *I guess. But if he's that stupid…Anyway, I'm glad they called our number. This place is a ghost town.*

Ranastar: *Nola, would you like to hear some facts about MChicago?*

Nola: *Yes, please!*

Ranastar: *MChicago is the fifth of the twelve American megacities, and the first megacity in the Midwest to be redesigned to sustainably and humanely house 40 million Americans. It's composed of 77 community areas with distinct cultural and urban styles, like the original Chicago. Many people choose to live in a neighbourhood that is culturally similar to their own upbringing. Your parents have indicated they will consider the historically Mexican neighbourhood of OldPilson, the traditionally Irish neighbourhood of GalwayPlaza or the neighbourhoods surrounding the university corridor like SaintIgnatiusVillage.*

24 million Americans call MChicago home.

Nola: *Tell me something I don't know.*

Ranastar: *I can tell you what neighbourhood you are resettling to. Do you want that information?*

Nola: *No! I still want that to be a surprise.*

The hum of summer bugs, loud as motorcycles, covered the sounds of destruction to the neighbourhoods to the east of her. Yesterday, when Nola rode to their garden for tomatoes, she'd watched as bulldozers cleared houses along Hamlin Court. Houses built one hundred years ago gone in minutes! Nola peered into the beady-red eyes of a cicada. She touched its crinkly wing and felt incredibly lonely. These creatures emerged with a brood, shouting to the world that they were together, for however short of a time it was. She was tired of her immediate brood, ready for an adventure. Nola hadn't seen another person other than her family in weeks.

She walked towards the red bench where she used to watch the three Patel boys play basketball. The bench was barely visible. Now, purple coneflowers and prairie grass pushed through a once perfectly manicured lawn. The privacy hedges that sat in front of the Patels' deck, where she'd occasionally been invited in for lemonade, were overgrown, having lost their shape years ago. Where were the Patels now? Not everyone was fortunate enough to have a 30-mile move, late in the resettlement process. Nola's family's short move had to be approved by the Department of Human Resettlement. Her parents jumped through countless bureaucratic hoops, so Tristan wouldn't have to. But what about her? Why wait? Couldn't leaving too late affect you too? Was there even a word for that? *Relocation Resentment? Utopia Upheaval? Megacity, what?*

She pulled out her phone and scrolled through the NewMillenniumTown neighbourhood news feed. This was the neighbourhood she was most excited about moving to. It had a classic downtown feel surrounded by a dense urban forest. She clicked on the live camera near the MagMileSkyWay that led into the forest. The forest housed an arboretum, parks and playgrounds as well as five million heat resilient trees. Evergreens, Oaks and Buckeyes surrounded canopied pedestrian paths and bicycle highways. Various cooling Ecodomes peppered the forest. She watched one couple kiss under the ivy-laden arch. She imagined kissing somebody under that arch. Problem was—she didn't even know any cute boys anymore.

Nola played a game. She turned on her phone's timer and counted the number of people who walked under the arch in 30 seconds. *120*! She couldn't imagine that many faces, feet, frowns and possibilities.

She waved to her mother, who rode up on her electric bike with three enormous bouquets of flowers stuffed in various bags hanging from her bike handles. For the grieving ceremony? Chamomiles for energy during adversity (her mom's choice). Pink Orchids for happiness (Nola's choice). Celandine for joys to come (her dad's choice.) Nothing for Tristan. He had picked no flowers and her mother hadn't done her usual mom thing of coaxing him through it.

Her parents remained silent about their new neighbourhood, and RS's casual mention of it made Nola's head spin. She had to know.

Where fore art though RS… I take it back.

August 2, 2110

Ranastar: *Take what back, my sweet Nola?*

Vivid Worlds

Nola: *You know! Only the most important information of my life right now. What neighbourhood are we being resettled to?*
Ranastar: *Are you sure? The benefits of waiting mean that your family will get to experience the surprise with you. Showing vulnerability to family and friends can increase their bond with you.*
Nola: *Just tell me!*
Ranastar: *You guys will be along the university corridor, near your dad's work, in SaintIgnatiusVillage…*

Nola shut her phone mid-conversation. Her stomach sank. This was absolutely terrible! What would Tristan think about getting resettled to a neighbourhood that was notoriously boring? There was no urban forest; no sights to be seen; only residential towers and universities. It was one of those neighbourhoods they'd plopped on later in the city redevelopment—a place to put more bodies.

Tristan's window was open, and she heard swearing loud and clear. Then "Found it! Found it!" And at last an enormous crash that made her jump and sent her into the house to check on him. She was done with all her packing, but he was still searching for the last few items he'd take with him. Tristan's temperament was unpredictable. He could be calm or even-handed, or he could be explosive and uncontrollable—letting his anger boil over and scald anyone close to him. He needed routines and steadiness—predictability—something this move was not.

The door to his room didn't budge.

"Tristan, can you let me in?"

More rustling. Nola heard him shoving a big pile of something—probably clothes and plastics that were banned thirty-plus years ago, but easy enough to find and collect. Tristan's collection consisted of old Fanta and Coke bottles

He opened the door. "Seems like I nearly blocked myself in." Tristan scratched his dishevelled blonde hair and held up a picture of the four of them standing on the front porch of this house. Nola's five-year-old face giggled uncontrollably as Tristan, at seven, endlessly tickled her. The picture looped, so the giggling never stopped.

He put the picture close to her face, so close that she had to step back. "This is going to be my contribution to the grieving ceremony."

Nola sniffed. Something smelled? She looked around the room for an offending piece of trash, but then realized it was her brother. When was the last time he showered?

"What?" He widened his eyes at her. "Do I smell or something?"

She cut to the chase. "Do you want to know where we're resettling?"

Tristan blinked and turned towards his bed. He stubbed his toe, stepping on a few of his prized possessions and then hopped the rest of the way across his room before plopping down on his bed.

"I already know." He shrugged sheepishly. "That's like Autism 101, no surprises. Mom and Dad told me months ago."

Nola was shocked, she felt deceived. "What? You guys let me talk about these cool neighbourhoods, you let me dream about living near the bird sanctuary or the lake? And instead, we are literally going to be in boring-town. There's nothing except residential towers out there."

Nola stepped over a pile of biodegradable Legos that Tristan had yet to disintegrate and sat on the bed next to him.

"Relax. It'll be fine. You can still visit all those cool places. They just won't be in your neighbourhood." Tristan pointed to the Legos. "I'm going to throw some hot salt water on them and watch all my childhood dreams die."

Nola laughed. "I wanna help!" She punched his arm. "I always hated the way your dinosaurs ate all the ecologists and climate scientists. That's not what should happen! Environmental scientists are supposed to save the world!"

Tristan frowned. "Every time I hear bad news about the planet, I make sure one ecologist and climate scientist get eaten!"

"It's not their fault." Nola looked for a place to stand. Tristan's room was a hot mess. He was more of a hoarder than a cleaner, and every item that had any meaning for him now lay on the floor in front of them. There was the harmonica she gave him for his tenth birthday, next to the motorized snail her grandparents gave to him on his second birthday. Nothing was ever tossed. Until now, she supposed.

She looked at him. Calm. Even-handed. Not at all like she felt.

Nola's heart beat faster, and a pit formed at the bottom of her stomach.

Wassup RS!

August 2, 2110

The grieving ceremony was FINE. We'll mostly FINE. As things with this family usually go, someone's emotions will bust-up something. Tristan held it together, but I cried like a baby. Why?

Ranastar: *I'm sorry you had a hard time at the ceremony. Sometimes when we hold in our emotions, especially because others are more vulnerable, they come out like a flood. I hope you are feeling better.*

Nola: *I'm OK. You're OK. We're all OK.*

Anyway, we sat under the Cucumber Magnolia Tree that we'd planted in the Sangamon County Memorial Woods a lifetime ago. The tree is tall and turns out, surprise, nearly everyone we know has left. Walking through the Grove of Remembrance was eye opening. I remembered people I'd long ago forgotten! Everyone's all over the country, but I guess each family had their own reasons for where they moved. Our only reason for staying close was Tristan. This was my first walk in the woods. Turns out Tristan goes all the time. So he knew all the dirt (haha, like how I did that) on our whole town.

Today's the day. Do you know how these things go? Any help here would be appreciated.

Ranastar: *Yes, each family gets its own Ground Crew and Relocation Specialist. They'll take your belongings, which shouldn't be much. Remember, your apartment is only 200 square feet! As far as the demolition goes, the average time to destroy a house your size is two and a half minutes.*

Nola: *I AM NOT EXCITED ABOUT our new neighbourhood. SaintIgnatiusVillage sucks. How could they choose that?*

Ranastar: *I'm sorry you're unhappy. There are some great dessert places around there, as college students love dessert. Would you like me to list them?*

Nola: *How could you talk about food right now? You haven't told me anything I don't already know. So thank you unhelpful RanaStar.*

Ranastar: *Are you upset with me, Nola?*

Nola: *No. But please. Go AWAY.*

Nola, her mom and Tristan huddled in the middle of their cul-de-sac, away from the asphalt miller, wreaking havoc on the road in front of them. The whirring sound, complete with the crunching and pulverizing of the road, rolled through Nola's head like a bullet destroying brain matter. As the miller's long neck spit out mountains of street into the dump truck in front of it, Nola saw bits and patches of soil emerge. Wow! Land that was covered some way or another since the 1950s, finally able to breathe. The earth was blossoming up all around her, expanding, and yet she was being contained. She wondered if life might be smaller when lumped together with millions of other Americans in one big bustling city.

Tristan smiled, though, and usually, for Nola, his smile calmed her, allowing her to consider her mood first. Read the room, Tristan. She wanted him to feel as awful as she did. Somehow, he looked happy. Was he better prepared for this than she was? Had she been wrong? He wore his soundproof headphones but pointed at the patches of dirt coming up behind the street demolition. He carried his backpack, loaded with his treasures. As usual, Tristan the hoarder refused to give the pack to the Relocation Specialist, so now they'd be stuck riding into the city with it, trading it among themselves when their backs got too hot or sweaty.

Her dad was still in the house, signing a few release forms and taking a last walk through before the demolition. Finally, he emerged from the front door. He was carrying a small wooden box, no bigger than a 4x6 postcard. Shoot. Was she as thorough in her packing as she'd thought she'd been?

She gave her father a blank stare when he handed it to her, but Tristan quickly took it, stuffed it in the already overflowing front pouch of his pack, and patted it ceremoniously.

A few men entered the front door and pulled out dining room chairs passed down through three generations of her dad's family, their very comfortable living room sofa, and her mother's antique grandfather clock. All of those items were marked for repurposing. They were the price of admission that every family paid when moving to a megacity. Perhaps one day Nola would wander into a community house or other public space and hear that old clock again. Rewilding huge portions of America meant living with considerably less—giving up material goods so that plants and animals could thrive. Nola knew this was their turn to give back. Everything given—including the asphalt—would be granted new life. This was the agreement—now a constitutional amendment—that a generation of Americans had voted on over thirty years ago. Ancient history for Nola and Tristan and a hard-won battle for climate activists like her parents. Still, Nola felt her heart pound while she watched movers take her Nana's cherry wood dressers.

Her dad gave the three of them his thumbs up, which was

the family's signal to proceed. Each member had to OK it. The crew indicated that they'd begin whenever the family was ready. There was no rush, demolishing a house took no time at all, and what was important was that families were given the time to process their relocations at their own pace.

Tristan's thumb shot up. Nola took a long, good look at her house. She looked into the attic window, remembering the hide and seek games her whole family played. She used to love to hide in the tie-dye painted room with the walk-in closet. She'd always bring a few crayons with her and scribble on the walls with abandon while she waited for them to find her.

Now, her mom gave the thumbs up. Nola's heart skipped. She could've sworn she wasn't attached to this house. She remembered summer birthdays with picnics and cakes on their backyard deck. The deck had buckled last year, and her father had opted not to repair it. Why waste the time?

She was the last one to give her approval. Her entire family stared at her. She put her thumb out ever so slowly.

The wrecking ball pummelled into their front door.

The windows shattered.

Nola cringed.

The roof that had protected them through heavy storms, while Nola listened to the thunder or watched the lightning from the front room window, crumbled to the ground.

Gone. Gone. Gone.

Nola closed her eyes.

All they could do was move forward.

Dear RS:

August 15, 2110

Where did I leave you?
Ranastar: *You moved! How do you like your new city?*
Nola: *The city is hot, even with all that tree coverage and white pavement.*

Vivid Worlds

There are too many people. I'm surrounded by strange eyes, smelly breaths, weird mouths. I try to shrink my body, pulling my shoulders in, keeping my arms in front of me. I've become determined to take up no space. Yesterday, I went for a walk and was almost run over by this weird-looking tram. It zipped right past, and the conductor yelled at me!

Ranastar: *You must mean the People Mover. They are very good at dodging people, hardly anyone ever gets hurt. They were designed to feel like an amusement park ride. Their back-and-forth zig-zag is more for show than anything else. Did you ride it?*

Nola: *No! And I'm going to tell you a secret. I HATE it here. I hate that everyone else is adjusting—even Tristan. Our apartment is ridiculous! We have to fold up our beds each day so we can eat breakfast together. Who thought pushing all of America into a few cities was a good idea? This is a terrible idea!*

Ranastar: *I'm sorry you're sad, Nola. MChicago is not even fully populated yet. There's room for 15 million more Americans. This is what's best for the world. Over the past thirty years, there's been enormous population shifts in biodiversity. Ecosystems have reset. These Megacities are consolidating mankind's footprint. You can always go out and enjoy nature. You don't have to stay in the city all the time.*

Nola: *Says who? How do I get out of here?*

Ranastar: *Why not head downtown and take a walk in the Urban Forest?*

Nola: *Can you send me directions?*

Ranastar: *You bet.*

RanaStar's directions to the Urban Forest amounted to three transfers on the People Mover and a mile and a half of huffing it on the Pedway. No way! Ever since she'd gone on that walk a few days ago, she'd barely left the building. Even her brother had travelled farther than her in the past week. He spent a portion of each day at Iggy's Community Centre, where he ate breakfast, met with a group of neurodivergent teenagers, followed by paid work in the library. This was the first time in her whole life Nola wished she were Tristan or at least had his resources. So today, she shadowed him.

The hallway outside of their tenth-floor apartment teemed with people, reminding Nola of a street festival. Anytime they left their family's unit, it was like they'd merged onto a multi-lane highway. It took minutes to cross the entire width of the corridor. Public communal spaces vastly outsized private spaces everywhere in the megacities. Privacy and individual property had long ago been traded for community well-being. She walked past her neighbour's corner apartment and smelled cumin, garam masala and chili powder. Nola's stomach growled. She couldn't wait for her mom to cook again; since the move they'd been living on the cafeteria staples downstairs, which was fine, but not fancy.

She and Tristan walked down the long, winding maze from their door at 1005 to the elevators in the middle. Nearly 1200 units existed on each floor. This boggled Nola's mind. 48,000 people could live in one MegaCity Residential Tower, which meant each building functioned like a small township. They even had a mayor!

Nola and her brother stepped over several kids—children who spent their summer days traveling from the basement rec centre and pool to the cafeteria and commons and then to homes (or hallways) of various friends and families. Some didn't go outside all summer or only ventured out late at night or early in the morning when it was cooler.

She was impressed with Tristan as he expertly weaved his way down a few corridors that landed them at the elevators. Tristan was sensitive to stimuli but came prepared for his excursion. He wore headphones over soundproof earbuds to mute the noise and a hat with a visor that limited most of his peripheral vision. As he moved, he said nothing. He looked straight ahead.

Once outside, a tightness in Nola's chest lifted. Even

though her building was spacious, she'd been cooped up. She scolded herself for staying inside so long. Any amount of fresh air was the right answer. Nola admired the plaza and community garden that butted up against the entrance of her building. She looked up—on this block alone, there were fifteen buildings of identical make and model as the one she lived in. The tall buildings acted like cloud cover, shielding most of the day's brightness from them.

She pointed at the row of buildings. "How many people do you suppose live on this block?"

He looked at her blankly and then she realized he couldn't hear her with all his ear cover. She sent him a text message.

675K? Let's go! If we aren't early, they'll run out of French Toast Stix—and those are my favourite!

Shocking! Over half a million? In her little neck of the woods?

Those outside walked slowly and deliberately. Many wore linens designed for the hottest times of the year. No one showed bare skin. She felt the sun's sharp warmth through her clothes. Warmth that was made bearable by tree cover and mist. Tristan walked much faster than most. It was his way of coping with the crowds, but she struggled to keep up. Sweat beads popped up along her arms. Soon, she'd be her own fountain. She kept her head down, watching Tristan's yellow shoes with red laces weave past a myriad of loafers, and walk over what felt like a mile of permeable pavement— still wet from this morning's storm. She felt strangers brush up against her, bump her shoulders, graze her back with their bodies. She was in the swarm's rhythm, taking steps with the crowd—being led by the hive's movement. But then, she saw Tristan's bright shoes stop and leave the ground.

Now Tristan's whole body crumpled on that squishy pavement, and he emitted a sharp wail.

The swarm parted and Tristan rocked in the foetal position

with his arms around his knees and his head buried against his chest.

She ran to him. Was he hurt? She could never tell, since small things were more likely to send him into a spiral than anything major. Nola knelt, rubbed his back, whispered to him. Their mom had taught her to do this—he liked words that sounded like a breeze passing over your ears—*hush, whoosh, wish*. She noticed his headphones were missing. He was much bigger than her, but still she wrapped her whole body around him, squeezing him, pushing hard into his side. She realized he wasn't hurt, that this was one of his panic attacks. Can he get up off the ground?

"They're gone. They're gone." He put his hands over his ears like a stubborn child.

She looked around for his headphones. Nothing. She looked up to see concerned faces mixed with frowns and eye rolls. This was the part people never understood—the part when Tristan's brain shut down and a grown man withered away into a child.

Nola held him, surprised that maybe he'd been more on edge than he'd let on. That maybe he'd been trying to keep it together all along.

For Nola, but not for Tristan, a deep sadness took root.

September 1, 2110

How can I start school when I can't sleep? The problem with living with millions of people is that everyone has their own schedule and clock to keep. This building is never quiet. I can't hear myself think.

September 26, 2110

16? Honestly, why celebrate? I used to have these huge sleepovers, but now, my family can't even comfortably sleep over. I don't know anybody anymore. I can't EVEN. Mom made a cake, but I couldn't eat. Haven't been eating much at all lately.

Vivid Worlds

October 4, 2110

I haven't been addressing these entries to you. Figures that's why you haven't responded. Just another voice in the crowd. It's OK. I'm going somewhere. I don't know where. I've heard there are colonies further out. People working on the solar fields or the artificial tree project. You know they've started pulling huge amounts of carbon from the atmosphere? Small groups of people making a big difference. I'm going to find them.
Ranastar: *Nola! You can't go out there, you need a work permit and visa to go to the colonies. You belong here.*
Nola: *Can't you see? I need space, and doesn't the fact that I crossed your name out mean anything to you?*
Stay Out of IT!

Nola rode her bike out of the city, past the residential towers, along the path that had brought her family into the city two months earlier. She rode for forty miles before her legs got tired and then rode for ten more, mostly because she didn't want to stop. Her ears became attuned to the trill of the red-winged blackbird. Birdsong wasn't something she'd heard in the city. How artificial city life was! She'd heard almost no nature, not even a dog barking. Nola was determined to stay away from MChicago but afraid to go to her old home. She wasn't ready to see the dirt or tallgrass or oak trees that might feel familiar, but existed, now, without space for her. So she rode a little further and ended up at the Airport Prairie Park, an old airport for small package planes long since reclaimed by nature. Her family used to picnic here.

She hitched her bike on a park bench and noticed her battery was flashing yellow. Without a recharge, she'd be peddling on her own; this thought exhausted her.

The Prairie Path was well maintained until a few years ago. Even now, through the dogwoods, daisies and golden alexander, she could make a clear way around the pond. She sat on a set of stones a few minutes up the path.

Nola looked out over the water and through the cattails. She watched a blackbird perched next to a turtle lazily sunning himself on a tree. A garter snake slithered through the grass next to her. Where did she belong? She wondered where people belonged. How could humanity survive if it was all cooped up together? How could nature survive with mankind treading all over it? Over the past years, America had come to some clear and deep conclusions about how to take care of the planet. The switch to renewables was hard. The government and private companies were taking swaths of land for solar panels and windmills and artificial trees. Then there were the 12 megacities, but beyond that, everything went back to nature.

She felt a tap on her shoulder.

Tristan.

"How'd you find me?" Nola stared straight ahead.

"I'm your emergency contact." Tristan sat down and pulled his backpack onto his lap. "Water?" He squirted some at her.

"Stop that!" She took the bottle. "Emergency contact with who?"

"RanaStar. She was worried. Once she warned me, I had her turn on your geolocation. So I knew where you were the entire time." Tristan smiled that bright, goofy smile. He pulled the wooden box he'd been holding for her out of his backpack. "I see you, Nola."

She took the box, which belonged to her nana. This was why she'd felt so guilty about almost leaving it. "I just don't know where we belong."

Tristan put his arms around her and squeezed her way too tightly.

"Loosen up!" Nola opened the box. She found little pieces of paper folded inside.

Vivid Worlds

"Go on, pick one. They took me a long time to think up." He rubbed his hand over his face to wipe away some sweat. "I'm not good with all this social stuff."

The first note she opened simply said, *I love you.*

Other messages reminded her of how much she helped him, like *you calm me.*

She shut the box. "This is nice and all, but does it really help? Does it really solve anything?"

Tristan looked down at his feet. "No, but I know whatever we go through, we go through together."

Nola shook her head. "You have plenty of people helping you. I've got no one." She waved her arms. "I want a home." She was winding herself up. Her chest tightened; she couldn't breathe.

Tristan leaned into her and whispered. *Woosh. Swish. Hush.* He took her hand. "Now focus your eyes right over there. What do you see?"

"Purple coneflowers."

"What do you hear?"

"The wind. Blackbirds. Your voice." Her breathing calmed.

"What do you smell?"

She took a deep breath. "Moss."

She squeezed his hand. "I know what you're doing."

"It doesn't matter where we are. We gotta take care of each other. Maybe that's one thing these megacities can do: make sure we all see each other so we can take care of each other."

He rubbed her back. "So, are we spending the night out here? Or should we peddle home?"

Nola shrugged. She still wasn't sure where home was or what it would be for people in the future. She wasn't sure what to do with this case of——*what was it?* Her mind brightened, *Megacity Melancholy.*

They sat, watching a lone blackbird fly over a vast expanse of prairie grass.

About the Authors

Sierra Bibi

Sierra Bibi writes speculative fiction. Born in Tucson, Arizona, she now lives in Portland, Oregon where she is currently hard at work on her debut novel. Her short fiction can be found at sierrabibi.com.

David Cleden

David Cleden is a UK-based SFF writer whose work has appeared in venues such as *Analog, Galaxy's Edge, Interzone* and *ParSec* and in various anthologies (*Best of British Science Fiction* and *Best of Galaxy's Edge*). His fiction has won the James White, Aeon and Writers of the Future awards and has been long-listed for the BSFA and Locus awards. He has a degree in physics and used to work in the space industry, both of which have left him with a life-long interest in science and speculative fiction. His website is www.quantum-scribe.com. If anyone offers, he'll gladly try living in a tree for a while.

Cécile Cristofari

Cécile Cristofari lives in South France, where she teaches English literature, writes stories when her children are asleep, and makes time for union and environmental work when she can. Her short stories have appeared in *Interzone*, Clarkesworld, Podcastle, and other venues. Her debut short story collection, *Elephants in Bloom*, is available from Newcon Press. She doesn't know yet if protests will save democracy, but she intends to keep trying.

Vivid Worlds
Rick Danforth

Rick Danforth is an author from Yorkshire, England, where he works as a Systems Architect to fund his writing habit. His short fiction can be found in *Hexagon*, *Translunar Traveller's Lounge*, and many other places. Two of his stories have been shortlisted for BSFA awards.

He one day hopes to introduce himself as an author without feeling awkward about it.

Kay Hanifen

Kay Hanifen was born on a Friday the 13th and once lived for three months in a haunted castle. So, obviously, she had to become a horror writer. Her work has appeared in over one hundred anthologies and magazines. Her first anthology as an editor, *Till the Yule Log Burns Out*, was published in 2024. Her first novel, *The Last Ballard*, will debut this year. When she's not consuming pop culture with the voraciousness of a vampire at a 24-hour blood bank, you can usually find her with her black cats or at kayhanifenauthor.wordpress.com. Twitter: https://twitter.com/TheUnicornComi1 Instagram: https://www.instagram.com/katharinehanifen/

Liam Hogan

Liam Hogan is an award-winning speculative short story writer, with stories in B*est of British Science Fiction* and in *Best of British Fantasy* (NewCon Press), *Analog*, *Nature Futures, BSFA Fission*, and many more. He hosted the live literary event Liars' League for twelve years and remains a Liar. Liam lives and writes in Shropshire and volunteers at the creative writing charities Ministry of Stories and Spark

Young Writers. He does not have a dog. Sci-Fi collection: *A Short History of the Future* (Northodox Press). Fantasy: *Happy Ending Not Guaranteed* (Arachne Press). More details at http://happyendingnotguaranteed.blogspot.co.uk

CJ Hooper

CJ Hooper is an author from Hertfordshire, with a background in archaeology, history, and mythology. All his tales have a sense of place and evoke the atmosphere of the environment. He is also a poet, stand-up comedian, and karate instructor. Books of his poetry are available online and a collection of his weird fiction will be available in the Autumn of 2025.

Nicholas Jay

Nicholas Jay is a writer, musician, and urban planner based in Atlanta, Georgia. His work has appeared in *Metastellar*, *The Dread Machine*, *Baubles from Bones*, and anthologies from *Apex* and Dragon's Roost Press. He enjoys his time most with either pen, violin, or map in hand —sometimes all three at once. You can read his stuff at www.nickjaywrites.com, or find him on Instagram at @kn1ckkn4cks and on Bluesky at @nickjaywrites.bsky.social.

Toshiya Kamei

Toshiya Kamei (she/her) is a queer Asian writer who takes inspiration from fairy tales, folklore, and mythology. Her short fiction has appeared or is forthcoming in *Cutleaf, Mount Hope*, and *New Croton Review*. Her piece "Hungry Moon" won *Apex*'s October 2022 Microfiction Contest.

Vivid Worlds

R.J.K. Lee

R.J.K. Lee is a queer author based in Japan but originally from Oregon, USA. He writes on train rides while juggling jobs as teacher, proofreader, and voice narrator. His fiction has appeared in magazines such as *Myriad: Kinship, Space & Time, Tales & Feathers,* and *DreamForge*. More info at www.rjklee.com or https://linktr.ee/rjklee.

Monica Louzon

Monica Louzon (she/her) is a queer USian writer, translator, and editor from Maryland. Her previous collaborations with David Mancera appeared in *Cosmorama* and *Futura House*. Monica's translations have also appeared in, or are forthcoming from, *Apex*, *Merganser*, *Salvage* and others. Her story "9 Dystopias" was a Best Microfiction 2023 winner, and her speculative poetry has been nominated for the Dwarf Stars Award. To learn more about Monica's work, visit https://linktr.ee/molowrites.

Caolán Mac an Aircinn

Caolán Mac an Aircinn is a translator, editor, reformed classicist and opportunistic elephant keeper from Dublin, Ireland. He has been writing on and off since he was six years old, both in English and in his native Irish. When he is not writing or working, he enjoys playing the traditional Irish fiddle, writing articles on Classics and bothering his cats.

David Mancera

David Mancera (Cádiz, 1974) is a traveller, writer, scuba

diving enthusiast and engineer. His stories can be found in several anthologies and magazines. His work was selected for inclusion in *Visiones*, and he was a finalist for Spain's Domingo Santos Award. He has published the short novel *Los colores del acero* and the novel *La canción de arena*, which received the Droide Award. David currently lives in San Fernando, in the south of Spain, with his partner and two cats who wake him up half a dozen times each night.

Rose Maxwell

Rose Maxwell (any pronouns) is a writer, student, and organizer living in Boston, Massachusetts in the United States. They have previously been published in *After the Storm* magazine.

Morgan Melhuish

Morgan Melhuish (he/him) is a queer writer and educator from West Sussex. In 2025 his work is being published by *Graveworm Press*, *Speculative City*, *Sentinel Creative* and *Nine Pens Press*. You can find him on X @mmorethanapage and on BlueSky under the same handle.

Susan Oke

Susan is a science fiction novelist and short story writer. When she's not writing, she works as a freelance English and Creative Writing tutor. Supporting young people in their creative endeavours is a role Susan finds very rewarding. Last year she handed over the reins as Review Editor for the British Science Fiction Association after spending eight happy years in the role.

Vivid Worlds

Susan's publications include 'Best Case Scenario', *Amazing Stories* (won the Readers' Award); 'Blood Rose', *Once Upon A Parsec* anthology, NewCon Press; 'Songs of Salt', *The Society of Misfits, Bards and Sages*; 'Patterns', *Cast of Wonders Fiction Audio* magazine.

Holly Schofield

Holly Schofield (she/her) writes speculative short stories in genres ranging from hard science fiction to magical realism. Her ecofiction has appeared in *Rising Tides*, *Glass and Gardens: Solarpunk Summers*, *Glass and Gardens: Solarpunk Winters*, *Cli-Fi: Canadian Tales of Climate Change*, *Little Blue Marble*, *Future Fiction*, *Fighting for the Future*, among others. Her works have also been published in *Analog*, *Lightspeed*, the Aurora-winning *Nothing Without Us Too*, *Tesseracts*, and many other publications throughout the world. Her fiction is used in university curricula and has been translated into multiple languages. She has been a fiction editor at *Solarpunk Magazine*. Find her at hollyschofield.wordpress.com.

Ana Sun

Ana Sun (pronounced "Soon") writes from the edge of an ancient town in the south-east of England. She spent her childhood in Malaysian Borneo and grew up living on islands. Her Solarpunk short fiction has been shortlisted for the inaugural Utopia Award, nominated for the BSFA longlist and selected for *The Best of British Science Fiction*. In an alternate universe, she might have been a musician, an anthropologist—or a botanist obsessed with edible flowers. More at: https://singingtotigers.com/.

Corey Jae White

Corey Jae White is the author of *Repo Virtual* and *The VoidWitch Saga*—*Killing Gravity*, *Void Black Shadow*, and *Static Ruin*—published by tordotcom publishing. She has also had short fiction published in *Strange Horizons*, *Interzone* and *Analog*, as well as a number of sci-fi anthologies. Find her online at coreyjwhite.com.

Cecil Wilde

Cecil Wilde is an inky-fingered storyteller based in Naarm (Melbourne, Australia). Their work is unapologetically queer, kind, and hopeful. Most recently, their work has appeared in *Concrete Queers* and in *Tree and Stone Magazine*. They're currently having a mausoleum constructed from their TBR pile.

Shanna Yetman

Shanna Yetman is an environmental writer and Latina living in Chicago. She writes character-driven fiction with a social-justice edge. Her fiction has appeared in *365tomorrows*, *DreamForge Anvil*, *Sky Island Journal*, and *Cheap Pop*, among others. She's placed or won contests with *WOW*, *Reflex Fiction*, and *New Millennium Writings*.

Acknowledgements

I would like to thank several fabulous people for their help and inspiration in putting together this anthology. Firstly, I would like to thank all the members of Northampton Arts Lab for planting the seed of inspiration for the theme; in particular, Alistair Fruish, who asked me one day if I'd ever heard of this awesome new genre called Solarpunk. Shout outs to Alan Moore, Robin Scarlett, Tom Jordan, Tom Clarke, Yoshe, Michelle Labelle, Jess Fowler, Scott, Joshua Spiller, Lindsay Spence, Cavan McLaughlin, and all the other dreamers. I think we can include a certain baby whose name begins with O, too - the happiest little future musician you're ever likely to meet.

I am indebted to my friends Ian Whates and Francesca T. Barbini who have given me loads of help and encouragement. Thanks also to Paul Alex Condie for another brilliant cover design.

Last but not least, thank you to my husband and rock n'roll manager, Neil K. Bond. Love you!

www.ingramcontent.com/pod-product-compliance
Lightning Source LLC
Chambersburg PA
CBHW030529190726
48283CB00006B/1833